MASKS OF BETRAYAL

KENT SIEVERS

 This story is a work of fiction. Characters and events are the product of the author's imagination. Any resemblance to persons, living or dead, is purely coincidental.

ISBN: 978-0-9976189-3-8

Dedicated to Sally J. Walker and the talented regulars at the Nebraska Writers Workshop.

Special thanks to-

Barry Ellington
Mark Kinsey
Tracy Hawkes
Mark Davis
Jolene McHugh

1

Blinded by rust flakes and sweat, Eugene Fellig smiled as he felt the bolt's threads finally take hold. Nothing about this morning had been easy.

After two more turns just to be sure the bolt would hold, he let go of the car's starter motor to shake the ache from his trembling arm. Filthy fingers tugged his t-shirt to wipe the salty sting from his eyes. Arizona heat shimmered from the parking lot's asphalt. Two bolts to go. *Two bolts and she's gone for good.*

The repairs were taking longer than planned. His heart wasn't in it. Fixing the old Ford Tempo was his way of helping the girl he'd fallen for broach their inevitable break-up conversation.

Trish and her best friend Lainey had blown into town in a whirlwind of rebellion that left them stranded in the parking lot of a Denny's near Eugene's apartment. In coming to their rescue, a white-hot love affair was born. Outside of work, Trish and Eugene had done little more than make love, sleep and eat. But, as the weeks went by and the excitement and adventure became routine, Eugene saw Trish longing for the comforts of home.

Yesterday before work, he'd purchased the needed parts for the car and this morning, as they lay together for what he feared would be the last time, he announced his gift. Her eager reaction confirmed his suspicions.

Now, as he caterpillared out from under her car, eyes stinging, he prepared himself for the pain and awkwardness of the inevitable breakup conversation. Gathering tools and wiping the grease, the words that had been an endless loop in his head the night before returned. *It's been fun but you need to get back home . . . .*

In Trish's bathroom, which was already packed for the move, he washed the lingering filth from his hands then scrubbed a little at his face. He paused to stare at his reflection in the mirror. Flecks of dirt still peppered his forehead and dark circles under his eyes betrayed his lack of sleep.

He had always been baffled by women's attraction to his unremarkable face. His nose, broken in the many fights of his youth, sat slightly crooked. A tiny scar nestled in his left eyebrow and his brown hair, with its barber college cut, just lay there. The one thing he did have going for him—at least according to a topless dancer he'd once met—were his intense green eyes. "You've got real pretty eyes," she'd said, while seductively undulating before him. Although he'd always been fairly sure she was fishing for tips, he'd taken the compliment to heart.

When he emerged from the bathroom wearing a fresh shirt and jeans, Trish offered to buy a late breakfast.

At the Denny's where Trish and Lainey had picked up graveyard shifts, the girls slid together into one side of the booth and Eugene sat opposite. Conversation lagged. Orders were placed. Food arrived. No one wanted to make the first move. When their waitress cleared the last plate from their table, Trish took the leap.

"I don't know how to say this," she said then took a sip of her soda.

"Not to worry Trish, I've seen this coming. We had a good time, but you two need to get back to Oregon and I need to get back to my old routine."

Saying it aloud hurt more than anticipated.

Tears welled in Trish's eyes. Eugene blew on his coffee, vowing not to mimic her. "Really, it's okay," he said, his throat tight. "All I ask is that you let me keep that cool chef's hat you stole."

Both girls laughed, Trish wiped tears. "I'm really going to miss you."

A foot caressed the back of Eugene's leg. "Your car should be good to go. When you stop for gas just check the oil and coolant like I showed you. I put a little extra of both in the trunk."

"How'd you learn so much about cars?" Lainey asked.

Eugene shifted in the booth, uncrossing his legs. The foot followed.

"I kinda grew up in a junkyard. So, do you know which way you're driving back? Still have your maps and everything?"

"Yes," said Trish. "I-10 west then hang a right at I-5. Pretty simple, I think."

Eugene caught a look in Lainey's eyes as she tongued the straw in her drink. He realized that the foot massaging his calf belonged to her.

For an instant, his libido conjured visions of a three-way. He dismissed them quickly. Trish had shown no sign of wanting anything more than to get back home. This was all Lainey.

"So, I guess this is it," he said, letting Lainey's flirtation become little more than a risqué memory.

They crawled from the booth in unison. Awkward hugs followed. Eugene dropped a tip on the table as Trish headed to the register to pay the bill. Lainey trailed behind, glancing back with a look that said, "Last chance." Eugene's smile and shrug said, "Thanks, but no thanks." Then the two were out the door, in their car and headed out of his life for good.

Deep breaths held back the still-threatening tears as he stepped from the air-conditioned restaurant. Their love affair was over as quickly as it had arrived. *God, Trish was something . . . her scent . . . the sweat glistening in the small of her back.*

Lost in thought, he reached his Jeep before he knew it. After fumbling for his keys he turned off the car alarm then unlocked the Jeep's rear hatch and the lockbox within. He removed a pair of digital cameras, one with a wide-angle lens, the other a telephoto. He checked for their memory cards and charged batteries before placing them on the front passenger seat. He glanced at his watch. He'd have to hurry or he'd be late for work. It would be a miserable night. As usual, he'd made things easy on everyone but himself.

Eugene had overcome a lot in his twenty-six years. At twelve, he'd been a middle class kid working summers and weekends at the family warehousing business with his older brother, Ray. By fifteen—thanks to a thieving, runaway father and a drive-by shooting—it was just his alcoholic mother living with him in welfare housing. Had it not been for Albert and Carl Fodoni, two old black men who'd taken him in, Eugene knew it was likely he would have been dead or in jail.

Firing the motor on his old Jeep, Eugene heard a slight lifter tick. He made a mental note to check the valves on his next day off. *Man, it'll be good to get back to normal.*

The air conditioner blew hot. Sweat trickled to join the tears rimming his eyes. He wiped away the moisture before turning off the Jeep's stereo and switching on a portable police scanner hidden between his front seats.

Hearing radio calls to minor car accidents and shoplifting arrests flipped a switch in his brain. His newsman mode had his hands doing an automatic check of his pockets. Pen, Sharpie marker, notepad and phone.

On the scanner, the Scottsdale PD dispatcher's normally monotone delivery shifted with the slightest edge of desperation as she requested units to answer a burglary call. Eugene ground his teeth at the lack of response. *Shift change. The lazy bastards want to go home.* In her second plea, the dispatcher broke protocol, her voice cracking, "C'mon, I really need your help here, folks."

Pencil Dick. She thinks it might be Pencil Dick. His foot pressed into the gas pedal as his mind calculated the quickest route.

"Pencil Dick" was the nickname the cops had given a serial rapist who had plagued the city for over a year. His victims all described their attacker as a young, white male with small and hairless genitalia. He wore a ski mask and leather gloves and chose the young and beautiful. He'd beat them into submission, don a condom then choke his prey to unconsciousness during sex. When his victims awoke, all found the word "BITCH" scrawled on their foreheads.

Anger colored the dispatcher's report that the caller had taken refuge in her bedroom closet and could hear her roommate being savaged. More maddening seconds of dead air was followed by, "3-Adam-15, we'll take it." Two more units chimed in then a "David" unit joined the hunt. Eugene recognized the voice from the David car as a friendly, young detective named Harry Aronson.

Eugene's phone buzzed and chimed with a text from the paper's cops reporter, Andrew Brinkmann. *Pencil Dick North Miller and First.* Cursing, Eugene tossed the phone to the passenger seat. His dull drive to work had just become a race against time. Weaving through traffic, thinking multiple moves ahead, he timed lights and pushed the speed limit.

Screaming obscenities at less than attentive drivers, he broke free of a knot of cars. His tires squealed as he made the diagonal cut through Papago Park. *Hope the cops aren't working radar today.* An excruciatingly long stoplight increased the pounding of his heart and clenched his jaw even harder. He checked his cameras. All was ready.

Nearing the scene, he slowed, seeing the unmarked detective's car heading his way.

They rolled up on each other with windows down. "Is it Pencil Dick?" Eugene asked.

"We think so," said Detective Aronson.

Aronson's new partner, Eddie Ibarra, leaned forward. "There's a good chance he's still on foot and armed with a knife." Ibarra was much older than Aronson, yet was a new hire to the force. "If you see him before we do, stay clear and holler."

"Will do," said Eugene.

The hunt quickly lost momentum, but Eugene's frustration still had him wound tight. *Lazy sons-a-bitches let him get away again . . . .*

After forty-five minutes of his cruising, the scanner fell silent but for a faint buzz as it rolled through channels. Eugene parked in the shade then pulled up a map on his phone. The neighborhood was a curving maze of fenced backyards with swimming pools and heavy foliage.

The dispatcher broke in with a disheartened request for a roll-call. Units responded with their numbers and location. The information showed no obvious holes in their net. But Eugene and probably the dispatcher knew they'd given Pencil Dick a big head start by taking their sweet time to respond to the first call.

A text from Michael Specht, the paper's photo editor, pestered. *Think they lost him again?*

Looks like, Eugene thumbed back. *Coming in. C u in five.*

The exhilarating smell of newsprint and ink greeted Eugene as he entered the *East Valley Herald* through the side pressroom door. Exchanging waves with Kurt, the head pressman, Eugene pushed through a pair of battered, swinging doors into the cacophony of a newsroom dealing with speculation on the serial rapist.

Michael Specht sat at his desk staring at a police artist's rendering of the man they'd officially dubbed the Scottsdale Rapist.

Breezing up to Michael's desk, Eugene stated the obvious, "Lazy cops let the creep get away again."

"Thought for sure they had him this time," said Michael. He cocked his head. "Seems like he always does his thing just before you come to work."

"That's because he's probably leveraging the afternoon shift change. He knows no one wants to work late."

Michael sat a little straighter. "Have you mentioned that to—"

"THREE-ADAM-15 IN FOOT PURSUIT." squawked the scanner clipped to Eugene's front pants pocket.

He made it back to his Jeep and was pulling camera's from the lockbox when the dispatcher cleared the air for emergency traffic.

A breathless officer, his feet pounding fast, huffed out, "SECOND AND CARHILL. EASTBOUND. WHITE MALE. FIVE-NINE. BLUE SHIRT."

Eugene's tires bounced and squealed as he tore out of the paper's lot. He envisioned the direction of the pursuit. At Osborn Road, he slowed for a traffic signal, gauged the risk then ran the light. Head whipping, eyes scanning, his gut told him he was in position. This was the place to be.

The scanner fell silent again. Eugene's heart pounded in his ears. *Calm down. Check cameras. Think.*

A sweaty, blue t-shirted man burst from the bushes in a side yard. Eugene slammed on the brakes, one hand on the wheel, the other keeping his cameras from flying off the front seat as he slid to a stop. Blue t-shirt hurdled a short brick wall thirty yards to the west as Eugene piled out, camera in hand.

The man closed fast—too fast to get off a picture—Eugene tossed the camera to the Jeep's front seat just before they collided, locking arms to begin an awkward dance for control.

"Gimme . . . the Jeep," growled the attacker, stinking with fear, his arms slick with sweat.

Screaming, Eugene drove forward with all his might. The attacker twisted, tangled in his own feet. Together they fell. When they hit the pavement, Eugene's forehead smashed into the man's nose. Blood gushed.

Cops flew in from all directions. Eugene rolled free as a knee flew past to land on the man's chest, forcing a spray of red from his ruined nose.

Ignoring the scorching pavement and rush of bodies, Eugene scrambled to retrieve a camera. Time slowed as he turned back, firing on instinct, picking his moments, hunting for focus, his ear telling him the camera's shutter would freeze the action. For an instant, the tangle of uniforms parted and the man's face was painted with light. Eugene's index finger punished the shutter button as the viewfinder blinked. The camera captured eight frames of blood-smeared rage.

His camera remained on target until the suspect was locked in a cruiser. Only then did he turn his attention to the phone pestering him from the front seat of his Jeep. He glimpsed Managing Editor Pete Cunningham's texts *On scene? Get the arrest?* before grabbing the camera with the telephoto to capture a few frames of the suspect in the police cruiser. The light was shit, but the man's rage still shined through.

Hands shaking from the adrenalin rush, he hit the play button on the camera with the wide-angle. The LCD flashed to life and he spun through his take. His exposures and focus were erratic, but in the second-to-last frame, all the pieces came together. Simultaneously, his heart soared and he breathed a sigh of relief.

His phone rang. "What?" he barked an answer without looking at the screen.

"Catch the arrest?" asked Michael Specht. "Pete's driving me nuts."

"Christ, you're not the only one . . . Can't you guys . . . " He caught himself and laughed, realizing he was still tense and it was coming out as rage against the desk jockeys. He took a calming breath. "Yeah, I caught the arrest . . . Caught it in more ways than one."

"What do you mean?"

"He ran straight at me. Well, we grabbed each other. Then I shot—"

"What?"

Eugene shook his head, "I caught the arrest. I'll explain when I get there. Is Brinkmann coming to the scene?"

"He should be there already," said Michael.

A hand touched his shoulder from behind. Eugene flinched and spun, fists raised. A shocked Andrew Brinkmann raised his hands in retreat, "Whoa, cowboy, are you gonna bust my nose, too?"

"Sorry, Andrew. Just a little cranked."

"Yeah, no shit. Are you driving the pics back?"

"It'll be quicker than firing up the laptop. Cops haven't asked any questions. Maybe I should wait."

"Umm, if they haven't nabbed you at this point, I'd make my escape."

"What? Why?"

"They may try to take your cameras for evidence." He glanced around. "It's not worth the risk. Better to beg forgiveness, you know."

"Shit. Right. I didn't think."

Back at the paper, the entire newsroom had gathered, waiting as Eugene placed his camera's data card in a reader at the photo desk. As the grid of images popped up on screen, he scrolled to the end of the take, magnifying the second to last image. A collective gasp rolled through the crowd.

"Whoa," said Michael. "That's goddamned spooky. Those eyes knife right through you. Quick, save that frame just in case."

Eugene did a "save as."

The crowd parted for Oliver Condon, the paper's owner and publisher. Condon stared at the screen. "You tackled that animal?"

"Well, he grabbed me and we sorta danced until he tripped. I know I'm not supposed to get involved in—"

"Bullshit," said Condon, unfolding crossed arms to lay a hand on Eugene's shoulder. "First you have to be a human being and do the right thing. Damn good job."

Eugene blushed. A "damn good job" from Condon was on par with winning a Pulitzer Prize.

Seven years earlier, Condon had seen something in Eugene and had taken a chance on him. A college scholarship contest brought them together. College wasn't on Eugene's radar until his yearbook advisor urged him to try for the scholarship. He didn't know how much college would cost, but figured the $500 prize would go a long way towards getting him there.

With the deadline for applications being midnight of the next day, he worked late into the night choosing images and writing a cover letter. He ditched the next afternoon's classes to take a series of buses to the *East Valley Herald*, the appointed collection point for entries.

Book bag slung over his shoulder, wearing his cleanest blue jeans and his dressiest thrift shop polo shirt, he marched into the newspaper building, not knowing what to expect. An elderly receptionist greeted him from her desk behind the front counter.

"Hi, uh, I've got an entry for the Press Association scholarship," he said, pulling an Ilford photographic paper box from his bag.

"Well, you're just in time," said the receptionist. "I was about to take today's batch back to Mr. Condon's office, just—"

"I'll get them," said a grandfatherly man approaching the desk.

"Oh, Mr. Condon, you don't have—"

"It's no bother, Mildred," said Condon, hoisting a box filled with envelopes from beside her desk. He wore a tweed jacket with leather patches on the elbows. A pair of reading glasses hung on a cord around his neck. The old man's intelligent eyes scanned Eugene with more interest than pity or distaste.

"Is that your entry?" he asked Eugene.

"Yes, sir." He held out the box.

"Ah, my hands are full, c'mon back, son," he said. "Have you ever seen the inner-workings of a newsroom?"

"No, sir." Eugene glanced at the receptionist to make sure it was okay. She smiled and tilted her head in permission.

The click of computer keyboards and the newsroom's intensity mesmerized him. In the background a police scanner added a knife-edged significance.

These people are doing something really important.

He followed the old man back to his office. Condon set the big box of entries on a corner of his messy desk. "My name's Oliver Condon, and you are?"

"Eugene Fellig, sir." He shook the old man's offered hand, taking care to stiffen his grip and look him in the eye just as the two brothers he lived with had taught him. Condon accepted the portfolio box then sat down, his leather office chair creaking as he settled in.

Eugene remained standing, entranced by a large black and white photograph on the wall behind the desk. The image showed a Japanese woman cradling a horrifically deformed girl in a large wooden washtub, her love for the girl obvious in soft morning light.

"What do you want to do with yourself?" asked Mr. Condon.

Still standing, staring at the picture, Eugene forced himself to focus on the task at hand. "I want to go to college and learn to be a photographer," he blurted, not sure where the words came from.

"I *see*," said Condon, "but can you? Sit, son. Go ahead and sit down." Condon pointed to a chair in front of his desk.

Eugene smiled and raised his eyebrows in return, unsure what the man meant by emphasizing the word "see".

Condon opened the portfolio box, setting the hand-written cover letter aside to go straight to the pictures.

The compact and comfortable atmosphere of the office settled Eugene. It smelled like a library. Leather and old paper, black and white pictures, awards and military memorabilia.

Condon pored over the images, considering each carefully. He held up a black and white picture of a homeless man feeding a dog beneath a wall painted with dancing cartoon pigs. "Where'd you take this?"

"Farmer John Meats near where I live."

"Why?"

"Excuse me?"

"Why did you take it?"

"I just thought it was interesting. The guy was really nice to share his food and those pigs are funny, I don't know, I guess I thought it was kinda sad, but kinda happy, too. I see stuff like that all the time and people like looking at it."

"And this?" Condon asked, holding an image of an angry little girl. Her face was big in the left foreground of the picture, her eyes filled with defiant tears. Behind the girl, two little boys trampolined on a discarded, threadbare mattress.

"That's Dayshawn. Her brothers wouldn't let her have a turn on the mattress."

"I gathered that from the story you told with this image," said Condon. "What do you shoot with, Canon? Nikon?"

Eugene reached in his book bag and pulled out an ancient Canon ftb camera with a 50mm lens. "I use this. It was the best one they had at the Goodwill. My school has a bunch of old film and they let me use the darkroom."

"No digital?"

"I wish," said Eugene.

"I noticed you were drawn to that photograph on the wall behind me."

"Yes, sir. Is that the girl's mom in the water with her?"

"Yes, the girl's name is Kamimura Tomoko. They lived in a Japanese fishing village called Minimata."

"What happened to her? Was she born like that?"

"Yes, her deformity was caused by mercury poisoning. Greedy men were dumping it into the ocean. But, they were forced to stop once the world saw that picture. You see, a photograph can be a very powerful thing."

"Ah, I do see," said Eugene, smiling as his mind sparked to life with sudden understanding.

"Yes, you certainly do." Fascinated excitement showed in Mr. Condon's eyes as he rested his chin between his thumb and forefinger, pausing their conversation to study the boy. "Eugene's a good name for a photographer," he said, breaking a brief silence. "The man who took that photo was named Eugene."

"Really?"

"Yes, Eugene Smith, one of the fathers of photojournalism. I actually met him a few times in Tucson before he died. Helluva guy." Condon fell silent, his eyes locked with Eugene's. "Do you know anything about the function of journalism in society? Why we do what we do?"

"No . . . I guess not. But when I walked in here, I could tell there was something really important going on."

A broad smile creased the old man's fatherly face. "What we do is very important. Journalism is a life of service. We serve our readers by telling them what's going on in their city. We hold the powerful to account and alert people when there's a problem—"

"So you're like a guard dog," interrupted Eugene.

"In a sense. Like a guard dog we make noise when something's wrong. But we also tell people about good things, things that shouldn't be taken for granted. Take that picture for instance," he pointed to the Minimata print. "Not only did that image bring an end to illegal dumping, it also showed the boundless love between a mother and her child. Wouldn't you say a moment like that should be appreciated?"

"Yes. It makes me sad, but it makes me happy, too."

Condon held up Eugene's picture of the homeless man feeding the dog. "Kind of sad but kind of happy, right?"

Eugene beamed, sitting up a little straighter. "Yes, sir. Thank you. Ah, do you think I could work for you someday?"

"Yes, possibly, but you're young and it seems employers think college is more important than the person these days. Let's take it one step at a time."

"All right," Eugene said, feeling a little less hopeful.

"So, where do you go to school?"

"Tech High, in south Phoenix."

"How'd you get here? Did you drive?"

"I took the bus and walked."

"Tell you what, Mr. Fellig, how about we take a tour of the paper, then I give you a ride home. I need to see a friend who lives on the south side, anyway."

Embarrassed by his mother and the public housing projects, he'd asked to be dropped off at what he said was his after-school junkyard job. Beaming with pride, Eugene introduced Mr. Condon to Albert and Carl Fodoni as well as King, the junkyard dog. The publisher shook their hands and kneeled to trade a little affection with the dog. He then asked to talk to Carl and Albert alone. Eugene nodded and headed for the office with King at his heels.

Carl and Albert entered the office a few minutes later. "You impressed that man, Eugene," said Carl. "He says you have an incredible eye and a talent for storytelling."

Eugene's heart soared, feeling special. For the first time in his life, he thought he might have value to the outside world.

A month later, as high school graduation approached, Albert and Carl presented a very surprised Eugene with a Mazda pickup truck. They had cobbled it together from several salvage-titled vehicles.

"It's a graduation present," said Albert.

"We wanted to get her painted but ran out of time. Figure we can finish her out together in the next couple a weeks," added Carl.

Wide-eyed and slack-jawed, Eugene stared at the truck in all its beautiful, rusted glory. "Sure, that'd be terrific. Sand out that rust on the rear fenders and add a little primer and paint. She'll be a real classic. Man, I can't believe—"

"It's our pleasure, son," Albert interrupted. "You earned every bit of it."

"By the way," said Carl, beaming, "that fellow from the newspaper called. Told us you didn't win that scholarship."

"Oh," Eugene murmured, a bit deflated but confused by the broader smiles on the brothers' faces.

"Good news is," Carl continued, "he offered you a paid, summer internship at his newspaper."

Eugene blinked. "Is that a job?"

"Just for the summer," said Albert. "He said it's like a tryout, but they pay you, too."

"Did he say what I'll be doing?"

"Well, not exactly, but he did say he'd have cameras if you could get transportation." Albert handed Eugene the keys to the truck.

Eugene was a quick study. The summer internship became a full-time job. Now, years later, he sat at the photo desk of the *East Valley Herald*, working an image of the city's most notorious serial rapist.

"Got a few minutes to tell me about your valiant capture of Derek Schaefer, a.k.a Pencil Dick?" asked Andrew Brinkmann.

"Schaefer. Is that Pencil Dick's real name?"

"That's what the cops tell me."

"Sure, just let me finish this caption and I'll come over."

Brinkmann probed Eugene from every possible angle, asking similar questions in different ways to make sure he had a clear picture. Eugene answered patiently. He'd been an observer of countless interviews over the years and knew the drill.

"The cops never said anything to you immediately afterward?" asked Brinkmann.

"Nope, not a thing. You were there, remember?"

"Yeah, and I still think it's strange."

"You don't think they're pissed that I grabbed the guy, do you? I really didn't have a choice. He came right at me."

"Well, I wouldn't think so. But, they can be thin-skinned and we've been pretty rough on them on the editorial page lately. I could see them getting pissed about you getting credit for taking him down."

2

Sitting in the air-conditioned comfort of a Starbucks, sipping an iced tea, Eugene finished processing and transmitting pictures of a high school baseball game, his only assignment of the evening.

Phone calls from other media outlets asking for interviews had come in all afternoon. He'd said no to all, saying he preferred the anonymity of his side of the camera. In reality, he knew Condon wouldn't approve of the celebrity status TV was so fond of.

To finish out the remainder of his shift, he popped in a set of ear buds to monitor his police scanner while surfing for the other local news outlet's take on the arrest of the Scottsdale Rapist. Everyone, including Andrew Brinkmann had made him sound like a hero.

Geez, Andrew, you have no idea . . . that little shoving match was nothing . . . Still, snagging that photo was pretty cool . . . I wish Trish were here to share in the fun . . . .

He plucked his phone from its holster and opened the Find Friends app. Trish was gone for real, just a pulsing blue dot on I-10, crossing the California border. Depression wedged in, casting a shadow on his otherwise amazing day.

Knock it off, dumb ass. You made a hell of a picture. Don't ruin it now.

Rather than going home and letting depression tighten its grip, he headed for the Prickly Pearadise Bar and Grill. Once a regular at the Prickly, he'd grown tired of the hefty bar tab and the constant bitching of fellow journalists who didn't appreciate how good they had it working for a real newsman like Mr. Condon.

Two steps inside the front door, Eugene found himself wrapped in the arms of Sandy Carter, the Prickly's lead waitress and daughter of the bar's owner. Sandy's breasts strained her tied-above-the-midriff shirt and Daisy Duke cutoffs showcased her long, firm legs.

"Where have you been hiding?" she asked, her chest warm and firmly against his.

Waitresses were Eugene's weakness. Sandy was a beauty, but on their one and only date, he'd seen that she was a high maintenance, daddy's girl. Not the hard working, self sufficient type he preferred.

"Oh, here and there," Eugene said, taking in her intoxicating scent, "I moved to an apartment on the south end of town. The Prickly just kinda fell off my radar."

"So, how are you dealing with the fame? You're all over the TV news."

"For that thing this afternoon? I don't remember TV—"

"Have one on me!" bellowed a huge man in a Hawaiian shirt plowing through the crowd to shake Eugene's hand. It was Chris Carter, Sandy's father. As usual, Chris had been drinking the profits. Tonight the alcohol conjured his happy-go-lucky persona rather than the dark brood feared by his employees. He handed Eugene a tumbler with at hefty pour of whiskey, neat, just as he liked.

"I've wanted to do something like that my whole life," slurred Chris. "You really nailed that scumbag."

"Honestly, the whole thing happened really fast. I just grabbed him and the cops jumped in. We're not supposed to get—"

"Don't be so modest, bud. That take down was really something."

Chris' 100-proof breath hung heavy as the he wrapped his thick, hairy arms around Eugene and Sandy's necks, pulling them into a boozy group hug. Sandy caught Eugene's eye, offering an "I know, Dad's been drinking" look.

"Thanks, Chris, but, really, I didn't do that much," Eugene said. He extracted himself from the bear hug, careful not to spill his drink. "Fact is I'm not supposed to get involved at all. I should be in trouble."

"Screw the rules, man. That head-butt was a thing of beauty. Just what the raping motherfucker deserved. Hell, I DVR'd it back in my office. You gotta see yourself on TV. Come on back."

Chris Carter's dank little office reeked of stale cigarettes. On a desktop dotted with cigarette burns, two ashtrays overflowed with snubbed-out butts. Liquor boxes and pictures of family and parties at the bar covered the walls. Someone in Chris' family—probably his brother by the looks of it—was big-time military.

"Sit down. I'll get this fired up," Chris said, tossing a box full of papers from a chair to the floor. He then turned the little TV so Eugene could see.

Sandy drifted in behind, laying a hand on Eugene's shoulder. It drifted to his neck. Then her fingers wriggled through his hair. He pressed into her touch. *God she smells good.*

"Tonight on Action Eight News we have exclusive video. Police may have the alleged Scottsdale Rapist in custody, thanks to a local photographer."

What the Hell? I never saw TV there.

The video looked nothing like he remembered. They showed only the last seconds of the awkward dance, staying with the action. He and Pencil Dick grunted, twisted, and fell to the pavement. The angle and tight framing made Eugene wince. He looked like a professional fighter as his forehead demolished Pencil Dick's nose.

"Oh, for heaven's sake," he said, as Chris replayed the head-butt again and again. Sandy's hands raked through his hair and tugged on his ear before sliding down inside his shirt to play with the hair on his chest.

"First of all, I didn't mean to whack him in the nose. I fell on top of him. It was an accident."

“Damn fine execution of an *accident,* if you ask me,” said Chris before taking a hefty sip of his drink.

“The rules are we’re not supposed to become the news, just cover it.”

Chris leaned back in his chair and offered an approving wink to his daughter. “Regardless of the rules, you did a good thing, man. Most guys would love to be in your shoes. Hell, every woman in town will be thinking of you when they go to bed tonight.”

Sandy’s breath blew hot in his left ear. Her breasts pressed warm and firm on the back of his neck. One hand worked some sort of magic on his right ear. The tumbler of whiskey Chris had handed him found his lips. *Every woman in town might be thinking about me, but Sandy will be the one taking me home.*

As the night rolled on, free drinks came from all directions. Some he sipped, others he shared with nearby revelers, wanting to keep his happy drunk on an even keel. With a drink in each hand he strolled through the bar, maintaining his life-of-the-party persona. At one point a drunken Andrew Brinkmann thrust out an arm and pulled him up to the bar. Eugene offered him one of his drinks. Andrew took it without hesitation.

“You know I’m proud of you kid,” he mumbled through the booze.

“Thanks, Andrew. I—”

“You know, there were some people that didn’t want you on staff.”

“Yeah, but that was a long—”

“Hang on. You need to hear the whole story, buddy.” He paused to take a sip of his new drink and winced. “What the hell is this?”

“I don’t know. Some sort of tequila thing, I think.”

Andrew forced down another sip and continued, “The day before they offered you the job there was a big-assed s-s-screaming match in Condon’s office. Michael called you a stray dog and a welfare case. That really got Condon steamed. Pete argued that you were uneducated and didn't have a degree . . . I thought Condon was going to punch him for that. The dumb bastard forgot that Condon didn't go to college, either."

Sobered, Eugene smiled. "Good to know, Andrew. Thanks, I'll—"

"You don't get it do you?"

Eugene tried to walk away but Andrew pulled him back. "You proved the dick heads wrong. Pete never shoulda been made a manager and Michael? Shit, that brown-nosing fool shoulda retired years ago."

Eugene tried to dull his crushing disappointment with a long sip of whiskey. "Guess that explains why Mike was so hard on me at the start. He was trying to prove Condon wrong."

"Damn right he was. Hell we all saw it. You should know you have a lot of friends in the newsroom. A lot of us were rooting for you all along."

Eugene wrapped an arm around Andrew's back, hugging him tight. "Thanks, man," he said.

Members of the copydesk arrived, carrying fresh, off-the-press papers bearing the photo of Pencil Dick's arrest. The party started anew and Eugene downed drink after drink.

At last call he slurred, "I should head home. W-who wants to drive me?"

Sandy swooped in, grabbing his keys the second they appeared in his hand. She ceremoniously pulled open her shorts to drop them into her panties. The overtly suggestive act brought loud approval from the bar. Sandy glanced to her father who smiled, offering a drunken nod and a muttered, "Go ahead. Knock off early."

As they weaved the half-a-block walk to his Jeep, Eugene asked, "Can you drive a stick?"

"I guess you'll have to teach me."

Their lurching, stalling, laugh-filled ride ended in front Sandy's apartment building. In a brief moment of fresh-air clarity, he wondered if this was a bad idea. Sandy wasn't his type. If she was hoping for more than just a good time . . . Then they were inside. As the door closed, perfect breasts jiggled free. She pulled him close and slipped a leg between his. He felt her warmth through his blue jeans and desire overpowered better judgment.

Sandy was in a mood to please. Delightfully long and playful lovemaking led to sleep with Sandy nuzzling his neck, her arm draped on his chest.

He woke sometime later, badly in need of the bathroom. Feeling his way through the dark, memories of the lovemaking brought a new erection that made peeing a messy affair. He closed the bathroom door and flipped on the light. Stuffed animals stared at him from all corners of the gaudy bathroom. Expensive lotions, perfumes and makeup filled the counters and shelves. He cleaned up, lowered the seat and took hold of his penis, whispering, "What the hell have you done?"

Later, he would face the damage control. For now, he had to get dressed and head home.

Shoes in hand, he kissed Sandy's cheek. She woke, smiling sleepily.

"I have to work in a few hours. Got to get home to sleep, shower, and change clothes."

She raised a hand to his face. "Will you call?"

"Sure and I'll stop by the bar when I get off work tonight."

Sandy rolled over, pulling her comforter up tight. "See you then, sweetie."

As he stepped outside, sprinklers hissed to life, startling him. Sandy's apartment opened on a courtyard swimming pool surrounded by grass and palm trees. At the front gate he paused to pull on his shoes then quietly worked the gate latch.

Worry for his camera gear turned to relief at seeing his Jeep untouched and secure. After crawling into the driver's seat and rolling down the window, he hauled in a chestful of fresh morning air, cranked the engine, and set off.

Wind whipped his hair as the first rays of sun broke the horizon, saturating the world with color. This was his city. He was no longer the scruffy-haired welfare kid from the projects. He had colleagues with college degrees who treated him with respect. Memories of Condon's pat on the shoulder brought tears to his eyes. He marveled at his uncanny luck.

At home, he carried in his cameras and computer, setting them in a pile next to the bed. It was good to get back to his messy, one-bedroom apartment. Something about Sandy's place . . . uptight . . . too perfect. He kicked off his shoes, stripped down to his boxer briefs then dropped on the bed to set his iPhone alarm to noon before tumbling into sleep, satisfied and happy.

* * *

At first, the pounding on the door seemed like a dream. Eugene rolled over, a slight hangover nagging, as mid-morning light slipped past his heavy bedroom curtains. A second round of louder knocking rattled the pictures on the wall. He sat up in bed.

What the hell?

"Mr. Fellig, this is the Scottsdale Police. We need to talk!"

He pulled on his pants. "Hang on, I-I'm coming!"

He opened the apartment door to two uniformed policemen. One had a hand on his holstered pistol. "Mr. Fellig, show us your hands, please."

Eugene lifted his open hands out to his sides. "This is a joke, right? A little payback for yesterd—"

The officers burst in hard and fast, throwing him to the floor, grinding his face in the carpet as they ratcheted a pair of cuffs to his wrists.

"WHAT THE FUCK, GUYS. THIS ISN'T FUNNY!"

"It's not supposed to be," one of them growled.

His cheek stinging from the carpet facial, he stared across his living room floor to see two pair of dress shoes walk through his open door.

"You were told to wait till we arrived," said Detective Aronson. He kneeled near Eugene's face. "Sorry, bud. You okay?"

"Sure, just a prank gone bad, right, Harry? A little payback for my getting in the way yesterday?"

Eddie grabbed one of Eugene's arms. "Help me out, officer." They lifted him to the couch and stepped back.

Their somber expressions gave Eugene a sick chill. *Something's wrong, something's very wrong here.*

"Eugene Fellig, you have the right to remain silent. Anything you say can and will be used against you in a court of law—"

"Damn it, Harry, it's not funny anymore."

Harry held up a hand to silence him and finished the Miranda speech.

"Of course. I understand my rights, Harry. What the hell is going on?"

"You are acquainted with Sandy Carter, correct?" asked Detective Ibarra.

"Oh, I get it. Sandy put you up to this. You can tell her I will call. But, first I really need to get some sleep. I work the late shift, remember?"

"Eugene, shut up and listen," said Detective Aronson. "Sandy's dead. Murdered in her apartment this morning and you were the last person seen in her company."

A sick, warm rush rose from the pit of Eugene's stomach. "What? That's bullshit, I just left her. She was fine. What time is it?"

"10:30," said one of the uniforms.

"I just kissed her goodbye . . . a few hours ago." His voice wavered as his throat tightened.

"So, you admit you were with her early this morning?"

Shoving grief and the urge to vomit aside, Eugene refocused. Problem solving replaced panic. "Yes, she took me back to her place after we left the Prickly Pearadise last night. We had a few hours of fun then I came home to get some sleep before work. Jesus, Harry, does Chris know yet?"

"It's Chris that found her," said Harry. "He pointed us to you. We almost had to lock him up he's so crazy. Can't blame him, walking in on his daughter like that."

"Like how? What do you mean?"

The detectives looked at each other then Harry snapped, "Let's just get you dressed and down to the station."

Eugene was escorted to the bedroom and the handcuffs removed. "If those are yesterday's pants, take them off and get clothes from your closet. We'll need everything from last night for evidence."

Pulling a clean shirt from a closet hanger, Eugene turned to see Harry shining his flashlight on the day-old clothes in a heap on the floor. Eddie pointed to the Sharpie marker in a shirt pocket. Harry's face tightened.

"Some of your colleagues are outside," said Harry. "For your sake I'll leave the cuffs off. But, just so we're clear, you run and we'll Taser the shit out of you. Let's just keep this light and friendly, okay?"

"Harry, you're scaring the hell out of me. I didn't do anything wrong."

"Light and friendly, Eugene. Do you understand?"

"Yes, sir."

As they stepped outside, the blinding summer sun sent Eugene's hand to shade his eyes. Across the street, television cameramen and on-air talent jumped to life.

"Let's put him in the front seat," said Harry. "I'll ride in back."

"Thank you for that, guys," said Eugene, latching the seatbelt buckle Harry had found for him.

Rolling by the line of media, Eugene caught the eyes of Andrew Brinkmann and another of the paper's photographers. Andrew waved. As the photographer put the camera to her face, Eugene gave them a jaw-clenched thumbs up.

3

A small lizard sunned itself on the wood railing of Jack Carter's front porch. Sluggish from the desert night's chill, the lizard's eyes remained closed. Jack placed his warm coffee cup near the little creature to speed its transition from night to day.

He broke the yolks of his eggs, mixing the yellow with the salsa and beans of his *huevos rancheros*. Forking the mixture into a soft, flour tortilla and taking his first bite, he gazed out at two thousand acres of mesquite, creosote, and cactus, all of it his.

Instructors atop four-wheelers buzzed around the property, hauling supplies, checking and repairing targets and shooting stations. From the storage barn, a tractor hitched to a hay wagon headed out to deliver bottled water and collect trash from the fifteen separate gun ranges of The Breech Firearms Training Academy.

Binoculars sat on the table next to his breakfast. After a few more delicious mouthfuls, Jack put the optics to his face. He immediately spotted a small, special ops group on their way back to camp from a night-long training session in the far reaches of the facility.

He wished all his customers were as disciplined as this bunch. Soon the vanloads of new students would arrive. Sprinkled among the rich hobbyists, military wanna-bes and corporate assholes, would be one or two men who proved capable, but most were naive. A few days of training and a piece of paper declaring they'd cleared "The Breech" would never put them on par with those who devoted their lives to such pursuits.

Still sluggish but able to move, the lizard backed away as Jack stood, picked up his coffee, and drained it before retrieving his breakfast dishes. With a pinky finger, he pulled open the screen door of his little house on the hill then slipped a foot inside to push it open the rest of the way. As his wife, Graciela, watered the houseplants, she listened to a morning news show on TV.

"Did you inhale that breakfast?" she asked, refilling the watering can.

"*No, mi bonita*, I tasted every delicious bite. The chorizo was a nice touch, by the way. I've got a busy day," he said. "There's a fresh class coming in this morning. They'll all want to meet me before I set the instructors loose on them."

He set the dishes in the sink then wrapped his arms around his wife. *God, I love this woman. How could I be so lucky?*

Graciela had stayed with him through it all. He'd landed in her care at Walter Reed Medical Center, a physical and mental wreck shot to pieces in a foreign land. Many said it was the ceramic plate in his body armor that had saved him, but he knew it was his love for Graciela that had brought him back. Since then she'd been there through all the years of not knowing where he was or if he'd come home. First he'd belonged to the military then to his private security work. Now he was all hers and never again would she hear, "Honey, we have orders."

He felt warmth rise within Graciela as she melted in the strength of his embrace. She gazed up at him. "You know the class could wait a few more minutes."

The telephone interrupted their amorous moment. A call on the private line this early cast a sudden feeling of dread on the morning.

Jack grabbed up the phone. "Hello?" His posture stiffened at hearing his brother, Chris, drunk and sobbing. In the edge of his vision, he saw Gracie's face darken with worry. She moved close to better hear.

After coaxing what he could from his brother, he said, "I'm two hours out but I'll be there ASAP." He met Gracie's eyes as his brother blubbered. "No. Chris, you stay put. Don't you do anything till I get there. And, for God's sake, lay off the booze."

It had been two years since Jack's eyes had leveled with their "mission" look. Jack saw Gracie's face pinch when she caught it. "What is it, Jack? What happened to Chris? What's going on?"

"It's our little Sandy . . . She's been murdered."

Gracie took a step back. "Jack, what the hell?"

"Some little media puke, from what Chris says. She took him home and he killed her."

"Is Chris all right? He's not going to do anything stupid?"

"Not if I can help it. I'm sorry, Gracie. I need to get down to Phoenix. Can you pack me a bag? I've got a few things to get together downstairs."

The little house on the hill was really the little house *in* the hill. Two floors below the surface, Jack opened the heavy metal door of his armory. The walls held a mix of weapons, pictures, flags, and plaques. In the center of the room an eight-foot long, waist-high cabinet displayed a tripod-mounted M2 Browning .50 caliber. Workbenches bristled with reloading presses and guns in various stages of teardown, many of them, new models sent to Jack for testing.

Opening a daypack, he collected several boxes of round-nose .45 ACP for his sidearm then added binoculars, radios, and other familiar tools of clandestine surveillance.

"I packed for two days. Is that enough?" Graciela yelled down the stairs.

"That'll do for now. I might have you bring more stuff when you come . if I need it. Shit, I'll need a suit coat for the funeral. Do you mind bring—"

"I'll handle it. You just get down to Phoenix and keep Chris from doing something stupid."

At their front doorway they held each other in a long embrace. Tears glistened on Gracie's cheek. She cried for Sandy and Chris and she cried for Jack. "You be careful. You know how Chris gets."

"I'll do what I can to shut him down and let me do what I do best. I don't do stupid, remember? I'll call when I get there to give you an update."

He marched down the long wooden porch to his SUV, thinking of Sandy and the hell he'd rain down on the asshole who killed her.

* * *

Eugene sat in a small, sterile interview room deep inside Scottsdale Police headquarters. Right foot tapping to fend off nerves and the need to pee, his gaze darted between the locked door, the beige walls, and the gray metal table anchored to the floor. Two hours had passed since he'd talked to anyone. He used the paper towel given to him during intake to wipe Sandy's scent from his fingers and face.

Officers and detectives watched via closed circuit television.

"Why do you think he's wiping his hands and face?" asked Harry.

"I could smell the sex on him back in his apartment," said Eddie. "Maybe he's trying to hide it."

"Wouldn't a serial rapist want to enjoy that as long as possible?"

"A rapist wouldn't want *us* to smell it," said Eddie.

"But he's already admitted to being with her."

Exasperation played on Eddie's face, "I know you're friends with this Eugene kid, but if it turns out that Schaefer's innocent and the real rapist was under our noses the whole time, the chief will put our balls in a vice."

"Schaefer's our guy," Harry declared.

"I wouldn't bet your career on that. Your friend was there every time our rapist struck and now the girl that took him to her apartment ends up dead and marked up just like our rape victims. He had a Sharpie marker in his shirt pocket, for Christ's sake."

Harry shook his head. "He's being set up or it's a coincidence."

"Fat chance . . . And just how would Schaefer set him up from jail?"

"Maybe Schaefer had an accomplice."

"Sure, and if he did, it was probably Eugene."

The video monitoring room phone interrupted. Harry picked it up. "His lawyer is here."

Eugene rose to greet the detectives as they entered with a stranger in tow.

"Eugene, this is Ely Rosenthal. Your publisher sent him over to act as your attorney," said Harry.

"Sorry we have to meet under these circumstances," said Rosenthal, shaking Eugene's hand. "How are you holding up?"

"Fine, sir," said Eugene, relieved to finally have someone on his side present. "Before I asked for a lawyer I let them sample my DNA. I hope that was okay. I told them I don't have anything to hide, but then I got scared."

The short, heavyset attorney tugged at his expensive suit coat while silently eyeing Harry and Eddie.

The detectives took the hint and moved to the door. Harry glanced at Eugene. "We're gonna step out now and leave you two to talk."

As soon as the door closed, Eugene blurted, "Good god, I hope that DNA thing—"

Rosenthal held up a hand to silence him then pointed to the red light on a video camera in the corner of the room. When it went dark, he settled into the only other chair and looked deep into Eugene's eyes.

"You realize the seriousness of your predicament?"

"I didn't kill Sandy. She—"

"Miss Carter's only part of it. They also suspect you to be the Scottsdale Rapist."

Eugene jerked upright. "What? That guy Pencil Dick, uh, Schaefer's the rapist. What the *hell* are you talking about?"

"Why do you carry a black Sharpie marker?"

"What does that have to do with anything?"

"My sources tell me the word bitch was scrawled on Miss Carter's forehead. It's not public knowledge, but the Scottsdale rapist wrote that same thing in black, permanent marker on each victim's forehead. I'll ask you again, why the black Sharpie?"

Eugene blanched. Crime scene-like images of Sandy filled his imagination. "To take notes, mark my spot at sporting events. In the old days guys used them to mark film."

"I'm told the police claim you were nearby *every* time the rapist struck and that last night you were extremely drunk when you left with Miss Carter."

"I was there because it's my job. I listen to the police calls . . . and, yes, I was drunk, but not insane. I could never hurt Sandy—"

"When you left her, did you see anyone around her complex?"

Eugene thought back to the night before, hearing the sprinklers, smelling the night air. "No . . . it was just before sunrise, the sprinklers came on . . . I put my shoes on outside, got in my Jeep, and went home. I didn't see anyone or anything out of the ordinary."

"Well," said Rosenthal, trying to sound upbeat, "the bright side of this is that Oliver Condon believes in you or I wouldn't be here. That said, is there anything you need to tell me? I'm your lawyer so it stays in this room. If there's anything—anything in your past or present, good, bad or embarrassing—now's the time to tell me."

"No, nothing. Nothing at all. I wish I'd never gone to that damn bar. I don't even like the place."

"Then why did you go?"

"Why does anybody go to a bar? I was a little depressed because I'd just broken up with my girlfriend. I'd had a great day and didn't have anyone to share it with."

"All right then. Let's take the first step toward clearing this up." Rosenthal's cordial, businesslike demeanor suddenly turned shark-like. "Did you kill Sandy Carter?" The attorney's eyes drilled deep.

Eugene refused to shy from the lawyer's piercing gaze. He carefully stated, "Hell. No."

Rosenthal lightened. "All right then, I need to know every detail. I need an exact timeline of what happened from the moment you saw Schaefer until they hauled you in here."

They talked for forty-five minutes, the lawyer taking notes and stopping frequently to clarify detail.

"Okay, I think we're ready to make a statement. Let's bring in the detectives and you tell them what happened. Don't embellish. Stick to exactly what you've told me. If I stop you, don't interrupt.

Remember, they are not good guys and they are not your friends. They'll hang you if you give them any rope."

"Okay." Eugene nodded with confidence. "Then can I go home after?"

Rosenthal's eyes dimmed. "They can hold you here for seventy-two hours without pressing charges. Expect to spend at least one night in jail."

"Christ, a night in jail?"

"Or more. Like I said, they can hold you for three days without charges, so prepare yourself. I'll know more in the morning after I talk with the district attorney. If they do charge you . . . and that's a big if, considering everything they have is circumstantial. I'll ask for bail."

"Bail? I don't—"

Rosenthal held up a hand. "Oliver will take care of it, if need be." He stood and opened the door to signal for the detectives.

Eugene crossed his arms and sat forward. He met Harry's eyes as they entered then mentally switched off the fact that he considered him a friend. Slowly, methodically, questions were asked and answers were given until every detail of the night before was made official.

Eddie and the lawyer left together. Eugene was alone with Harry.

"I'll tell you right up front," said Harry, "you won't like the intake procedure. We gotta do it to keep everyone safe. Turn around, put your hands behind your back."

Wide-eyed and holding down the urge to vomit, Eugene obeyed. Harry steered him from the room and through the halls to the jail's intake area. Eugene stared at the floor the whole time, trying to isolate himself from reality.

Harry escorted him to the jailer, a heavyset man sporting big-framed glasses and a bushy, graying mustache. The man directed them into the cold, beige intake area. He removed Harry's cuffs then handed them off before telling Eugene to remove his belt and empty his pockets. His personal belongings were placed into plastic bins.

"Strip down," said the jailer.

"Everything?"

"Naked as the day you were born."

Arms crossed and hands sheathed in latex, the jailer appeared unimpressed by Eugene's look of disdain.

It's just like the doctor's office, he told himself as he disrobed. As each piece of clothing was removed and handed off, the jailer felt through it then dropped it to the floor. Naked, cold and defenseless, Eugene felt latex fingers probe through his hair and behind his ears. He closed his eyes wanting to shut out the world.

"Open your mouth."

"Huh?"

"Open up. You got any false teeth, plates or partials?"

Eugene shook his head, opening his mouth like a horse at auction. He caught a whiff of the jailer's lunch and saw crumbs in his mustache as the dull-looking man peered into his mouth. *This is no doctor's office.*

"Good. Tongue up." The jailer then stepped back, "Arms up and turn all the way around."

Eugene did as he was told.

"Now, lift up your cock and balls. Spread your legs." Acutely aware of Harry's presence, Eugene wanted to scream and lash out. Swallowing his frustration, he lifted himself to give the jailer a look.

"Now, drop just your balls and hang onto your cock. Thanks. Now, turn around, bend over, spread'm and cough."

Eugene narrowed his eyes. "What?"

"Turn around, bend over, spread your ass cheeks and cough."

Harry averted his eyes. Eugene complied. When he was directed to stand, Harry handed him an orange jumpsuit.

"Keep your socks and underwear," said the jailer.

His underwear and socks on, he stepped into the jumpsuit. The ill-fitting uniform halved his scrotum when he stood tall. "Got anything a little bigger?" he asked, embarrassed by the squeak in his voice. His face grew hot as his eyes began to tear.

The jailer offered a look that said, "Yeah, right." He held out an odd-smelling pair of rubber and canvas slip-on shoes. "Over there, step on the footprints facing forward," he said, pointing to two sets of shoe prints painted on the floor.

After Eugene found his mark, the jailer stepped behind a counter that held a digital camera tethered to a computer. "Look up here."

Eugene tugged at the crotch of his jumpsuit so he could stand straight and stare into camera's cheap plastic lens.

The jailer tapped the mouse. "Good. Now step on the other two footprints and face to the side."

Eugene complied. "I could show you how to get the most out of that camera," he said, trying to distract himself from the urge to sob. "This overhead light is anything but flattering."

The jailer only stared at the computer screen, his right hand clumsily fingering the mouse.

Multiple pairs of handcuffs hung on the wire mesh at the jail's entry. Eugene's face fell when the jailer reached for a pair.

"It's routine," repeated Harry, "and it's just till they get you into a cell."

"I didn't do anything wrong, Harry. You've got to believe me," he cried, his vision blurring as tears streamed down his cheeks. "The lawyer says you're going to try to keep me in here for days."

Forcing a smile, Harry offered, "Eugene, it's for your own good. We're still trying to sort all this out. Besides, we're uptown compared to most jails. How busy are we, Max?"

"If you're wondering about a private cell, that ain't gonna happen tonight," Max-the-jailer said, expertly cuffing Eugene's hands behind his back.

"Look at it this way," said Harry. "Once this is all cleared up, you'll have a great story to tell."

"Is this going to get cleared up?" Eugene's hands writhed in the metal cuffs. "I've never had much luck when it comes to help from the police."

"Are you talking about your brother?" asked Harry.

"You know about him?"

"Yes, we know what happened."

"No, you don't. The cops never checked. They just wrote him off."

"I'll admit I've only glanced at the reports," said Harry. "But I saw that your brother's death was gang related. You can't blame—"

"That's what I mean. They wrote him off. He wasn't in a gang. We moved into the projects like two days before it happened. Those cops just made shit up."

Harry's jaw tightened. "This is Scottsdale, not the projects. Just ride it out tonight and we'll talk in the morning."

Max-the-jailer nudged Eugene toward a hallway with shiny beige walls. They reached a three-way intersection. Long lines of individual cells stretched off in opposite directions. It reminded him of an animal shelter.

"See you in the morning," Harry called, his voice echoing from beyond the steel mesh and concrete cages.

"Now, here's how it works," explained the jailer. "I'll unlock the cell door and you'll walk in. I'll lock the door and open the port for you to put your hands through then I'll take off the cuffs."

"Is Derek Schaefer in this jail, too?"

Max sighed heavily. "Yes, but he's in his own cell way down at the other end of the block." He unclipped a ring of keys from a carabiner on his belt and used a wide, flat, brass key to turn a big lock in the cell door. "Step on in, son." He added a nudge.

A fat man in a wrinkled dress shirt and pants lay face down and snoring on one of two metal bunks bolted to the concrete on either side of the ten-by-ten cell. Withering at the smell of vomit and the sound of the cell door closing, Eugene dutifully backed up, placing his hands through the portal to be relieved of the cuffs. The jailer slapped the little door closed and moved on without saying a word.

Harsh light glared from buzzing florescent fixtures in the ceiling outside the cell. Claustrophobic panic gripped as Eugene stared at three concrete walls, a steel mesh front, the two metal bunks and a combination stainless steel sink and toilet.

Fear had masked his need to pee, but now his body nagged for relief. Taking advantage of his cellmate's slumber, he sidled up to the toilet, unzipped and peeled his jumpsuit down to his waist. Like a scared turtle, his dick had withdrawn. He stretched it out, aimed and tried to relax. Nothing. His entire body ached with tension. Eventually, he coaxed a trickle and soon the contents of his bladder thrummed into the metal receptacle. Pressing a button on the wall brought a loud flush that caused his cellmate to roll to one side and fart.

Eugene sat on the empty bunk, trying to ignore that it lacked a mattress, pillow, or bedding of any kind. He placed his head in his hands. A loud curse came from somewhere down the line. Voices mixed with the echo of flushing toilets, conversation and occasional laughter. He wanted to cry. A loud bang made him flinch.

"That'll be the dinner cart," said his cellmate, hauling his girth upright. He discovered then chose to ignore the vomit on his shirt. "Forgive the cliche, but whadda ya in for?"

"I guess you'd call me a person of interest," said Eugene. "Yesterday I was a hero and today I'm in jail."

"Hey! You're that guy from the TV that caught the rapist, aren't you? What the hell are you doing in here?"

"Long story."

His cellmate grew even more enthusiastic. "You know that asshole rapist is in here, just down the line. He's quiet now but he was cursing a blue streak earlier. Some really racist garbage."

A small, Hispanic man sporting a hairnet rolled a tall, catering service cart past their cell.

"He starts at the far end and works his way back," said the cellmate. "He'll feed us in a minute."

Metal clanged as the little portal doors opened and closed down the line.

"How come you got to keep your clothes?" asked Eugene.

"I'm a short-timer. They're moving me to county in the morning."

Eugene slumped even more on his bunk. "Guess that means they plan on keeping me."

"That's a logical conclusion."

The man with the cart arrived at their cell, unlatching the portal door, shoving in a thick plastic tray. Eugene retrieved it, politely handing the first tray to his cellmate, and grabbing the second for himself. The portal door slammed shut and the hairnet moved on.

Dinner was noodles and chicken with a cookie and a small carton of milk. A plastic spork was the eating utensil.

After a couple of bites, Eugene offered, "Better than I thought it would be."

"Beats the hell out of the county lock-up where I'm headed. By the way, my name's Duke, Duke Ellington."

"Eugene Fellig. Pleased to meet you. I take it you're not from the musical side of the family."

Ellington let loose an acidic belch then hauled in a breath, letting it out slow. "What was your first clue?"

"Pale complexion for starters."

"Heh, yeah. You don't want to see me dance, either."

Eugene smiled, relaxing a bit. "So, you're headed to the county jail?"

"Yeah, did thirty days last time I got picked up for DUI. This is my fifth go-round. They'll hang onto me for a while this time. It's mostly baloney and bread and dog food over there. Guess I'll have to get used to it."

A sudden clatter and a stream of curses echoed from down the line.

"I ain't eat'n this shit, you fuck'n spic!"

"That would be your dance partner," said Ellington.

Eugene peeled open his milk carton, ignoring Schaefer's outburst, "Fifth DUI? Have you tried to get help?"

"Been in a couple of programs. I'll straighten out for a few months then go on a bender. Gonna cost me my job this time." He stared at his food tray a moment. "Just as well. My wife left me last week. That's what set me off."

"Sorry," said Eugene. "So how does it work in here?"

"It'll be lights out in about three hours. Breakfast is early. It's hard to say just when since there's no clocks. Then you wait for lunch."

"That's it?"

"Yessir, other than the guards walk-through every half hour. Over at county they give you rec time outside every couple a days and there's a TV room. They don't do that here because nobody's around long enough."

"Jesus."

Hours later, the jailer made the final tour of his shift. He peered into each cell to make sure all was well. Eugene tried to meet his eyes but found them closed to human contact.

"LIGHTS OUT!"

A few lights went dark, but not the fixture outside their cell.

Eugene lay down on his bunk, trying to silence his mind and ignore the ball-biting crotch of his jumpsuit.

"YOU DOWN THERE! PAPARAZZI DUDE?"

Eugene lurched from the first touches of sleep.

"THAT'S RIGHT! I KNOW YOU'RE THERE COCKSUCKER! HOW YA LIKE BEING LOCKED UP, YOU SACK OF SHIT? WATCH YOUR ASS, MR. PAPARAZZI! I'M COMIN FOR YA!"

Eugene looked to the locked cell door then to his sleeping cellmate. The smell of disinfectant, vomit and caged men—all of it amplified by the pallid green glare of humming florescent light—conjured a lonely, desperate ache deep into the marrow of his bones. He wanted to scream. He wanted to go home. He wanted to go to Starbucks for coffee. He balled into a fetal position, crying quietly on his way to restless slumber.

A thunderous, metallic fart followed by diarrhea and the loud flush of the toilet woke him. *Morning? No way to tell.*

"Sorry," said his cellmate, slumped on the toilet, offering another courtesy flush that barely muffled the sickening sound and smell.

Eugene rolled over, tugging at the crotch of his jumpsuit. His own need to shit was making the suit even tighter. Ignoring his body's needs, he drifted back to something just shy of sleep, waking what seemed like seconds later to the crash of the jail's main gate. He sat up, head swimming, feeling like he'd barely closed his eyes.

"That'll be breakfast," croaked Ellington.

The peanut butter sandwich and carton of orange juice delivered by a hair-netted worker brought Eugene's already cramped bowels to agonizing attention.

"You want my juice?" asked his cellmate. "My stomach's a bit disagreeable this morning."

"I heard," said Eugene, waving off the offer.

"Sorry about that. You know, my first time in, I made myself sick by holding it. So, don't be afraid to—"

"I'm okay," snapped Eugene. "How the hell do you do it?"

"I relax and pretend I'm alone. Courtesy flushes are big help. You—"

"No, I mean how do you keep from going crazy? I barely slept. The light, the sound, nothing to do. These bunks are cold as hell. I just want to go for a walk, hit the coffee shop, surf the internet—"

"You get used to it. I sleep a lot. Some guys exercise." He stretched as if that qualified. "I never asked yesterday. Have they charged you with anything?"

"No, I don't think so. My lawyer said they can hold me for three days, though."

"Three days is nothing. It'll go by quick. Before you know it, it'll be lunch then dinner. They'll come to take me to county, eventually. That'll be a distraction."

Eugene settled back on his bunk, wondering if he'd ever go home again.

4

"Rise and shine, asshole!"

Eugene sat up, his head pounding. He blinked. Eddie and Harry stood outside his cell. Eddie smiled, adding a cage-rattling slam of his fist on the cell's steel mesh door. Ellington cursed then rolled over, facing the wall.

"What the hell, guys? What's with the attitude?" asked Eugene. "Do you have some news?"

"We have good news and bad news," said Eddie, a small scar on his upper lip making his smile more of a sneer. "The bad news is we're on to your little game with Schaefer."

A sick, warm rush of pending doom rolled in like a wave, leaving fear in its wake. "What the hell are you talking about?"

"I was going over old reports, you know, bringing myself up to speed on our elusive rapist. Surprising how often the guy slipped through our fingers. Time after time we'd close in and poof, he'd just vanish. It's like the guy's a magician."

Eugene stood and walked to the front of the cell, threading his fingers through the mesh, his cramped bowels amplifying his foul mood. "Didn't see much magic when I grabbed him yesterday. Where are you going with this?"

"You were always hanging around when Schaefer disappeared."

"Oh, Christ. My lawyer told me all about this. I am not a rapist. I—"

"We know. You're pecker doesn't fit the description. Harry tells me you ain't got much but you got Schaefer beat."

Harry shot his partner a look of disbelief, "What the hell's wrong with you, Eddie?"

"You stuck me in here just for a look at my dick? Goddamnit, Harry, you—"

"No, that's not why I—"

"Water under the bridge," said Eddie, a satisfied grin riding his fleshy, brown face. "It's likely though that Schaefer had a partner helping him escape." He put a hand to his chin and stared at the ceiling, "Seems like he sure thought he'd catch a ride with you yesterday."

"You've got to be kidding. I told you yesterday. He said he wanted my Jeep."

"Uh-huh. I think what really happened was you and your best buddy, Pencil Dick, cut it too thin. You didn't want to get caught, so you tossed Derek under the bus. Then you tried to make it look like we had the wrong guy by killing the waitress."

"Are you listening to yourself, Eddie? You're fucking insane. Everyone at the bar saw me and Sandy leave together. I'd have to be an idiot to—"

"Witnesses say you were extremely intoxicated. Maybe your judgment was impaired. Or maybe you were working up the courage. Or maybe you didn't think of it till you were alone. No one's claiming you're a mental giant. In fact, a few of your colleagues say you're not even qualified to be working at a newspaper. They say you're a charity project. A sad little stray dog your publisher felt sorry for."

Eugene's fingers tightened on the wire cage door. *Stray dog. He's been talking to Michael. Cocksucker.*

"Ah, hit a nerve, didn't I?" Eddie's scalp glistened through his short-cropped hair, accentuating his sneering smile. "What is it? What trips you trigger? Are you pissed off at the world because chicks don't dig welfare trash?"

"Fuck off, *pendejo*."

In a flash, Eddie's right fist hammered the wire mesh a fraction of a second after Eugene yanked his fingers back.

"Getting a little slow, *abuelo*?" snarked Eugene.

Eddie re-cocked his arm and Harry stepped in, pushing him back, "Knock it the hell off, both of you! Eugene, we're letting you go."

Eugene brightened. "Now, I get it, Eddie. You're pissed that you're losing your scapegoat. Guess you'll actually have to do your job now."

"Eugene!" snapped Harry.

"You'll be back," said Eddie. "Your boss and his fucking son-in-law senator can only pull so many strings—"

"What do you mean?"

"I mean, you're only getting out because your publisher has powerful relatives."

"Eddie, you know that's not the only—"

"Mr. Condon wouldn't do that."

"Face it, asshole. You're a rich guy's pet project, a fucking stray dog that'll end up biting the hand that feeds him."

"Knock it off, Eddie," Harry growled. "Eugene, we also found red fibers in the bed. They're inconsistent with anything in both your apartment and hers. It's not much, but combined with the favors Condon called in, you're a free man. You'll be processed out in a few minutes. I called Brinkmann. He's coming to get you."

"Thanks, Harry." Eugene shot Eddie the finger.

"Don't thank me," Harry said. "I wanted to keep you in here, safe and out of trouble. There's a lot more going on here than you realize."

When Max-the-jailer arrived, Eugene turned to Ellington, still rumpled on his bunk, watching silently. "You take care," he said, reaching to shake the man's hand. "And try to use your time in county to get straightened out, maybe get in some kind of a program."

"Sure," said Ellington, his tone bored and uncaring.

* * *

In the beige Southwestern-styled lobby of Scottsdale Police Headquarters, Andrew Brinkmann waved to Eugene as he emerged from jail looking wrinkled and tired.

"How you holding up?" asked Brinkmann, simultaneously shaking Eugene's hand and slapping his shoulder.

"I'm all right. Didn't get much sleep. Schaefer's in there and he yelled all night. Worse, I couldn't get Sandy out of my head. Then this morning, Harry's new partner was a complete asshole. The guy's off his rocker."

"Eddie Ibarra? I've picked up some very interesting shit on him . . . What did he do to you?"

"Weird shit. Claims I'm Schaefer's partner and that I killed Sandy to get him off the hook."

"That doesn't surprise me. He and Schaefer have a history."

Eugene stopped him. "What?"

"They're both tangled up in that . . . Hang on, cops are coming. I'll tell you more in a bit." The detectives approached. Brinkmann turned journalist. "You pick up any leads on the Carter murder?"

"I'm looking at my lead right now," said Eddie.

Eugene rolled his eyes. "Jesus, Eddie, chill."

"Piss off, asshole."

"Hey," snapped Brinkmann, "that's out of line."

Harry stepped in between his partner and the newspapermen. Picking up on the tension, uniformed officers paused like kids anticipating a schoolyard fight.

With an eye on the gathering crowd, Eugene took a deep breath. "Look, guys, if you're pissed that I got in the way yesterday, I'm sorry. I never should have stopped him like I did. But, you have to take some of the blame. Your slow response gave Schaefer a hell of a head start."

"Bullshit," said one of the uniforms.

"Hey, we all heard the dispatcher begging," snapped Eugene. "Three freaking calls before anyone bothered to get off their ass and help."

"Eugene!" interrupted Brinkmann.

"What?"

"This isn't helping your situation. Remember where we are." Brinkmann turned his back on the lawmen. "Where do you want to go? Your apartment or the paper?"

"Home, I need to shower and change clothes."

"Good luck with that," said Eddie, tacking on a vicious chuckle.

"Why? What do you mean?"

"The guys got a little aggressive at your place," said Harry, sheepishly. "You'll need a new TV and mattress. Your manager says you'll have to pay for the broken toilet and water damage."

Eugene shot a jaw-clenched glance to the crowd.

"We had a warrant," reasoned one of the uniforms. "It was lawfully executed."

Eugene looked to Harry, whose shrug said it was beyond his control.

Eugene sighed, letting it go. "Classy guys, real classy. Hey, I gotta hit the restroom."

"Over there by the drinking fountain," Harry said, pointing, as the crowd began to disperse.

"Do what you gotta do and let's get back to the paper," said Brinkmann. "Everyone's eager to see you."

Eugene headed off.

Eddie's phone rang. He spoke briefly and hung up. "We have reports waiting at the crime lab. I'll meet you upstairs."

"Works for me," said Harry.

When he and Harry were alone, Brinkmann asked, "What's got Eddie so wound up?"

"The usual politics."

"Could it have something to do with Eddie and Schaefer's previous involvement in the old Luchador case?"

Harry stiffened, trying hard not to show his surprise. "You know about Schaefer?"

"That he's one of the abused Luchador kids? Yeah, we figured it out early this morning."

"None of the kids' identities was ever released to the media."

"Not officially, but word gets around. Besides, we didn't need the name. Condon recognized him. He says he's the kid that actually stole the photos that broke the case. He and a social worker brought them to us. Rumor is Eddie was involved in covering up for some very powerful people. You've got a public relations nightmare on your hands."

"You don't know the whole story. The foster kids weren't the only victims back then."

"Giving me the details would help your case."

"Honestly, I don't know everything and I couldn't tell you if I did. What I can tell you—off the record—is that Eddie and the chief go back a ways and I trust the chief's judgment on this."

"Fair enough. Trashing Eugene's apartment was a cheap shot, though. You need us on your side."

"That goes both ways. Your publisher's hindering our investigation by pulling strings with his senator son-in-law isn't making you any friends."

"Um, Harry, the crooked foster parents and the social worker who fed them kids died while in custody. Oliver wasn't going to take any chances with Eugene's safety."

"You might want to check out your buddy before you go too far out on a limb for him."

Brinkmann stiffened. "Save me some time then. What do you know?"

"Schaefer and Eugene grew up together. We think they're friends."

Brinkmann's eyes widened. "Okay, you've got my attention."

"Eugene and Schaefer lived in the same welfare housing project. They were almost neighbors. They went to grade school together until child protective services put Schaefer in foster care."

Brinkmann crossed his arms and shook his head.

Harry continued, "Honestly, I never thought Eugene killed Sandy Carter. We were just playing it safe. Then we find this childhood connection and I have to wonder if he was helping his friend."

"But he tackled the guy."

"Only after Schaefer ran straight for him . . . like he was expecting a ride."

Andrew processed the new information quickly, replaying in his head what he'd seen on the previous afternoon. "Shit—all right, say I buy your theory—I don't, but if I did, what do you suggest?"

"Go to him as a friend and lay it all out. If he is only guilty of helping Schaefer and he cooperates, it'll go a lot easier. Hang on, he's coming back."

Eugene approached looking relaxed. Brinkmann made an effort to brighten, unfolding his arms and smiling.

"Sorry if I let my temper get the better of me a minute ago. I'm over-tired and I was literally, full of crap. You know, the one thing they never mention in prison movies?"

"Enlighten us," said Harry, obviously surprised by Eugene's sudden mood change.

"In jail, everybody's afraid of what could get shoved in their butt, but nobody talks about what has to come out. I was miserable all night because I wouldn't use the shitter in front of my cell mate."

Harry forced a laugh. "Ah, thanks for sharing. Listen," he said, reaching out to slap Eugene on the shoulder, "I have to get back to work. Eugene, you take care of yourself. Don't leave town or anything. This mess is far from over."

"Not going anywhere, Harry, believe me. I want this solved way more than you do." He waved Harry goodbye, heading for the exit with Brinkmann taking the lead.

"So, Andrew, what did I miss while I was in the bathroom? You looked a bit preoccupied just now."

"I'll tell you once we're out of here and headed back to the paper," Brinkmann said, urging Eugene forward.

Stepping into the sunshine, Eugene reveled in the fresh air, the sound of traffic, and the afternoon heat. Passing under a eucalyptus tree on the way to Brinkmann's car, he pulled off a leaf, crushed it, closed his eyes and took in its menthol scent.

"Was it bad in there?" asked Brinkmann.

"Not terrible, just stressful. Boring more than anything. Way too much time to think." Eugene fastened his seatbelt and cracked a window to vent the heat. "I don't think I'd do too well if I had to stay for very long."

Brinkmann's hands danced on the sun-baked steering wheel, the car's turn signal clicking as they merged into traffic. The first minutes of the drive were quiet then Brinkmann broke the silence. "Remember the *Luchador* sex scandal a few years back?"

"Yeah, sure. I came on staff right after. Mr. Condon was obsessed with it."

"Mr. Condon's fairly sure that Schaefer was one of the child victims."

"No shit? I mean, what are the chances? How many kids were there?"

"God, dozens that we know of," said Brinkmann. "A lot of kids just disappeared and were listed as runaways."

"I always felt kinda shut out of that whole thing," said Eugene.

"Not surprised. You were young, not even twenty-years-old, right?"

"I was eighteen when I started the internship."

"Geeze, that's right. I forgot. The whole *Luchador* thing was *reeeeally* nasty stuff. Mr. Condon insisted you be kept out of the loop."

"He actually told people not to tell me about it?"

"Sure. Look, those sick bastards were preying on kids. You were just a kid. Get it?"

Eugene swallowed his frustration at the "kid" label he'd never been able to shake. Before coming to the paper, he'd already seen more of the world's ills than most of the newsroom would see in their lifetime. "I think I can handle it now," he said, patiently. "Give me the lowdown."

"Okay, but it's not pretty. Schaefer stole a box of incriminating photos and gave them to a social worker who brought them to us. She was filling in for a real scumbag who'd had a heart attack. This scumbag kept an eye out for the right kind of kids, you know, the hard-to-place boys who were acting out sexually."

"Probably victims of sex abuse at home," said Eugene.

"Yup, most definitely. Well, he'd funnel the kids to the home of Kyle and Mary Buckingham, two more giant pieces of shit. The young ones were pimped out to pedophiles who came in from all over the country. The older boys got tossed to the Luchadores and when they aged-out of the system, these poor kids who'd been abused for what was probably years, wound up dead in a landfill."

"Where'd the Luchador name come from?"

"They wore Mexican wrestler masks to hide their identities. The box with the pictures that Schaefer took had their name written on it. *Los Luchadores de Niños*."

"The . . . wrestlers of children?"

"Yep, only boys probably. Girls would be niñas, I think."

"So let me get this straight. You think the guy I tackled yesterday was responsible for our breaking the story on the Luchadores?"

"Yep. We're pretty sure it's the same Schaefer. He risked his life to steal the photos from the Buckinghams and not one single sick Luchador bastard was ever identified. It's one of the reasons Condon is so obsessed with the story. He feels like we let young Schaefer down."

"But I thought people went to jail."

"Three were convicted, but they were the enablers like the Buckinghams and their caseworker. By the way, they all died mysterious deaths in prison. Whoever the big boys are, they didn't want to leave any loose ends."

"Isn't Schaefer a loose end?"

"Not really. All the abusers wore masks, remember? He did claim that one of the big wigs in the foster care system was one of them. Said he recognized his voice, but that got shot down. The guy's lawyer made Schaefer out to be mentally unstable. Besides, he had no hard evidence."

"If it went on for years there had to be some sort of trail."

"Well, that's where Eddie comes in."

"Eddie Ibarra? Harry's new partner?"

"One and the same. He was an investigator for the State Patrol back then. Rumor is he made evidence disappear and did whatever else was necessary to protect the big boys. Anyway, he lost his job over it. Condon, Pete and I dug like hell, but the whole thing was kept extremely hush, hush."

"That slimy son-of-a-bitch! I knew he was crooked. How the hell did he wind up in Scottsdale?"

"Harry says he's friends with the chief."

"Well, leave it to Scottsdale's finest. Christ, can you imagine how betrayed Schaefer must have felt? No wonder he turned into such an asshole."

"Yep, pretty amazing shit. Even more amazing is that it's come back to haunt us. Condon is sure this happened for a reason. He believes we're gonna nail these Luchador assholes this time."

Eugene's mind flashed to his own feelings of betrayal at the hands of the police. He stared out the window in silence, biting his lower lip.

"Hey, you still there?" asked Brinkmann.

"Yeah . . . Just thinking . . . Why didn't we know who Schaefer was right off?"

"The Luchador kids were minors. The names were never officially released, but we got 'em on the down low. Plus, Schaefer's grown up a lot since then."

"Then how do we know for sure he's one of them?"

"We didn't, not for *sure.* But a minute ago I tricked Harry into confirming it. Shit, that reminds me I've got to call Condon." He tugged his phone from his belt and speed-dialed.

"Mr. Condon, it's Andrew. Cops just confirmed on Schaefer and they're aware that we're onto Eddie Ibarra's involvement . . . Yes, Harry just told me . . . Yes, I have Eugene. We're headed back . . . No, no signs of trouble . . . Yes, he looks a little wrinkled and he smells like jail, but I think it's an improvement," he said, winking at Eugene. "Yes sir, see you in a few."

"I'll bet that made his day," said Eugene, ignoring Brinkmann's jab at his smell.

"Yep, like I said, he's pumped."

"When did you figure all this out?"

"Early this morning, like two a.m. early. Condon put it together from your picture of the arrest. He thought Schaefer's face was familiar but couldn't place it. Then he wakes up in the middle of the night with the answer. But here's the scary part. When he came into the office to compare our copies of the Luchador Polaroids with your picture, he discovers our copies missing from the database. When he digs out the backup CD from a locked drawer in his desk, he discovers it's been scratched all to hell."

"Somebody broke in and stole the photos?"

"No signs of a break in, but whoever it was had seven years to make those photos go away. I've thought for a long time that the Luchadores have somebody planted at the paper."

"Jesus, any thought's as to who?"

"Nah, could be anybody in the newsroom, or advertising. Heck, even the janitors. But get this, stealing the photos didn't do them any good. They didn't know Condon had copy negatives in his safe at home. He called a friend with a darkroom and by 7 a.m. he had prints in hand."

"There's something in those photos they don't want us to see."

"Bingo," said Brinkmann. "He wants you to have a look at the pictures. Says you have a unique eye. That's the other reason he pulled strings to get you out of jail."

"Eddie was bitching about strings and a senator, what did he mean?"

"Condon used his connections, to get you out. I think he called his state senator son-in-law, Gordon Bartholomew."

"He shouldn't have done that. I can take care of myself."

"Maybe so, but no way was he leaving you in there, not with Eddie Ibarra in the mix and not after somebody broke into our newsroom. He wants to make sure we're all safe and working 24-7 on taking these guys down."

Brinkmann steered into the side parking lot of the *East Valley Herald*, parked, put the car in gear but did not shut off the motor. He stared out the windshield in silence.

"What?"

"I have something I have to ask. Don't get mad."

"What, Andrew? I know I need a shower." He plucked at the shirt sticking to his chest, wrinkling his nose. "My cellmate had vomit all over him."

"No, it's not that. Do you know Derek Schaefer? Harry told me you two grew up together."

"Uh, no, not hardly. What time frame are we talking?"

"He didn't say when, just that you were neighbors in a housing project."

Confused, Eugene's face twisted. "Nope, never met the guy until yesterday . . . And why? What's this all about?"

"They think you were helping him."

"Oh, that's bullshit. Eddie was yapping on about it this morning."

"Eugene, you're a nice guy, sometimes too nice."

"Jesus Christ, Andrew, you know me. How could you possibly think—"

"Wait, let me finish. Harry says to tell you that if you know Schaefer and were uh . . . helping him, well, you need to tell them now. I mean, if you knew . . . I mean, after what the Luchadores did to him, maybe you felt sorry. I get—"

"What does Mr. Condon say about this?"

"He doesn't know yet."

"Well, for the record, my only contact with Schaefer was when I caught him. Fucking cops never change. Crooked Eddie's behind this. Hell, maybe he killed Sandy and set me up."

"Wait, Eugene. Just hold on. They don't think you had anything to do with killing Sandy. They're only interested in your association with Schaefer."

"Wow, Andrew, they're using you."

"What the hell are you talking about?"

"You've never been on the wrong side of a police investigation have you? Cops pull this shit all the time."

"Pull what?"

"Make shit up to chip away at credibility, create doubt and suspicion then use it to their advantage. They pulled the exact same crap when my older brother was killed. It made my life a living hell."

"What? What are you talking about? I didn't even know you had a brother."

"That's because I don't talk about it. My life sucked back then, okay?"

"Okay, sorry. I really didn't know."

The idling car's air conditioner struggled to keep ahead of the punishing heat and the radiator fan kicked in.

"His name was Ray."

"Eugene, you don't have to—"

"No, I think I do. It's the only way I can make you understand. I was fifteen and he was shot by mistake in a drive-by."

"Geez."

Eugene's eyes narrowed as the memories stabbed. "We'd just moved into this shitty little apartment. We were sitting outside because the air conditioner didn't work. One minute I'm joking with Ray and the next, he's on the sidewalk with part of his head missing. Blood was everywhere. All I could do was cry. Mom came out and started screaming at me. When the cops showed up, one of them pulled me aside. He claimed my brother was a gangster and that I'd get it next. Said he'd protect me if I'd be his snitch."

"Did you take him up on it?"

"That's my point, I didn't *know* anything. Like I said, we were new. We'd moved in like two days before. Didn't know anybody, let alone gangsters. My brother was killed by accident plain and simple."

"Did you tell him that?"

"Sure I did. That's when he switched gears. In a loud voice he says, 'Thank you for cooperating, son. I look forward to working with you.' I look at him like he's crazy. He says in a whisper, 'You're mine now, you little cockroach. All your neighbors think you're a snitch, so you might as well be my bitch in exchange for my protection.'"

"What did you do?"

"I told him to fuck off. Said I'd report him. He just laughed and joked about letting nature thin the white trash from the herd."

"Jesus, I'm sorry . . . Harry laid out a pretty convincing case."

"They always do. You know, because of that one asshole cop labeling me a snitch, I got the shit beat out of me every couple of weeks for like a whole year. Now it's happening all over again, only this time they're trying to turn my coworkers against me."

"Weird though, you and Schaefer growing up so close together."

Eugene's jaw tightened. "I suppose, but have you checked the sex offender database lately?"

"No, why would—"

"I'll bet there's a registered sex offender living on your block. Look it up, you'll be amazed. You probably walked your dog right past that sex offender's house. Maybe even shot the breeze with him on your way by. In fact you and your sex offender neighbor are probably planning to rape some poor girl this weekend."

"Okay, okay I get it—"

"See how easy it is to use a minor coincidence to cast doubt?"

"Point taken," said Brinkmann. "Let's get inside. This car's an oven."

The ink and paper smell and the air-conditioned comfort of the pressroom brightened Eugene's mood as he and Brinkmann entered through the building's side door, only to find their path blocked. Kurt, the paper's burly head pressman waved as he steered a forklift laden with a huge roll of newsprint clamped in its hydraulic jaw.

"Hang on, Eugene," hollered Kurt, as he rotated the roll to the horizontal position, lowered it and released the 1500-pound bulk to rumble the floor as it rolled to a set of chock blocks. Kurt shut down the forklift and dismounted, a broad smile riding his bearded face.

"They treat you all right in there?" he asked, automatically pulling a rag from his back pocket to wipe his right hand before grasping Eugene's.

"Bunks are hard and cold, but other than that it was uneventful."

"I hear Scottsdale's new digs are a step up," said Kurt. "The place you don't want to go is Sheriff Joe's Durango jail. My uncle works there. He says that place is a hellhole."

"My cellmate said the same thing. Hopefully neither one of us will ever have to find that out personally." Eugene smiled.

"You got that right." Kurt ran the rag over his left hand before giving Eugene a rough slap on the shoulder that turned into a macho, headlock sort of hug.

"Kurt, you gonna talk all day or are we gonna load this roll stand," said an older pressman sporting a traditional, folded newspaper hat. "Hey, Eugene, good to have you back," he added with a wave.

"Hey, Jerry!" Eugene waved.

"Give us a minute, we'll mount this roll and get out of your way," said Kurt, stowing his rag and pulling a wrench from his back pocket.

Brinkmann leaned into Eugene and whispered, "That missing pinkie finger on Kurt's right hand, you think that was some sort of biker initiation?"

"Nah, Kurt's okay. Hey, Kurt!"

"Don't just ask him," hissed Andrew.

Eugene waved him off. "Kurt! How'd you lose that finger?"

Kurt looked up from behind the roll, stern-faced. "I cheated on a mob boss' daughter. I was lucky the finger's the only thing that got cut off."

Brinkmann's face blanked, his reporter's instincts urging caution until his suspicion was confirmed by Eugene's sly, sideways glance.

Jerry guffawed, "Ha! See? I told you nobody believes that one, Kurt."

"I don't know. I think I almost had him."

Brinkmann tried to smile, almost, but not quite.

"I keep telling you to work the shark attack angle," said Eugene. "Chicks would dig that."

"No, no, go with humor," added Jerry. "Chicks really dig funny. Shark attack's good but tell it with a pirate voice."

Kurt fell into character. "Aye, laddie, I'll tell ye how I really lost me pinky finger." Face twisted and elbows raised as though he were about to dance a shanty, he said, "Truly it was a table saw, so it was. The saw was angry that day, my friend . . . ."

The group froze. Kurt's face went from pirate to surprise in a heartbeat.

"Oh, that works," said Eugene. "A little honesty, humor, and a Seinfeld hook. Chicks will definitely dig that."

Everyone nodded agreement.

"Eugene would know," said Brinkmann "There isn't a graveyard-shift waitress in Scottsdale that hasn't fallen under the spell of the great Eugenie. All the single guys in the newsroom talk about it. Every time they turn over a new rock, there's a little note that says, 'Eugene was here.'"

"Oh, now, it's not that bad," said Eugene, as the pressmen gave nodding approval and went back to work.

Jerry shoved a metal spindle through the roll's core and Kurt wrenched it down then used the press' winch to transfer it onto a metal contraption that held three of the massive rolls set in a pit at the head of the press.

"You ever see the flying paster do its thing on a roll change?"

Andrew whispered, "No, that old press scares the hell out of me and I get the feeling they just tolerate us newsroom types."

"Oh, they're not that bad. You gotta be a little rough around the edges to wrestle that press every day."

"Uh-huh."

"No, really. They're sort of a mix of artists and machinists. Take the flying paster for instance. Complicated as hell. When one roll runs out, the next one in line spins up to match the speed of the first then rotates in to be snatched and cut. That's the loud pop you hear sometimes. It's really amazing if you think about it."

"Thanks, guys, and sorry for the wait," said Kurt, climbing aboard the forklift. "You know the building does have a front door," he added, only half joking.

"Then I wouldn't get to see you work your pirate magic, Cap'n Kurt," joked Eugene, offering the pressmen a wave before heading off to the newsroom.

"Try to hang onto that smile," said Brinkmann, pushing through the swinging doors into a hall leading past the break area and the photographer's workroom. "The pictures you're about to look at are really gross and Pete's in a pissy mood."

"When is he not in a pissy mood?"

"True." He paused at the entrance to the newsroom. "You ready? Everyone's been worried about you."

Eugene rolled his eyes and stepped in.

The newsroom staff descended on him like five-year-olds on a birthday cake. Questions, back slaps and handshakes came from all directions until Mr. Condon's powerful voice beckoned Eugene to his office.

"Good to be back, everybody," Eugene said. "I better go answer his call."

When he entered, the big-framed publisher went beyond his usual, finger-crushing handshake and wrapped Eugene in his arms. It felt reassuring but surreal as Eugene hugged back, smelling cedar and pipe smoke.

"You appear to have weathered your night in jail. It's good to have you back safe," said Condon.

"I'll bet he slept better than I did," said a voice from the periphery.

Eugene turned to see Pete, standing near a coat rack draped with Condon's leather-elbowed tweeds.

"Pete, geeze, I didn't see you there. You do look like you've had a hell of a night."

"I've been staring at these little glimpses of hell since before sunrise." Pete motioned to Condon's desk, where a collection of glossy 8x10 prints showed terrified young boys in the throes of a variety of sexual abuse.

Eugene's face twisted. "Aww, Andrew, you were right. That's pretty gross."

"I told you," said Brinkmann, standing in the doorway. "Ready to hear what I gleaned from police headquarters?"

"Yes, Andrew. Step in, close the door, and bring us up to speed."

"There's several new developments," Brinkmann began. "First, Harry Aronson confirmed that Schaefer was one of the Luchador kids. He also acknowledges Eddie Ibarra's questionable behavior on the original Luchador case and knows we're aware."

"Are they doing anything about it?" asked Pete. "He really shouldn't be anywhere near this case."

"Apparently the chief thinks otherwise. Eddie and the chief are old friends. Harry wouldn't elaborate, but he says we don't know the whole story and that he trusts the chief's decision."

"What's your take on this Detective Ibarra?" asked Condon.

"I'd say he's an unprofessional hot head, judging by the small confrontation we had in the headquarters lobby."

"What happened?"

"Oh, not much really, just a little name calling and—"

"Eddie wants everyone to believe I'm Schaefer's accomplice," blurted Eugene. "He's going to try to turn you all against me."

"I'm sorry," said Condon. "You'll have to explain that—"

"It's true," Brinkmann interrupted. "The police believe there's a tie between Schaefer and Eugene."

"Not just a tie, sir. They think Schaefer ran to me expecting I'd help him escape. It's Eddie Ibarra looking for a scapegoat."

"What on earth leads him to that ridiculous conclusion?"

Eugene started to speak, but Brinkmann interrupted again. "Apparently, Eugene and Schaefer were neighbors and went to school together."

Pete came to attention. "Do you know him, Eugene?"

"No, I kept to myself in those days. This . . . uh . . . This was after my dad split and we were evicted. You know the history, Mr. Condon."

"Yes, I see. Certainly a difficult time for you. Andrew, tell me more about what Harry said regarding the chief and Ibarra."

Eugene held up a hand, "Wait. Is no one concerned about this claim that I'm connected to Schaefer?"

"Well, yes," said Condon, patiently, "but only because they're wasting time. You say you don't know Schaefer and that's good enough for me."

"Sir, I'm not worried about you. It's the rest of the newsroom. I told you what the cops did to me as a kid. I think Eddie's trying to use half-truths and coincidences to turn my friends against me."

Hand on his chin and brow furrowed, Condon considered the possibilities as Pete spoke up. "This could put our credibility at risk." Condon shut him down with an abrupt wave of his hand.

"He's right. I hate to admit it," said Brinkmann. "But it only took Harry two minutes to convince me that Eugene and Schaefer were partners. Others in the newsroom will have similar doubts and—"

"And if they do charge me with Sandy's murder," interrupted Eugene, "they'll leverage those doubts in court."

Condon took a deep breath and leaned back, his old leather chair creaking. "Very well, I'll draft a memo to the newsroom."

"You might consider preparing a statement for the other media outlets. You know they'll be all over this," said Pete.

Eugene withered, a sick feeling in the pit of his stomach.

"Pete, you can knock that crap off right now," snapped Condon. "We're a team and I'm in charge. Right now the only one in the room showing a lack of integrity is you. I suggest—"

"You're right, Oliver," moaned Pete. "I'm sorry, Eugene. This has been a helluva long couple of days."

"No problem," said Eugene. "We're all a little strung out."

5

"So, Mr. Condon," Eugene said, purposefully brightening, "do you think I'm *old* enough to be looking at these now?" He swept his hand at the pictures spread across the desk.

"I won't apologize for being concerned back then. You *were* too young, regardless of what you think."

"I know and I appreciate your concern. Andrew brought me up to speed on what happened to the digital files. Good call on making copy negs."

"Call me a curmudgeon for mistrusting digital, but in this case it paid off."

"Who made the prints?" asked Eugene. "Your average lab wouldn't touch this stuff."

Condon smiled. "I woke a good friend with the needed equipment. He's an artist. My granddaughter worked with him for a couple of summers—but I digress. The point is the Luchadores are desperate enough to commit murder and burglary to throw us off their trail. Now's the time to go for the throat and figure out what it is in these photos they don't want us to see."

"It's gotta be something that identifies either a place or a person, but for the life of me, I can't figure it out," said Pete.

"Eugene," said Condon, "you see things a little differently than most. Take a good long look and tell us what comes to mind."

Eugene moved to Condon's side of the desk to better see the images. The 8x10 pieces of paper bearing blurry, square images sat in neat rows, five across and four down with one spot empty on the bottom-left corner.

"Square format. I'm guessing the originals were Polaroid by the quality. Jesus, this is sick." His eyes locked on an image of a teenage boy, whose eyes were filled with rage as he gritted his teeth against his torture. His tormentor was a big-bellied, thick-chested monster wearing a black, fabric mask emblazoned with a skull and crossbones. "Wait. That's Derek Schaefer, isn't it?"

"Yes, I believe so," said Condon. "When you see what he endured you can almost understand why he felt compelled to lash out and hurt others."

"No. That's no excuse for what he did," said Pete.

"Okay, but let's not forget the paper's motto, 'Providence favors the open mind.' Schaefer's actions deserve punishment, but I believe the greater portion of the blame falls on the evil that created him." Condon pointed to the man in the skull and crossbones mask. "We wouldn't have these photos had this tortured little boy not risked his own life to get them to us."

"The rage I see in his eyes . . . It's the same rage I saw yesterday," Eugene said, pointing to the young Schaefer.

"Interesting that those angry, terrified eyes stuck with me all these years." Condon shook his head.

"The masks they're wearing. Can you buy them?"

"Luchador masks. Yes, you can buy them online but most are cheap knockoffs," said Condon. "I'm told these are high quality, custom work. Unfortunately, I've been unable to track their source."

"Let go of the masks for now," said Brinkmann, "and take a look at the people and the surroundings. There's gotta be something they don't want us to see."

Eugene placed both palms on the desktop and leaned in, his eyes poring over the pictures. "Okay. Looks like at least two locations. One could be a warehouse. The other looks like it could be the basement of a public building, maybe a church. There's a big coffee urn in what looks like a serving window there in the background. See? I count seven separate wrestlers. That pirate guy's a real hard belly. This guy's got gym muscles, so he probably has a cushy desk job."

"Gym muscles?" asked Brinkmann.

"They look good, but some middle-aged, barrel-chested lumper could—"

"Lumper?" asked Condon.

"Sorry, warehouse slang. That's the name for the guys who load and unload semi trailers. They'd eat that pretty boy for lunch."

Eugene returned to the images. "Judging by this guy's calves, he's a runner." He picked up the picture for a closer look. "Odd, I see band-aids on at least three of these guys—"

"We think they're to cover tattoos or birthmarks," said Condon.

Pushing a cart loaded with donuts, bagels and an insulated, plastic urn of coffee, Millie, the newsroom secretary, peered in through the office window. Brinkmann opened the door.

"You want something before I offer this up to the newsroom?" asked Millie.

"No, but thank you, Millie" said Condon. "Go ahead and park it in the conference room then let everyone know refreshments are here. We'll be along in a minute."

Pete stretched with a growl. "I'm starving and I've gotta hit the restroom."

"Very well," said Condon. "I suppose we could all use a break. Go grab some food and coffee, everyone. We'll reconvene in thirty minutes."

Eugene hung back with Condon.

"They tell me you pulled strings to get me out of jail."

"Yes, Eugene, I broke a personal rule and called my son-in-law for help. I was worried for your safety." Condon had a large magnifying glass in his hand and was over the photos.

"I'm sorry you had to do that, I—"

"No apology needed. Your catching Schaefer may have ripped the scab off a wound that's nagged me for years."

"Well, thank you anyway. I know how lucky I am." He shifted his weight. "You were in the middle of the Luchador thing when we met, weren't you?"

Condon looked up from the photos. "Yes, and I was very upset. The cover-up at the State Patrol, the lack of convictions . . . I felt like I let a lot of people down, Schaefer most of all. Now that failure has most likely led to murder and rape."

"Sir, you put too much of this on your shoulders. We'll get them this time. They've screwed up and shown us what they're afraid of."

"I hope you're right. I'd be lying if I didn't admit I have a good feeling about this."

Eugene nodded agreement.

"Eugene, Andrew came to me this morning, embarrassed about what he told you at the bar the other night. I'm sorry you had to hear that. You've been nothing but an absolute source of pride for me from the first day you poked your head in the newsroom. Remember that day?"

"Seems like a lifetime ago," Eugene said, blushing.

"You know," Condon straightened to look him in the eye and continued, "if you're thinking my interest in you back then was based on pity for those boys in the photos, you're wrong. I saw raw talent and didn't want it to go to waste. Was I feeling bad for the child victims? Certainly, but it was your God-given talent and good decision making that made you the successful young man you are."

Eugene breathed back a sudden teary urge. "It may all be for nothing, Mr. Condon. It wouldn't be the first time the police railroaded an innocent man. I'm worried—"

"That won't happen. Not on my watch it won't. Now buck up, grab some food and let's get back on these photos."

Pats on the back, prison jokes and short conversations followed Eugene through the newsroom, trailing off once he approached his boss' desk. Michael Specht stared at his computer, making printouts for an upcoming news meeting.

"I'm gonna grab a donut. Michael, you want something?"

"A plain bagel and cream cheese would be nice. And welcome back. We've missed you."

"Sorry if this mess has screwed up the schedule."

"It hasn't been too bad. The summer intern's decent. She's even picked up the late shift."

Brinkmann waved a half-eaten glazed donut to get Armstrong's attention. "Mike, the digital files of the foster kid photos. When was the last time you actually saw them in the system?"

"Not since I filed them seven years ago. They're disgusting—"

A horrific, high-pitched shriek ripped them from conversation. Millie stood outside Mr. Condon's office. The sheaf of papers she'd been holding littered the floor at her feet.

Pete and Eugene arrived in Condon's doorway simultaneously, gently urging Millie aside. Condon lay on his back on the floor, his shirt splashed with coffee as he writhed, his mouth gulping for air like a fish out of water, his hands clawing at his throat.

"Heart attack?" cried Pete, dropping beside the distressed man.

"Allergy, I think," said Eugene. "SOMEONE CALL 9-1-1! NOW!"

"His coat," squeaked Millie, white as a ghost and pointing at the jacket hanging on the corner rack. "He has a pen thing."

Pete jumped to his feet to search the pockets of the jacket. Eugene took his place beside Condon as the man's red face darkened to purple. He raised a big hand to grab Eugene's shirt, pulling him close. The old man mouthed something Eugene couldn't understand. He shook his head, not comprehending. Rage and fear filled the old man's eyes as he made one more attempt. Eugene turned his head, laying his ear to Condon's blue lips.

"P-p-p . . . A-a-ass clown . . . It's—" The words were lost in a gasp.

Confused, Eugene pulled back, looking into Condon's staring eyes.

"Do you have it?" screamed Millie, as Pete fumbled.

"Epi Pen. Is that it?"

"Yes. For God's sake, hurry." Millie clenched her fists to her breast, tears sheeting down her cheeks.

Eugene held out a hand and Pete thrust it forward. The Epi Pen flew from its protective plastic tube striking Eugene in the chest before falling to the carpet and rolling under Condon's desk.

"Oh, for Christ's sake!" Eugene stretched across Condon's legs to retrieve the pen.

"I'm sorry!" cried Pete. "Oh, God!"

Condon's legs and arms twitched and trembled. His eyes rolled back in his head as the rest of him arched and convulsed.

Millie leaned against the wall outside the office and slid to the floor, fists to her temples, oblivious of the gathering crowd.

Eugene raised the pen, deducing its function in an instant and slammed the tip into Condon's left thigh.

"It says hold it for ten-seconds," said Pete, reading the pen's protective tube.

Eugene kept the pressure, holding the leg as best he could, counting to twenty to be sure his racing brain hadn't counted too fast.

All watched with anxious anticipation as the violence of the convulsions weakened.

On her knees, Millie crawled to Condon and patted his darkening face. "Oh, Oliver, don't you leave me now," she whispered. When Condon's face went slack, pallid and lifeless, she cried out, "It's not working. Do something. Somebody do—"

"Pete, I need you," said Eugene in a tone that snapped Pete from his glassy-eyed panic.

"Tell me what to do."

"Tilt his head back. See if anything's stuck in his throat." He snugged his knees against the big man's chest. "I'll pump, you breathe."

Pete's eyes rounded. "I-I can't Eugene, I—"

"PETE, GODDAMN IT!" barked Eugene. He leaned down to grab Condon's face then tilted it back to look in his mouth. He thrust a finger past Condon's blue lips into his throat, but felt nothing but tight tissue constricting the airway. Hands on Condon's chest, he pumped then slid sideways to breathe for his mentor. The scratch of the old man's whiskers and faint smell of aftershave tugged at Eugene's sense of reality. His own pulse pounded in his ears.

"Now, push there like I did," he growled at Pete.

Pete's hands hit Condon's chest like a jack hammer.

"NO! You'll break ribs." Eugene shouldered Pete aside. "Like this." He pumped with a firm rhythm. Pete took over and Eugene resumed his intermittent mouth-breathing chore.

Lead pressman Kurt pushed through the crowd "Make room, everyone. The paramedics just pulled up in back. They're coming in."

As the paramedics pushed him aside, Eugene offered, "We did the allergy pen thing but it didn't help." He retreated from the office to watch through the doorway as they ripped open Condon's coffee-stained shirt and applied patches and wires. Injections were given and a rubber mask sealed over his mouth and nose. A football-shaped ventilation bag was attached and squeezed in a slow rhythm. When they lifted the mask to see if he breathed on his own, a moment later the mask was reapplied, a bad sign Eugene knew, from covering countless car accidents.

6

"It's my fault he's dead," said Pete, staring out the glass facade of Mountain View Memorial hospital's emergency entrance. In the half-circle drive outside, paramedics restocked and cleaned their rescue squad.

"No," said Eugene. "You heard what the doctor said. The allergic reaction probably caused a heart attack. None of us knew about his allergy. How were we—"

A commotion burst through the doors from the emergency bay and hospital staff scrambled into action. Thankfully the incoming patient's face was hidden behind straps and blood-streaked foam stabilizing blocks.

"Jesus," groaned Pete turning away from the mess.

"He probably won't make it, either," Eugene murmured.

"God, shut the hell up. Don't you feel anything?"

"Sorry," Eugene said, knowing full well grief would consume him once he dared to relax and stop problem solving. "Guess I process this stuff a little differently. Covered one too many accidents, I suppose."

"I took too damn long finding that Epi Pen." Pete knuckled his forehead. "Then-then I dropped it . . . and I goddamned freaked out over the CPR thing."

"Pete, that took three seconds, four at most. It wouldn't have made a difference."

Pete's cell phone vibrated. He jerked it from his shirt pocket, looked at the screen and ignored the call. "Did Millie order the donuts?"

Eugene frowned at the question. "She usually does."

Overhead Muzak played a generic happy tune. Eugene's greasy scalp itched and his two-day-old clothes reeked of sweat and fear. He blinked to moisten his sandpaper eyes then saw Harry and Eddie parking in the patient drop-off zone. A bad feeling climbed his spine as they marched to the emergency receiving area. A volunteer directed them to the lobby.

Pete stood. Eugene followed suit, too tired and drained to feel nervous.

"Sorry for your loss," Eddie stated automatically rather than sincerely.

Shaking Eugene's hand, Harry looked him up and down. "You okay?"

"No," said Eugene. "I don't think life could get any shittier."

"I assume you have questions," said Pete. "Let's get them over with. The Condon family is on their way in."

"Take a seat," said Harry, turning a pair of the lobby's fabric and chrome chairs to face Pete and Eugene. "First of all, we've dispatched a team to your office. Since we're already acquainted with you, Eugene, we'll handle your interview."

"We get it," said Pete.

"Okay then." Harry opened a small notebook and clicked a pen. "Did either of you know about his allergy?"

"I didn't," said Eugene, looking at Pete.

Pete shook his head. "Not really. I knew there was a medical condition of some sort because he wore a medic alert bracelet."

"Mr. Cunningham," Eddie spoke up, "you've worked for Condon for quite some time. You're telling us in all those years he never mentioned that he was allergic to peanuts?"

"No, I don't think so. He's a fairly private guy and my boss. And, well, he's in his eighties."

"What was Mr. Condon doing at the time of his attack?" asked Harry.

"Looking at those awful *Luchador* photos," said Eugene. "We wanted—"

Eddie bolted upright. "You have photos from the *Luchador* case?"

"Yeah, we wanted—"

"Where did you get them?"

Pete's expression turned cold. "At Condon's request, we made copies before we turned the originals over to you."

Wide-eyed, Eddie whipped out his phone, stood, and walked out of earshot.

"Looks like somebody has a problem," Pete said.

Harry held up a hand, rose and walked to his partner.

When Eddie returned, Pete asked "What's the matter?"

"Looks like you have the only remaining photos from that case. The originals were destroyed."

"Really?" Pete locked gazes with him. "Weren't you the guy who got canned for destroying evidence?"

"I resigned over a personal matter. And, no, I did not destroy evidence before leaving. I wouldn't go around making accusations without knowing the whole story, mister. Someone—not me—sent them in a load of trash to the landfill, supposedly by accident . . . a clerical error."

Pete assumed a deliberately thoughtful expression. "And the State Patrol didn't make digital copies?"

"Missing as well," Eddie snapped.

"Funny thing," Eugene spoke up, "Our digital copies disappeared, too, and the backup CD was destroyed. Luckily, Mr. Condon had copy negs nobody knew about."

"That so? Where are the photos now?" asked Eddie.

"On Condon's desk in his office."

Eddie punched in a number and put the phone back to his ear.

Harry looked up from his notebook with tired eyes. "In light of the timing and this new info, I think we have to classify Condon's death as suspicious."

"Consider, hell," snapped Eddie, hanging up. "The techs have the photos bagged and tagged. Let's take their statements and get over there."

"Eugene, take a walk with me," said Harry. "Pete, you stay with Eddie."

"Why split us up?" asked Eugene.

"Eugene, don't argue," snapped Pete, "The Condon family's on the way over here and I need to get back to the newsroom. I have an obituary to write."

Eugene shrank at hearing the word obituary. He inhaled deeply and complied.

"I was hoping we'd get a minute alone, detective," Pete said to Eddie when Eugene was out of earshot.

"Why's that?" asked Eddie.

"I need an honest assessment . . . I mean . . . Is the paper's credibility at risk? I'm the head of the newsroom now and . . . ."

Eddie watched his partner walking away with the photojournalist. "What do you think of him?" he asked.

"Eugene?"

"Yes."

"I've always thought he was a good kid . . . A little rough around the edges . . . Condon certainly liked him." Pete drew a deep breath and crossed his arms. "But to look at him now, it just feels like something's out of place."

"Can you expand on that?"

"I don't know." He shrugged. "It's just a feeling. His connection to Schaefer . . . Do you think he has ties to the Luchadores? I mean, that backup CD. No one but a newsroom employee would have known, plus he was alone with Condon minutes before he fell ill."

Eddie offered a crooked smile. "Are you accusing Eugene of murdering Condon? Is there something you're not telling me?"

"Oh, heavens no. I just want to be sure you have every detail."

"Uh-huh. Well, he is a person of interest in Sandy Carter's murder, so if something comes to mind . . . ."

"Of course."

"Walk me through what happened this morning," said Eddie, opening his own notebook and pulling the interview back on track.

Eddie finished Pete's interview just as Harry and Eugene returned to the lobby, smiling and gesticulating. Their lightened mood vanished when the lobby doors slid open and an older, well-dressed couple entered, accompanied by a younger, more casually dressed woman.

"That's the Condon family. Can I go talk to them?" asked Pete.

"Sure. I've got what I need," said Eddie. "Thanks for the honesty."

Pete and Eugene rejoined and approached the solemn group. The two detectives trailed along at a respectful distance.

"Mr. Cunningham," said Margaret Bartholomew, "I'd like you to meet Oliver's granddaughter, Olivia. Of course, you know my husband, Senator Bartholomew."

"Yes. Senator, I'm so sorry for your loss," said Pete, shaking the senator's hand. "And Olivia, it's nice to finally meet you, although I wish it were under better circumstances. I'd like you all to meet Eugene Fellig, one of our photog—"

"Ah, the famous photographer. Or should I say infamous?" said the senator. "Oliver and I conversed about you just last night."

Eugene smiled and nodded, awkwardly shaking the senator's hand. When he let go, Olivia stepped in and extended her hand. Eugene grasped it, instantaneously aware of a sudden attraction, followed by a tinge of guilt. "Sorry I'm such a mess," he said. "It's been a rough couple of days and—"

"No apology needed," said Olivia. "My grandfather talked fondly of you."

"He was an amazing man," said Eugene. "I-I'm really sorry we've lost him."

"My condolences, as well," Pete chimed in.

"What on earth happened?" asked Margaret. "Was it his allergy?"

"Yes, to start with," said Pete. "They think the reaction brought on a heart attack."

"He was always so careful," said Margaret. "But, I suppose the mind dulls with age."

"We used his Epi Pen and did CPR," said Eugene.

"Did he say any . . . you know . . . last words?" asked Olivia.

"He whispered something to Eugene," said Pete. "But in all the confusion . . . I forgot to ask. Eugene, what was he trying to tell you?"

"It was gibberish." Eugene shook his head, feeling the red rising in his cheeks. "I couldn't make out what he was saying. I'm so sorry."

"What was he working on before the attack?" Olivia pressed. "The murder of Sandy Carter?"

"It was the Lucha—"

Margaret Bartholomew interrupted, "We don't need to go into that now."

Eugene picked up on Olivia's irritation. She had her grandfather's eyes, intelligent and patient. She wore her dark hair tied back into a ponytail. Her white cotton blouse, blue jeans and silver conchoed belt added a southwestern flair.

"If it's any consolation," said Pete, "he died doing what he loved. He had that gleam in his eye. You know the look he got when he was on a big story."

"I know it all too well," said Margaret. "Growing up as the daughter of a newsman, there was always another big story. Frankly, we all wanted him to retire and enjoy himself after Mother died. But . . . I think he loved that damn newspaper more than he loved any of us."

A weary, solemn-faced doctor emerged from behind heavy double doors. He introduced himself, apologized for their loss and invited the family to a room where they could have a moment alone with the deceased.

"I'd like to remember him like he was," said Olivia, wiping her eyes, hanging back as her parents went with the doctor. Eugene poured a cup of coffee from the machine at the volunteer's table and extended it to her. She sipped, watching the two detectives approach, her expression not particularly welcoming.

"We're going to make sure those pictures are secured," said Eddie.

Harry spoke to the newspapermen, "You two are headed to the paper as well, correct?"

"Yes," said Pete. "I just want to make sure Margaret and the senator are all right."

"We'll see you in a few minutes, then. I'm sure we'll have follow-up questions, so be prepared."

"Sure, whatever you need." Pete sighed with a half-hearted wave to the exiting detectives.

Olivia gazed at Eugene for a long moment, her teary, green eyes oddly brimming with curiosity. "So, the Luchadores are back?"

Eugene frowned a moment. "You knew about that?"

She merely nodded and looked expectant, so Eugene continued." Schaefer—the guy we caught yesterday—was one of their victims."

Her eyes turned to saucers. "Interesting timing. So, what did Grandpa whisper in your ear?"

"I'm sorry, I don't—"

"He said something that you were too embarrassed to repeat. I could see it on your face."

Eugene put his hands in his pockets and stared at his feet. "It didn't make any sense."

Pete straightened, crossing his arms and glaring a challenge.

"To you, maybe," Olivia lifted a determined chin as she stood. "What did he say? I don't care if it's embarrassing. I deserve to know."

"It was . . . well . . . he kinda went p-p-p and then said ass clown . . . or something like that."

"What?" snapped Pete. "Eugene, that's just—"

"I know it's weird, but I'm telling you the last two words out of his mouth sounded like ass clown."

"Thank you," Olivia said, placing a gentle hand on his arm. "Let's keep in touch." She pulled a business card from a small leather purse and handed it to him.

He glanced at the card. It read *Arizona Providence*. *President* was printed above her name. He tucked it into a shirt pocket. "Believe me, I am really sorry about all this. I loved your Grandpa. He did a lot for me."

"In case you didn't know, he loved you, too." Tears again welled in her big green eyes. Obviously embarrassed, she turned and walked toward the exit.

Eugene glanced to Pete, who looked both embarrassed and angry. "Let's get to the office," he snapped.

Together they headed for Pete's car, Eugene's mind a confusion of grief, fear and a subtle tinge of guilt at his thinking of Olivia's soft touch and sweet scent.

* * *

In the passenger seat of Pete's car, parked in the street in front of the paper, Eugene watched the man's jaw flex as he glared at the collection of police cruisers and crime lab vans.

"It pisses me off, too," Eugene offered.

"What's pissing you off?" barked Pete, jamming the transmission into park.

"Losing Condon and all the cops invading our space."

"Maybe they're hunting for *ass clowns*."

"Pete, she asked me point blank. I wasn't going to lie."

"Whatever." Pete yanked the keys and crawled from the car, Eugene on his heels. "Don't go passing that 'ass clown' thing around. We don't want Mr. Condon's legacy to become a crude joke."

"Of course not." As they neared the front door, Eugene spoke to Pete's back. "You know, if you want help on Mr. Condon's obit, he did a lot for me, I—"

"Noted, but I have a good idea where I'm going with it." Pete stopped and turned. "Did you know he hadn't paid himself a dime for the last three years? Advertising's been weak." He paused, obviously worried about facing the newsroom. Both hands stuffed into his pockets, his right hand jingled his car keys.

"I didn't know, but that sounds like him. Captain of the ship sort of thing, I guess . . . . You know, the newsroom's gonna have a lot of questions about our future."

"I'm well aware." Pete hauled in a deep breath, letting it out slowly before pushing through the glass front doors into lobby.

From behind her desk, Millie simultaneously wiped her eyes with a tissue and stood brave-faced to greet them. Her attempt at stoicism melted as soon as Eugene's eyes met hers. He pushed through the little gate by her desk and pulled her into a hug. She felt like a frail little bird trembling in his arms.

Newsroom staff gathered near Millie's desk, their eyes anxious and pleading.

Andrew Brinkmann, flanked by Michael Specht and Gordon Reynolds, the sports editor, spoke first. "The detectives won't tell us a damn thing. Did he ever regain consciousness?"

"No, Mike, I don't believe so," answered Pete.

"It was a heart attack, right?" asked Reynolds.

"Yes, but it was likely brought on by an allergic reaction to nuts."

The crowd stilled. Millie sniffed and sobbed quietly. Eugene held her tight.

"What's going to happen to the paper now that Mr. Condon is gone?" asked Reynolds.

"Way too soon to know, Gordon. I'm sure the Condon family—"

"Are we gonna be sold to a damn chain?" asked an anonymous voice from the back.

"Listen, everybody," said Pete, holding up his hands. "I promise I'll keep you all informed. Let's try to make Condon's last edition of the paper the best one ever. As soon as I know anything about future plans, I'll share it with you. Word of honor."

Beyond the dispersing crowd, Eugene noticed Harry and the crime lab techs in Condon's office. His gut tightened on a sudden surge of anger at their intrusion.

"You gonna be okay, Millie?"

"It's my fault, you know. There must have been peanut oil or dust in the bagel I gave him." Millie's hands continued to tremble slightly. "The police were asking about it."

"I'm sure they're just being thorough." He gave her a squeeze ending in a gentle rub on the back. "I'm gonna go see what they're up to. Are you sure you're okay?"

"Yes," she said, her head showing the same tremor that afflicted her hands as she visibly fought for emotional control, "but I don't really have much choice in the matter . . . Choices tend to die off as you get older, Eugene . . . just like the ones you love."

"I'm so sorry, Millie." Eugene hugged her again adding a kiss to the top of her head then leaned back to look deep into her eyes.

"Go, Eugene. I'm okay. Go figure out what happened to Oliver."

A crime lab tech swept a flashlight beam across the floor behind Condon's desk. Harry wrote notes on a yellow legal pad. Clear plastic evidence bags sat in a bin on Condon's old chair, his leather-elbowed tweeds lay in a chair next to the coat rack. Remnants of the paramedics' work littered the floor. As if symbolizing a final assault, Condon's favorite Gene Smith Minimata print hung off kilter on the wall behind his desk. Eugene swallowed back the urge to cry.

"Stay out," warned Harry.

He stopped in the doorway. "I am." Embarrassed at the weakness in his voice, he wiped tears from his eyes.

Harry glanced up from his notes. "You okay?"

"Yeah, sorry." Eugene cleared his throat, sniffed and stood straighter.

The female tech set her flashlight on the floor and reached for an evidence bag.

"Where's Eddie?" asked Eugene.

"Test results came back and the chief wanted a briefing. He'll be back in a bit."

"What's she looking at?" He pointed to the tech. "Assuming you can talk about it."

Harry shot Eugene an irritated look. "Witnesses reported that during Condon's attack you said it was an allergic reaction. Tell me your basis for that conclusion."

"He couldn't breathe. I was just guessing—We went through all of this at the hospital."

"Humor me. Had you used an Epi Pen before?"

"No."

"How did you know what to do?"

"Like I told you at the hospital, I saw one used on a TV show, plus Pete read the instructions off its container. He said to jab it in Condon's thigh and hold it in for ten-seconds. I counted to twenty to be sure."

"You fumbled with the pen before administering it, is that correct?"

"Yes, just like I told you. I had to grab it from under the desk because it flew out of its container when Pete tried to hand it to me."

"It flew out of this tube?" Harry picked up an evidence bag containing the pen and its case. Fingerprint dust still clung to the plastic. "Had he tried to open it before handing it to you?"

"No, I don't think so. He just pulled it from the coat pocket and sort of shoved it at me."

"How did he know to look in the coat?"

"Millie told us."

"How long did it take to retrieve the pen from under the desk?"

"I don't know. A second, maybe two."

"Did you look to see if the pen was operable?"

"No, I just grabbed it from under the desk and jabbed it in."

"Where did you learn CPR?"

"I've shot pictures at Red Cross events and EMT training. I just sort of picked up the basics."

"And you and Pete initiated CPR after the pen had no effect, correct?"

"I started it . . . well . . . ."

"Well what?" said Harry.

"It wasn't Pete's finest hour. He kinda panicked."

"Why didn't you mention that before?"

"I don't know. Maybe I was embarrassed for him."

Harry nodded then checked his notes again. "Why didn't you tell me you were alone with Condon before the attack?"

"I did. Maybe not right out, but I mentioned Pete and Andrew had left. I was only in there with him for a few seconds."

"What did you talk about?"

"I asked him why he pulled strings to get me out of jail and we talked about Schaefer." Eugene's throat tightened and his face went hot. "Shit." He wiped his eyes. "I don't know what the hell's wrong with me."

Harry put down his pen and pad and stepped through the office doorway to put a calming hand on Eugene's shoulder. "Was Mr. Condon doing anything besides talking when you were with him?"

"He was looking at the photos with a magnifying glass."

"The Luchador photos?"

"Yeah."

"Did he say anything about them?"

"No, not directly, but he did try to say something before he lost consciousness."

"As I recall, you said you couldn't understand his words."

"I was embarrassed to say it in front of the family. What he said sounded like a stuttered 'p-p-p . . . a-ass clown.'"

The tech on the floor paused but never looked up.

"Are you sure?"

"Yeah, I've played it over in my head about a million times. I mean, it was kinda distorted, but it was 'ass clown or p-p-pass clown,' something like that. He stuttered on the p, you know? I told Condon's granddaughter after you left because she cornered me. Now Pete's angry at me for telling her. He told me not to spread it around, but I thought you should know."

Eugene watched the tech use a pair of plastic forceps to grasp a pale chunk of something from the coffee stain in the carpet. She placed it in an evidence bag with several others. He stiffened. "Are those peanut chunks? Were they in his coffee?"

"I can't talk about it," snapped Harry.

Eugene's rage rose hot and fast. He pushed forward. Harry moved to block him. "Did someone do this on purpose?" He pushed again and saw a touch of surprise—*or was it fear*—flash on Harry's face. "Sorry," said Eugene, dialing back his anger, taking half a step back while consciously slumping to look less threatening.

"Eugene, maybe you ought to go some place to cool down and relax. You've got to be exhausted. Give us some time to get to the bottom of this."

Eugene nodded and turned, hating himself for letting his darkness escape.

"Wait," said Harry. Eugene froze. He faced the newsroom and was quickly aware that his colleagues were watching. "What's that in your back pocket?"

"My wallet."

"No, your other pocket. Back up to me. Slowly."

Eugene stepped backwards until he felt Harry's hand on his neck and felt something slide from his back pocket.

"Why are you in possession of a Luchador photo, Eugene? Are you trying to hide something?"

Eugene turned to see Harry holding a folded and creased piece of photo paper. He turned it to Eugene. It was the image of the young Schaefer being brutalized by the man in a skull and crossbones mask. The tech rose to her knees, holding out a plastic evidence bag. Harry dropped it in.

"I did not put that in my pocket."

"Eugene, you're a suspect in the murder of Sandy Carter and now it appears you are tampering with evidence. I'm going to have to pat you down."

"Harry—"

The detective's kind expression had transformed into professional hardness. "Shut up and empty your pockets."

"Okay, okay." Bile roiled in Eugene's stomach and he felt a noose tightening as his trembling hands placed his phone, multi-tool, wallet, keys and pocket change into an evidence bag on Condon's desk.

"That it?" asked Harry.

"Sure, I think so." Eugene patted his pockets to be sure they were empty.

"Arms out and turn around."

Once again, he faced the watching newsroom.

Harry squatted to run his fingers inside Eugene's socks, working his way up each pant leg, probing each pocket. When he finished he placed a hand on Eugene's shoulder and turned him so that they were face to face. "What the hell aren't you telling us? I want to believe you, but the evidence—"

"Nothing, Harry. I'm not hiding anything. I didn't put that picture in my pocket. Someone's setting me up."

Harry plucked the bag of belongings from the desk, removed the multi-tool and handed everything else back before stepping to the office doorway and signaling for a uniform. "This officer will escort you to the conference room where you'll wait for further instruction."

"Christ," Eugene muttered, turning to head for the conference room with the uniform in tow.

7

Head spinning, a cop at his heels, Eugene lumbered through the newsroom. Through tears and crushing embarrassment, he saw his friends gathering in twos and threes, staring and whispering conspiratorially.

After pocketing what was left of his personal belongings, he dropped the empty bag on the conference room table and slumped into a chair. He glanced up to see the back of the officer filling the doorway.

"Fuck this shit," he whispered to himself, laying his head and arms on the cool Formica tabletop. In the distance, a warning bell rang out and the floor rumbled as the newspaper's big printing press started a run.

Exhausted sleep came in a wave of white noise. The unnatural and abrupt tumble into oblivion jerked him back to consciousness as if he fought to protect himself. In his brief return to the present, his guilt that always lurked waiting for a weak moment, rushed in. He resisted by trying to relax. Once again his exhaustion sucked him back into a deep sleep and the reliving of his dark childhood memories.

He was a teenager, standing at the delivery yard gate of his family's warehouse watching his father and brother drive off for the morning's deliveries.

For two weeks he'd been left behind, forced to work on a construction project with Hank, an ignorant, ass-kissing bully. Hank's cute, young wife, Lacy, answered phones and assisted Eugene's mother in the warehouse office. More than once, he'd seen

Lacy and his father emerge from a remote corner of the warehouse after *assisting* each other in the shadows.

Hank's head was too small for his body, but his fists made up any deficiencies in his own mind. He used them on Eugene to vent his frustrated suspicions of his wife's cheating. The man routinely delivered hard jabs to the kidneys, thighs and groin, all disguised as horseplay.

Resigned to another day of paying for his father's screwing the hired help, Eugene turned away from the departing trucks, thinking about the ride home the night before. As they'd rolled out of the south Phoenix squalor toward middle class mid-town, he'd complained about Hank to his father. All he received in return were placating words followed by a fatherly jostle of his painfully bruised thigh.

A jolt of pain shot from his tailbone to the top of his spine as Hank's kick lifted him off the ground.

"Knock it off! Goddamn it, it's not funny," Eugene yelled.

"Whaddaya gonna do, crybaby? Run and tell your daddy again? That's right, he told me all about your little pity party when he met me at the bar last night."

"Was that before or after he fucked your wife?"

Hank froze like a kid caught with a girlie magazine.

Seeing the effect, more words poured from Eugene's mouth before he could stop them, "You beat on me, 'cause you're too chicken to take on my dad."

"Fuck you," Hank huffed, turning on his heel to walk away in a loping, cartoonish stomp.

For the remainder of the morning they kept their distance, but Hank's mounting curses showed a slow boil of anger.

At their lunch break visit to the mobile roach coach, Eugene bought a package of lemon Zingers and a chocolate milk, planning to enjoy the delicacies with King, the delivery yard guard dog.

During the day, the huge Shepherd-Airedale mix stayed tied in the shade of the dilapidated house trailer at the back of the yard. After dumping and refilling King's water bowl, Eugene picked a patch of shade and sat down in the dirt with the dog for the shared meal.

Eugene never saw the short chunk of 2x4 sail in. It caught him above the ear in a sharp explosion of pain. "Fuck!" Filthy hands rushed to rub the pain as he blinked away the stars edging his vision.

"You gonna keep fuckin' with that dog or help me rip a sheet of plywood?" Hank asked, grinning with arms crossed

"Fuck you, Hank!"

Hank gave him the finger and turned for the table saw.

Eugene picked up the two-foot chunk of pine and hurled it with all the might a teenage boy could muster. It bounced off the middle of Hank's back, causing him to grunt and stumble. Obviously thinking it was a game of fetch, King raced to the end of his tether to pounce on the board. Hank yanked it from his mouth then sent it crashing down on King's left eye.

Eugene leaped up, screaming, "NO! ASSHOLE!"

King went down with a yelp then sat up, one eye closed and bloody, the tip of his tail twitching nervously.

Hank shot Eugene a maniacal smile and raised the board for another strike, but Eugene barreled into him, sending the killing blow off target.

For a moment, all three participants stood frozen. Out on the dirt road in front of the warehouse a truck rumbled and air brakes hissed.

Dad and Ray are back . . . It's now or never. "What's it like kissing Lacy after my dad's cock has been in her mouth? What's he taste like?"

Hank's murderous rage came out as a scream that put Eugene's feet into motion. After dodging a roundhouse fist, he raced for the trailer, launching himself up and through the open door with Hank closing fast. He turned and kicked. The heel of his boot crushed Hank's nose.

Eugene howled with joy at the powerful rush of seeing his enemy fall back on his ass with his nose bloodied. The joy was short-lived. Hank was up in an instant. Blood smeared his face and murder glittered in his eyes. He managed two strides before King took him down, yapping and growling then grabbing an arm to drag him through the dirt like a child's broken pull toy.

"No! King, don't!" Eugene jumped to the ground and tugged at the dog's cracked leather collar. King released, his muzzle flecked with red foam.

Hank rolled to his knees, arm dangling and blood dripping. "I'll fuckin' kill you and that dog." Hank blew a spray of red from his nose, shook his head and picked up the board. A growl vibrated from deep inside King's chest.

"I don't think so," said an angry voice from behind. It was Eugene's father, a revolver in hand.

Lacy and Eugene's mother came running. His mother sounded breathless and a little frantic as she yelled, "What the hell is going on?"

"I tried to tell Dad, he—"

"Shut up, Eugene."

"That dog's vicious. I'll sue you if you don't put it down," growled Hank.

"No!" cried Eugene.

"I told you to shut up," ordered his father. "Hank, you leave now or I'll put *you* down."

Hank's shoulders slumped as he whined, "Fuck this shit" He turned to stomped over and confront his wife. "You screwin' him?"

"I-I . . . Baby, you know I . . . ." She looked to Eugene's father for help. He shook his head no.

Hank's good right hand dropped her to the ground. With his small-headed, cartoonish stomp, he marched for his car. The vehicle roared off in a plume of dirt and gravel.

Eugene looked to his mother. She shot back an icy glare as if blaming him for all of it then turned and walked away in silence.

"You happy, now?" asked his father.

Choking on injustice, tears and adrenaline, he couldn't answer.

"Go clean yourself up. I'll deal with the dog." He cocked the pistol. King looked on obediently.

"No, you can't shoot him. I won't let you." He kneeled, wrapping his arms around King's neck.

"He's just a dog, and now he's half blind. Hank could sue us. Take everything we've got . . . I'll give you ten minutes." His father released the gun's hammer and shoved the weapon in his back pocket before walking for the office.

Wasting no time, Eugene unhitched King's tether and ran with the dog all the way to the Fodoni Brother's Junkyard.

"What in tarnation happened to you two?" asked Carl Fodoni when Eugene and the dog appeared, bloody and breathless.

"King saved me and now my dad wants to shoot him."

"What? What the hell is your daddy up—"

"I can't talk. Will you take him?"

"Well, sure. I always liked that dog. Y-you okay? You're both bleedin'. I'm thinkin' I ought to call the cops."

Panic clutched his chest. "No, that'll just make it worse. I'll be fine. Don't call anybody. The fight's over. I'll tell Dad I untied him and he ran off."

One week later, Eugene's father cleaned out the family's bank accounts and disappeared. Two months after that, the business went under. Eugene, his mother and older brother, Ray, had to move from their mid-town apartment to a welfare housing project just blocks from their former business.

In the newspaper's conference room, his head still on the table and consciousness tugging him out of the past, Eugene heard his mother's boozy, cigarette-rasped voice calling from his dream. "You just couldn't keep your worthless little mouth shut, could you? It's your goddamn mouth that put us in the projects and it's your fault your brother's dead."

The ring of his cell phone fully pulled Eugene back to reality. He plucked the phone from his belt while wiping drool from the corner of his mouth. Caller ID listed the number as "Unknown."

"Hello?"

"I just heard a very interesting conversation."

"Who is this?"

"DNA doesn't lie. The cops found out that you and Derek are blood relations. Eddie's on his way to arrest you."

"This isn't funny."

"Stay there if you want. I just thought you'd like a heads up. This time they'll lock you up over at county. There's a good possibility you'll never make it out of there alive."

Eugene came to his feet. "Who-who are you?"

The line went dead.

The uniformed cop stared at him from the doorway.

"Need something?"

"Nah. Wrong number. "He feigned a yawn and a stretch. "Ruined a perfectly good nap."

The cop turned back to face the newsroom. Eugene calculated his chances of escape. *They'll track my phone.* He carefully set it down and pushed it away.

Through the conference room glass Eugene saw Harry still in Condon's office. A pair of crime lab technicians were packing their kits. The newsroom had gone back to work.

The caller's voice played in his head. "You'll never make it out of there alive."

A clamoring of noise and a commotion in the front lobby drew the newsroom's attention. Eugene craned around his guard to see Eddie and a cadre of uniforms burst in. Millie jumped to her feet to hurry to the little swinging gate entrance. "Can I help—?" The uniforms' forward momentum knocked her to the floor.

Eddie froze. Several coworkers from the newsroom jumped to her aid, shouting objections.

"I-I'm all right," she loudly told them, sitting up, cradling an elbow.

Eugene's guard started toward the crowd, stopped, and turned back just as Eugene shot past him at a dead run.

Eddie hollered, "EUGENE FELLIG, STOP!"

As Eugene burst through the double-swinging doors into the pressroom, Eddie's voice was swallowed by the freight train noise of the press running at full tilt.

Kurt looked up, confused. Eugene flung open the door to the parking lot then turned on his heel, took three long strides and leaped head first into the pit just as a roll change commenced. Spinning like a buzz saw, the quarter-ton roll of paper slammed into Eugene's forehead, flinging his body back onto solid concrete. His world went black.

When he came to, Eugene's head sang a chorus of pain. The press sat silent. From somewhere above, Kurt sounded distant and tinny as he argued with Eddie.

"You saw Eugene Fellig run out that door, correct?"

"Yeah, he ran like a bat outta hell. Newsroom employees are not allowed in here during a press run. I figured there was a big fire or something going on."

A new voice entered the conversation. "What's with the full stop? We were just gettin' her dialed in."

"Ask the cop," Kurt snapped.

"Did Eugene Fellig come in here?"

"Didn't see him on my end."

"I already told him he ran out that door." Kurt snarled. "I guess screwing up the press run wasn't enough. Now he's calling me a liar."

"Hey, Mr. Pig! Why don't you leave him alone and go eat a donut," spoke up Kurt's brother Mikey, the flyboy.

Eddie raised his voice with, "I'll arrest every goddamn one of you, you don't start cooperating."

"Don't mind Mikey," said Kurt as if calming a kid, "He's simple. Doesn't mean any harm. Look, nobody's dicking with you. You asked me if I saw Eugene and I told you. You told me to stop the press and I did. Sorry if I was asshole, but stopping a press run costs money."

"I need your names."

"Sure. I'm Kurt Wragge, lead pressman. That's Jerry Francis—he's my second—and Mikey here is our flyboy."

"Mikey, what's your last name?"

"Same as his, dummy."

"Mikey, cool it," Kurt ordered. "Let the man do his job. Mikey's my brother. We take care of each other."

After a short silence Kurt's face appeared at the edge of the pit. Eugene looked up, seeing double. He closed one eye and the two Kurts became one.

"You should be dead, dude. What were you thinking?"

Eugene carefully shook his head, not understanding.

"Jerry's checking the dock to see if it's clear. Take my bike if you want." He held out a ring with two keys.

"I can't hear you."

Kurt held a finger to his lips. "You're too loud, dude. Take it down a notch or three."

"Is it clear?" Eugene asked, his voice quieter.

Jerry's face appeared. "Dock's clear." The two pressmen reached down to give him a hand up.

Kurt again held out his keys. "Take my Harley, dude. Get out before they come back."

"Is the paper warehouse door open?"

"Yeah. Just. Take. My. Bike," he enunciated each word slowly.

Eugene rubbed his head. "No, this is on me. Don't take any more chances."

Keeping one eye closed to hold nausea and double vision at bay, Eugene stepped through the plastic strip doorway. Looking around for searching cops, he hobbled through the mountain of stacked rolls of newsprint to the back door. He pressed the side of his face to its warm metal surface to steady himself and tested the knob. Taking a fortifying breath, he pulled open the door and stepped out. Expecting a wall of flashing lights, cops and guns, he found only a picnic table and Kurt's Harley chained to a pole. In the distance, a reddening sunset bathed the beige stucco of Scottsdale with color and shadow.

8

Inside his cell, Derek Schaefer laid back on the cold, steel bunk, his mind a storm of anger. Minutes before, Eddie had come by to taunt him with news of his DNA link to Eugene.

"Quit trying to mind fuck me, asshole," he'd said. "There's no fucking way I'm related to that paparazzi dude."

Alone with his thoughts, his certainty crumbled.

Memories of his ma and pa and the Luchadores flooded in. *I deserve this . . . I'm just like them . . . .* Surrounded by quiet, trapped in concrete and steel, he drifted to sleep, inviting his punishment, letting his mind take him back to his tortured past.

He was nine, maybe ten, out on a scrap run with his ma and pa. Oil burned off the engine of his father's old truck, invading his nostrils. Seated between his parents, rusty seat springs stabbed at his skinny legs through a frayed horse blanket. From the truck's rattling, door-mounted speakers, Conway Twitty howled of honky tonks and angels.

Ma was silent as always. She looked tired but pretty in the new, flowered dress he'd plucked from a Goodwill donation box days before.

"Well, looky there," said Pa, spying a pile of cardboard at one of their regular stops. He turned down the music and slowed, dropping the truck out of gear and setting the parking brake. "Stay put," he said, crawling out.

Pa approached a short, fat, bald man with the wooden grip of a revolver poking from his back pocket.

"Lookin' to trade today, mister?" Pa said to the man while holding his hands out to his sides. The man's ugly smile, and a lone pickup truck parked in front of the building told Derek there would be a trade and his mother would have to earn her keep.

The short man stepped close to Pa saying something Derek couldn't hear.

Pa walked back to the truck and placed a hard, boney hand on the window sill. "Hop on out, darlin'. He wants to see what you're wearin'. You better make it good. We need that cardboard."

Ma stared blankly out the windshield. Without a word, she opened her door and crawled out. The thin fabric of her pretty flowered dress pinched between her butt cheeks, exposing the lack of underwear. Her flip-flop sandals clapped at her heels, kicking up dirt as she sauntered to the ugly little man with the gun.

Derek turned in the seat to better see. The ugly man nodded to Pa then took Ma's hand, leading her to an old house trailer in the back of the warehouse delivery yard. A huge dog appeared from under the trailer, its tail wagging. The fat little man brushed it aside.

"Hop on out, boy. It's time you learned how she does it. You watch a little. You're gettin' old enough to start earnin' your own keep." His pa urged him from the truck with a thump on the shoulder.

From the yard gate Derek watched his Ma drop to her knees in the trailer's open door. The short man undid his pants and put his thing in her mouth. His ma's head began to bob as the man swayed into her with his head back and eyes closed. Derek's fingers moved to the tiny boner rising in his pants.

"You seen enough now. Quit diddlin' yer little nub of a pecker and start loadin' the truck." Derek went to work in silence. A grunt from his ma made him glance back. The short man was behind her now, his belly resting on her ass as he humped like a dog. Her face was red and mouth twisted as her boobs jiggled below the dress pushed up to her armpits.

A hard slap from Pa's hand made Derek wince and stumble. Pushing down anger, he turned his attention back to the cardboard.

Ma appeared at the back of the truck a short time later, a stack of cardboard under her arm and tears in her otherwise blank eyes.

Cardboard loaded and tied down, Derek climbed to the middle seat, wincing as a rusty spring clawed his leg.

"She's still a good'n ain't she?" Pa hollered at the short man. He goosed the engine then released the parking brake as blue smoke billowed. "Same deal in the next week or two? . . . Okay, I'll check back."

Pa slammed the truck's four-speed into second. The shifter whacked Derek's shin and his hand moved to rub at the pain.

"Keep your leg the hell outta my way," growled Pa." And you, bitch, clean yourself up." He pulled a dirty rag from the dash and threw it at her. She wiped between her legs then dropped the rag to the floor. Her teary, blank eyes found a scab on her arm. She picked at it. Derek covertly patted his ma's leg, eager to start earning his keep so she wouldn't have to cry.

His mind recalled hearing that an anonymous report of child sexual exploitation led the state of Arizona to place him in foster care. Fighting and acting out sexually in the system earned him a series of placements, the last of which was in the home of Bob and Mary Buckingham.

Two days into his new life with the Buckinghams, an older boy woke Derek just before sunrise. Naked, erect and angry-faced, the boy's fists were at the ready. His anger dissipated when, rather than fighting, Derek demonstrated the skills learned from watching his ma.

Afterward, the boy said, "My name's Reggie. I'm gonna be your roommate and teach you the rules."

"I'm Derek."

Reggie shook Derek's hand like a grown-up. "What happened to your dick? Were you born like that?"

"Yeah," Derek said, casting his eyes to the floor.

"Don't be sad. It's a good thing. Pervs like little kid dicks and you got the tiniest pecker I've ever seen. Combine that with your talented mouth . . . Heck, the Buckinghams are gonna love you."

Derek beamed. "Really? I've got talent?"

"Uh-huh. But you know, if you don't do what the Buckinghams want, you'll go to juvy. That's like jail. Really bad."

"Yeah, I know."

"There's only one way you can stay here and be part of the family."

"Earn my keep?" Derek said, feigning oral sex.

"Yeah. It's not so bad when you're little though. The pervs give you lots of tips and the Buckinghams let you keep them."

"What's a tip?"

"Gifts the pervs hand out if they like you."

"Gifts?"

"Yeah, iPods and shit."

Derek smiled. "I never got a tip before, I was just helpin' out my ma."

"Well, enjoy it while it lasts. When you get to be a big kid like me, it's not so easy."

"Whadda ya mean?"

"Well, there's little kids and big kids. Little kids are worth more and they don't have to do all the stuff us big kids do."

"I'm sorry."

"That's okay, I'll be eighteen soon. That's when you age out. No more pervs. I'll be able to do whatever I want. The Buckinghams say because I've been good, they'll help me get my own place."

"Cool."

"Yup, now help all of us out by doing whatever the Buckinghams need. The one rule above all is that we don't talk to rubes."

"What's a rube?"

"Nosey outsiders and do-gooders who don't have a clue."

"Okay, but what about school?"

Reggie grinned, "We don't have to go because we're home schooled."

"A teacher comes to our house?"

"Nope, the Buckinghams just tell the do-gooders they're teachin' us. Our school is really stayin' home all day watchin' TV and playin' video games."

"That's awesome," said Derek.

"Yup, Mr. And Mrs. Buckingham are great. We got a good thing goin' but you gotta keep the customers happy."

"Cool. I can do that. I've got talent."

Derek's talent and his deformity made him a novelty act much in demand. He reveled in the notoriety and soaked up the Buckinghams' praise while staying in the ranks of the little kids much longer than most.

On the day of Reggie's aging out party, it was announced that Derek would be taking his spot with the older boys.

"You're lucky you lasted as long as you did," said Reggie. They were in the Buckingham game room, seated on beanbag chairs. Reggie was showing 15-year-old Derek how to smoke weed from a bong, a perk of joining the older boys.

"Now that I'm a big kid I figure I'll have to do butt sex, right?"

Reggie took a long pull from the red glass tube while feigning fellatio. Both boys laughed and smoke shot from Reggie's nose and mouth. "Anal mostly, but you—"

"Ha, ha. You said anal's mostly butt."

They fell into a round of coughing, pot-induced giggles until teary eyed and gasping for air.

Reggie finished his thought. "You'll be cool. It's not that bad and it's waaaay, better than juvy or risking your ass on the street. There's a Luchador party tonight. You'll see."

"What's a Luchador?"

"Just another bunch of pervs. We're not supposed to talk about them, but since you're going I figure it's okay. It's kinda like a costume party."

The roommate produced a small foil of cocaine. "Best thing about a Luchador party is the coke." He loaded a thumbnail with white powder then snorted it in. His eyes widened with pleasure. "This is really kick-ass stuff." He handed Derek his own foil of white powder. "Now hold onto this and don't use it 'til you're about to start the party. Suck it up your nose just like I did. It'll make things way easier and a lot more fun," he said, stretching back in the beanbag, obviously enjoying the high.

That night after a light dinner, Mr. Buckingham ordered Derek and six other boys into the family's panel van. All sat on blankets and pillows spread on the hard metal floor. Mr. Buckingham crawled into the driver's seat and cranked the engine.

Derek looked at the boy sitting next to him. "Luchadores?"

"Yup, we all gotta take a turn." The boy put a finger to his lips. "Shhh, no talking."

After the van rolled to a stop and Mr. Buckingham had shut down the motor, all the boys snorted their coke with practiced ease. Derek followed their lead, fumbling his foil and inhaling the white powder.

It burned going in. He had to fight back a sneeze, but a sudden, pleasurable rush soon followed.

"Everybody out, and don't do anything stupid," ordered Mr. Buckingham, popping open an old plastic camera.

They stood in a large, nearly empty warehouse. Derek's head whipped all directions, his reflexes heightened, his mind quick and nimble yet his knees oddly weak. The slam of the van door echoed in the vast space. A glaring, bright light dangled from the rafters illuminating a large, rubber mat in the middle of the cavernous space. A table covered in black cloth sat at the far side of the mat, filled with tubs of ice and beer, piles of cigars and bottles of serious liquor. Comfortable chairs had been positioned beyond the table.

"Go earn your keep," ordered Mr. Buckingham.

The boys shuffled to the mat, formed a line and waited silently. Derek's eyes darted to every dark corner.

"Where are they? Let's start this party," Derek blurted, feeling euphoric.

Mr. Buckingham tapped the back of his head. Derek turned and received an approving wink, followed by a flash and a whir as Mr. Buckingham took his picture like a proud father at a school program.

Rusted hinges groaned from somewhere deep in the building. A boy-sized creature appeared, dressed in black from head to toe. Shiny ringlets dotted his suit. Silently, he padded to the table and pressed a button on an old boom-box radio. Odd marching music filled the space as seven naked men strolled in, their faces hidden by weird fabric masks. Derek clapped his hands, hooting at the spectacle.

The men formed a line on the opposite side of the mat, facing the boys. They stretched and stroked themselves until the marching music fell silent.

"Strip," ordered a fat man in a black skull and crossbones mask. Gray hair curled on his sagging chest.

The boys complied, piling their clothing at the edge of the mat.

A boy whispered into Derek's ear, "They like it when you fight. Keep away from the guy in the clown mask if you can. His cock can really do some damage and he's into breath games."

"What's a breath game?"

"Choking. It won't kill you but you'll think it will. That's what gets him off."

Rivulets of fear trickled into Derek's mind. The air suddenly turned warm, thick, smothering. The open space seemed smaller, closed in.

The clown stood like a statue, his eyes scanning until he and Derek locked gazes. His mask's red sprouting hair and bulbous nose accompanied big squared teeth set in a permanent grin. The bravado conjured by the cocaine vanished and Derek averted his eyes.

Skull-and-Crossbones pointed to Derek and ordered, "I get the new kid's cherry."

"Hell, he's got a toothpick for a pecker. You're welcome to him," said a man in an electric-blue mask emblazoned with silver lightning bolts.

"Smaller the pecker the bigger the fight," joked Skull-and-Crossbones, "which, by my estimation, makes you a warrior chief."

The men laughed, shoved, and slapped each other on the ass until someone yelled,"WRESTLE!"

Derek followed the scramble to the center of the mat. The Luchadores circled their prey. Then it turned into a free-for-all of grabbing and twisting, laughter and squeals of pain. Derek stood wide-eyed as Skull-and-Crossbones strolled through the melee, his sagging girth blocking out the light as he stepped close. Derek moved to please him and was rewarded with a hard slap in the middle of his skinny back. Eyes tearing with pain, he back-pedaled. The huge man lashed out, his wide palm striking Derek hard on the face. Before he could stop himself, Derek punched the man in the crotch. The man released a pleasured grunt then grabbed Derek by the hair and slapped him again. Screaming with rage, Derek kicked with all of his might.

"That's it, that's what I need, boy. Show me what you got!"

Rage powered Derek's hands and feet, punching and kicking until he fell to his knees, exhausted and sobbing.

With unexpected quickness, the big man hoisted him high overhead. The dangling light spun into a blur as the man turned round and round. Suddenly falling, Derek hit the mat hard, Skull-and-Crossbones landing atop him. The air rushed from his lungs just before a big arm wrapped around his middle forcing him around onto all fours.

Just do it, asshole!

The next moment Derek's mouth gaped in a silent scream, His eyes closed to shut out the world. A shadow crossed his face. He flinched, his eyes opening in a frightened glance. The clown loomed over him, the stitched, fabric smile widening as the monster beneath smiled.

* * *

Derek endured six months of Luchador parties before salvation arrived in the form of a heart attack. John Loundy, the social worker who fed the Buckinghams' sex business, was forced to undergo a quadruple bypass. His replacement discovered problems with the paperwork. That same week, the body of Reggie, Derek's former roommate, was found rotting in a landfill.

Loundy's eager young replacement insisted on making a surprise visit. Her supervisor, Riley Mitchell agreed and insisted he accompany her, issuing a caution to tread lightly because of the Buckinghams' willingness to take on the hard cases.

Derek and Jamie, the newest Buckingham foster child, were watching television in the living room when Mr. Buckingham called a house meeting.

"Gentlemen, your case manager, Mr. Loundy is ill and two rube replacements are paying us what they think is a surprise visit. Act surprised and treat them accordingly. If they ask questions, remember your lines. I can't stress enough what's at stake."

"Juvy," spouted Jamie like a proud student.

"Yes," said Mr. Buckingham, smiling. "Or worse. It could mean getting tossed to the street where we can't protect you at all."

Hours later when the doorbell rang, Jamie jumped from his chair, a ball of excitement.

"Whoa, little dude, take it down a notch," Derek advised. "They're just going to look around and ask some questions. Remember what we were taught to say to rubes."

Mr. Buckingham answered the door with his wife at his heels. Derek almost laughed when he saw her wearing an apron. Earlier they'd aired out the house, carefully arranged schoolbooks at the kitchen table, and made sure all signs of drugs had been eliminated.

"Hi, we're with the state foster care office," said a friendly looking young woman who was accompanied by an older and taller man. "Sorry for not calling to let you know we were coming, I'm Annabel Marshall and this is my supervisor, Riley Mitchell." Both had shiny, photo ID cards hanging around their necks.

Derek smiled to himself. *Fucking rubes are clueless.*

"Well, this is a pleasant surprise. Is Mr. Loundy coming, too?" asked Mrs. Buckingham.

"No, I'm afraid he's in the hospital," said Annabel.

"Oh, no. Is he going to be okay?"

"Yes, but he had a heart attack and underwent bypass surgery. We're hoping he'll be able to return. In the meantime, I'll be taking over his caseload."

"Where's he at, I mean which hospital? I'd like to send flowers. Maybe the boys could make him a card."

"I believe he's at St. Joe's, right Mr. Mitchell?" asked Annabel.

Mitchell nodded. "Like Ms. Marshall said, we're sorry for the ambush. We have another bit of unfortunate news, but first we'd like to visit with each of the boys. You know, to get them acquainted with Ms. Marshall."

Derek blanched. He had heard that man's voice somewhere in his past. He picked up a magazine, flipping pages as he scoured his mind for a clue.

"Not to worry," said Mr. Buckingham. "Your office is welcome anytime. We just roll with the flow around here. Please come in, sit down. What can we do you for?"

"Can I get you two some coffee? Maybe a soda or bottle of water?" asked Mrs. Buckingham.

"No, but thank you," said Mitchell. "I don't anticipate this will take long. We just need a minute alone with each boy. After that we'll sit down together and talk."

That voice . . . He's a perv, but from where?

The social workers set up at the kitchen table while the Buckinghams sat in the living room, casting warning looks to each boy as they were called in. Jaime went first. On his return, he offered an eager thumbs-up and a huge smile.

Derek, being the oldest, went last. Seeing Annabel up close, surprising memories of his mother surfaced. The social worker had kind eyes and a soft voice. When she pulled a card from her purse and handed it to him, he caught hint of perfume.

The questions were brief and superficial. Derek put on his best, big brother act and got an approving wink from Mr. Buckingham.

"Well, that's all the questions I have," said Annabel. She smiled at the Buckinghams. "Looks like you're holding up well under difficult circumstances."

"It's a labor of love," said Mrs. Buckingham. "But it's worthwhile. In fact just last week we received a letter from a boy we cared for about ten years ago. He's married and has a family. I could get it for you if you like. We—"

"That won't be necessary," Mitchell interrupted. "We've got one more bit of business that shouldn't be discussed in front of the boys."

Mr. Buckingham stood and made a shooing motion with his hands. "You boys head into the game room. You can watch your show in there. Derek, you've got your school work done, correct?"

"Yessir," said Derek, doing his best to sound sincere.

Jamie jumped from his chair. Derek followed, a little more slowly, his peripheral vision catching Mitchell's gaze as it followed little Jamie's ass down the hallway.

Yep, he's a perv. Probably another Buckingham plant, putting on a show for this new lady.

Derek strolled slowly down the hall until he was certain he was out of sight. Already in the game room, Jamie poked his head from the doorway. Derek put a finger to his lips then to his ear. He pointed to the living room. Jamie nodded with understanding.

Stepping back to within earshot, Derek leaned against the wall, surprised by his tension.

"There's no easy way to say this," said Mitchell. "Reggie Johnson, one of your former charges . . . He—"

"Don't tell me something bad happened," cried Mrs. Buckingham.

"I'm afraid so," said Mitchell. "His remains were discovered in a landfill south of Buckeye. He—"

"Oh, good Lord!"

"That just makes me heart sick," moaned Mr. Buckingham. "Can't say as I'm surprised." He let out a long, slow breath.

"What do you mean?" asked Annabel.

"Well, there was no controlling the boy. He was damaged goods when we got him. As you know we take the difficult boys."

"Something we truly appreciate," said Mitchell.

"I assume foul play was involved?"

"Yes, I'm afraid so. The coroner's report points that direction. His remains had been there for some time. It was a fluke that his body was discovered at all."

In the hallway, Derek slid down the wall, his insides twisting and hands fisted against his temples. *Reggie, Jesus . . . a landfill . . . No wonder he didn't keep in touch.*

"We thought Reggie'd turned a corner. But . . . a few weeks before he left us, we discovered he'd been prostituting himself again."

"I'm sorry," offered Mitchell. "I know how dis—"

"It was partially my fault," interrupted Mrs. Buckingham. "I was the one pushing to give the boy more freedom. He claimed he had a job, we—"

"And he paid back your faith with lies and sick behavior," snapped Mr. Buckingham.

Derek's mind spun. *It's all a lie. Reggie was awesome. He did everything they asked . . . Oh God.* His hands covered his mouth to hold back a scream.

"I'm very sorry," he heard Annabel say, grief clouding his ability to comprehend. "I have to ask . . . Mr. Loundy, my predecessor . . . His reports were, well . . . almost nonexistent in regards to this family. Why is that and why was there no record of Reggie's errant behavior?"

"I'll take the hit there," said Mr. Buckingham. Jeff . . . uh, Mr. Loundy . . . We've worked together for so long . . . Well, I guess we got a little lax on the rules. When we discovered what Reggie was up to . . . Well, he was so close to aging out that—"

"That you thought it better to cross your fingers and hope for the best," inserted Mitchell.

"Yes, that's about it. Some boys need to get out on their own before they find their footing."

"Had you reported his behavior and had Mr. Loundy done his job, this boy might still be alive," insisted Annabel.

Mrs. Buckingham let out mournful croak.

"Ms. Marshall, that's uncalled for," said Mitchell. "You're inexperienced. The Buckinghams have given—"

"No, no, it's true. It is our fault," Mrs. Buckingham squeaked. "But, Ms. Marshall, honey, you're are young and I'm afraid you'll learn soon enough that regret is probably the hardest part of giving yourself to troubled kids."

Giving . . . hell . . . You sick bitch! On his knees now, Derek recalled Reggie's aging out party and the two men in the van who'd picked him up for work the next day. Horrific imaginings of his friend's body, lifeless and rotting on a mountain of garbage rushed in. He pushed down the urge to scream with thoughts of revenge. *I have to get out. Burn these sick freaks to the ground . . . Jesus, little Jamie. I talked him into this bullshit. He trusted me.*

Derek stood, then tiptoed down the hall. He once again shushed the watching Jamie, before entering the Buckingham's bedroom and removing the bottom drawer of a dresser where he'd seen Mr. Buckingham hide his insurance policy, a cigar box with extra pictures he'd pocketed from the Luchador parties.

Racing back to the room he shared with Jaime, he wrapped the box in a t-shirt, opened the window and dropped it into the bushes outside.

Later, tales of evil and nosey government bureaucrats living on fat government checks filled the evening dinner conversation. Derek doted on Jamie while plotting his escape. It was only a matter of time before the theft of the pictures would be discovered.

At sunset, under the pretext of taking out the trash, he stepped from the Buckingham home for the last time, veering for the bushes to retrieve the box before jogging six blocks to a convenience store pay phone where he dialed the number on Annabel's card.

"Hello, this is Annabel."

"Are you alone?"

"Yes, who is this?"

"Derek Schaefer from the Buckinghams. I'm at a pay phone. Can you come get me?"

"I don't understand. Are you hurt? Where are your foster parents?"

"I couldn't talk in front of them, I think they killed Reggie because he got too old. Just come get me, please. They make us do sex stuff. I have pictures. I'm at 32nd and Oak. I'll be in the bushes in back of a check cashing place. If I see cops I'm gone. Please, they're gonna kill me, too."

Sitting in her car by a dumpster outside the check cashing store, Annabel maintained a condescending air until Derek opened the cigar box. She fell silent, lingering on each image and letting out a gasp at seeing the image of Derek at the mercy of a monster.

"That's Mr. Mitchell, your boss," said Derek, pointing to a picture of the man in the blue, lightning bolt mask. "I recognized his voice at the house . . . He's in on it."

Annabel was crying when she closed the box's lid and placed it back in Derek's hands. Continuing to cry, she dropped the car into gear.

"Where are we going?"

"Someplace that will make sure the world knows about this."

"Will I have to go to juvy?"

"No, Derek, you've done nothing wrong."

Almost an hour later, they parked in front of the *East Valley Herald.* "There's a man in here that I trust. My father knows him. I'm going to leave these with him then take you someplace safe. Do you trust me?"

"Yes," said Derek.

An old man in a brown jacket stepped from the newspaper's front door and looked up and down the street.

Annabel held out her hand and Derek handed her the box. She crawled from her car and locked the doors then met the old man, showing him her ID badge. When he opened the box lid he slumped then stood tall and squared his shoulders. He motioned for her to come inside and she pointed to the car. He nodded and shielded his eyes to better see. A moment later he stepped back inside and she returned to unlock the car door.

"What did he say? Is he going to do something?"

"He's going to write a story and he's calling the State Patrol. They'll make sure all the boys are safe."

Three years later, the Luchadores were still a mystery. That betrayal by the authorities had left a giant chip on Derek's shoulder. On his 18th birthday, the state of Arizona washed their hands of him. He walked away from the foster care system with only a small, monetary settlement, most of which went to cocaine. With no discernible talent beyond what he'd learned in the sex trade, Derek turned to prostitution to pay the rent.

His rapid descent to rock bottom ended in a cocaine-fueled rage in the bedroom of an elderly pawnshop owner who couldn't pay for a weekend's fling. Rather than endure a beating, the old queen offered a battered pickup truck and lawn care equipment as trade.

Honest, hard work suited Derek well. His once pale, soft body became tanned and strong as he earned his living in the Arizona sun. The smell of fresh-cut grass and customers who paid cash were more cathartic than any of his state-ordered counseling sessions had ever been.

One hot summer afternoon, while cutting grass in the pricey suburb of Scottsdale, he dreamed of painting his name on his truck and buying a riding lawn mower. A young college-age girl steered her convertible into a driveway across the street. Climbing from her car and retrieving her book bag from the back seat, she caught his eye, smiled and waved before heading inside. Minutes later, she appeared in front of him holding a glass of iced tea. Her tan skin glistened and he caught the scent of coconut oil. Their fingers touched as she handed him the sweating glass.

"You work here every week?" she asked, as Derek downed the cold drink.

"Yes, this is one of my many regulars," he replied proudly. He wanted to tell her all about his business plans, but held back, fearing he'd sound foolish.

"Well, I just wanted to say hi. Guess I'll see you next week." She touched his hand again in parting, sending a shock of electric lust through him. He'd never thought much of women and he'd never really considered his own sexuality. But now, for the first time in his life he ached with desire. *This is clean, and right. This is what love is supposed to be.*

A week later Derek drove his freshly waxed and gleaming truck to Scottsdale with his heart in his throat the entire way.

He'd nearly finished the job by the time she rolled up in her convertible, offering a smile and a wave before parking. She wore a yellow cotton sundress that haloed her form in the afternoon light as she crossed the street.

"I was hoping I wouldn't miss you," she said, coming in close. "Wearing a shirt today, I see." She reached out to slide a hand under the shirt.

His loins fluttered at her touch. He wanted to pull her in tight and never let go.

"Why don't you take a break, come over? Have a little iced tea and cool off in the pool."

"Sure," Derek squeaked, abandoning his mower and following with his head in the clouds.

At poolside he sipped his tea while sitting on the end of a metal lounge chair. After less than a minute of awkward small talk she stepped close and pulled down the straps of her sundress exposing erect and wanting nipples. She pulled his head in to caress them and moaned as he put his mouth to work. She pulled his shirt off over his head. He stood, pulling her in tight. After a long, probing kiss, she reached down to unbutton his pants, sliding her hand into his underwear, sending his mind into orbit. *My god, this is what it's supposed to feel like.*

She giggled.

"Is that it?" she asked, holding his tiny little rock-hard penis in her hand. "It's so . . . small—"

"I—I'm sorry," Derek croaked, suddenly a small, frightened boy again.

"That's what I get for picking trash off the street," she laughed, shaking her head.

Shame crashed over him. He pulled away, tears flowing before he could stop them.

"What, you're crying? Christ, what's wrong with you? Are you retarded or something? It was just supposed to be a quick screw—Jesus, you need me to call your mommy or something?"

Decades of abuse ignited in fury. His left hand flew to her throat and his right hand delivered a punch that rolled her eyes back as she fell to the pool deck. Hands that seconds before had been gentle and loving now ripped away her dress and yanked down her panties.

Her focus returned as his fingers probed. She hauled back her legs as if to give better access then kicked him hard in the face.

Fireworks went off in his head, but he stayed on task, fueling his rage with the pain. "That's it. That's what I need. Gimme what you got!"

She delivered a glancing kick then tried to crawl away, but he grabbed her and punched her into submission.

"This is how the street trash does it, bitch!"

Mounting then thrusting with every ounce of his strength, his hands found her throat and squeezed. Submission became panic as she bucked into him. Her expression flicked from startled desire to terror. In that instant, Derek understood the ecstasy of power made sweeter by fear. He climaxed, firing decades of pain and fear inside her as the light fluttered from her eyes.

With reality's return came his own panic, only slightly offset at seeing the shallow rise and fall of her chest. He grabbed his iced tea cup to fill it with chlorinated pool water, then used that and her panties to scrub away any sign of himself.

Back in his truck, he tossed the cup and the soiled panties to the floorboards. In a memory flash he saw his mother tossing a wet cum rag to the floor of his father's truck.

During weeks of laying low, the fear in the little rich bitch's eyes became an obsession. He now understood all the men who reveled in dark pleasures at his expense. Now it was his turn. With careful planning, he could relive that feeling of power and pleasure again and again.

In the harsh light of the Scottsdale jail, Derek Schaefer woke from his dream, his heart aching with regret. *How could I? I'm just like them.*

He squirmed to a sitting position on the hard, cold bunk, wiping sweat from his forehead as he looked at the concrete and steel of his well-earned punishment. Soon he'd be transferred to county jail where he'd be everybody's bitch. With any luck, the Luchadores would have him eliminated.

9

Amazed that he'd slipped through the cop's fingers, Eugene was a mile south of the paper before his double vision and nausea settled into to a dull ache and ringing in his ears. His stride became even and sure. He tried to exude a look of nonchalance but in a resort town where the only people on foot were joggers in expensive workout clothes, he worried that he looked like a turd in a punch bowl.

Waiting for a light at McDowell Road, he relaxed enough that his thoughts turned to the mysterious caller's claim that he and Derek were related. *Dad did like skanky whores . . . I suppose.*

The low-blood-sugar sick of waning adrenaline brought vertigo. He caught himself, shaking the dizziness from his head as he realized he'd held his breath. He drew in a chest full of hot evening air and blew it out slowly. The night sky glowed cerulean blue, blending at the horizon with the last traces of sunset. Beyond his slitted eyelids, cars on the street seemed to flow as a stream of warm, white and red, trailing off to feed the color on the horizon.

A mechanical behemoth whooshed up. Eugene stepped back. Air brakes hissed and a door swung open. He blinked and shook his head then realized he'd been standing at a bus stop. Grabbing the opportunity, he climbed the narrow metal steps, searching his pocket for change. He hadn't been on a bus since high school.

"Buck seventy-five," said the driver, with a mistrustful glare.

Eugene pulled a wrinkled dollar bill and change from his pocket. Swaying a bit, he stared at the fare box and slid the bill home, following it with three quarters. He looked down the center aisle for a seat and saw he was the only rider. *Empty, on its return run back to Phoenix.* He took a seat halfway back. The hard, cool bench felt good against his aching muscles. Outside, night quickly settled over the city, like it always did in the desert.

As the bus pulled away from the curb, he realized he'd exited a bus at this very intersection many years before. That was the day he'd met Oliver Condon. A smile swept his face then unexpected tears escaped his eyes. His breathing hitched as he fought for control.

Embarrassed by the sudden wave of emotion, he wiped at the tears and looked to the bus driver. The man probably hadn't seen his little breakdown, his attention on driving while he talked into his radio microphone.

Is he calling the cops? The next moment the man glanced at him in the big mirror above his seat.

At 68th Street, the bus filled with a sweep of light and shadows cast by the bright overhead lights of a used car lot. Shiny pennants waved and painted windshields beckoned with offers of "Low Mileage" and "Special Financing."

The bus slowed and eased to the curb as its passenger door swung to open. Certain cops were about to board, Eugene was surprised to see only a tired-looking man in mechanic's uniform climb in. After a friendly high-five, the driver and the mechanic exchanged a few quiet words. Eugene caught the new passenger's glance and yawned, rubbing his eyes before nonchalantly turning his gaze out the window.

"You okay, buddy?" the approaching man asked. The patch above his shirt pocket said his name was Fred. A fading tattoo on his forearm spelled something in Spanish. The grease under his fingernails confirmed his profession.

"I've had better days, but, yeah, I'm okay. Thanks for asking."

Eugene's polite response eased the tension. The mechanic took a seat across the aisle. Now ignoring him, the driver's eyes darted between the rearview mirror and the road as they hit a dark stretch near Papago Park.

He turned to stare at the passing darkness then flinched at his own reflection in the window. His hair stuck out in all directions. Filth streaked his face. At the edge of his scalp, an oozing wound sat atop a huge, goose-egg bump. *No wonder I scared the hell out of them.*

At 35th Street the bus stopped in front of a bright little Liquor Wheel store. Fred the mechanic stood to exit, Eugene gave him a friendly nod.

"A little advice," offered Eugene.

The mechanic shot him a wary look.

"Never cheat on a Mexican girlfriend. Especially one who has big brothers."

A knowing smile spread on the mechanic's face. "Ibuprofen and ice," he said. "A beer or three wouldn't hurt either."

"Beer's what got me in trouble in the first place," said Eugene.

"Moderation helps, too." The mechanic laughed. "Learned that the hard way myself."

"Hey, Fred, do me a favor and tell the driver not to worry. I'm just heading to my parent's house for the night."

"Will do," Fred said, with a wave and kept on to the front of the bus.

At 15th Avenue, Eugene pulled the cord to signal the driver to let him off. With the bus at the curb he rose and walked stiffly to the forward exit. He hesitated beside the driver. "Sorry if I scared you. I've had a reeeally lousy day."

The driver chuckled and slapped his thigh, "Yep, you did have me goin' there for a bit. I get all kinds of crazies on this bus."

Eugene feigned amusement and ran a hand through his hair, "Yeah, sorry for that, I didn't realize how bad I looked until I saw myself in the window. I take it Fred clued you in."

"Yep, do yourself a favor, young man, and marry yourself a round woman. A girl with a little meat on her bones will keep you warm and appreciate you more than the skinny ones. Hell, I've been married twenty-seven years and mine gets sweeter by the day."

"Thanks," said Eugene. "But I think I'll lay off girlfriends for a while."

"Not to worry," said the driver. "You take care now." He pulled a lever to swing open the door.

Eugene stepped from the bus into the hot summer night. He needed water and rest but his destination was still miles away. Across the street, a Circle K store beckoned with its brightly lit coolers filled with bottles of cold water. He forced down thoughts of quenching his thirst. A man in his condition would draw too much attention in this part of town.

Wearing his best, 'moving-on-meaning-no-harm' face, he crossed McDowell on the green light to head south. Ahead, tall palms dotted the skyline above a mix of quaint Craftsman and Tudor style homes in the historic Story neighborhood.

Traffic whizzed past, swirling sand and cigarette butts in the gutter. The carbon-heavy exhaust of an ill-tuned truck caught in his nose. He considered the cash in his wallet and made a mental shopping list. Ahead, in the amber streetlight, the massive Papago Freeway overpass loomed. The big ribbon of concrete cut the city in two and was the dividing line between chic and shabby.

In the distance a heavyset woman laden with shopping bags walked toward him. Little more than a dot in the distance, he felt her sizing him up. He moved a little farther to the right to give her the full sidewalk. Soon they were close enough to trade a quick glance.

"*¡Hola,*" she said, pausing to offer a look of concern and a bottle of water from her bags.

"*¡Hola,*" replied Eugene, smiling.

"*Gracias, uh, mi español es muy malo,*" he said, humbly accepting the water. "Uh, "*Mercado?*"

"A store?" asked the woman, in heavily accented English.

"Yes, for water and food."

"On Grand Avenue," she said, pointing.

Eugene downed half the bottle of water. "*Gracias*," he said again then pulled out his wallet to pay.

The woman looked offended. "No, is my gift."

Eugene bowed and nodded his thanks before moving on.

The first house he saw after clearing the overpass had a red-tiled roof and a neat little courtyard hemmed by a low stucco and wrought iron fence. Concrete pillars lined the home's driveway. Atop the six pillars, concrete lions perched, two white, two gray and two terra cotta.

"Awesome," he said aloud, thinking of the hissy fit the snooty Scottsdale homeowners associations would throw over something so quirky. Continuing south, gang tags became more prevalent as did battered chain link and prickly pear cactus fences.

At Grand Avenue, he turned left, passing a boxing club and a pizzeria before spotting the small, bag-your-own grocery. At the checkout, the clerk appeared relieved to see Eugene pull money from his wallet. After paying, he triple-bagged his provisions of two liters of bottled water, trail mix, Fat Freddie meat snacks, a Bic lighter and a cheap paring knife.

With fourteen dollars and change to his name, he exited the store and headed for a trash dumpster in a distant corner of the lot. There he hoped to secure the last item he'd need to ready himself for the dangers of his old neighborhood.

The scurry of roaches and the stench of rotting fruit gave him pause as he lifted the dumpster lid. *You've gotten soft,* he told himself. His skin prickled as he thrust his hand into the dark mix to retrieve a yellow plastic binding strap from a broken fruit box. Working quickly, he tied the strap to the handles of his plastic shopping bags then draped them over his shoulders. Not only did it spread out the weight, it left his hands free to fight and thereby made him a less inviting target.

As he headed southeast on Grand Avenue, poverty deepened further and streetlights grew fewer and farther between. He felt more alone than ever. No car, no friends, no phone. Fear tapped him on the shoulder.

What the hell am I doing? I don't belong here anymore . . . I'm weak now . . . I'm running away . . . just like my Dad.

He plodded on, lost in fearful imaginings until at 15th Avenue and Washington, he caught sight of the State Capitol's copper dome to the west. Turning his head to look east, the multi-storied, concrete and glass buildings of Phoenix's law enforcement community loomed. Phoenix PD, Maricopa County Sheriff, FBI, Homeland Security. All stood within blocks of where he'd grown up and not once had any of them lifted a finger to help a teenage boy labeled a snitch by one of their own. He straightened with anger and continued on towards home.

Approaching Madison Street, groups of anonymous shadows traveling in twos and threes formed a shuffling stream of humanity heading for the St. Vincent de Paul homeless shelter. All kept a safe distance. None spoke or made eye contact. He knew Vinny's well. He had dined there whenever his mother had gone on a bender and traded their food stamps for booze.

At Madison Street, looking east beyond the slow rise of the 7th Avenue bridge, he caught sight of Chase Field. The last time he'd been in the big domed ballpark, he'd had a press credential, rather than the suspicion of rape and murder hanging around his neck. He broke away from the homeless stream to embark on the last leg of his journey.

Nearing the railroad switchyard, he breathed in the familiar stench of a hide rendering plant that hung in the air. A distant train horn blared. Then the whimsical Farmer John's Meats building came into view. It was here that he'd taken the picture of the homeless man and his dog under the dancing, cartoon pigs that had so impressed Mr. Condon.

Thoughts of Condon, then Sandy, quickened his pace. *The sooner I'm settled the sooner I can . . . I can do what? Hide like a rat in the sewer?*

At Jackson Street—across a huge expanse of barren ground—sat the railroad switchyard. Beyond the yard his family's former warehouse stood, looking as dark and depressing as ever. Approaching the tracks, he saw the beacon of a train still half-a-mile out, reflecting on the shiny ribbons of steel. He'd spent countless hours watching this switchyard from the warehouse as diesel engines pushed and pulled graffitied boxcars and tankers to hitch and unhitch with metallic thunder.

It was from the warehouse dock that he'd seen his first dead body, a homeless man cut in two after passing out drunk on the tracks. It was in the yard itself where he'd first stared down the barrel of a gun. He'd been helping his father and brother offload a boxcar in the small hours of the morning. They'd left him to stand watch on the siding as they trucked load after load to their warehouse. By 2 a.m., Eugene was asleep on his feet. He didn't hear the car pull up or the man step out.

"Can I help you?" a voice had said, sternly.

Eugene's eyes flashed open to the black eye of a revolver's muzzle backed by the glare of a flashlight.

"Railroad police. You'd better have a good explanation."

"My dad and brother will be right back," Eugene had said, swallowing hard, angry at himself for falling asleep. "These recliners are going to our warehouse." Eugene tilted his head toward the dock where his father and brother could be seen offloading their truck. "My dad says this car's getting pulled from the siding at 8 a.m. That's why we're here tonight . . . I mean . . . this morning."

The flashlight flicked off. The revolver lowered. Eugene saw the square, silhouetted jaw of what his father referred to as a "railroad dick."

When his father returned, the cop took him aside for a terse discussion of safety and school nights. When Eugene's English teacher caught him napping the next day in class, he'd blamed video games. No one at school would have believed the real story.

Now he stood at the intersection of Buchanan Street and 9th Avenue, where train tracks took a diagonal turn out of the switchyard. His head thumped with a dull ache, his feet screamed for relief and the plastic strap holding his provisions had rubbed his neck raw. He adjusted the strap and looked east beyond the 7th Avenue bridge to the Fodoni Brother's Junkyard. King, his old, one-eyed canine friend was likely watching from the shadows. It had been almost two months since he'd paid him a visit. His heart soared at the thought of scratching that wiry old face.

A dome light inside a police cruiser flashed to life beneath the bridge. He dropped to his haunches.

Did they track me? No, I left my phone . . . Mr. Condon was the only one besides Mom who knew about the brothers.

The officer slid low into his seat, obviously preparing for a nap then reached up to flip off the light.

Sleeping on the job. Some things never change.

Hopes dashed for seeing King, he turned his thoughts to where he'd hide out. He quickly dismissed the nighttime favorite of warehouse rooftops as being too hot and too exposed in sunlight. His second favorite, a little hidey hole up in the bridge's southern abutment was blocked by the napping cop. Frustrated and tired, he turned west toward his family's old warehouse.

Blacktop gave way to dirt and gravel. His crunching footfalls conjured childhood memories. Then he was in front of the old warehouse. Large, dark and foreboding. Squaring his shoulders and crossing his arms, he let the reality of it sink in. Chain link, razor wire and graffiti covered the building's cinder block front. Behind the fence, steel casement windows—some still holding shards of glass—looked like broken teeth in the skeleton of what had been his family's run at the American dream.

His parents had saved for years to finance the start-up. Lured by cheap lease rates so close to railroad siding, they hadn't realized that the former cold storage building sat in a war zone hemmed by a welfare housing project to the south and the city's largest homeless shelter to the north.

Thinking he might climb the fence at the rear of the building and spend the night on the dock, he rounded the west side of the structure. He could hardly believe his eyes. Standing in ramshackle defiance to the neighborhood's industrial decay sat the tiny Morning Star Baptist Church. *Good God, this place should have collapsed years ago.* The little church's green-shingled roof sagged and its wood frame leaned. Somehow it had survived.

As a child, the mid-town Sunday morning Lutheran services his mother forced him to attend were boring, staid affairs. He always thought of them as punishment compared to the music and dancing he'd seen in this tiny church. Congregants streamed in once a week, some in Cadillacs and others on foot, all wore fancy clothes and elaborate hats. Services were held in lantern light for want of electricity. Many a night Eugene had slipped into the weedy expanse between the warehouse and the church to peek in at the swooning and testifying and, best of all, the powerful gospel music pounded out by the congregation and its out-of-tune piano.

All that remained of the church's joyful noise was a silent, off-kilter shell. Summoning all his courage, he waded into the weedy, dark space between the buildings. Worried he'd stumble into a snake or sleeping bum, he crouched and stepped carefully.

Like a blind man reading a Braille bible, his fingers traced splintered clapboard siding in search of one of the church's two side windows. One was covered with plywood; the second gaped, its wooden cover long gone.

"Hello. Anyone home?" he asked into the darkness. "Just need to crash. Mean no harm."

Hearing no response, he pulled the lighter from his pants pocket, extended an arm through the window and flicked it to life. In the small orb of light he saw no threats, just dusty, warped pews piled with trash. He put the lighter back in his pocket then transferred his bags of provisions from his sore shoulders to the pew just inside the window.

"Hello. Anyone home?" he called again before crawling inside. The smell of dry rot and body odor that may or may not have been his own mixed awkwardly with the sudden loss of street sounds. In the brief flare of his lighter he made out the nearby old piano, its keyboard now broken and its guts torn out.

One sweep of his arm cleared the trash from the pew. He sat, groaning wearily. Every inch of his body hurt and his feet throbbed. He drank the remainder of a half-empty water bottle and managed a few bites of a Fat Freddie meat snack before stretching out and letting sleep take him.

10

Inside the *East Valley Herald*, night had turned the lobby window into a mirror reflecting a somber newsroom still reeling at the loss of their publisher. Outside a line of television trucks sat with microwave masts thrust high while crews pulled cable and set up lights in preparation for the ten o'clock news.

Tony Burke, a paunchy, middle-aged graphic artist rose from his chair to peer through his collection of super hero action figures lining his cubicle walls.

"The detectives have commandeered our conference room and they're interviewing people," he reported, like a submariner who'd gone up-periscope.

"Do you really think Eugene is a killer?" asked Mark Tetely, a digital imager.

"No," said Burke, slumping back into his chair. "This whole thing is way too much like the time Spiderman was framed for killing J. Jonah Jameson."

"You're comparing Eugene to Spiderman?" asked artist Mike Poole, not bothering to look up from his computer.

"It fits. Innocent photographer and hero set up by evil-doers."

"Interesting little toys you have," intruded a commanding voice from outside their walled space.

The art department turned to see the hulking frame of Sgt. Bryan Simpson.

"They're not toys," said Burke. "They're collectable action figures."

"Ah, a connoisseur. So then this area must be your fortress of attitude."

"You mean fortress of solitude," corrected Burke, not seeing the smiles cross the faces of his colleagues.

"My apologies. Did any of you witness the goings on surrounding Condon's office or the food delivery this afternoon?"

"I had a cruller," said Poole. "Tony had a sprinkle donut."

The sergeant sighed with a flicker of frustration and shifted his feet. His eyes peered a bit harder. "Anything else?"

"What exactly are you looking for?" challenged Burke. "We all loved Mr. Condon. Without him, we'd have probably been sold to a big newspaper chain a long time ago."

"And a big chain is a bad thing?"

"The worst . . . I mean, some are better than others but they're all greedy corporate bastards. They cut back and lay off then give big bonuses to management for chopping heads."

"What happens now that Mr. Condon is gone? He was the owner, correct?"

"His family will take over," Burke asserted more hopeful than confident.

Always the realist, Tetely offered, "That's gonna be a problem. His daughter and her politician husband have wanted to cash out for years. This newspaper is—or—*was* a lot more than money to Mr. Condon. Word was he hadn't paid himself a dime in the last two years just to help keep us in the black."

"Who's the leader now that he's gone?"

"I guess it's Pete, right guys? He's the city editor," said Burke. "He reported directly to Condon. That's another reason we're still profitable. Fewer managers and more worker bees."

"What's Pete's last name and where does he sit?"

"Cunningham," said Burke, pointing toward a cluster of desks in the middle of the newsroom.

"Thank you, gentlemen. By the way, I was always more of G.I. Joe type myself."

"Twelve inch version or the three-and-a-quarter?" asked Burke.

"The big ones, of course. Those little ones were just cheap, plastic army men."

Burke and the other artists gave an approving nod.

The sergeant headed for the city desk then stopped and turned back, "I almost forgot. You were discussing Eugene Fellig when I interrupted."

The artists merely stared back in stoic silence. Burke crossed his arms.

"I noticed a bit of contention. What's your opinion of him?"

Burke raised his chin. "He's a great guy and somebody's setting him up."

Poole huffed.

The sergeant honed in. "You don't agree?"

Poole's face tightened. "What I *think* is none of us really know him. My *impression* is that he's a good guy who takes great pictures."

"But there's something else, right?"

Poole scoffed. "Talk with Michael Specht, Eugene's boss. He's the one that's bad-mouthing him."

"Why don't *you* just tell me?"

Poole glanced to his coworkers.

"Look, all we're interested in is finding the truth," said the sergeant. "Debunking the gossip is a part of that."

Poole stared at him a moment before shrugging. "Okay . . . They got off to a rough start,"

"But they got over that a long time ago," inserted Tetely.

Poole turned. "Then why is he still running his mouth about Eugene being Condon's welfare project that came back to bite him?"

Tetely looked startled. "He's saying that? He's—"

"Hang on," interrupted the sergeant. "Let's start from the beginning."

Burke took the lead. "Mike Specht wanted to hire a friend who was some big award winner. Condon insisted he hire Eugene instead."

"I see," said the sergeant, making a note on a spiral-bound notepad.

"Eugene was barely out of high school when Condon hired him. He was kinda rough and he always seemed to be wearing the same clothes. Some people—not me—mind you, called him a charity project. They thought maybe Mr. Condon hired him because he felt sorry for those foster kids in the Luchador case. Me, I just thought the kid shot great pictures."

"Where does this Michael Specht sit?" asked the sergeant.

"Up there, near Pete, on the city desk," said Poole, pointing.

* * *

In the conference room, Eddie, Harry and the department's youngest detective, Luke Jeffers, interviewed Amy Becker, the summer intern who had taken Eugene's place on the late shift.

"So then you'd describe Eugene as a loner," said Jeffers, trying to hurry along the petite, young brunette.

"I wouldn't say loner. He keeps to himself. But that's partly because he works the late shift, and partly because he's a very old soul. He's content with his own company."

"You two ever date?" asked Eddie.

"No, not that I haven't been tempted. I've seen the waitresses over at the Pancake Palace trip all over each other to get his attention. But . . . you know . . . I don't want to be one of *those* interns. Understand?"

"Well, thanks for the insight," Jeffers said, standing to show her the door.

When Amy was out of earshot, Eddie asked, "What the hell is a 'very old soul?'"

"I was gonna ask you that same question, old man," laughed Harry.

"Don't know about the old part, but I do have soul," said Eddie, standing to shuffle out an awkward dance move.

Jeffers reddened and looked downward.

"Wait, wait. Let me picture it," said Harry, placing an index finger on his upper lip. "Hub cap-sized, mirrored sunglasses and a porn star mustache."

"Screw both of you," said Eddie. "I was more of a clean cut Latin lover. You know, a Frank Poncherello type. Had my uniform shirts tailored to show off the tight abs and big guns. The ladies loved me."

Harry poked Eddie's middle, "Well you've certainly got the paunch part of it covered."

Eddie sucked in his gut and rolled his eyes.

"Who's Poncherello?" asked Jeffers.

"CHiPS. You know," said Eddie. "Eric Estrada from that California Highway Patrol show."

"I didn't think they had TV back in your day," said Harry.

"Bite me."

The detective's attention was drawn to Sgt. Simpson's bulk filling the conference room doorway. "You interviewed Pete Cunningham, right?"

"Yeah, twice, Once at the hospital and a follow-up here," said Eddie.

"Did he say anything about a conflict between Condon and his family?"

"No, he never touched on that. What's up?"

"You might want to ask him about it. I just picked up on a power struggle. Condon's daughter wanted to sell and he didn't. Sounds like Cunningham is stuck in the middle. I also picked up on a little resentment between the Fellig kid and his boss, Michael Specht."

Raised voices jerked their attention to the newsroom.

Millie, the newsroom secretary, stood at Pete Cunningham's desk, trembling with anger and shaking a piece of paper in his face.

"How dare you soil Oliver's final edition with this garbage," Millie said, crumpling the paper and throwing it at Pete. "What in God's green acres would make you say this about Eugene?"

"I'm just presenting the facts, Millie," Pete said, slumping back into his desk chair and crossing his arms. "We can't look biased towards one of our own."

"Well, you skipped a few facts in your damn story. You didn't say anything about Oliver mentoring Eugene or how much Eugene looked up to him."

"She's right Pete," said a nearby voice from the watching newsroom staff.

"This is a hatchet job," said Millie. "Oliver never would have allowed crap like this to see the light of day."

"Millie, I'm sorry if—"

"You are most certainly not sorry," she accused. "And don't think for a second that Oliver wasn't aware of your actions behind his back."

Pete blanched.

"What's going on, Pete?" asked Gordon Reynolds, the sports editor who had stepped closer. "Is there something you're not telling us? Are we being sold?"

"It's nothing new," said Pete, sounding tired. "Nothing has changed. You all know that the family wants more involvement in the paper—"

"Involvement hell," spat Millie. "His daughter wants to sell it to a group of vultures."

"Now Millie, that's not—"

Pete's words were swallowed by the newsroom's loudly disapproving voices.

Watching from the conference room window, Harry said, "I'm thinking we might have a motive."

"Yeah," said Eddie, yawning and running his fingers through his hair. "But proving those peanut chunks were more than an accident will be tough unless a witness—"

"There's the Epi pen," said Harry. "I'm eager to see Condon's toxicology report—" A yawn interrupted his sentence.

"How long has it been since either of you slept," asked Jeffers.

Harry struggled to calculate. "Hell, almost 30 hours, I suppose. Let's get what we can from Cunningham and call it a day, guys. We can dig into this family fight more tomorrow."

"Aren't you working something in Phoenix tomorrow?" asked Jeffers.

"Oh. Yeah, that's right," said Harry, rubbing tired eyes. "Medical examiner's autopsy on the Carter girl. We're hoping to get preliminaries and maybe have a look around Eugene's old neighborhood."

"Yeah, but I was thinking we should rattle Schaefer's cage a little before he gets transferred to county jail tomorrow," said Eddie.

"Not a bad idea. Hey, you never told me. What was his reaction to our discovering his DNA link to Eugene?" asked Harry.

"He told me—and this is a direct quote—'Don't think you can brain fuck me you old spick.'"

"Classy guy."

"Okay, sounds like you two have a full plate," said Jeffers. "How about I dig into this family thing and you and Eddie deal with Schaefer and Phoenix."

"Works for me," said Eddie. "You might take another run at that old lady secretary tomorrow, too. I get the feeling that she and Condon were knocking boots. Maybe you could leverage the embarrassment factor to make her tell us a little more than she has about the Fellig kid."

Harry's jaw tightened. He looked to Jeffers who offered an understanding nod. "She kind of warmed up to me earlier," said Jeffers, "Don't think I'll have to strong arm her too much."

"You hungry partner?" Harry asked.

"Yeah, I could eat."

"Pancake house?"

"That's a good thought," said Jeffers. "If Eugene was *knocking boots*—to use Eddie's cowboy reference—with the waitresses, they might know more about him than anyone."

"It's on the way. You can drop me at my house after," said Harry.

"Cakes it is," said Eddie, "but let's poke that Cunningham fellow before we split. Give the kid here a head start on tomorrow."

Jeffers looked back patiently, "I'll tell him to come back."

"And tell him to bring a copy of the story that pissed off the secretary. I want to see what that's all about," said Eddie.

* * *

Pete entered the conference room, shoulders back and standing tall. He handed Harry a printout. "I assume you want to talk about Millie's little blowup. Let's get this over with, I've got a paper to get out and, if we bust deadline, I have no idea where the overtime money will come from."

"This won't take long," said Harry, scanning the story.

Eddie went first. "So, the rub between Condon and his daughter—this thing about selling the paper—how long has this been going on?"

"Years. Margaret's wanted Oliver to sell ever since his wife died. He refuses to talk to her about it, so she talks to me and I talk to

Condon and we go round and round . . . while I take a beating from everyone involved."

"Why didn't you tell us about this conflict earlier?"

"I didn't think of it. It's just part of the landscape—wait—Don't tell me you're thinking this . . . I mean, that's ridiculous. Everyone here loved the old guy."

"We have to look at everything."

"Then you're officially calling Condon's death a murder?"

"We're still calling it suspicious," said Harry, without taking his eyes off the printout. "I think I see what has Millie so riled up. You make some fairly large assumptions here—for a journalist, that is."

"Look, we can't afford to appear to be playing favorites. I'm in charge now and Eugene's not telling us about his link to Schaefer hurt our credibility. I feel that putting it all out there is the right thing to do."

"Do you know something we don't? You're assuming Eugene knew he's related to Schaefer."

"How could he not know? I-I mean, why else would he run?"

"Off the record?"

"Yes."

"Maybe he was scared off by my partner and a bunch of uniforms, barreling in like a lynch mob."

Eddie's face sharpened.

"Eugene ran off before we could tell him about the DNA link," said Harry.

"Maybe that's because he already knew."

"So, let's be clear, Mr. Cunningham, you have no proof that Eugene was aware of the connection."

"No," Pete said, his shoulders slumping. "I don't . . . hell . . . Millie was right. I'm an idiot. Condon would have nipped my stupid assumption in the bud. Jesus, and we've already gone to press."

11

News crews across the street from the *East Valley Herald* had just packed up and pulled out for the night as Harry and Eddie stepped from the air-conditioned newsroom.

"Lynch mob?" Eddie growled loud enough to qualify as a yell. He threw up his arms, stomping out to their car parked at the curb in front of the building.

Harry froze in place, leering at Eddie's wide back before following, careful to keep his hands at his sides. It was time to have it out with the aging, arrogant prick once and for all.

Eddie turned to face him, arms crossed, his butt against the cruiser's hood, ready for an argument.

Harry obliged. "If you'd called, you'd have known I had him contained. And you're goddamned lucky that *old lady*—Millie is her name by the way—didn't break a hip or worse when you knocked her down. What the hell were you thinking?"

"It was an accident."

"Bullshit. It was pure ego. You wanted to be the star, taking down the bad guy."

Eddie remained silent, eyes narrow as he turned his head to gaze up and down the wide street. The incessant buzz of cicadas rose and fell in the windless summer night. Harry felt the day's heat, stored in the concrete sidewalk rising up through the soles of his shoes. He calculated his chances as poor if this were to turn into a brawl.

"So I screwed up and let the kid escape."

"No, you chased a good kid into harm's way. You know it's the Lucha—"

"Take it down a notch," interrupted Eddie. "We don't need the whole world hearing this."

Confused, Harry lowered he voice and continued. "You know damn well the Luchadores are involved here. Framing Eugene to take the heat off Schaefer makes him just another lowlife. Nobody's the wiser."

"How do you explain the DNA?"

Harry crossed his arms and kicked at a crack in the sidewalk. "It has to be some weird coincidence. If you hadn't chased him off maybe we could've asked him about it. What the hell were you thinking?"

"I already said I fucked up. What more do you want?"

"Quit acting like king shit. You're just pissed off 'cause this Lucha—"

Eddie's arms shot up again as he yelled, "Look if you don't like the—"

"No, goddamn it! I don't like . . . You're dangerous! Tomorrow morning I'm gonna ask to be reassigned. I can't trust you. No wonder the state canned your ass." Harry stepped deep into Eddie's personal space, expecting a punch.

Much to his surprise, Eddie deflated and sat back against the hood of their car, palms down, head drooping. "You can trust me Harry. Question is, can I trust you?" he said in a near whisper.

Harry just stared, wondering where this was going.

"I'm serious, kid. Can I trust you? Because I need you *with* me."

Harry looked long and hard into Eddie's eyes. "I'm not a kid, and, yes, you can trust me. What the hell do you mean, need me with—"

Eddie held up a hand to stop him. Under his breath he said, "Eugene's sleeping tonight in an abandoned church in his old neighborhood last I heard."

"What? Don't mess with me right now, Eddie. I—"

Eddie's hand again stopped him. He lowered his voice even further. "I ain't messing with you, partner. There's shit going on you don't know about—couldn't know about because I don't know you."

"Jesus, Eddie, what's going on?"

"Anyone who's watching thinks I'm a hotheaded asshole who couldn't find my dick with both hands. We need to keep it that way because last time, these assholes went after my family. I had no choice but to be their scapegoat."

Eyes narrowed, back stiffened, Harry said, "Okay, go on."

"I have a friend. He's had eyes on Eugene since we orchestrated his escape."

"Wait . . . you orchestrated . . . How high up does this go?"

"The chief knows the basics and I have full approval. If anyone makes a move on Eugene, my friend will take them down and find out who sent them by whatever means necessary."

"Who's your friend?"

"Right now I'll just say he's got major skin in the game. Look, we can't beat these guys if we play by the rules. I need somebody to work off-leash. If this all goes to shit . . . Well, I'm toast, but I want the chief, and now you, to have plausible deniability."

Arms crossed and slack jawed, Harry blinked, slightly shaking his head as he tried to comprehend. "So, what's the next step?"

"Hope someone moves on Eugene so we can get our hooks into them. Beyond that, we continue like nothing's changed. My friend will watch over him and reel him back in when it's safe."

"Eddie, this is a lot to take in . . . Can't say I'm comfortable with using Eugene as bait."

"He's street smart. He'll be okay and my friend's a pro."

Eddie suddenly jerked his head up, his expression angry. He jumped from the hood of the car, throwing his arms in the air and yelling, "Then go ahead, asshole. In the meantime we have one more stop to make."

Harry backpedaled, his jaw tight and eyes blinking until he saw Eddie wink. The crooked smile that appeared on his aging partner's face was the first real one he'd ever seen. He followed the man's lead. "Fuck you, Eddie! Maybe I'll just do that. Let's get this bullshit over with so I can go home."

Eddie's eyes twinkled in the dim light. His smile broadened. It was the smile of a man who'd been through hell and was glad to be alive.

"Excellent . . . Now let's get off the street. We're sitting ducks out here. I'm driving."

Harry glanced up and down the street, imagined threats now lurking in every shadow. "Yeah, you've got a point," he said, still feeling slightly off balance by his partner's transformation, but suddenly glad to have him in his corner.

* * *

Waiting for a left turn arrow at Scottsdale Road and Drinkwater Boulevard, Harry mulled over the new information and cataloged the day's events. "Shit, Eddie, I forgot to tell you. Eugene told me what Condon's last words were."

"I thought it was gibberish." The light changed and Eddie turned south.

"Might as well have been. It was something like ass clown or—"

Eddie stabbed the brake pedal and yanked their Crown Vic into a strip mall parking lot as car horns blared from behind.

"What the hell, Eddie!" Harry unlatched his seat belt to retrieve his legal pads and printouts from the floorboards.

"Ass Clown . . . The red fibers . . . We were right!"

"Right about what? What are you talking about?"

"Ass Clown's a Luchador . . . A clown mask with bushy, red hair." Eddie was almost hyperventilating. "There were no pictures—"

"Slow down a little. So you think Condon saw something that identified this Ass Clown?"

"Had to . . . Why else would he use his dying breath to say the name?"

Harry sat in silent thought, his eyes blinking rapidly as he fit the pieces together.

"What? What are you thinking?" asked Eddie.

"I'm thinking I thought it was weird that the chief gave into that hack senator's demands so easily. You knew what those red fibers were from the start."

"I had a pretty good hunch," said Eddie.

"Damn it, Eddie, I hate playing catch up to this circle of trust crap—"

"I'm sorry, I—"

"No, I understand. I just don't like it. Now, you say there were no pictures. What the hell was it that Condon saw that made him say the name?"

"I don't know. There has to be something we missed."

"I've looked at those pictures for hours. There's nothing in there that looks like a clown."

"Maybe it was a reflection or a shadow. I've always thought the Ass Clown wouldn't allow pictures because he had a physical deformity that couldn't be hidden with a mask or a band-aid."

"Are you sure we have all the pictures? If they poisoned Condon to shut him up, they likely took what he saw."

Eddie stared out the windshield and counted on his fingers. "Eighteen, pretty sure—"

"Wait, wait." Harry thumbed his phone to life, "I made copies." He flicked through the images, counting them, and ended on eighteen then did it again to be sure.

"I could be misremembering. It's been a lot of years."

"Heck, coming in late like you did, a lot of stuff could have disappeared before you ever saw it."

"True . . . Well, I guess all we've got left is Eugene and what pictures we have in hand. I still want to show them to Schaefer in the morning. Maybe we'll get lucky. You still up for pancakes?"

"Yeah, I'm hungry and we have to go through the motions just in case we're being watched."

* * *

In a secluded corner of the Pancake Palace, slabs of butter puddled atop steaming pancakes set before the bleary-eyed detectives. Both stared at a gleaming, chrome syrup caddy loaded with flip-top dispensers.

"What's boysenberry taste like?" Eddie asked.

"Tart, I think. I prefer plain old maple," Harry said, hoisting the biggest dispenser, "No point in messing up good cakes with some fru-fru syrup."

Eddie followed his partner's lead, pouring the maple then returning the dispenser to its chromed rack.

"So, Eddie, in the interest of our newfound trust, what're the details of what went down at the State Patrol?"

Eddie kept his eyes on his pancakes. He used a fork to steer a butter glob through the syrup. "Wasn't my proudest moment." He cut a wedge of pancake from the stack and forked it into his mouth, chewing contemplatively. "I was a rookie detective. They brought me in late and from day one the whole thing smelled bad. But, my real trouble started after I asked Riley Mitchell for a look at his left thigh."

"The foster care muckety-muck?"

"Yep. The kids said he always kept a big square band-aid on his left thigh. I saw it in the pictures and figured it was to hide a scar or a birthmark or something."

"Was he willing?"

"Nope. Told me to piss off and lawyered up. It went downhill from there. I made some noise about a warrant. The next day my daughter gets pulled over and, lo and behold, they find cocaine in her trunk."

"Oh, shit, Eddie."

Eddie held up his fork, "It gets better. While I'm at the jail trying to sort it out, I get an anonymous phone call. This guy tells me that either I take the heat for the missing Luchador evidence or they'll send her to prison. I say, 'What missing evidence?' He laughs and says, 'Guess you haven't heard.' Then he raises the stakes, saying there were plenty of bull dike cons that would stick a shiv in my little girl for a few bags of chips at the prison commissary."

"What did you do?"

"It's my daughter. I collapsed like a dollar store lawn chair."

"Is she okay? Did they—"

"Yep. Oddly enough, they kept their word and made it go away. Just an unfortunate lab mistake. A week or so later I'd lost my job, my pension and my good name, but managed to stay out of jail, probably because taking me to court would have been too risky."

"Eddie, I'm sorry."

"Eh, I lived. Worst part of it is, they were free to keep hurting kids. That ate me up so bad I started drinking and that cost me my marriage and even my daughter for a while."

"But you both lived to fight another day. How's she doing now?"

"Daughter's great. She got her master's degree last year."

"And your wife?"

"She remarried a couple years ago."

"You dealing with that okay?"

"Oh, sure. It's tough though. Her new husband's a hummus-eating liberal pansy-ass who wants me to join his drum circle . . . You know, to work out my issues."

Harry choked, nearly shooting coffee from his nose. "You know, we're kinda having our own little drum circle moment right now."

"I guarantee this is about 99-percent less stupid. So, now that we've got it all out there, are we good?"

"Yeah, we're good."

They turned their attention to the cakes, saying little until a chubby, balding man with a pit-stained shirt and grease-spotted tie approached. "Hello, I'm Paul Harbin, the night manager. The girls tell me you have some questions. If it's about Eugene, I'll tell you I still can't believe what's happened."

"Please, have a seat if you've got a second," said Harry. Eddie slid over in the booth to make room.

Harbin sat, an ample portion of his oversized ass hanging out of the booth. "I know Chris Carter, the murdered girl's father, through the restaurant association. Is he okay?"

"He's having a pretty rough time of it," said Eddie.

"Surely he doesn't think Eugene had anything to do with Sandy's death, does he? I mean . . . We all love Eugene. He would never hurt a soul."

"We'd like to talk to Eugene about it, but unfortunately he ran away. There's a warrant out for his arrest," said Harry.

"Yes, I heard . . . No offense, but I can't blame him. You know, working in a coffee shop I hear things and—"

"What things have you heard?"

Harbin looked around then leaned in close, whispering, "Luchadores . . . and, like I say, no offense, but didn't some crooked cop get fired for covering for them a few years back?"

Eddie blanched.

Harry covered, "That was years ago and a different department altogether. And, as to the Luchadores being involved here we've seen nothing—"

Harbin held up a hand. "Hey, I'm sure you guys are on the up and up. Like I said, no offense. I'm just saying you might want to look into it. It could be his motive for giving you the slip."

"How long have you known him?" asked Eddie, obviously trying to get past the Luchador speed bump.

The manager pinched his fleshy chins while staring up at the restaurant's tall, A-framed ceiling. "Let's see, I started here three years ago and he was a regular customer then . . . I met him right after he cleaned our men's room."

"He worked here?"

"No, no, it was typical Eugene. We had a big chamber of commerce breakfast scheduled and a bunch of jerk high school kids trashed the men's room. It was a morning from hell with people out sick, so I stayed to help dayside. I hit the bathroom ready to do battle and there was Eugene wearing pink rubber gloves and pulling paper towels out of the urinals. Now, how many guys do you know who would clean your pisser as a favor?"

"Not many," said Eddie.

"What can you tell us about Eugene's past?"

"I won't be much help there. He's a good kid and all but not much of a talker. He dated some of the girls and even worked on their cars so they might be more help. Hey, Beth!" Harbin called waving a fat arm to catch the eye of a pretty, young waitress.

"Freshen your coffee?" Beth asked, approaching their table with a Bunn coffee pot in hand.

"Thanks," said Eddie, nudging his cup.

"Beth, these detectives are asking about Eugene. Can you answer some questions for them?"

Beth teared up and fanned her face with her free hand. "I-I'm sorry," she said, swallowing hard, setting the metal-bottomed pot on the table, "I-I'm friends with both Sandy and Eugene and there's just no way he—"

"I've gotta get the register," Harbin interrupted, hauling himself from the booth.

"Beth, what's your last name?" asked Harry.

"Carpenter."

"You and Eugene dated?"

"Yes, a few times. It was before I met my husband, of course."

"Did he ever talk about family, friends or previous employers?"

"Not really. He was more of a listener than a talker. And, honestly, he wasn't really my type. I was just curious as to whether the rumors about him were true."

"Rumors?" Eddie asked, eyebrows raised. "Were these rumors sexual in nature?"

It was Harry's turn to blanch. He shot Eddie a look that said, "Don't go there."

"I-I'm not sure what you mean."

As Eddie pushed on, Harry wanted to hide under the table. "Beth, I'm sorry to get so personal, but can I assume things went beyond dating?"

"Yes, not that it's any of your business."

"We have to ask and I'm sorry for this, but it's *official police business*. Was there anything odd about Eugene in a sexual way? How would you describe his penis?"

Beth's cheeks went from red to purple. Harry wished he was anywhere but here.

"N-normal . . . I guess . . . not that I'm a penis expert or anything. Why?"

"I'm sorry," Harry said, red faced. "My partner hasn't had much sleep the last couple of days. What exactly were the rumors about Eugene?"

She took a deep breath and settled herself. "The most incredible back and foot massage imaginable. Everyone talked about it. Let me tell you, after eight or ten hours on your feet, a good foot rub and a good listener are priceless." Her whole body appeared to relax just thinking about it.

"Was Sandy having problems with anyone? A boyfriend that might have been jealous of Eugene?" asked Harry.

"I hate to speak ill . . . She slept around, a lot. But, I hadn't heard of any problems. Most guys were scared of her father. He can be a real mean drunk."

"Was he ever a threat to Sandy?"

"Oh, no. He treated her like a queen."

"Was Eugene seeing anyone special recently? I mean, besides Sandy."

"I don't think she and Eugene were a thing, really . . . Like I said, she got around. Lately he's been coming in with a new girl from the Denny's, I think her name is Trish."

"Do you have a last name for Trish?" Eddie asked.

"No, they came in for breakfast a few times, but we never talked. She's really cute though."

Harry wrote *Trish/Denny's* in his legal pad. "Thank you for your time," he said, "and sorry if we embarrassed you."

"It's okay, but trust me. Eugene doesn't have a mean bone in his body."

When they were alone, Eddie smiled and popped a fork-full of pancake into his mouth. "Talk about a mean bone . . . Sounds like this Eugene kid's a stud."

"Jesus, Eddie. Official police business? Really?" whispered Harry.

Eddie's smile broadened as he chewed. He swallowed, following up with a big slurp of coffee. "They'll be talking about us dumb cops and our penis questions for weeks. Look at her, she's already telling people."

Harry looked down the aisle, past the register to see Beth gesticulating and nodding in their direction. "This dumb cop act's a real bitch, Eddie."

"That, my friend is what keeps us safe. I've been playing the idiot from the first time I locked eyes with Schaefer."

"So you knew right off?"

"Yep."

"Why didn't he recognize you?"

"Never had much contact with him. They brought me in late because they needed a scapegoat. Man, I need to hit the sack. All this food is putting me to sleep. What time do they transfer prisoners tomorrow?"

"Usually right after lunch."

"Whadda ya say I pick you up around 10:30 then?"

"Works for me."

Enduring the critical looks from the restaurant staff, they paid their bill then sauntered to the car.

Embarrassed and feeling sleep-deprived giggles coming on, Harry said, "Eddie, I think we missed an opportunity."

"What's that, partner?"

"Back when we had Eugene and Schaefer together in the jail, we should have asked for a penis lineup."

The twinkle returned to Eddie's eyes and an ear-to-ear grin spread across his face like watercolors hitting a thirsty piece of paper. Affecting a haughty, British accent, Eddie held up a hand with a pinky finger extended, saying, "Number One, please step forward and fluff your winky."

Harry answered, "P-please, can we call it a tally whacker? Penis is so . . . p-p-personal."

This urged a snort from Eddie that sent them both into a fit of uncontrolled belly laughter that lasted until they were in the car, teary-eyed and gasping for breath.

They'd almost gotten it under control when Eddie pointed and said, "Look, look."

Harry followed the finger to the window by the restaurant's cash register where the fat little manager glared at them disapprovingly. It set them off again, laughing and snorting until it hurt.

"Oh my god," Harry said, gasping for breath while holding aching ribs. Eddie fumbled the key into the ignition, cranked the motor and pulled away. They were back on the street before the sillies waned and both men wiped tears from their eyes.

"Geeze, Eddie, penis questions and Porky's references . . . We really need some sleep. What time are you picking me up again?"

Eddie cleared tears from his eyes and glanced at his watch, "Let's move it back half an hour, say, 11:00."

"Deal."

* * *

The family dog, Abby, greeted Harry as he stepped in from the garage. The sillies still coaxed a smile until guilt at not seeing his kids before they'd gone to bed mixed with worry for their safety. Pulling a blue plastic cup from the stack on the kitchen counter, he filled it with cold fridge door water and downed a couple of ibuprofen.

Abby danced at his feet, eager for attention. "Good morning, Miss Abigail," He said, bending to scratch under the chin of the little Westie. He let the dog out for a pre-sunrise sniff and piddle.

As always, his wife had left a light on for him in the living room. He switched it off after letting the dog back inside. Kicking off his shoes in the living room, he unbuttoned his shirt as he padded down the hall of the little three-bedroom house. He stopped to peek in on each kid, needing to see their peaceful slumber.

In the hallway outside the master bedroom, Harry ripped free the noisy Velcro straps of his body armor before entering. He smiled at Sarah's barely audible little snore and reveled in the comforting smell of soap and makeup and freshly washed clothes.

As quietly as he could, he plugged in his cell phone and slid his paddle holster from his belt, placing it inside a lockbox in the drawer of his bedside table. Shirt and vest went into a rustic-looking Equipale chair they'd bought while on vacation in Mexico. He let his dress pants fall to the floor and used his toes to strip off his socks. Sarah, stirred. Harry froze. The quiet little snore resumed. Harry slipped under the covers.

"Need me to set an alarm?" Sarah mumbled, rolling to drape an arm across his chest.

"No, Hon. I set my phone. Going in a little late." He lifted his wife's hand and kissed her dainty fingers then pressed them to his chest as his over-tired mind spun down to heavy slumber.

Urgent barking woke him in what seemed only minutes later. He registered screamed threats and heavy footfalls. The clock on his bedside table read, *9:10 a.m.*

Muttering curses, he opened the bedroom door to discover his thirteen-year-old daughter Sophie, hobbling down the hall with his ten-year-old son, Mitchell's arms wrapped around her waist. Abby barked her objections.

"What the heck is going on?" he demanded, blinking the muck from his eyes.

"Make her give me back my Playstation controller!" screamed Mitchell.

"Tell him to stay off my phone!" screamed Sophie.

"I didn't touch it. Now give it back!" Mitchell lunged for the controller held high over Sophie's head.

"BOTH OF YOU KNOCK IT OFF."

"See, now you're in trouble," said Sophie.

"Give him back the controller, Soph."

"Not until he admits his crime."

"Sophie Aronson. Give him that the controller, now." Harry's quieter tone held a more threatening note.

Reluctantly, she handed it back.

"Mitch, tell me the truth. What did you do?"

"I used her stupid phone."

"Say that again and look at me."

"He used my phone!" Sophie blurted. "He got into my Facebook account and posted that I like to smell butts!"

"How come she has a cell phone and I don't? It's not fair."

Harry fought back a smile. "That's not the issue, buddy. Did you post a rude message?"

"Yes, but she's always teasing me that she has a phone and I don't."

"Is that true, Sophie? We warned you about that."

"Maybe."

"Sophie, will you promise not to lord your phone over Mitchell?"

"Of course," Sophie said, a little too quickly.

"I'm serious, Soph. If I hear you teasing him even once, you lose your phone for a week."

She nodded submission.

Harry rubbed his eyes, "Mitch, you'll probably get a phone after your next birthday. Teasing your sister isn't helping. A phone is a big responsibility. If—"

The hum of the garage door opener sent the kids running for the kitchen. Harry followed. Sarah Aronson entered, plastic grocery bags dangling from her fingers as the kids tried to outshout each other. A stern look from Sarah shut them down.

"Don't tell me these two couldn't get along while I was gone," she said, setting the bags on the kitchen counter.

"I needed to get up in a bit, anyway." Harry scratched his scalp and rubbed his eyes.

"That's it, you two, I had one simple request. Let your father sleep."

"But, Mom!"

"I don't want to hear it. Now, go get the rest of the bags."

Both seething kids stomped for the garage.

Harry rubbed his temples. "God, I'm tired and it's gonna be another hot one. Maybe I'll just go to work like this, the hell with clothes."

"Well, you are quite an impressive specimen in those boxers, but you might want to take a shower. You stink and your hair's all over the place."

Harry caught his reflection in the microwave's glass and laughed. He danced to Sarah in search of a kiss, halting abruptly when the kids came in with more groceries.

"Thanks, guys. You know I love you," Harry said as they dropped their bags and went back for another load.

"Love you too—"

Harry's hand caressed his wife's bottom. She let him pull her close.

"Go ahead, make my day," Harry teased.

"Tonight, Stinky Harry. What is it about working too hard that makes you so horny? Is Eddie picking you up or are you meeting him at the station?"

"He's picking me up, at eleven. We've got something in Phoenix."

"I think your shower ought to be a cold one."

Harry glanced to the sideways pup tent pitching camp in his boxers and grinned. Sarah smiled longingly and moved in close again, running her fingers through his greasy hair before their faces came together in a kiss.

"Ewww," said Sophie, as she teetered in with both hands full of grocery bags. Mitch smiled as he hoisted his bags to the kitchen island.

"Move along. Nothing to see here," Harry mumbled. The kids turned on their heels for another load.

"Any progress on the case?"

Harry's insides tightened, hating the half-truths he was about to tell her. "Not really. Eddie went all bad ass and that made the Fellig kid run off."

"I worry about this new partner. What did he do this time?"

"Tried to make a big show of arresting Eugene. He ended up looking like an ass. Now, the kid's out there on his own."

Harry felt her tense. He offered a reassuring hug.

"Harry, this morning's paper made mention of those child molesters, the Lucha-somethings. If they're involved, we on the home front could—"

"I'm being careful. So far, the only connection to the Luchadores is that Schaefer was one of the kids they abused. Eddie might be an overzealous jerk, but he does know his stuff when it comes to staying safe. He is former Special Forces and SWAT, remember?"

"Still . . . I worry about—"

Sarah's answer was interrupted by Mitchell teetering in, arms laden with the last of the groceries. He frowned at his two solemn parents. "What's up, Dad?"

"Nothing, buddy. Just work stuff. Nothing to worry about."

12

Eugene woke, his head throbbing and crotch stinging with heat rash. His neck felt like a toy airplane's over-wound rubber band. One eye was mattered and fogged with the other glued shut. Gently, he peeled open the unwilling eye then rubbed away the goo and crusty bits. Shafts of light glared through the church's windows and stabbed through holes in the sagging roof.

A pigeon's throaty coo caught his ear. The bird sat atop the cross member of a rough-hewn wooden cross streaked with bird shit. Beneath the cross, a card table altar sagged. Beside it, the church's once joyful-sounding piano slumped, broken and silent.

The rotund bird stared down from on high, tilting its head, its orange eyes blinking curiously. Shafts of light reflected off the bird's feathers, giving them a rainbow sheen.

"Good morning," Eugene mumbled to the bird. His lips were cracked and his throat felt like 60-grit sandpaper. The bird hefted its bulk and trundled back and forth on the cross as Eugene coaxed saliva with a painful, dry gulp. Four, life-giving swallows of water washed away the sandpaper. He finished the last of his left over Fat Freddie and ate half another before losing interest and tucking the remnant into his shirt pocket.

Water and food brought focus. His sleep had been a weird jumble of dreams mixing past and present. He'd woken filled with regret and feeling the full weight of his predicament. *All right, now what? Where do I start?* Automatically, his hand went for the empty phone pouch on his belt. *That's right, I left it behind.*

The pain and stiffness associated with arranging his sore body on the pew made him long for his pillow-top mattress. He needed to piss.

Standing slowly, his feet screamed objection. He stepped into the aisle and unintentionally set off an explosion of feathers and flapping wings.

"Shit!"

The pigeon flew straight for his face. Its heavy breast skimmed the top of his head before the bird careened off the front wall and wheeled back. This time Eugene ducked letting out an odd, primal grunt as his hands moved to cover his head. The pigeon swerved, escaping through a hole in the back of the church.

Relieved no one had been there to see his panic, he turned back to the pew. He awkwardly brushed his fingers at his hair. A small, gray feather floated down to land on one of two tattered, red canvas shoes in the aisle. Before he could comprehend that the shoes were on feet connected to thick, hairy calves, a huge fist slammed into his right eye. Dust shot from the floorboards as he landed and rolled into a ball.

When the anticipated kick to the ribs didn't follow, he peeked out from between his fingers and saw a jumbo-sized version of the Phillip Seymour Hoffman character, Scotty in the movie *Boogie Nights*.

"AHHH! AHHH! AHHHHH!" Dust roiled as the giant stomped, his arms held high and head wagging like a threatening bear. The giant's too-small t-shirt exposed an ample belly, his long, dirty blonde hair swinging like greasy curtains over his acne-scarred face.

The glaring standoff continued until Eugene thought to offer his half-eaten meat snack. The giant scented the air. Ferocity became a child-like yearning. The huge man lunged, grabbed and retreated, greedily stuffing the Fat Freddie into his mouth. He chewed, swallowed and burped. The site made Eugene smile. His new friend smiled and giggled in return.

"What's your name?"

"Uhhhh."

"Can't talk?"

The big man shook his head. One eye lazed upward, out of sync.

Eugene crawled to his feet. The giant backed up and growled, his fists at the ready.

"It's okay, big dude." He pulled another meat snack from his stash. He peeled it open and held it out. This time the giant took the offering more gently before stuffing it into his mouth and rolling his eyes in ecstasy.

"You like Fat Freddies?"

"Uhhh huhh,"

"Mind if I call you Freddie?"

"Uhhh." Freddie smiled then licked the empty wrapper before letting it drop to the floor. He backed up a step and used a red sneaker to nudge a cardboard flat of unopened cherry yogurt containers into the aisle. He bent down, pulled one plastic cup free and offered it in trade. Eugene shook his head, wondering what dumpster the rotten yogurt had come from.

A putrid hiss accompanied Freddy's peeling back the foil lid. He tilted his head back, lifted the yogurt container over his mouth and let a runny, pink dollop fall in. The slimy remainders were wiped out with a filthy finger that he licked clean.

Apparently satisfied that Eugene was not a threat, Freddie yawned, stretched and lumbered to his rat's nest bed of paper and rags near the front door of the church. He settled in with a fart. Seconds later he was snoring.

The ancient floorboards creaked as Eugene shuffled to poke his head out the window he'd crawled through the night before. Graffitied railcars thundered in the switchyard to the north. To the south, an SUV sat parked in front of a cell phone tower surrounded by chain link.

Eugene unbuttoned and unzipped and sent a dark, yellow stream into the weeds outside. His nagging bladder satisfied, he stepped carefully around the trash on the floor to peer out the one grimy window not covered by plywood on the west side of the church. Pickups and stake-beds laden with roofing and fencing material exited the sprawling Southwestern Suppliers yard. Parked by the yard's front gate, a roach coach served up brunch. *I'll bet they've got chocolate milk and lemon Zingers . . . But, no going out until dark.* He returned to his pew in defeat to munch on the trail mix instead.

* * *

"No Pete this morning?" Charlie Hastings asked as the department heads assembled around the city desk for the morning news meeting. Charlie wore gray, polyester dress pants, a white, J. C. Penny button-down shirt and a funky, typewriter-themed tie.

"He called to say we should do the morning meeting without him," said Michael Specht, arriving with a handful of photo printouts.

Just as the meeting got underway, they were interrupted by a rush of activity in the front lobby. Margaret Bartholomew, Oliver Condon's daughter, ushered in a group in formal business attire. Pete, looking like a dog hoping for a fallen scrap, brought up the rear.

Millie stood to greet them, but Margaret Bartholomew ignored her as Pete threaded through the group to push open the gate beside her desk. He motioned the group to move through.

"Welcome to our operation." Pete's arm swept grandly over the newsroom. "Advertising and circulation are down that hallway over there and the pressroom and production areas are down that hallway there."

"Let's have a look at advertising," said an effeminate man in his fifties. He had neat, blond hair and wore a fine blue suit. His face had the glow of a morning spent poolside.

Heads lifting out of cubicles made the newsroom look like a prairie dog village under threat. Conversation and movement ceased, creating an atmosphere of everyone waiting and watching like prey eyeing the predators.

When the group returned from advertising, Margaret Bartholomew and the blond man were laughing, an awkward sound in the waiting atmosphere. Her smile faded when the newsroom department heads stepped up as a group to formally greet them.

"Pete, would you be so kind as to make introductions?" asked Charlie.

"Of course, Charlie. Gather round, everyone."

"I'd like you all to meet Marty Janck and his staff. They're with the Mid-States Investment Group and they're here on a little fact-finding mission."

"Ah, yes," said Hastings before making introductions all around. "So, this is a chamber of commerce tour?"

"Something like that," said Pete.

Hastings stiffened, knowing "something like that," was probably his worst fear.

"Charlie is it?" said the effeminate man. Smiling, he offered a limp, right hand that left Charlie wondering if this man expected him to bow and kiss it rather than shake it.

"Yes, I'm head of the copy desk." Janck's hand felt soft and lifeless.

"So, what exactly does your job entail?" asked Janck.

"Well, we're not a huge operation, so I handle my department's scheduling and budgets, as well as editing the higher profile stories. I also do some headline writing."

"I see. Then you dealt with this morning's story about the photographer. What was his name? Eugene, something?"

Silently cursing the weak, error-filled story, Hastings said, "That one was all Pete. My contribution was only a slight trim to fit the news hole."

"A very interesting story indeed. Have you seen the analytics of the online traffic?"

"Not yet, but I'm certain the analytics will be good."

"Shall we move on to the production area?" urged Margaret Bartholomew.

"Lead on," said Janck with a courteous bow.

Once the suits had filed out, Hastings broke the room's stunned silence, saying, "What the hell was that, and what the hell are analytics?"

"An online traffic report, you know, web traffic," said Michael Specht.

"Anyone heard of this Mid-States company?" asked Hastings.

"Says here they're an asset management company," said a copy editor. "Come have a look."

The group moved to his desk and stared at his computer screen.

Tony Burke and the rest of the art department arrived. "Are we being bought?" asked Burke.

"I've never heard of these guys," said Hastings. "I don't see any mention of journalism in these results."

"Google it again and add 'newspaper' to the search string," said Burke.

"Go ahead," said Millie, joining the group, "but I can save you the time. They're the vultures who Oliver's daughter has been courting."

"Damn it to hell," said Hastings. "Oliver isn't even in the grave and his daughter's cashing out."

"Looks like they've bought a few small to mid-sized dailies," said the copy editor, scrolling through the search results. "Not enough of a track record to tell what they're about. Wait, here's a quote from that Janck guy."

We believe the future of newspapers is nowhere near as bleak as some suggest. People will always want their local news and newspapers are perfectly positioned to deliver. Return on investment may not be as grand as it once was, but that will change as legacy costs are contained.

"What's a legacy cost?"

"Ink, paper, pressroom," said Millie.

"And copy editors," added Hastings.

"Well, I'm withholding judgment," said Specht. "If we are being sold, I'm just glad it's not to one of the big chains."

"At least some of the big chains understand journalism," said Hastings.

"As long as they keep the stockholders happy, they do." said Millie, hotly. "They'll want high profit and low cost, so be prepared to do a lot more with a lot less."

13

Harry winced as mid-morning light glared under the rising garage door. In the driveway, Eddie sat at the wheel of their cruiser, his eyes hidden behind dark Ray-Bans.

"Sleep well?" asked Harry, crawling in.

"Eh," said Eddie. "Couldn't shut off my brain. I finally gave up around eight and went to Safeway to buy flowers for Millie. Caught her at home before she went in to work."

Harry grinned, "And?"

"She can swear like a sailor."

"Ha! I knew I liked her."

"After dressing me down, she told me that Eugene broke off contact with his mother years ago and that last she heard Virginia Fellig was still living in the housing projects."

"Huh, strange we didn't see a listing for her."

"Well, we still ought to make a show of asking around about her. How'd you sleep?"

"Feel like I barely closed my eyes. The kids fighting woke me up."

"Heh, glad I only had one. I think the teenage years were the worst. A constant mother-daughter fight. It's a wonder any of us survive."

"Yeah, but the good times make up for the bad."

"Yeah," Eddie said with a sigh.

"Any news from your mysterious friend?"

"No movement. Eugene's still parked in the church. Apparently there's another homeless guy in there with him, so he's got a friend to keep him company."

It was a short, fifteen-minute drive to police headquarters.

"Morning, Max," said Harry, as he and Eddie stepped into the jail after depositing their weapons in lockers. "We're here to see Schaefer. Anything we need to know?"

Max sighed, pushed his glasses up his nose and put his hands on his hips, "We had to move him out of the main jail into isolation. Went nuts on the night crew after he learned he's to be transferred to county."

"Are we talking bat-shit crazy or just pissed-off crazy?" asked Harry.

"A little of both. He'll nod or shake his head, but that's about it. The dumb ass smeared his own shit all over his cell. Nightside put him in a restraint chair and hosed him down. This morning he seemed calm but he won't eat or talk."

"Well, shit. Pretty inconsiderate." Eddie's quip earned him puzzled glares all around.

"I figured it was only a matter of time. He's the over-compensating type, you know. Scared as hell and trying to look like a badass. I looked in on him about twenty minutes ago. He was just balled up in a corner."

"Think he'll talk?"

"You can try, but let me send in some guys to put restraints and a spit mask on him first."

"Good thinking," Eddie said.

"Yeah. That cell's got a camera and mic, right?"

"You betcha," said Max.

"Eddie, I'm thinking I ought to go in alone," said Harry. "If he remembers you it might set him off again."

"Great by me. I'll hang back. I could use the coffee. Hell, maybe I'll get a little nap in while I'm at it."

* * *

Harry peered through the little plastic window of the isolation cell. Clad in gym shorts and wearing a mesh bag on his head, Schaefer sat cross-legged in a corner, arms behind his back and head slumped.

"He say anything to you guys?" he asked the two jailers standing by.

"Nah, not a word," said the shorter of the two men.

"Weird. Max, he looks more like a little kid than a bad-assed serial rapist."

"Over-compensating, like I said." Max used a big, flat, brass key to unlock the door then pulled it open.

"You feel like talking?" asked Harry, cradling a manila envelope while trying to ignore the lingering odor of shit as he and two guards stepped in. He kneeled to minimize their imposing presence.

"Who the fuck are you?" Schaefer asked without raising his head.

"I'm Detective Aronson. I'd like to ask you some questions and show you some pictures regarding the Luchadores."

"You might as well kill me now. Save me the trouble of getting my throat slit at county." He pulled his knees to his chest, tucked his head and began to rock.

After several minutes of silence, Harry asked, "Derek, will you look at the photos? We're hoping you might see a clue that leads us to Ass Clown."

Derek's head shot up, his eyes wide behind the mesh spit mask.

"Will you look?"

"You're just another lying cop. He never let Buckingham take pictures . . . You all lie just like that Spic who tried to mind fuck me with DNA bullshit."

"That wasn't a lie. You are related. But that's not what I'm here for. Will you look at the pictures?"

Schaefer nodded.

"I have to warn you these might be upsetting."

"I lived it, dude. Pictures ain't nothin.'"

Harry pulled the photos from the envelope and fanned them like a hand of cards. Schaefer winced and buried his face in his knees, once again rocking to and fro. He mumbled, "They're gonna kill me."

"Not if we get them first."

Derek shook his head and croaked, "Yeah, right. Like that'll happen."

Harry set the photos down and pulled a plastic magnifier from the envelope. "Just give each photo a good look, that's all I'm asking."

The rocking stopped. Derek leaned forward to better see through the mask.

"Can we take the restraints and mask off him?" Harry said to the guards.

"I wouldn't advise it," said the smaller guard, his hand resting on a can of OC spray, holstered beside a collection of plastic restraints on his belt.

"Derek, if I have them take off the mask will I regret it?"

He shook his head. Harry turned to the guards and motioned for them to go ahead.

The larger guard shrugged, stepped forward and removed the mask and plastic cuffs. Derek sat motionless. Deep dark crescents underlined red eyes. *He looks like a sickly child.*

"I can't promise anything, but if you see something that helps us, I might be able to prevent your transfer to county jail."

Slowly Derek shifted his gaze to Harry's face. "It don't matter. They'll get me anyway."

"Things are different this time—"

"How can a cop be that fucking stupid?" Derek's dark eyes raged with anger. "They got it wired, dick head. Nobody beats them. Nobody."

The guards took a step forward but Harry waved them back. Schaefer balled into a sitting fetal position.

"Derek, what you did before, risking everything to steal the photos. Man, that was a brave thing. I'm sorry we let you down."

Derek met Harry's eyes, looking so tired, so defeated. "Yeah, well that don't matter now. I'm just like 'em."

Harry considered his next words carefully. "Are you referring to the attacks on the women?"

"Yeah, I raped all eight of 'em . . . and I enjoyed it. Little rich bitches didn't deserve it . . . But I didn't deserve what the Luchafreaks did to me."

"I don't believe you're like them, not in the least. I think you were acting out of anger. These Luchadores . . . Derek, they're the evil. You are not."

One of the guards huffed and Harry shot him a threatening look that shut him up.

"Can you two step out and leave us alone?"

The larger guard stiffened. "That's not procedure."

The smaller guard elbowed his partner and tilted his head to the door. "We'll be watching through the window."

Harry nodded and waved a hand without taking his eyes off of Schaefer.

"You ready?"

Schaefer nodded. Harry handed him the photos and in a show of trust, sat on the floor next to him. "What made you so sure the man in the blue mask is Riley Mitchell?"

"I remember his voice. He used to say things. He told me to call him papa."

"What else can you remember? It looks like they took you to different locations. Can you remember how many?"

"Two, but mostly this warehouse." He pointed to an image that showed a black expanse beyond the wrestling mat. "Mr. Buckingham would drive us. We were in the back of his van. We never got to see where we were going."

"How long was the drive?"

"Half-hour, maybe. It took a little longer to get to the other place. That one smelled like a basement. It was warmer in the winter, though."

"How about the Luchadores themselves. Can you describe them for me?"

Derek shuddered and took a deep breath. Pointing to a picture on the top of the stack he said, "We called this guy the Anal Pirate because of the skull and crossbones. He liked to be punished. Kicked in the balls mostly. The harder the better. Then he'd give it back twice as bad. Ass Clown was the worst though, he had a dick . . . "

Harry stiffened, his reaction stopping Derek.

"What?" Derek asked.

"Nothing," said Harry. "It's just an unusual nickname, you know?"

"Ass Clown liked breath games and he had this big horse cock. Said he liked to slide it in slow and listen to the bones break."

A look of disgust escaped Harry's face that he instantly regretted. Derek's eyes shuttered and he fell silent.

"Wait, I'm an idiot. It's important I listen to *everything* you have to say. We failed you the first time and you deserve—"

In a flash, the scared little boy was a man again, eyes raging, "You're fuckin' right you failed."

Harry sat cross-legged on the floor, his back to the padded wall and hands to his sides. "Please, Derek, tell me everything."

Schaefer glared into his eyes for a long moment then the rage slowly subsided.

It's like he's some sort of shape shifter. God, what they did to this poor kid.

They talked for nearly an hour. Harry did his best not to look shocked while inside the sadness and disgust grew with each new scene of Schaefer's real life horror show. Although Schaefer examined each image carefully, he identified no real clues. As the discussion came to a close, Harry could see a weight had been lifted from Derek. He sat relaxed, his eyes clear, his expression calm.

"One last question," Harry said, rising to his feet. "When you attacked those women, were you working alone? I mean, did you have any help, a lookout maybe?"

"Nah, it was all me. I beat 'em, raped 'em and wrote bitch on their faces. Always did it in the afternoon, 'cause that's when they got home from school."

Harry gathered up the pictures in silence as he tried to process the bits and pieces of new information.

"You're gonna do you best to keep me here, right?"

"Yes, I promise—"

"No."

"No what?"

"No promises."

"I'll do my best then," said Harry.

* * *

When Harry entered the break room, Eddie looked up from his coffee to share a knowing glance with Max-the-jailer before studying Harry. "I was beginning to think maybe you'd decided to take up residence in there."

"It was time well spent. He confessed to all eight of the rapes and said he was working alone. Max, can you pull a copy of the video for me for the chief?"

"Sure thing."

"Excellent. Congratulations," said Eddie, brightening.

Harry waved it off. "Feels hollow. If you could have seen him, he's just a little kid. He never stood a chance . . . and now he'll get tossed in prison with all the animals—"

"He won't stand a chance in the big house," affirmed Max.

"When's that bus supposed to be here from county?"

"Any time now."

"Can you keep him off it?"

"The wheels are in motion. I can't . . . County's got better facilities for the mentals anyway. You know, rubber rooms and a medical staff."

"Aww c'mon. There has to be something."

"What I can do is talk to the county medical team. They're good people who'll make sure he's isolated and safe for the time being. I'll even have one of my deputies follow him through intake if it'll make you feel better."

"Regardless of how it feels, Harry, we now know for sure that Eugene and Schaefer weren't working together. That's worth my congratulations."

"It was all him. I didn't do anything but show him small kindness as he looked at these." Harry held up the envelope of photos. "Max, everybody else has looked at these. Would you give it a go?"

"I'm betting the picture we want is gone," said Eddie.

"I know, but just in case. The *Herald's* publisher saw something and he tried to say but couldn't get it out before he died. His last words were ass clown."

Max's eyebrows rose above his metal-framed glasses. "Ass clown?"

"That's one of the Luchadores," said Eddie. "He wore a clown mask."

Max grunted his disgust.

Harry pulled the printouts and handed them over. Max set them on the table and adjusted his thick glasses to better see. For ten minutes he pored over the prints with the magnifier as all sat silent. Harry studied his face, a little surprised by Max's lack of revulsion.

"I got nothing, boys. All I see is a bunch of sick bastards."

"No reflections or shadows? Anything at all?"

"Nah. I think you're right, Eddie. The one you want isn't here." Max tapped the pictures. "Where'd these prints come from? The detail's pretty crappy."

"These are scans of prints we got from the *Herald*."

"Where'd the newspaper get them?"

"The publisher had them printed from copy negatives." Eddie jerked back. "Oh shit! Damn it, Harry, we screwed the pooch. The negatives. Where the hell are they?"

"We were too fucking tired last night to realize," groaned Harry.

* * *

Harry and Eddie exited Scottsdale police headquarters hard at work on their cell phones.

"All right, Millie. Thanks," said Eddie, ending his call.

Harry pulled his phone from his ear. "Lab guys say there were no negs in Condon's safe or his desk. But there's a file cabinet full of old negatives and—"

"They won't be in there. Millie says Condon had a friend print them. They're probably still at that lab."

Harry waved off the techs and ended the call. "So, where's the lab?"

"You know the Tradewinds motel in Mesa?"

"Yeah," said Harry, holstering his phone. "That place on Main with the great old neon sign."

* * *

Half an hour later the Tradewinds' beautifully renovated, retro signage came into view. Two neon palm trees loomed. Nestled into the tree's glowing green foliage, a vintage script read *The Tradewinds* in pink neon. Below, turquoise letters read *MOTOR HOTEL.* Best of all were the three blue neon monkeys frozen in an unending animated climb up the tree's scalloped-orange trunk.

"That's a sweet old sign," said Eddie, exiting the car. "See? Things do get better with age."

"True, of course. Unlike you, the sign just underwent a complete makeover."

"I got a sign for you right here," Eddie said, offering a one-fingered salute.

Eddie rang the counter bell in the empty front office. "Hello, anyone home," he called even before the bell had stopped ringing.

"Maybe we should have called," said Harry. Eddie rang the bell a second time, "Hello?"

From somewhere in the back a loud crash caused both detectives to draw their weapons. Eddie dropped to a crouch, his left hand wrapping his gun hand as he pushed through a swinging gate, his weapon sweeping in a fluid, practiced motion.

"Stop," whispered Eddie, pointing to several dark brown shoe prints on the vinyl floor of the hallway leading back to where the crash had emanated.

"That blood?" asked Harry.

Eddie looked for a long moment then shrugged. "Maybe."

"Could use some help!" came a faint cry.

Eddie moved down a narrow hall, clearing each room until they reached the open doorway of what looked like a small apartment with its contents tossed and tangled on the floor.

"Back here," called the weak voice. "My hip, I think it's busted."

"Call it in," said Eddie as he moved forward.

"Already on it," said Harry, dialing his phone.

"Sir! We're the police. Are you alone?"

"Near as I can tell. I'm all the way in the back. It's a photography darkroom. I'm on the floor."

A sharp acidic smell caught in Harry's nose as they stepped into a small room painted in black. The walls held stainless steel sinks, shelves filled with yellow and black boxes and dark-brown glass gallon jugs. In the middle of the floor, below a Formica counter, an elderly man lay splayed out. His shirt and pants were stained a dark brown while white crystalline powder clung in his hair. Shards of brown glass glinted in the floor's puddled mess.

"Check him," said Eddie as he finished clearing the space.

"Sir, medics are on the way," said Harry crouching by the old man. One eye had swollen closed beneath a puffing and purplish face. "Are you cut? Jesus, what is this stuff on your clothes?"

"C-41 chemistry mostly. The brown stuff is blix. I clocked one of 'em with glass jug of it before they dropped me."

"We're clear," Eddie said, returning. He grabbed a package of paper towels and gently tucked it under the old man's head.

"I don't know what to do for him," said Harry, desperate to ease the man's obvious pain.

"Best to just leave him be. What happened?" asked Eddie.

"Cocksuckers beat the hell out of me," the old man snapped. "What's it look like?"

"Judging by your knuckles, I'd say you managed a few good shots," said Eddie.

"A couple . . . Woulda given the chicken shits a run for their money back in the day. Hell, never woulda let 'em get the drop if they hadn't flashed ID."

"That I don't doubt, sir," said Eddie. "You say they had ID. By that do you mean law enforcement?"

The old man suddenly growled with pain. "Aaaaughh! Goddamned don't that hurt."

"Hip?"

The old man panted, visibly gritting his teeth. "Lightning bolts fucking running up my leg. Feels like my goddamn groin exploded. And, ahhhh, can't breathe deep enough. Ribs busted, too, maybe."

"I hear the sirens," said Harry. "The squad will have something for the pain."

"Were they law enforcement?" Eddie repeated more emphatic than before.

"I assumed, but they flashed their stuff so fast I couldn't tell you for sure."

"Did you see their car?" asked Harry.

The thinning gray hair shifted as he shook his head.

"Were they after Condon's film?" asked Eddie.

The old man turned his one working eye to Eddie then fell silent. His liver-spotted hands folded to shake against his stomach.

"It's okay. We're on Oliver Condon's side," Harry tried to reassure him.

"And I'm the queen of England."

"No, really, sir. We—"

"Where'd you serve? South Pacific?" interrupted Eddie.

"Yessir, some. Korea mostly."

Eddie let out a long whistle of admiration, "First Marines? Chosin?"

"Yessir. Oliver did, too."

Harry scanned the man's skinny forearms. The faded outline of a helmeted bulldog graced the left. His right displayed the eagle, anchor and globe of the Marine Corps.

"You serve, son?" the old man asked Eddie.

"Yes, sir. Force Recon. Long time ago."

The old man's eyes narrowed, obviously judging Eddie then they softened. He lifted a shaking hand. "Pleased to meet you. The name's Arthur Smith. Semper fi."

"Ooorah," said Eddie, shaking the man's offered hand firmly. "Eddie Ibarra."

"There were two of 'em. One white, the other Mexican, like yourself. They talked like cops, but as soon as they knew we were alone, they went after me. Don't know where they went. Like I said, they laid into me and I clocked one of 'em." He groaned then gritted his teeth again. "They wanted Oliver's negs. Told 'em Oliver took 'em with, but they tore me and my place up, anyway."

"You say Oliver took the negs?" asked Eddie.

"That's what I told them."

"What would you tell us?"

The old man cast a judging glance to Harry, considered him briefly, then blurted, "I still got 'em. Oliver left them by mistake. He was in an awful hurry . . . Those two assholes . . . They told me Oliver's gone. Is he?"

"Yes sir," said Eddie. "Heart attack."

Arthur's gaze went to the floor and the shaking in his clasped hands intensified. "He was a damn good man. Survived that frozen hell. Those chicken shit perverts killed him, didn't they?"

"Don't know for sure, but it's a possibility . . . I'm sorr—"

"No, he wouldn't want pity. Let's just finish what he started." The wrinkled face took on a determined look. "Assuming they didn't toss the rooms, the film should be in a stack of toilet paper rolls on a housekeeping cart in room 19. I was gonna drop 'em by the paper after I finished cleaning. Just started when those guys pulled up. I had a feeling."

14

"Will I need a mag-card for the room?" asked Harry.

Arthur let out another growl of pain, gritted his teeth and waited for it to subside before answering. "No cards. Keys." He plucked a ring of keys from a clip on his belt. "The master's stamped with an M. Works on all the rooms."

"Arthur, can we keep the existence of negatives between us?" asked Eddie. "The fewer people know the better."

"Yeah, no problem. Now bring the medics back. I'll be fine."

"Harry you go. Arthur, you're not getting rid of me until you're in the medic's hands."

The rescue squad rolled in as Harry stepped from the back.

Flashing his badge as he exited the front lobby, Harry announced, "Elderly male, all the way in the back, severe beating, possible hip and rib fractures." The paramedics removed the necessary equipment from their squad. "It looks like blood on his clothes but it's some sort of photography chemical."

"Show us."

"Arthur Smith's his name. Awake, alert, tough but in a lot of pain," said Harry leading them to the darkroom then stepping aside as they went to work with cool efficiency. As the two medics moved in, Eddie released Arthur's hand and gently smoothed the old man's wisps of matted hair. The two men exchanged the briefest of glances, then Eddie stood and made his exit.

Back in the lobby they saw a well-past-middle-aged sergeant emerge from a marked Mesa PD cruiser. "How do we play it, Eddie?"

"I'll engage the sarge. When I walk him to the back, you make a beeline for room 19."

"Got it."

Harry hung back as Eddie stepped out the lobby door, introduced himself and shook the officer's hand. When they strode back into the lobby, Eddie was talking fast, "The vic is the manager, an elderly male, name of Arthur Smith. Two male perps, one Caucasian, the other Hispanic. Vic said they flashed ID so fast he couldn't tell from where. He's back here," said Eddie, obviously trying to move the sergeant along.

The man stopped, staring at Harry.

"Sgt. Dempsey, meet Detective Aronson."

"Call me Harry. Good to meet you," Harry said, pocketing the keys before patiently shaking Dempsy's hand.

"What brought you two to our fine city?"

"I assume you heard about the death of Oliver Condon," said Eddie.

"Yeah, but I heard it was an accident."

"True, but a high profile guy like that—we've gotta dot the I's and cross the T's."

Dempsy nodded understanding.

"Apparently Condon and our—I mean, *your* vic was friends with Condon. Come on back. You'll want to talk to him before the medics transport. Anyway, like I said, we came over to dot the I's and cross the T's and found him in the back. Looks like he put up a hell of a fight."

Harry stepped from the office and scanned the street to make sure no one was watching. Satisfied, he walked the line of motel rooms sorting the keys through his fingers until he was at room 19 in the back corner of the complex. Inside, the cart sat between the foot of the bed and the television. He swung the door closed and went to work.

Towels and washcloths filled the lower shelf of the plastic cart with clear trash bags on either end. A neat stack of toilet paper rolls sat atop the cart, surrounded by tiny bottles of shampoo, conditioner and miniature soap cakes. Harry slipped a hand in, his heart pounding as he grasped the plastic sheet folded like an accordion between the paper-wrapped rolls of single ply.

"Gotcha," he said aloud.

Four brown/orange strips were held neatly on the page. Beside the factory's *PrintFile Archival, 35-7B* marking at the top of the page was the single, hand-printed, all-caps, *LUCHADORES.* Holding them up to the curtained window he fingered each frame. There were 19 in total. Heart soaring he refolded the page and tucked it behind his Kevlar vest.

Sliding the curtain aside he saw a few motel guests peeking through windows and half open doors. Tapping his vest for reassurance, he made his exit doing his best to look like he was just another curious guest.

Eddie had parked himself at a palm tree near their car, tucking one foot up against the tree's trunk as he nonchalantly stared at his Smartphone.

"You look like a big Mexican flamingo standing there on one leg," Harry said, leaning his back against the car and propping a foot on a tire to match his partner.

"You find 'em?"

"Yep, tucked 'em behind my vest. Four strips, nineteen pictures."

"Nineteen?"

"Don't get your hopes up. There could be a duplicate."

"Ah," said Eddie. "Hey, they're bringing him out."

The detectives caught the gurney just as they were about to load Arthur into the squad. "Semper Fi, Arthur," said Eddie, grabbing the former Marine's boney hand.

"Roger that," croaked the old man as Harry patted him on the shoulder then covertly tucked the ring of keys back into the old man's pants pocket. He gave Arthur a wink and got a faint smile in return.

Once the squad doors closed, Harry and Eddie stood in stunned silence for a moment, "Damn he looked a lot worse in the daylight," said Harry.

"Yeah, he's that age . . . a trip to the hospital . . . well . . . ."

Sgt. Dempsey emerged from the office, squinting in the bright sun before raising a metal clipboard box to shade his eyes, "You know he was one of the Chosin Few? I'd sure like to catch the son-of-a-bitches . . . He couldn't or wouldn't talk much. Tell me again what he said to you."

"Said it was two males, one Hispanic the other white—"

"I got that. Was it a robbery?"

"No, they flashed ID. He thought they were cops, but didn't get a close enough look to tell from where."

The sergeant lowered the clipboard. His face hardened. "You're accusing cops of—"

"No, Sarge, just relaying what the victim said. For all we know they were skip-tracers or thugs looking for someone. You know, the usual riffraff."

"Tell me again, why did Oliver Condon's death bring you two into Mesa?"

"To be honest," said Eddie, "the circumstances surrounding his death are a little hinky. We're still sorting it out."

"Okay, that makes sense. Your department's had more than its share of high-profile crap lately. But what's the connection here?"

"Condon and this guy were friends. Witnesses said they had an early morning, like before sunrise, meeting. We just wanted to know why."

"And?"

"And what?"

The sergeant's shoulders squared. "And did he tell you why?"

"It's the damn *Luchador* case, Sarge," admitted Harry. "We're still considering Condon's death suspicious. He broke the Luchador story years ago. Then we find out our serial rapist is connected and surprise, surprise people start dying."

"Christ Almighty, why didn't you just say that right off? You think the Luchadores did this? Shit, that darkroom . . . maybe he—"

"Nah. Kiddie porn's all digital these days and Condon and this fellow go way back," said Harry. "Probably nothing more than a couple of old soldiers whose aches and pains and memories wouldn't let them sleep."

The sergeant tilted a thumb to the hotel office, "So this guy gets worked over after meeting with Condon and Luchadores might be in the mix." He rubbed his chin. "You sure you're telling me everything? I find out this is some sort of kiddie porn thing and you didn't tell me we're gonna—"

"Look, Sarge, the meeting between the two old war horses was innocent. Clearly this attack was not . . . Are the Luchadores involved? Hell, we don't know. We just wanted to talk to the guy."

"Looks like you may have another Bob Crane on your hands," said Dempsy.

"Who's that?" asked Harry.

Dempsy shot Eddie a knowing look. "Kids," he said, tilting his head to Harry.

"Bob Crane was an actor in the TV series Hogan's Heroes," said Dempsy. "Somebody beat him to death in a Scottsdale motel back in the 70's. Never was solved."

"I was overseas when that one went down," said Eddie, "I've heard talk, but what really happened?"

Dempsy shook his head, "The media tried to paint it like your department screwed the pooch, but from what I heard, everyone involved pulled a Sgt. Schultz."

"I know nothing," Eddie clowned in an odd German accent before clicking his heels and standing at attention.

Harry stared at his partner, eyes narrowed and mouth open.

"Jesus, kids these days," Eddie said smiling, "Sgt. Schultz? Hogan's Heroes? Stalag 13? You're telling us you never saw it?"

"Nope, never."

"Sgt. Dempsey, I fear for the future of the human race."

"You should Google it on the You Tubes," said Dempsy, "Classic television."

Harry acknowledged the sergeant's suggestion, restraining a laugh at the old cop's jumbled internet references.

"So, are we cleared to head out?" asked Eddie.

"Yeah, we know where to find you if we have questions. Take it easy out there. Gonna be a hot afternoon."

"We'll try," said Eddie, handing the sergeant his card. "If you get prints or anything else that might interest us would you mind passing it along?"

"Sure thing, Detective."

Walking for their car, Harry said, "Whadda ya think? Hit the station and get a better look at the negs?"

"Yep, but let's have a quick look now. I grabbed a little something that should help." "Damn this car is an oven," Eddie said, cranking the engine and lowering the windows halfway as Harry turned the car's air conditioner to high.

Eddie pulled a small, plastic magnifier from his shirt pocket and handed it to Harry, then dropped the car into gear and pulled from the lot heading west on Main. "If there's a duplicate we keep heading to Phoenix. The day's gonna get away from us."

"Well, let's cross our fingers it isn't." Harry unfurled the sheet of negatives and put his eye to the loupe, moving it in and out before realizing the loupe had to be on the sheet before coming into focus. "Okay, here we go."

"What, you see something?"

"Nah, just figuring out this old school shit. Give me a sec." He shifted the loupe from frame to frame, then consulted the pictures on his phone before returning to the negatives.

"Anything?"

"It's hard to tell . . . Don't see a duplicate . . . Wait . . . This one's different. Show's more of the warehouse . . . And it's hard to tell, but there might be something in the background."

* * *

"Nice digs, guys," said Eddie admiring the view from the fourth floor window of the Scottsdale police computer lab. Ken Stoops, the technician tasked with digitizing Condon's copy negatives, ignored Eddie's remark as the film scanner hummed to life.

"Can we go straight to this picture?" asked Harry, pointing to the middle of the sheet of negatives.

"Sure, no problem," said Stoops, pulling the plastic film holder from the scanner. He donned a pair of white cotton gloves then pulled the strip of film from the middle of the page. He placed it in the holder then slid it into the scanner.

Eddie strolled over from the window and stood next to Harry, whose foot nervously tapped. The machine hummed as it digitized the film. After over a minute of waiting the image flashed onto the screen.

"Oh, geeze, what an asshole," murmured Stoops, staring at an image of a naked fat man in a skull and crossbones mask. Gray hair curled from his sagging man boobs. His hands were raised in victory and he appeared to be howling with a naked teenage boy crumpled at his feet.

"That's the guy the kids called the Anal Pirate," said Eddie, "but we're not interested in him. It's the guys in the background."

"A little dark back there. The on-camera flash could only do so much. I'll pull out what I can. You don't care about this pirate guy, correct?"

"Nah, we're actually looking for a clown."

Stoops shot Harry a glance then shook his head and went back to work. "Okay, I've saved the full image. Now let's eliminate Mr. Anal Pirate." Stoops adjusted the crop marks on the screen so that only the dim background was selected then hit the on-screen scan button. The metal box hummed to life. Slowly a massive blowup appeared on screen. "Well, heck, there's your clown right . . . Oh, man, is he peeing on that kid? What an asshole."

"Guys, this is like the holy grail for this case," said Eddie.

"Yeah, but Condon had this image all along," said Harry. "What the heck did he see in it that morning?"

"Can you take it up any bigger? Wait. Is there something odd about that hand?"

"Hang on," said Stoops. "This new scanner's amazing. Let me toss in a bit more exposure, maybe a little infrared."

The scanner hummed to life again and soon a brighter, more well-defined image flashed on the screen.

"That hand had to be what he saw," said Eddie. "He's missing a pinky finger, correct?"

"I don't know," said Harry. "Could just be a shadow."

Stoops' hands returned to the keyboard and mouse. "A little unsharp mask . . . Now bring up the shadows . . . A little clarity . . . Yep, that hand's either missing a finger or he's got it folded under."

Eddie let out a long, slow whistle then murmured, "I think I know who that is."

* * *

Long, sleepless hours in the front seat of his SUV gave Jack a pinched neck and a shirt soaked through with sweat. He hadn't done any long-term surveillance since his time in Afghanistan. His aging body ached its objections.

As he unscrewed the cap on a bottle of water, he eyed a paper sack on the passenger side floorboard holding two previous bottles filled with urine. His cell phone buzzed. He cleared his throat of cobwebs with a sip of water, screwed the cap back on the bottle while checking the caller I.D. then answered.

"Hey, Eddie. All's good here. You close?"

"Nah, we're still in Scottsdale. Probably won't get there for another hour. Any movement on your end?"

"Nope. His big roommate left the church about an hour ago. I did see our boy piss out a window a while back. Near as I can tell he's in there alone. Don't think he's going anywhere until sundown. What's cooking on your end?"

"We've got a picture of the Ass Clown."

"No shit? Are you sure?"

"Yep, Clown mask, red hair and, get this, the guy's missing a finger."

"Excellent. Any leads—"

"Yep, I'm pretty sure it's a pressman at the paper. We're waiting for backup before we go ask him to come in for questioning. Wish you could be here."

"Well, if he is who you think he is, it's probably best I stay away. Gracie would never forgive me if I got tossed in prison for murder now that I'm finally home for good."

"True," said Eddie. "Stay cool."

"That ain't happening, not baking out here in the sun. For your information, I've already turned two wide-mouth bottles of water to apple juice. If you get my drift."

"That's a mental picture I didn't need."

"I'm thinking of taking a break. Might take a run by the homeless shelter up the street. Maybe put my ear to the ground."

"You think that's wise? What if—"

"I'll keep eyes on him. I brought some surveillance toys. Besides he's gonna get suspicious if my vehicle's parked here much longer."

"Roger that. I'll be in touch."

Jack navigated his iPhone to a bookmarked web page and placed the phone in a cradle on the dash. He unzipped a camo duffle on the front passenger seat and removed a battered McDonald's soft drink cup with a small, ragged hole in the side. Inside the cup an Android Smartphone was held in place with Velcro and wadded napkins. He pressed the phone's power button and replaced the lid with its chewed straw. Within seconds the iPhone on his dash flashed to life with a video stream from the cup.

Sucking the straw for effect, Jack exited his vehicle. He set the cup on the ground in front of the cell tower's fence, checked his iPhone to be sure the aim was correct then made his exit, looking like just another nameless technician heading home for the day.

15

"I take it all's quiet at the church?" Harry asked as Eddie put his phone away.

"Beyond Eugene's pissing out a window, he hasn't moved."

Their car idled in the parking lot beside the *East Valley Herald* building. They waited for backup before approaching Kurt Wragge for questioning.

"How do you want to handle this?" asked Harry.

"Put backup on the front and rear exits. We enter through the pressroom door. I'm eager to see the look on his face when he realizes we've come for him."

"Works for me."

"Oh, and keep an eye on his little brother, Mikey. The kid's kinda special."

"What do you mean, 'special?'"

"He's retarded."

"The PC term is mentally handicapped, Eddie."

"Yeah, yeah. I can't keep up with all that bull shit. Just keep an eye on him. He's a little hot-headed. When I talked to him the other day he told me to go eat a donut."

Harry flashed a smile. "Oh, I would have paid to see that. What's he look like?"

"You'll know him; small body, big head, kinda looks like a cross between an angry old man and a kid. Gives me the hebegebees."

A marked, two-man patrol car rolled up. They lowered their windows. The driver did the talking. "Afternoon, detectives. What's the game plan?"

"We're going in the side door over there to question a suspect. I don't anticipate problems, but we'd like cars on the front and back. The guy we're looking for is a pressman named Kurt Wragge. He's around six-foot-one, 180-pounds, with a beard and brown hair."

"We saw a guy matching that description when we came around the building. He's back on the loading dock at a picnic table with a little guy."

Eddie's eyebrows shot up. He tilted his head. "Well, that'll make it easier. Tell you what. Give us two minutes then drive around to the east side. We'll approach from the west."

"Got it," said the driver. His window slid up and they drove off.

Eddie and Harry crawled from their air-conditioned car into the stifling summer heat. Eddie groaned and stretched as Harry double-checked his pistol.

Eddie frowned at him. "You nervous?"

"This is a big deal. I'd be crazy not to be nervous."

"Been a long time coming," said Eddie. "All right, let's do this."

Together they ambled for the back of the building. Kurt and Mikey sat alone on opposite sides of the picnic table on the loading dock, just like the officers described. Kurt lit a cigarette. Seeing the pair approach, he raised a hand in greeting. The detectives assumed stiff smiles, returned the wave and climbed the four concrete steps to the dock.

"Hey, detectives," Kurt said. He pulled the cigarette from his lips and used a finger to dab something off his tongue. "What's up today, guys? Any news on Eugene?"

Mikey turned with a mouthful of sandwich. His odd eyes and open-mouthed chewing reminded Harry of a goat.

"Nothing new on Eugene, but I do have some questions," said Eddie. "We'd like it if you'd come to the station."

Harry stepped around to the end of the table to better see Mikey's hands as the little pressman hurriedly stuffed the remainder of his sandwich into his mouth. His goat-like eyes narrowed. *Hebegebees is right.*

"Can we do it here or maybe in the morning? I've got a lot of work waiting today."

"No, we need you to come now." The cruiser rolled up behind and the two uniforms stepped out.

Kurt's face turned to stone. "What's going on? Why do you want to talk to me?"

With his left hand, Eddie pulled from his shirt pocket the small picture Stoops had printed for him.

"What's that?"

"You don't recognize your own photo?" said Eddie, his right hand now resting on the grip of his .45 automatic.

Kurt's stony expression turned dark. "I don't know what you think you have, but that ain't me."

Harry glanced back and forth between Kurt and Mikey, feeling less sure by the second.

"Until we get this cleared up, Kurt, we're gonna need you to come with us," said Eddie. "Mikey, why don't you step out from the table and walk over to my partner."

Kurt's posture stiffened. "Am I being arrested?"

"Only if you force the issue."

"Mikey, come on over to me," said Harry, trying to look less threatening.

Kurt looked at his brother, his eyes softening for a moment. "Go on, Mikey." He glanced at Harry. "He's simple, detective. Go easy on him."

"No problem. Come on over here, Mikey. We just have some questions for your brother. It's no big deal."

Mikey flicked his odd gaze from his brother to the officers to Harry. "Fucking donut eaters."

"No, Mikey. Be nice," Kurt instructed. "I'm gonna be right back. Nothing to worry about. Just do what he says."

Mikey stepped out of the table, eyes glaring. He took three steps toward Harry then turned an expectant look at his brother.

"Good job, Mikey," said Kurt. "I'm gonna go with these guys for a little bit. I'll be right back. You behave yourself. Maybe get back to work."

"Okay."

Eddie slipped a pair of cuffs from his belt. The polished steel flashed in the sunlight.

As if a switch had been flicked, Mikey jerked and shouted, "No!"

Harry put a hand on Mikey's shoulder. The shorter man spun and buried a fist into Harry's groin. A wave of liquid pain shot up into his kidneys. Gasping in agony, he grabbed the offending wrist and twisted.

Kurt lunged forward. "Mikey no! Stop it!"

Eddie wrapped an arm around Kurt's neck and tripped him forward. They hit the concrete hard, as the two uniforms leaped up to the dock to help. One went to Eddie. The other came to Harry's rescue, knocking Mikey to the ground then wrenching his arms behind him.

"Quit fighting," growled the uniform as he struggled for control. He sat on Mikey's legs and ratcheted cuffs on the struggling and growling smaller man.

Harry rolled free, his hands in his crotch. He looked to Eddie who still sat atop Kurt. "That was totally unnecessary! We just wanted to talk to you."

"Good job beating up a mentally handicapped guy, assholes," barked Kurt.

Harry caught sight of a female photographer moving in an arc around the dock snapping pictures. More newspaper employees joined the show.

"Kurt Wragge, you're under arrest," growled Eddie. "You have the right to remain—"

"I know my rights," said Kurt. "Mikey, you okay? Mikey?"

"Shut it. He's fine," snarled Eddie. Determined, he then finished his Miranda speech.

Harry crabbed over to Eddie, his groin and kidneys still singing. "Call a squad," he said in a low voice, "I think I felt Mikey's wrist pop."

"Jesus. Call it in," said Eddie to the uniform kneeling at his side.

"Did you all hear that?" shouted Kurt to the gathering crowd. "They broke my mentally handicapped brother's—"

"Shut up," growled Eddie.

"I won't shut up," yelled Kurt. "You broke my little brother's arm! He's handicapped!"

"Take 'em both in," Eddie barked to the uniforms. "We'll get them looked at at the station."

"What the hell is going on?" The pompous-as-ever Pete Cunningham called out.

"Now's not the time," said Eddie, rising to his feet as the uniforms led Kurt and Mikey down the dock steps.

"Are they being charged?" demanded Pete.

"This is police business," said Eddie. "We came to ask questions and Mikey attacked us. Beyond that, no comment."

Harry rose to his feet, careful to let the pain show on his face for the camera and its incessant click-click-click.

Safely inside their car and finally driving away, Harry said, "That was a freaking disaster. Mikey's a monster. He's got moves . . . God, I need to ice my balls . . . I swear, he felt no pain. I've never seen anything like it . . . We better hope—"

"Kurt's the ass clown. No doubt about it," snapped Eddie. "Why'd you have to mention the wrist in front of him?"

"Shit, Eddie, we already looked bad."

"I know, I know, but goddamn it . . . That fucking rag of a newspaper's gonna crucify us for this and we didn't do anything wrong."

* * *

Blood stains dotted the white name patch on Kurt Wragge's uniform shirt. He sat motionless in the same beige interview room at the same gray, industrial table they'd used with Eugene. Eddie and Harry stood, arms crossed, watching him on closed-circuit TV.

"I gotta tell you, Eddie, I'm a little worried we jumped—"

"Bullshit. That's the Ass Clown. There's no doubt in my mind." Eddie held up the blurry, pixelated printout. "Just look."

Harry stared at the photo for the briefest of moments. "Let's go talk to him before he lawyers up."

Elbows on the table, head resting against his manacled hands, Kurt shot the detectives a look of disgust. "So whadda ya gonna do? Fuck over the whole *Herald* staff one by one?"

Eddie smiled malevolently.

Kurt's face reddened. He folded his hands and placed them on the table, clearly trying to control his rage.

One by one, Eddie placed printouts of the Luchador party on the table. Kurt's face pinched. He sat up and squared his shoulders as Eddie placed the enhanced, but blurry image of Ass Clown on top of the stack jabbing a finger at the photo. "Missing a finger, just like—"

"You roughed me up and broke my brother's arm because of a blurry picture?"

"His wrist. And it's not broken, just sprained, so quit harping on that. You're missing the same goddamn finger and you have the right body type. You had access to Condon's office and I'm betting once forensics come back on the Carter girl, your DNA will be in the mix. This is you. You're the Ass Clown. You're the goddamned Ass—"

Kurt jerked back in his chair, flinching at Eddie's thrusting the print into in his face. "Wait . . . These are the Luchador photos right? From like, seven-eight years ago?"

Eddie smiled his crooked smile. "You almost got away with it, but we beat you to the negatives."

Kurt raised his cuffed hands high then slammed them down, the crash of metal on metal making Harry jump, as the confronted man screamed, "COMPLETE AND TOTAL BULLSHIT!" He stood, sending his chair tumbling backwards. In a rage, he tried to tip the table only to discover it was bolted to the floor. Eddie cocked a fist and Harry moved to block him.

"Kurt, sit the fuck down. Eddie, back off."

Detective Luke Jeffers burst in. "Everything cool in here?"

"I lost the finger like five years ago working construction. There's no way that's me. You can check with the fucking hospital."

All four stared at each other for a long moment. Kurt's chest heaved as the rage slowly drained from his face. Jeffers righted Kurt's chair and pointed. The pressman slumped into it.

"Harry, Eddie, we need to talk outside . . . like, right now."

In the hall with the door closed, Jeffers said. "He's not the guy."

"Bullshit, he—" Eddie started in.

"Shut up and listen. He's right about the finger. We should have waited for a warrant. Insurance records pointed us to Mountain View Memorial. He was treated for a severed finger trauma *five* years ago. Got that?"

Eddie deflated, "No, that can't be right."

"It is, Eddie. The chief wants to see both of you on the double."

"Shit," Harry groaned.

* * *

Fine Navajo blankets, Hopi kachina dolls and Remington bronzes lined the mahogany walls of Chief Carlton Royal's office. In the corner beside his desk a weathered wooden stand held a fine western saddle with intricate leather tooling and bright silver accents.

"Come in, detectives," said the chief, greeting them at the door, "I was just going over what happened at the *Herald*. Margie, no interruptions," he called out to his secretary.

"Carl, I just want to start by—"

Anger flashed. "I'm the Chief, Eddie. A little respect is warranted." He jabbed a finger at the chairs before his desk. "Take a seat."

"Yes, sir. Sorry, sir. Permission to pull my foot out of my mouth?"

"I'd rather you pull your head out of your ass. Both of you, sit *down*."

The Chief took his sweet time strolling to his side of the desk. His chair groaned as he sat, scooted in, then turned his computer monitor so they could see.

Eddie's shoulders slumped.

On the screen, the image of Kurt Wragge's bloody face accompanied a story with a damning headline.

"Eddie, where do we stand in the trust department?" He shot a glance to Harry.

"He knows," said Eddie. "We talked it through last night."

"Very well then. Eddie, we agreed that you needed to *look* like an idiot, correct?"

"Yes, sir."

"Care to tell me why you took that to mean *be* an idiot?"

"Sir, no excuse, sir. I got ahead of myself and made an assumption."

"He's not alone sir," said Harry. "I'm just as much to blame. The guy has the same build and the same missing finger of this 'Ass Clown' character. We wanted to move before word got out that we had the negatives."

"I've looked at that photo. It's far from conclusive."

"Yes, sir," both detectives mumbled in chorus.

"I understand your need for speed. But you two made a serious mistake in not waiting for the background check. I figured we'd take heat for yesterday's play-acting with Eugene. But, damnit, Eddie, did you have to knock down Millie in the process? We're lucky she's not suing. God only knows what this Wragge fellow will do."

"I know, Chief, and I feel terrible. If it's any consolation, I paid Millie a visit this morning to apologize."

"I heard. We've talked. The flowers were a nice touch. Probably the only good move you made recently. Am I safe in assuming she led you to the missing negatives?"

"Yes, sir," said Eddie. "She told me about Condon's photographer friend. But in all honesty, what I feel the worst about is not buttoning down the film angle sooner. We were over tired . . . Maybe if I hadn't been playing the fool so hard, we'd have saved the motel owner a beating."

"True . . . That's something we'll all have to live with. I'm just as responsible for approving your plan." He sighed heavily. "Any news from your unofficial friend?"

"All is well. There's nothing new to report."

"All right then . . . Since the Luchador issue is fully in play, I have no other choice but to keep you a million miles away from the case."

Eddie sat up straighter. "But, sir, I—"

"No, Eddie, you're too hot and your past made this inevitable. Didn't I tell you this could happen?"

"Yes, sir. Ah, would suspending me be a better option? I'm willing to—"

"Nice try, but you know as well as I do that you'd only use your time off to pursue them directly. I think we'd all be better off keeping you two in the aimless hunt for Eugene. In the public's eyes at least, he is still very much a suspect in the murder of Sandy Carter."

Confused, Harry looked to Eddie who wore a sly smile.

"Tomorrow morning I'll hold a press conference announcing Schaefer's confession. Good work on that by the way, Detective Aronson," he said, nodding to Harry. "I'll make it clear that Eugene and Schaefer's connection is merely coincidental. For the time being, because of Eddie's previous entanglements, you two will have nothing official to do with the Luchadores."

"Yes, sir, I understand," said Eddie, "and thank you."

Harry felt a little desperate. "Sir, I *don't* understand. Maybe I'm not picking up the backchannel here."

"It's simple, detective. Officially, you're off the Luchador case. You will walk out of here and maintain an attitude of just having had your asses handed to you. Unofficially, you hang back, let Eddie's original plan run its course and, if that leads back to the Luchadores, well, so be it."

Harry sighed in relief. "Sir, I appreciate your confidence in—"

"No need to kiss my ass, detective. Just do me a favor and don't let the rope I've given you end up wrapped around my balls."

* * *

After a theatrically sullen walk from the chief's office and several, "I don't want to talk about it" responses to curious cops, Eddie and Harry were in their old Crown Vic heading for Phoenix.

"Well, that was fucking amazing," said Harry. "I thought I'd be back in uniform."

"It ain't over yet. Carlton's a hell of a leader, but you do not want to see him pissed off. Our asses really are on the line here."

"You two went through academy together, right?"

"Yep . . . plus we crossed paths in the military, saved each other's asses, yada, yada, yada. I'll tell you about it sometime, but for now let's try to do right by him."

They drove on in silence, passing a yellow and green Cash America Super Pawn store. Eddie steered the car into the left turn lanes on McDowell to catch the Hohokam Expressway into downtown Phoenix. Pale pink gravel hemmed by concrete curbs shimmered with heat. Wispy palo verdes shifted in a light summer breeze. Afternoon was well on towards evening, but the long summer days meant the punishing sun still hovered high on the horizon.

"Weren't you as sure as I was that Wragge was our man?" asked Eddie, breaking the silence.

Harry hauled in a breath and let it out slowly. “I don’t know what to think anymore, Eddie. Was I sure? Hell, yes, but now I’m not sure if it was instinct or pride.” He yawned and rubbed his face then scratched his scalp. “Christ, I could have used a couple extra hours of sleep.”

“Traffic’s heavy. We’ve still got another forty-five minutes of drive time. Grab some shuteye.”

* * *

Eddie’s long, high-pitched whistle pulled Harry from his nap. “What’s up?” he said, blinking himself awake, trying to make sense of where they were.

“This is not the shit hole I remember.”

“What do you mean?”

“I mean, this is where the projects were, but they never looked this good.”

Green space edged by stately metal fences surrounded modern, Mexican-villa style duplexes with red tile roofs and faux, wrought iron balconies.

“Doesn’t exactly fit with the rest of the neighborhood,” said Harry. “I remember seeing something about this on TV. This is part of that Federal Hope Six project, I think.”

“The HUD thing. Yeah, guess I never realized that this was its location. I’ll be damned, the old Bucket of Blood is no more.”

“Bucket of Blood?”

“Yeah, that’s what we called it back in the day. Hell, the gang wars got so bad on the weekends, the street cops wouldn’t go in unless a SWAT team was there as backup. My, how times have changed.”

“Dang, and Eugene lived right in the middle of it. Think we’ll find his mom in here?”

“Nah, but we need to make a good show of asking around.”

“Looks like the new stuff ends here at 11th,” said Harry, seeing a rundown cinderblock grocery store clad with security bars and tagged in graffiti. Turning south, the sharp contrast continued with bright and new on one side of the street and weeds and chain link on the other.

"Hey, pull over. Let's talk to this guy," said Harry, pointing to an elderly black man seated in the alcove entrance to his duplex. The old man slumped in a cheap, plastic chair, his chin resting on his chest.

"You sure he's even alive?"

"He's probably just napping, like I wish I was."

The old man lifted his head as they approached. He wore thick glasses, the lenses held in heavy black frames. A cigarette dangled from his right hand. His long yellow fingernails needed trimming as did his gray-blotched hair. The scent of mothballs wafted from his clothes.

"Good evening, sir," said Eddie.

"If'n you say so," said the man, his words mushed for lack of teeth.

"We're police detectives," said Harry, squatting to seem less intimidating and to better see the man's eyes. "We were looking for the Buckeye Street housing project, but it seems things have changed."

"Tore it down 'bout a year ago. Put this new Hope project up instead. Chased out the riffraff and put 'em in what they call 'scattered site' housing. Made 'em somebody else's problem."

"Did you live in the old projects?" asked Eddie.

"Yessir, for almost twenty years. My Tilde and I qualified to come back, I got a little pension and social security. I kinda miss the old place. This just don't feel like home and Tilde don't let me smoke inside."

"Is Tilde your wife?"

"Yessir . . . She died about a month ago now. Still can't bring myself to smoke inside. Don't know nobody around here no more. A lot of good people moved out with the bad." He pulled a handkerchief from his pants pocket, removed his glasses, and wiped damp eyes.

"I'm sorry about your wife," said Harry, putting a comforting hand on the man's boney knee. "My name's Harry. My partner here is Eddie."

"William Jefferson," mumbled the old man, holding up a weak hand. Harry shook it gently.

"In the old projects, did you know a woman named Virginia Fellig?"

"What the hell she do now? That woman's nothin' but trouble." The old man wrestled the arms of his chair, anger straightening his posture. "Always wigglin' her skinny white ass for all the young bucks. City chased her out with the riffraff. Good thing, too. Always tradin' food stamps and sex for booze. Why you lookin' for her?"

"We have some questions about her son, Eugene," said Eddie.

The old man brightened, lifting his head, suddenly wide-eyed and hopeful. "How's that little fella doing? Can't believe a good boy like that came out a mess like Vaginia. Damn shame about his brother."

"Eugene's all grown up now," said Eddie, surprised by the old man's sudden transformation from down-trodden to proud. "What can you tell us about him?"

"Fine boy, damn fine boy. Fixed my Oldsmobile a few times back when I was still drivin'. Got me parts for cheap from the junkyard." He drew back a little to eye them suspiciously. "Don't tell me he's in trouble."

"Just some questions on a case. Has he been by to visit?"

"No, sir. Ain't seen him since he went off to work for the news. He's got himself a real important job now. Prob'ly couldn't find me in this new place, anyway. Don't know folks around here no mo' and they don't know me. My Tilde, she died 'bout a month ago. Ain't got nobody to talk to now."

"I'm sorry about your wife," Harry repeated, patiently. "Would you have any idea how we'd find Virginia?"

"Some'a the riffraff been sleepin' in the condemned places over there," he said, pointing to the far side of 11th Avenue where a line of squat, cinderblock houses deteriorated behind a failing chain link fence. "Ain't seen her comin' or goin' from there, but I seen her around . . . Knowin' her, she's workin' out a trade. She ain't much to look at no more, but some folk ain't picky. You should check the party house down on Tonto."

"Do you know the number?"

"No, sir, but the front yard's a burned up trash heap. City tore everythin' out after a fire. Folks still squattin' there, though. Ain't no power or water, just drugs and booze. Don't know why the city don't do somethin'."

"Thank you for your time, Mr. Jefferson," Harry said, standing while offering his hand. The old man shook it vigorously.

"Is there a number where we can reach you, if we have more questions?"

"No, sir, ain't got no phone. Got no family to call, anyway. My Tilde could never have kids. She died a month ago now. Ain't got nobody to talk to an' I can't smoke inside."

"When we see Eugene, we'll tell him hello for you and that he should come by for a visit," said Harry.

"That'd be fine. That'd be just fine," the old man said, smiling. "He's a good 'un, that one."

16

In the monotony of earth tones and desert landscaping, the Tonto Street party house stuck out like a burnt fleck in a bowl of oatmeal. A blackened mattress draped the frame of a charred couch in the front yard. Burnt bedding, papers and trash had been heaped all around. In the driveway a rusty pick-up truck with four flat tires squatted under the weight of a bed full of crumbling shingles and tarpaper.

They parked thirty yards to the east in front of a vacant lot. A small Hispanic boy in dingy Sponge Bob Square Pants underwear and red, rubber flip-flops poked a stick into a swarming anthill at the edge of the lot.

"Be careful, son," said Eddie, "Those ants will sneak up and bite."

The boy dropped his stick into the angry red mass and backed up, smiling sheepishly.

"How old are you?" asked Harry.

The boy held up four tiny fingers. With great care, he then folded three to his palm, leaving the middle finger erect. A huge smile spread below the boy's dirt and snot-caked nose. Harry's face went blank. Eddie laughed. The boy ran for home.

"That's quite a welcoming committee," said Harry.

Edging past the sagging truck and into a bougainvillea-covered walkway, Eddie unsnapped the thumb break on his .45 and Harry followed suit. The house's screen door lay to the side, torn from its hinges. The front door hung slightly ajar. Hand on his pistol, Harry prepared to knock, first making eye contact with Eddie whose pistol was now out of his holster. Eddie nodded. Harry tapped hard and the door swung open.

"Police!"

There was no answer. On a ratty couch in full view of the open door, a bone-thin white woman lay sprawled in an over-sized t-shirt looking dead to the world. The cigarette in her right hand had burned down to the filter and the ash still hung precariously.

A crash from somewhere deep in the house brought Harry's Glock from its holster. "Got it," said Eddie, stepping inside, his weapon in hand. "*POLICIA! POLICE!*" he barked, taking aim down a dark hallway where a rotund and nearly naked black man charged toward him with a Louisville Slugger held high overhead. Seeing Eddie's pistol, the fat man's eyes widened. He immediately dropped the aluminum bat making it ping off the bare concrete floor.

"What the hell you doin' in my place?"

"We knocked and announced ourselves," said Harry, "plus, the door was open."

Eddie remained silent, his sites holding firm on the man's bulbous center mass.

After tugging white headphones from his ears, he let them dangle from the mp3 player tucked somewhere inside his piss-stained Fruit of the Looms." I didn't hear, had my tunes goin' in the bathroom. What the hell you want?"

The house smelled like a burned out port-a-potty in full summer bloom. Fast food trash, broken bottles and remnants of drug use littered the floor.

"Anymore in here or is it just you two?" Eddie asked.

"Just us. You gonna jack us for squattin'? 'cause that's bullshit."

His pistol still on target, Eddie threw a glance to Harry. "Take a gander out the front, make sure no one's coming around."

Harry stepped to the doorway to look then shook his head.

"We just want to talk to a Virginia Fellig. Is that her? What's your name?"

"Call me Leroy and yeah, that's her on the couch. Vaginia! Git the hell up." Failing to stir the unconscious woman, Leroy looked to Eddie, "You mind if'n I give her a shake?"

Eddie lowered his pistol a few inches and motioned his head toward her.

Leroy kicked the arm of the couch then shook the woman's leg. "Git yo skinny ass up. You bringin' the fuckin' police to my door now."

"Fuck you, Leroy," croaked the old woman, coming to life. She scowled at her cigarette and knocked the long gray ash from its end. "Where's the fuckin' fire? I . . . ." She stopped mid- sentence to suck back a breath then emitted a wet burp.

"You got police here who wanna talk to you. Wake the hell up."

She glanced at Eddie. "I didn't do shit!"

He lowered his weapon but maintained a taut stance. "Ma'am, we just need to ask a few questions about your son, Eugene. Does he have any friends or favorite hang-outs in the neighborhood?"

"What did that little shit do now? Everybody says he's such an angel." She reached into a big vinyl purse on the floor in front of the couch.

"Stop, ma'am. I need to see your hands," ordered Eddie, his stance swinging slightly her direction.

"I got her," said Harry, aiming his weapon.

Eddie turned back to the fat man. Leroy's right hand now unabashedly scratched at his balls through his sagging underwear.

"Don't get your panties in a knot, Officer Pedro. I just need a smoke," said Virginia. She withdrew a half-crushed pack of cigarettes then paused to scratch her boney arms before attempting to straighten her rat's nest hair.

"I gave that boy life and what the hell's he done for me? Huh? What the hell's he done for me?" She jabbed a thumb at her withered chest. "I gave him life!"

"I'll ask again, have you seen Eugene or know anyone else he might stay with?"

"Hell, no. And, if you see that goody-two-shoes, you tell him don't bother comin' home no more. I done all I can for him." She laid back and settled on the couch, her t-shirt sliding up past her waist exposing the ratty underwear flossing her crotch. The cigarette pack fell from her hand as she faded back to unconsciousness.

"That all you need?" asked Leroy, his gaze locked on Virginia's crotch.

Eddie stepped forward to shake Virginia's shoulder.

"What?"

"Eugene's father. Was he seeing any other women before he disappeared?"

Virginia cackled, exposing yellow teeth and receding gums, "The only one he wasn't fuckin' was me. I cut him off after my third dose a crabs. He liked 'em skanky. He'd stick his dick in any . . . " her weakening voice trailed off as she slipped back to sleep.

"*Now* you done?" asked Leroy, his hand now fondling the bulge growing inside his underwear.

"Yes," said Harry. "Jesus fuck! What's wrong—"

Eddie interrupted, "Leroy, do you know Eugene?"

"Never met him. Don't wanna meet him. Now if'n you ain't gonna arrest us, leave us be."

* * *

In the field near their car, the little boy in the Sponge Bob underwear waited. This time he waved with all of his fingers and smiled. Eddie and Harry waved back.

"I'll never understand how people can live like that," said Harry, hesitating at the car door. "The place smelled like a goddamn outhouse."

"You grew up in the East Valley, didn't you?" Eddie leaned against their car.

"Yeah, in Mesa. Graduated from ASU then took my academy training in Maricopa County . . . It's not like I haven't seen crap like that before. It just pisses me off."

"Hey, watch the street. I need something from my briefcase in the trunk," said Eddie.

Harry obliged.

"You probably had parents that set ground rules and expectations, right?" said Eddie from behind the open trunk.

"Sure. How about you? Normal childhood? Or were you raised by wolves or something?"

"Or something," said Eddie, pulling an odd little toy badge from his briefcase.

"For the kid?" Harry asked tilting his head to the little boy watching intently from his weedy playground.

"Yeah, just a little something," said Eddie "He reminds me of somebody I once knew."

Eddie approached the lot, kneeling at the curb, holding out the little badge shaped like a triangle with a lightning bolt dagger through its middle. The boy approached with caution. Eddie said something in Spanish and pointed to the brass and copper badge attached to his belt. The boy stepped closer and Eddie pressed the little plastic badge into the boy's hand then stood and saluted. The boy imitated the gesture.

Once they were back in the car, Harry said, "That was nice. Where'd you get that fancy badge? All I get from the department are those cheesy gold stickers."

"Around here something less cop-like makes fewer waves. 'Snitches get stitches,' as they say."

"You think he stands a chance? I mean, look at where he's growing up."

"If someone shows him he has value," said Eddie, fastening his seat belt. "You'd be amazed the difference one person can make to a kid like that."

"Speaking of kids, what did that, 'or something,' mean when I asked about your childhood?"

Eddie smiled. "What would you say if I told you my parents were illegals?"

"Really? You aren't bullshitting, are you?"

"My dad pushed my mom across the Rio Grande in an inner tube near Brownsville, Texas. I was born a U.S. citizen one day later."

"No shit?"

"Honest to God."

"Are your parents still around?"

"Sure. My dad will probably outlive me. Mom's doing well. Her heart's not all it should be. They live in Hermosillo."

"Mexico?"

"Yeah."

"You said they were illegal. Were they—"

"Deported? Yes, busted in a packing plant raid. That's when things got ugly for me. I was about that little guy's age back there."

"Were *you* deported?"

"Nope. They wanted me to grow up in the U.S., so they sent me to an aunt and uncle here in Phoenix. Turns out those two just wanted the welfare money. He split shortly after I arrived. Aunt Estelle stuck around, but she was a crack addict. I remember being hungry and moving a lot. For a while, I'm pretty sure we were even squatters just like them." He nodded to the party house.

"So how did—"

"Ever hear of Santa cop?"

"Sure. Cops take kids shopping at Christmas."

"My Santa Cop was a sergeant named Tim McPauly. I got to ride in his squad car and he handed me a $100 gift card to go Christmas shopping at Wal-Mart. I thought I'd won the lottery. Anyway—long story short—it was Tim who steered me toward the military. That's how I got out. I was lucky. I could have ended up a gangster just as easily."

"Damn, Eddie. What else don't I know about you?"

"All in good time, partner. All in good time," Eddie said, smiling. "Well, we've put on a good show and in an amazing stroke of luck—

if you can call meeting the party house residents luck—actually tracked down Eugene's mother. Never thought that would happen."

"Yeah, no shit. I can certainly see why he broke off contact—hey maybe you ought to check in and see if anything's going on with your mystery friend."

"I talked to him while you were napping on the way over. Told him we might be doing a drive-by. He said all is quiet. You snore when you sleep by the way."

"Since we're driving by that church, well . . . Now that the Luchadores know we're onto them, maybe it's time to bring him in."

Eddie considered the option. "Nah, we've gone all-in on setting the trap. I think we ought to leave it set a little longer. If he survived the old bucket of blood, another night in an empty church'll be a cake walk. A drive-by though—if anybody's watching—might steer them his direction."

"Works for me," said Harry, secretly hoping Eugene would spot their car and come in on his own. "Where's it at?"

"Near 9th and Buchanan. Not far."

Turning north on 9th Avenue from Grant, the landscape transformed into an industrial mishmash of weedy vacant lots and warehouses surrounded by chain link topped with razor wire. An old Hispanic man in a floppy straw hat pedaled a bike pulling a two-wheel trailer filled with trash bags bulging with crushed aluminum cans. Further north, a Union Pacific train engine blocked the street as it pushed a line of boxcars through the intersection.

At 9th and Buchanan they rolled to a stop.

"Which way right or left, I don't see a church," said Harry.

"My friend said it's across the road from a cell tower so it must be down there," Eddie said, pointing left. "Thing is, I also see a junkyard down there under the bridge."

"Old Mr. Jefferson mentioned a junkyard. Gate's open. Wanna check it out?"

"Yeah, but let's make a loop around the church first."

Turning left, they rumbled over a set of railroad tracks. Soon their tires crunched on gravel as they rolled by a small vacant lot, a metal

Quonset hut style building and a large old metal and cinderblock warehouse with most of the windows broken out.

"Where's your friend hiding?"

"Don't know, but he's around. He has a knack for hiding in plain sight."

"Hey, there it is," said Harry. "Not as big as I had imagined. It looks more like a shack than a church."

They rolled to a stop then stared at the building for a long moment. In the fading evening light a hint of red brake lights shown on the church's gray wood front.

Come on, Eugene. You know it's us. Just come on out and let us take you home.

"I know what you're hoping," said Eddie, "but clearly he wants to stay put."

Eddie plucked his chirping phone from his belt and smiled at the screen. He turned it to Harry.

"Damn, your guy's a ninja," he said staring at picture of the ass end of their car parked in front of the church.

"Yep, none better. I'd say I taught him everything he knows, but he outpaced me years ago. Whadda ya say we go check that junkyard."

As they rolled up on the battered metal sign reading, *FODONI BROTHERS*, two elderly black men were in the process of leaving. One worked the gate for the other who sat behind the wheel of a classic old pickup polished to perfection.

As Harry and Eddie stepped from their car, the man at the gate called out, "We're closing up for the day."

"Sorry to hold you up, but we're the police. Got a minute to talk?" asked Harry.

The old man genuinely smiled. "If you lookin' for Eugene, he ain't here."

"I take it we're not the first to come by?"

"No, seems everybody's lookin' for him."

"Who's everybody?"

"Couple a state cops and some rough lookin' toughs from the hood. I'll tell you what I told them. We haven't seen him for goin' on a couple a months, now."

"We're from Scottsdale. I know it'll be hard to believe, but we are friends with Eugene. We'd like to bring him in and keep him safe until we get things straightened out for him. I'm Harry Aronson and this is Eddie Ibarra."

The driver of the truck hopped out and strolled to share in the handshakes.

"My name's Carl and this is my brother Albert."

"Good to meet you," said Harry.

"Pleasure," said Eddie.

"These two fellas say they're friends with Eugene," said Albert.

"Well, then I'll tell you what we told everybody else, I doubt we'll see him until he gets right with the world, which I'm sure he will do," said Carl.

"How'd you come to know Eugene?" asked Eddie.

"That's a long story," said Carl, "and it's been a long, hot day." He paused, first looking at the ground then into the eyes of the detectives. "But we'll make time. Come on in. We'll talk. Good thing we DVR'd *Dancing with the Stars*, Albert."

In the fading evening, a yard light flashed on, illuminating an oily dirt path leading to an office that was a cobble-together, plywood affair. Hubcaps hung from any surface that would hold a nail. Out of the darkness and without warning, a huge, one-eyed dog bounded from behind a pile of car batteries. His ferocious barking froze Harry and Eddie. The dog's wagging tail did little to allay the chilling effect.

"Don't mind King. Ifin' his tail's a waggin', you're all right," said Albert, unlocking the door and stepping in. He flipped on the office light as Carl punched an alarm keypad near the door. The oddly comforting smell of old men, cooking oil and plywood welcomed them.

Behind a well-used, plywood front counter with its ancient cash register hung a mix of girlie calendars, cartoons and yellowed newspaper clippings from the *East Valley Herald.* Below, a sleek, brushed-metal iMac computer sat atop a battered wooden desk.

"Come on in and sit," said Carl, motioning to a small sitting area with an ancient turquoise refrigerator and a heavy, chrome-legged table with matching turquoise upholstered chairs. "And just so you know, I got a .38 in my pocket and there's a shotgun behind the counter. You two don't look like the nervous type, but some cops are and—"

"No worries," Eddie stopped him. "In this neighborhood, I'd be more concerned if you weren't armed."

"Can I get you gentlemen some pop or a bottle of water?" asked Albert. "Got some diet Cokes and cherry Fresca in here, too." Carl pulled open the ancient refrigerator. "I assume a cold beer is not on your on-duty menu?"

"Water's fine for both of us, thank you," said Eddie.

Harry took the offered bottles as he and Eddie settled at the table. The two of them looked out a large picture window that framed a breathtaking view of the downtown Phoenix skyline.

"That's a great view," said Harry.

"It does look best at night," said Carl with pride. "In daylight you gotta look past all the junked cars."

"'Course all them cars look like money to us," added Albert, taking a seat across from them. "Been building our little business for goin' on forty years, now."

"How'd you get started?" asked Eddie.

"It was that Studebaker you saw out front," said Carl, motioning to the yard. "We was scrapin' like a lot of folk do down here. One day this fella offered me three-hundred dollars for a rear fender. That was a lot of money back then so we sold it to him. Heck, we didn't pay more than two-hundred for the whole truck. Wasn't long after, other folks started calling . . . Made a decent chunk of change sellin' it piece by piece. We used that money to buy another truck, then another." Prideful smiles graced both men's faces.

"It was our boy, Eugene, that suggested we rebuild the old girl 'bout five, six years ago. All we had left at the time was the frame," added Albert.

"Ah, and now we're back to the reason for our visit," said Harry. "What can you tell us about Eugene?"

Carl and Albert exchanged what appeared to be telepathic glances.

"King liked 'em and they both seem okay to me," said Carl to his brother. "Go ahead, give 'em the lowdown on our boy."

Albert took a pull on his can of cherry Fresca then began, "He came from what some might call a dysfunctional family."

"I call 'em assholes," shot Carl.

Albert ignored his brother and continued, "We met the boys, Eugene and Ray, when their daddy bought a used battery from us. Even then we could see the boys had a way with mechanics. Their daddy paid for the battery and they set to work putting it in lickity split. But we didn't get real close to Eugene until things went bad for the family."

"Care to elaborate?"

Carl picked up where his bother left off, "Their daddy was always cattin' around. From what we gathered he was messin' with the wife of an employee and that man took it out on Eugene. Anyways, there was a big blowup. Eugene and his dog, King showed up at our door beaten and bloody—"

"King is Eugene's dog?"

"Yep, Eugene's daddy intended to kill that fine animal, so our boy brought him to us for safe keepin'. Wasn't two weeks later the boy's daddy split. Cleaned 'em out. The boys and their momma disappeared for a while. Figured they were gone for good, especially after we read in the paper that Ray, Eugene's older brother had been killed. Then one night our boy came flyin' over our fence. Bunch a hoodlums was wantin' to beat on him. After we chased 'em off . . . Well, he pert near lived here."

Eddie shook his head and slouched into his chair, shifting gears as he cracked the cap on his water bottle and took a swig. "You mentioned some state police came by."

"They asked if we'd seen Eugene. We told 'em the same thing we told you."

"M-hm," hummed Eddie, taking a longer drink from the water bottle. "Forgive me for asking, but did they see that paper bag in the refrigerator with Eugene's name on it?"

Albert went stone-faced, but Carl didn't miss a beat, "We just wanted to have a few things around in case he did come callin'. Let's call that bag a wish for his well being, rather than proof that he'll come home."

"Our boy don't realize it," added Albert, "but there's a lot of folks down here who are proud of him and would do anything to help. A' course he ain't the sort to take advantage of that."

"And ifin' he does come around," said Carl, "you'd be hard pressed to catch him . . . but then I got a notion you may not want to catch him." The old man's bright eyes spoke volumes as he stared squarely at Eddie until out in the yard they heard King barking as though he had treed a bear.

"Something you need to deal with out there?" asked Eddie.

"Nah, that's his rabbit bark. Sometimes he'll spot one in the yard, he'll make a good show of chasin', but he don't really want to catch 'em."

"Yeah, sometimes catching only complicates things," added Harry. Carl smiled and gave a barely imperceptible nod.

King's huge head appeared in the window seconds later, his paws resting on the sill as his long tongue bobbed from one side of his wide, panting smile. The old men gave the dog a wave of recognition. He blinked, gave a half-hearted bark that Harry thought sounded more like a laugh as he hopped down and loped back into the yard's dark maze of metal.

17

The crunch of tires on gravel caught Eugene's ear as he woke inside the little church, head pounding and skin as dry as a turkey left too long in the oven. Bright daylight had given way to evening, but the little wood structure refused to let go of the heat. Brake-light red washed down the narrow alley between the church and the warehouse. Dizzy at standing too quickly, he shook it off and quick-stepped past Freddie's empty nest to press an eye to a hole in the plywood covering the church's front door.

Shit! Harry and Eddie! How the hell do they know?

His feet wanted to run, but his brain said it was too late. After a few agonizing seconds, their car rolled ahead, made a wide turn on the gravel road and drove off.

Now, that doesn't make any sense. Why not have a look around?

Curious, he strode for the window and crawled out into the evening. A slight breeze, cool and heavenly, greeted his parched skin. Edging to the front of the warehouse to peer down the road, he watched the detectives make a brief stop at 9th Avenue before continuing on to the Fodoni Brothers' yard.

Certain this was a trick to draw him into the open, he craned his head in all directions. The only thing moving was a feral cat sniffing at a fast food drink cup on its side next to the cell tower gate.

At the junkyard, Albert and Carl greeted the detectives then all four walked for the office. The distant sound of King's amiable bark brightened Eugene's mood. He realized the detectives' drive by the church was probably just a wrong turn. Relaxing, he stood and leaned through the church window, pulling the bag of trail mix and a bottle of water from his provisions on the pew.

He drank half the liter bottle then poured a little into his hair, relishing the sensation of it trickling down into his shirt to be cooled by the light evening breeze. Dinner in hand he walked back to the edge of the warehouse, dropped to his haunches and settled in to watch the junkyard while munching on nuts, raisins and M&Ms.

Thirty minutes later the group reappeared, shaking hands and laughing. Harry and Eddie drove off into the night. Albert and Carl buttoned up the office and followed suit a short time later.

Eager to see King, Eugene decided to take a chance and walk straight down Buchanan Street rather than take a more judicious route around the back of his family's old warehouse.

In his years away it seemed only the graffiti had changed. A careful examination of the landscape revealed all of his old escape routes and hidey holes were still there should he need them. As he approached the 7th Avenue bridge, a favorite hidey hole came into view. High in the southern abutment, powerful quartz lamps drew a frenzy of insects. Behind them sat a small crawl space. The lights amplified the heat, but if you ignored that, their incessant buzz, and the layers of bird shit and bug carcasses, it was a good hiding spot when need be.

Many years before, that filthy little niche had led him back to the Fodoni brothers. During his time in the projects, he'd avoided the yard, not wanting to bring his troubles to his friends. The night they were reunited, he'd had no choice.

He had been on the run from a carload of Mexican gang bangers. He thought he'd gotten away and planned to spend the night up under the bridge, but before he could make the climb, their low rider cut him off. Out of desperation, he scaled the Fodoni brother's fence, tearing clothes and ripping skin on the razor wire as he rolled over and dropped to the ground.

King knocked him down and was delivering a welcome home tongue bath when a blast from Albert's twelve-gauge sounded.

"That first round was birdshot. The rest are buck and aimed straight at your heads," Albert had yelled at the carload of gangsters. Carl soon joined him, revolver in hand.

"You *cabrónes* mutha-fuckers don't need to be protectin' no snitch!" called a Hispanic voice.

Carl took careful aim. "You know the rules. Do what you want out there, but you bring trouble to this yard and us old *cabrónes* will kill you. No cops, no dickin' around. You and your car'll be ground up with the scrap."

After the low rider screeched off down the street, Eugene had stepped from cover.

"Where you been, son? We missed you," squawked Albert. "More importantly, that dog's been missin' you." He'd smiled, set down the shotgun, and held out welcoming arms.

"I'm sorry for bringing my troubles to your yard."

"Shit, them little punks?" Carl had said, "We deal with them kind a couple times a week. Now, where you been? I heard about your brother and I'm sorry."

"That was my fault," Eugene had blurted, crossing his arms and staring at the ground. "And it's my fault my dad ran off."

"Son, your pa runnin' off ain't nobody's fault but his own. And your brother's death is on the fool that pulled the trigger. Don't be puttin' that bullshit on your shoulders. Come on in the office, have a cold pop, and we'll get you patched up."

Eugene had tears in his eyes as he was yanked from his memories by King's yelp for joy just before the dog's paws collided with chain link.

Tears now streaming, Eugene ran for the gate, shoving his hands through the narrow opening to scratch King's muzzle and receive a saliva-laden greeting. After a few joyful moments he stood, put a shoe on the gate chain and hoisted himself up and over, deftly avoiding the loops of razor wire. Just as he had so many years before, King knocked him to the ground.

"We have to quit meeting like this," Eugene joked, before burying his face in the dog's wiry coat as he wrapped his arms around his middle. King paused to sniff and lick at his boy's wounded face. "That's right, buddy, my eye's a bit messed up now, too," he said, roughly scratching at King's hindquarters to make the dog's butt dance.

With King wagging and prancing behind, he walked around the battery pile to the back of the office. Out of habit, he dumped and refilled King's water pan. He then stuck his head into the hose bib stream, feeling the water turn cool as it washed the salt and dirt from his skin. He drank until he could drink no more. Since King insistently leaned against him, he ruffled and patted the big dog one more time before marching for the office door. The safe place, the water and the loving dog had him feeling semi-human again.

"Stay," Eugene whispered to King before retrieving the office's deadbolt key from inside a Studebaker hubcap hung near the door. The dog sat back on his haunches and cocked his head in concern. "I'll be back. Don't worry."

The smell of the brothers and the beep of the alarm system greeted him. Dim light glowed from a wall sconce down a short hall leading to the bathroom. Much to his relief, the alarm code had not changed. He moved to the makeshift kitchen where he opened the old turquoise refrigerator and smiled at a paper sack with his name on it.

"I'll be damned."

The sack contained two ham and cheese sandwiches, a package of lemon Zinger snack cakes, a quart of chocolate milk and a note that he eagerly unfolded.

> *Figured you might come by. Also figured you'd want some lemon Zingers, ha ha. Remembered they were your favorite from the roach coach. Thugs from the neighborhood looking for you. Cops too. If you need it, there's a Walmart cell phone in the drawer below the register. Carl loaded it up with a bunch of minutes. Bye for now, all our love, Albert & Carl.*
>
> *P. S. Two detectives from Scottsdale came by tonight. We told them we ain't seen you for a couple months which is true. They said they're on your side, but you can't never tell with cops.*

Eugene stuffed the first sandwich into his mouth, washing it down with a cold bottle of water. The second one he ate more slowly while sipping the chocolate milk. With the remaining half carton of milk and the package of Zingers in hand, he moved to the desk and fired up the iMac he'd given the brothers. While the computer booted, he retrieved the pre-paid phone and charger, pulling them from their plastic packaging and placing them in his pants pockets.

Back at the computer, he fired up Safari and clicked the brothers' bookmark for the *East Valley Herald*. The lead story was a punch in the gut.

"What the fuck guys," he said aloud at seeing his booking mugshot next to the headline, *POLICE HAVE NO LEADS ON DISGRACED EV HERALD PHOTOGRAPHER*.

Disgraced? So much for having my back, shit, this is a lynching. Condon never would have let this bullshit see the light of day. Pete? You slimy sonofabitch.

Beside the three graphs that offered little more than no-comment statements from the Scottsdale Police he found a smaller, "Related Stories" link. He clicked through. The same, guilt-tinged booking photo loaded next to the headline, *TRUTH REVEALED: EV HERALD PHOTOG ESCAPES-WARRANT ISSUED by Pete Cunningham, Acting Managing Editor*. Reading more like an editorial, the story laid out the familial link between himself and Derek Schaefer. The wording inferred the paper's disgraced former employee may have been helping his brother elude capture.

Fuck you Pete, you goddamn wannabe. I'll hand you your ass, you son-of-a-bitch.

Heart in his throat, he leaned back in the ancient metal office chair, closed his eyes and breathed slowly. He ran his fingers through greasy, wet hair, then scratched his scalp in frustration as he fought for focus.

Calm down and think. Panic won't solve anything.

For a long time he stared at the dark ceiling, playing it all over in his head. Then he sat up straight, tore open the Zingers, and took a bite, washing it down with a swig of chocolate milk. As the sugar hit his system, he wiped his hands on his pants then put his fingers to work at the keyboard.

He searched for everything he could find on the Luchadores, sending his finds to the nearby printer atop a metal file cabinet. He then looked for addresses for Harry and Eddie and the Condon family. From there he cast a wider search net on Mexican wrestlers, prostitution, sex offender data bases, Craig's List personal ads . . . He listened to the laser printer's satisfying hum as he finished his Zingers and chocolate milk. King's angry bark launched him from his chair.

He folded his printouts and tucked them into the back of his pants before peering out a window with a view of the gate. King was launching himself at the fence, barking and yapping. *More cops?*

After resetting the alarm, he stepped outside to better view over the battery pile. A hulking figure moved in an awkward bob and weave, turning round and round as he fended off three attackers.

"Oh shit, it's Freddie."

An attacker lunged. Freddie shrieked with pain then lashed out clumsily, "Ahhhh, Ahhhh, Ahhhh!"

Laughter followed. The attackers circled like wolves on a bear.

Eugene grabbed a handful of lug nuts from a box on a workbench and stuffed them in a front pocket. From the battery pile he yanked free a cable with a heavy, lead terminal clamp and draped it around his neck. In his run for the gate, he paused to break off the steel whip antenna from an Oldsmobile.

The smallest attacker showed off now, bouncing like a boxer, laughing and dancing. He launched into a flying kick. Freddie caught him, lifted him high and slammed him to the street, triumphantly chanting his "Ahhhh, Ahhhh, Ahhhh!" He tried to stomp the guy in his own victory dance, but his attacker rolled away.

Eugene hit the gate at full speed. One foot found the gate chain as his hands gripped the top of the posts, King continuing his lunges and barking. Up and over like an Olympic vaulter, he tucked into a roll as he hit the ground and came up running. Thirty yards out he slowed to identify his targets and start launching lug nuts. One attacker turned away, yelping with pain then cursing.

"Run, Freddie! Get out of there!"

Freddie stood his ground. Eugene let the last three nuts fly in unison, shotgun-style to cover his approach. He transferred the antenna to his right hand and yanked free the battery cable with the other, spinning it up to speed.

He attacked without hesitation, screaming with rage. The surprised attackers evidently expected some sort of macho standoff with an easy target, not this serious fighting. The lead terminal clamp whistled into the cheekbone of the largest in the group as the steel whip—impossible to see at night—cut deep into the face of the smaller show-off, who had slowly gained his feet after Freddie's body slam.

Eugene felt pressure slide across his right shoulder as his momentum carried him through the group. He turned, whipping the cable back up to a whirring circle just as Freddie landed a roundhouse punch to the kidneys that lifted an attacker off his feet. The guy stumbled forward right into Eugene's lead terminal clamp that caught him in the ribs. He went down shrieking in pain.

A muzzle flash registered at the same instant the bullet whizzed past Eugene's ear. On his knees, the littlest attacker pressed one hand to his bloody face. A small caliber pistol wavered in the other hand. He staggered to his feet firing two more shots. Eugene zigged and zagged.

A blinding light and the roar of an engine filled the night. Everyone but the shooter jumped for cover. The shooter turned to face the light just before the vehicle's collision sent him flying. He hit the pavement face first, his body rolling limply to a stop.

"Who sent you? *Comprendo*, mother fuckers?" barked the driver, exiting the SUV. Light reflected off the pistol in his hand. He kicked the little gang banger's .25 auto a safe distance away. "Who sent you?" he repeated more forcefully.

The attacker with the shattered cheek stared at the ground, a hand clutching his wounds. His partner just stared around, totally confused.

"Go on, *Vamanos*!" barked the driver.

The two collected their unconscious friend and limped off into the night.

Eugene slipped back, out of the wash of headlights.

"You stay put!" the driver ordered.

For a moment there was only King's continuous barking, the SUV's throaty idle and the sobbing of Freddie, who was on the ground, rocking and holding his gut. Eugene and the driver sized up each other.

"*Pinche su madre*!" came a shouted insult from the darkness.

The driver's square-jawed face changed with a broad smile. "*Chinga pendejo*!" he shouted back.

Eugene heaved a sigh of relief and held up his now empty hands. "Thank you . . . I think . . . sir."

"You hit or cut?"

"No, sir. I don't think so."

"Eugene Fellig, right?" asked the driver.

"No, my name's Jimmy, Jimmy John—son."

"Nice try, kid. You are freaky fast, I'll give you that," said the driver with a laugh. "Before we talk, I'd appreciate it if you'd drop to your knees, cross your ankles and put your hands on top of your head, interlacing your fingers. I'd like to make sure you don't have any more surprises tucked away."

Eugene complied, glancing at the moaning Freddie. "We need to help Freddie, I think he's cut pretty bad."

The driver studied Freddie and his too-small t-shirt and hands covered with blood. He turned his glare back to Eugene, "Gimme a hand. You try anything and I'll rip you a new asshole."

Now shaking from the adrenaline let-down, Eugene stood. King's bark had turned hoarse with prolonged effort. He turned to point a shaky finger at the agitated dog. "King! Stop! Sit!" A whine answered him.

He marched to Freddie, knelt and put a hand on his bloodied shoulder. "It'll be okay, buddy. Let us take a look at it. Can you do that?"

"Uhh huh," Freddie grunted.

The driver approached, carrying a large first-aid bag bearing a military name patch that read CARTER. It chilled Eugene to the bone.

The driver expertly examined Freddie's gut wound with its oozing blood glittering in the SUV's headlights. "He's lucky he's got a bit of padding." He pulled a roll of gauze and a pair of snub-nosed scissors from the bag. "Here, cut me off two strips, each about two feet long."

Eugene did as he was told.

The driver wadded one piece to clean away the gore then packed the other into the wound. "Hold this in place," he said.

Feeling calmer, Eugene put his fingers to the gauze. The driver tore open a large, square bandage and applied it to the wound. "His shoulder's next," said the man.

Freddie sat as still as a frightened fawn as they worked.

"I didn't kill Sandy," Eugene blurted, as they worked on the shoulder.

The man paused in his work, but didn't bother to look up. "Sandy was my niece, by the way. I'm Chris's brother, Jack."

"I-I've seen your picture in his office. Why not just let 'em shoot me?"

"Why'd you risk your skin to help this guy?"

"Couldn't just let those assholes kill him."

"Funny."

"What?"

"I kinda came to the same conclusion about you. By the way, what were you after in the junkyard office?"

"Food and water," Eugene lied.

"Nothing to do with the papers shoved down your pants, huh?"

"I, ah . . . How long you been watching me?"

"Since my phone call sent you out the back door of that newspaper building."

Eugene blinked and sat back on his heels." You're shittin' me. Why?"

"Wanted to see who came after you. I was hoping for a little bigger fish than those dickheads."

"Well, I think your brother wants me dead."

"Chris wants a lot of things . . . Kid, there's more you don't—"

Sirens and red/blue flashing lights interrupted him. Speeding, one police cruiser hit the railroad crossing to the north fast enough to go airborne. The other braked hard and managed to keep its tires on the ground. On his feet, Eugene slinked back out of the headlight's glare.

King resumed his frantic barking and jumping at the fence.

"Get around the back of the vehicle. Stay low," shouted Jack. "When they take me down, get the hell outta here."

Eugene stared from the dark, confused, "You didn't call them?"

"No, cop's shot tracker probably picked up the gunshots. Now move!" Jack stood and put his hands out to his sides, providing a distraction. Keeping to the shadows, Eugene slid to the SUV's tailgate.

Tires screeched to a stop amid wailing sirens.

"Gun!" yelled an officer.

"Gentlemen, I have a permit—"

Now on the ground peering under the SUV, Eugene saw a jumble of legs then Jack's face as he was taken to the ground hard. Their eyes locked for an instant. In spite of the rough treatment, Jack calmly nodded and blinked. Eugene slipped off into the night.

18

Safely out of sight, running for the back side of the Buchanan Street warehouses, Eugene heard Freddie's growl just before Jack Carter yelled, "Go easy on him. He's—" The staccato crack of a Taser followed and Eugene winced as Freddie cried out in pain.

In the shadows and weeds behind the warehouses, Eugene considered his options and decided the best course was to move to the rooftops where he could watch and listen.

Staying low he moved quickly to a spot where a new, tilt-wall constructed warehouse connected to an older, concrete block building. It looked a bit more daunting than he remembered. Shaking off his fear and adjusting his sweaty computer printouts hugging his butt in his pants, he scaled a weak fence then splayed his feet and hands between the walls.

Twelve inches at a time, he worked the slow, wedge-and-step ascent. Minutes later he was thirty feet up, his arms and legs shaking with fatigue. He hooked one arm over the old warehouse's wall then swung to hook his other to pull himself over. Rolling onto the warm asphalt rooftop, he heaved a sigh of relief. *Son of a bitch, that was easier when I was a kid.*

He managed only a moment of calm before the distant drone of a helicopter sent him running for the cover of one of the four swamp coolers dotting the warehouse's shallow-pitched rooftop.

Heart pounding and body weak from exertion, he slipped under the cooler's ductwork just before a bright circle of light washed past. *That's it. Use the spotlight, not the infrared.* The copter briefly hovered over the street, providing a few seconds of illumination for the cops below before it moved off.

When the noise of the chopper blades faded in the distance, he rolled out into the open and lay flat on his back, deep breathing away the urge to vomit. Ever so slowly, he recovered. His breathing slowed as the shaky, cold sweat sick diminished. Laughter on the street below brought him back to attention.

By the sound of it, the cops below were having a party. He crawled up to the roof's peak then down to the gutter on the far side. After following the gutter to the front of the building, he lay down to look through a drain hole with a clear view of the street.

Freddie lay strapped to a gurney that was being lifted into a paramedic squad. When it pulled away, he was surprised to see Jack leaning against the hood of a police cruiser. He casually conversed with officers who appeared to hang on his every word. Eugene could only hear fragments, but enough to understand Jack was telling war stories. Funny ones if the laughter and fist bumps were any indication.

Relieved that they weren't looking for him and slightly confused by Jack's bromance with the cops, he returned to the roof's peak to take in the view. Up here he'd always felt on top of the world. Tonight was no different.

Looking east, eight shallow-pitched, white-painted roofs spread out before him as they peaked and valleyed all the way to the 7th Avenue bridge. Sirens wailed in the distance. Trains rumbled and banged, sounding air horn warnings at each street crossing. Aircraft streaked in an out of Sky Harbor airport, marker lights blinking. Life went on, oblivious to the problems of the rooftop king.

Feeling slightly more in control, he strolled to one of swamp coolers to quench his thirst. With practiced ease, he lifted away one of the cooler's louvered side panels, set it aside then pulled away the calcium-encrusted excelsior pad beneath. One hand found the plastic water line connected to a pump in the cooler's water pan and traced it up to a copper distribution line at the top of the box. He pulled the plastic hose free as his other hand found the water pan's float valve and pushed down. Warm water squirted from the hose.

He let the water run until it cooled then sipped as the sense of coming full circle hit him. The spout of water reminded him of the drinking fountain at the *East Valley Herald*, which had always made him think of the rooftop fountain.

Memories of Mr. Condon rushed in. He saw Oliver at his desk, poring over the Luchador photos . . . then panic filled the old man's eyes as he gulped for air like a fish out of water. *What were you trying to tell me, Oliver? What the hell is an ass clown?*

Unable to coax the answer, he tucked the thought away and pulled the folded and now sweat-sodden printouts from the back of his pants and sat down against the swamp cooler. In the dim light all he could make out was the headline.

POLICE HAVE NO LEADS ON DISGRACED EV HERALD PHOTOGRAPHER

The word, "disgraced" stuck in his craw. Heat crept into his face. Before he could swallow back the sudden tightness in this throat, tears escaped streaming down his cheeks. He wanted to be furious, but the emotional floodgates had finally opened. He sobbed for Oliver and Sandy then finally for himself.

I did my best, Oliver, just like you said, but it wasn't enough for them. Welfare case, stray dog, uneducated . . . The words burned like acid in his brain . . . *Fucking uppity cocksuckers . . . Did any of them come to my defense? Probably not. They're all gutless wonders.*

* * *

Derek Schaefer sat in a bland concrete isolation cell inside the Maricopa County jail, clad only in his underwear and considering how best to kill himself. There really was no other option. *Better to go on my terms than theirs.*

Through the haze of scratches on the hardened plastic window at the front of his cell, he looked directly into the guard's control booth.

A multi-chinned man in a khaki shirt sat watching from behind greenish glass, looking like a fat little ghost in the video monitor's light.

It had been hours since he'd been told he'd be taken to psych for evaluation. In that wait time he'd worked out a plan to play it cool until he was issued enough clothing to fashion a noose.

A floor guard holding a handful of papers and a light blue wad strolled up to the control booth. He talked briefly with the fat little ghost then shrugged, turned, and walked straight to Derek's cell.

Jaw clenched and eyes narrowed in fear, Derek watched the floor guard key the lock and slide open the door.

"Whadda *you* want?" Derek said as the guard tossed the blue wad at his feet.

"Put that on. I'll escort you out."

Confused, Derek donned the papery blue pants and shirt that resembled hospital scrubs without saying a word. He followed the guard's directions, exiting the cell, turning to the right and following a yellow line to the same pair of heavy sliding doors he'd walked through hours before.

Head down, the concrete flooring cold on his bare feet, Derek assumed he was headed to his psych evaluation. *Keep it cool and even.* He passed cell after cell, ignoring the screamed threats and pounding on the plastic windows.

At the heavy doors of the sally port entrance, the guard called out, "Hold up."

A buzz and thunk sounded. The first door slid open. They stepped in together and waited for the door to close behind. After another buzz and thunk, the front door opened. Stepping out, they passed another guard and an inmate dressed in a striped shirt and pants walking the opposite direction.

"Is that the uniform I'll be issued after the psych evaluation?"

"Nope." The guard held up the paperwork in his hand. "These are release orders. It's your lucky day. You're going to processing. You'll be back on the street shortly."

Stifling the urge to ask questions, Derek shuffled along with the guard at his heels. His brain spun with thoughts of who and why. Soon they were back in the large bland room where he'd been processed in. Two guards—one male, one female—sat behind a high counter that ran the length of the room's back wall. In the middle of the room sat an x-ray machine beside a walk-through metal detector.

Fearing the female guard might recognize him and sound an alarm, Derek relaxed when his escort steered him to the male. He kept his face down answering only yes and no. His gaze followed his paperwork across the counter to the processing guard whose fingers worked his computer keyboard.

Papers spit from a nearby printer. The processing guard snatched them up, put them on the counter then launched into a speech about court dates and warrants and failure to appear. The words barely registered as Derek's mind spun a mile a minute.

"Are you listening?" asked the guard.

"Uh-huh," Derek replied with a nod. He took the offered pen and signed where the guard pointed.

A plastic bag containing his wallet, keys, and a copy of the paperwork he had just signed landed in front of him. Derek took it then dared to look up. "How about my clothes?"

"In Scottsdale. Held for evidence."

"Shoes?"

"Them, too. You should have asked whoever's picking you up to bring clothes."

"Oh, yeah, right," said Derek, as though he'd forgotten. "So . . . are we good?"

"Yeah, *we good*," snarked the guard. "Door's behind you."

Plastic bag in hand, Derek turned and marched for the door, not looking back, terrified that someone would catch the mistake.

In the darkness outside, bugs swarmed around a streetlight. The sidewalk's warmth met his bare feet and the city's stench greeted his nose as he took his bearings. Tall buildings all around meant downtown, not the Durango jail he'd expected. Across the street, closed-for-the-night bail bond offices dominated a line of unwelcoming concrete storefronts.

Stepping out to the curb, he looked back over his shoulder. Stainless steel letters on the brick wall above him read, *4th AVENUE JAIL.* He scanned the street peering into every dark corner for signs of a sniper or a carload of drive-by shooters. *A screw-up this big . . . It has to be the Luchadores.*

A light flickered on from the line of cars parked across the street. He tensed and backed to the brick wall of the jail. *Just a man lighting a cigarette . . . No eye contact. There's gotta be cameras all over this entrance . . . They won't try anything here.*

"Fuck me . . . fuuuck meeeee."

Clutching his paper and plastic bag of belongings, he slid down the side of the building. Frantic, he searched the street for a dark alcove in which to hide and think.

An older, red and yellow minivan turned onto 4th Avenue from Madison, a taxicab sign glowing atop its roof. The van did a slow roll past Derek then stopped and backed up. The driver's side window slid down. "If you got cash, I'll take ya where ya need to go," said the driver. He looked to be a tall man with oversized gold-framed glasses and an acne-riddled face.

"I'm all right," Derek said. "Just waitin' for my ride."

"Okay, I'm gonna go gas up. I'll make one more pass afore I head home if'n your people don't show, I'll be back . . . oh, and if a homeless shelter's what you need, it's about six blocks east 'a here. They got boxes of donated clothes . . . in case you wanna get out of that paper suit." The driver waited a second longer, his elbow hanging out of the window.

Derek ran through his options. *I'm a dead man anyway.* Just as the driver pulled his elbow inside and began to roll away, Derek raised his arms and dashed for the cab, his paper suit flapping. "I got money," he said holding up his plastic bag. "My apartment's near 30th and Fillmore, over by the Celebrity Theater."

"That'll be 'bout twenty bucks, but I need to see cash first."

Derek pulled his wallet from the bag and fanned it open.

"You got yerself a ride, man. Come on up front if you want."

Derek yanked open the sliding side door and crawled in.

"Oh-h-h kay. Back works, too. Make sure you buckle-up."

Sliding the door closed, Derek settled into the seat. He hauled in a deep breath and let it out slowly as the van pulled away from the jail. They headed south.

"So, whadda ya do for a livin'?" asked the too friendly driver.

"What?"

"Sorry, just makin' small talk. I'll shut up if'n you don't feel like talkin'. Looks like you've had a rough night."

"Lawn care. Got my own business," Derek offered. He noticed the cabbie's operator's license picture was partially covered by a McDonald's hamburger coupon clipped to its plastic frame. Below, the bright LED meter read *156.40.*

"You gonna reset that meter?"

"Sorry. Thanks," said the driver as he clumsily poked at buttons until the amount changed to the minimum 2.50.

Derek's neck hair prickled, "Been drivin' long?"

"First week, believe it or not. Got laid off from the city parks department. Gotta pay the bills somehow, but this ain't hardly makin' it for me."

"Yeah, drivin' a hack's a tough way to make a livin'."

"You got that right," said the driver, turning north onto 1st Street. "You buckled in?"

"Yeah." Derek held the unlatched belt across his chest, catching the driver's eyes in the rearview mirror. When the driver looked away, he glanced to the driver's empty floor-mounted seat belt receptacle. When he looked back to the mirror the driver was watching him again.

"Don't worry about me," said Derek. "I'm no bad ass. Just got busted for drunk and disorderly out on the river. Got caught skinny dippin', believe it or not. Had some hot chicks out there, man. Too bad I don't remember much after the first case a beer." He smiled and shook his head. The driver smiled in return but his eyes stayed worried.

They turned right, onto Jefferson Street. Derek feigned a look out the window at a bright neon guitar jutting from the Hard Rock Cafe while he tested his door latch.

It's busted. Kid lock?

Blooming Palo Verdes and skinny-trunked palm trees lined the brightly lit but mostly deserted sidewalks. The shuttered storefronts offered nowhere to hide even if he could make his door work. Ahead, the big green arch of Chase Field's roof loomed. *Grow some balls, Derek. Choke the guy out. Steal the van. Wait. What if he's got a gun?*

"You ever been to a game there?" asked the driver, pointing out the window to the ballpark.

"Too rich for my blood, man. I mow lawns for a livin'. Hey, what'd you do for city parks? Lots of grass to mow there. Maybe you could hook me up."

"I was a painter."

"Oh, ain't never done much of that."

Stopping for a red light at 7th Street, the driver said, "Hey, almost forgot your complimentary bottle of water." He leaned forward, lifting the lid of a little ice chest. Derek twisted sideways in his seat, ready to grab the gun that he was sure would come out. He was thrown off balance seeing only a cold, wet bottle of water in the man's hand.

"Thanks, man. Beer woulda been better, but that'll do."

The driver turned his body, handing the bottle back. Derek didn't notice the tiny muzzle of a .22 pistol peeking from under the man's right armpit until a bright flash and a sudden, searing pain made him shriek.

Fear exploded to rage. Derek's left hand came over the headrest to jam under the driver's glasses. His middle finger sank deep into an eye socket as his right hand grabbed the driver's flailing wrist. Feral screams mixed with the gun's repeated flashes and pops, all creating a slow motion, strobe light horror show.

In the struggle, the driver's foot slipped from the brake. The van rolled into the intersection. Neither man heard the blare of the eighteen-wheeler's air horn or the screech of tires before the powerful rig slammed into the van's passenger side. The van continued to slide sideways, until it shuddered to a stop, pinned against a traffic signpost in the median.

Blackness.

In Derek's rising consciousness, the smell of steamy, sweet antifreeze registered first, followed by the ticking of hot, twisted metal. Pain throbbed in his chest, arm and leg. Blinking, he realized where he was and what was happening. Seeing the grill of the semi truck through the mangled passenger windows, his reality fully kicked in. Adrenaline coursed and the need to escape overrode his pain. The driver lay face down on the front passenger seat, the hair on the back of his head thick with blood.

A metal signpost blocked Derek's shattered window. Looking to the back, he saw the rear hatch hung open. A few cars had stopped and others were slowing. Derek rolled from his seat into the van's center aisle, clutching his plastic bag of meager possessions. He ignored the shooting pain in his thigh and the nagging ache in his chest as he crawled over the back bench seat. He awkwardly tumbled onto the street. The smell of gasoline added to his panic as he struggled to his feet amid puddling fluids. Shards of plastic and glass cut at his bare feet but that pain was nothing compared to his drive to get away.

A tall black man walked hesitantly toward the accident. Others were exiting their cars. He took a staggering step in the opposite direction. The world took a slow-motion spin then tilted sideways. He gritted his teeth determined to continue traveling in a dizzied arc toward the shadowy sidewalk. Panting, he swallowed the rising nausea and miraculously the horizon settled.

"Sit down, man. You're hurt," said the black man behind him.

When a hand settled on Derek's shoulder, Derek swung a wild fist that caught the man in the throat. He fell back, choking.

Path clear, Derek steered his barely cooperative limbs toward the back of an office building and a red brick church just beyond. *I'll find a dark doorway,* he thought, plodding on, *I just need to lay down and catch my breath.*

Discovering the church's side door locked, he propelled himself hand over bloody hand down a metal rail to the front of the church. The edges of his vision turned fuzzy, then stars sparkled. *I just need to lay down for a second . . .*

19

"Eugene, if you can hear me, I'm not your enemy. We need each other's help."

The voice sounded distant as Eugene crawled out of a deep slumber. He'd cried himself to sleep on the rooftop. Every joint in his body ached. He lifted a sweaty arm off his face and sat up, blinking the world into focus.

Was I dreaming? He pulled the cell phone from his pocket and powered it on. The little LCD said it was 12:45 a.m.

"Kid, I'll be here all night. It's just us. No cops. I'm gonna park under the bridge and catch some shut-eye if you want to talk."

Eugene shuffled to the front of the building to peek out the gutter's drain hole. The street appeared empty but for Jack, standing beside his SUV, his back against the front fender, arms crossed and one foot propped on a tire. He stayed that way for a long moment, eyes closed, head tilting back, obviously listening for a response. Hearing none, his shoulders slumped and he crawled slowly up into his SUV. The engine fired. He rolled down his window and gave one more glance up and down the street. A moment later he made a U-turn and rolled slowly toward the bridge. Eugene peered over the roof's edge to watch the SUV. Under the bridge, Jack parked and shut down for the night.

Returning to his swamp cooler, Eugene took a long drink and washed his face. He considered how Jack had come crashing into the fight only to let himself be roughed up by the cops. *He did a shitload more for me than the newsroom pansy-asses.* He indulged in thoughts of punishing Pete, imagining the feel of his knuckles crushing the cartilage in the slimy little shit's nose. In that instant, he made up his mind.

Again, he pulled the little flip phone from his pocket and dialed.

"Hello?"

"Albert?"

"Why hello Eugene, we was hopin' you'd call."

"Sorry for calling so late. Thanks for the Zingers and everything."

"No problem. It's the least we could do. How—"

"I didn't do it."

"You don't have to tell me that, son, I know you didn't hurt nobody . . . I'm awful sorry about Oliver. He was a good man."

"I just called to say thanks for everything, Albert. Gotta few things I have to do. Don't know when—"

"You do what you gotta do, son. But don't be thinkin' you're all alone. I know you ain't one to ask for help, but ain't nobody ever made it through life without it. Don't let pride get in your way."

"This isn't about pride. Well, maybe it is a little. I am gonna ask for help, but it means taking a chance. I'm just gonna have to trust my instincts and maybe force a few things to go my way."

"Uh-huh, I get that. Sometimes you gotta use a big hammer and a little heat to bust things loose. Just make sure you listen to your heart. You've got a good one, son. I don't think it'll lead you wrong. In the end, that's all any of us can do."

"Will you tell Carl I love him and thanks for everything?"

"Sure, son. We love you, too. This'll all work out in time."

Tears leaked down his face at hearing Albert's calming words. Eugene fell silent for what felt like a lifetime.

"Eugene, you still there?"

"Yes, Albert, I'm here. Once I come out the other side of this mess we have to make time. I miss you and Carl and the yard, now more than ever . . . I'm gonna pull the battery on this phone to be safe. I'll call again when I can. Bye for now."

"Goodbye, Eugene. Good luck. Know our prayers are with you."

He removed the phone's battery, shoving all into his pants pocket. After reassembling the swamp cooler, he climbed from rooftop to rooftop until reaching a pair of metal handrails cresting the top of a warehouse halfway down the block. The handrails accompanied a short metal ladder meant to aid the use of an extension ladder.

With the street below clear, he used the handrails to go up and over, lowering himself with practiced ease to dangle from the lowest rung. He swung a foot to a set of metal bars protecting a window then his right hand grabbed a horizontal electrical conduit. Nimbly shifting his weight, he sidestepped on the bars until he could safely drop to a concrete landing at the building's front door. For a long moment he crouched like an alley cat, scanning the street. Neither man nor beast moved anywhere. He stood and walked toward the bridge.

The parking lights on Jack's SUV flashed. Eugene waved in return. *Okay, here's hoping nothing's off and this Jack guy says the right things.*

The SUV's motor cranked to life. The driver's side window slid down. Jack waved a beckoning arm. Eugene stopped within talking distance.

"You ready to come in and get a little help?"

"I'm willing to talk about it."

"Well, climb in and let's talk. I'm not the only one looking for you, but I am one of the few on your side."

"That was you parked across the street from the church, wasn't it?"

"Yeah."

"Why? Why just watch me?"

"To be blunt, you were Luchador bait, but things have changed. Look, it's clear the risks outweigh the rewards, so I'm switching to plan B. Climb in. I'll tell you what I can."

The metallic rattle of chain link and King's high-pitched whine drew Eugene's attention.

"All right, but first let me say goodbye to an old friend."

"Don't take long. We're exposed out here."

Eugene nodded and walked for the junkyard gate where King stood with his front paws propped on the fence.

"Hey, old buddy, hate to leave so soon, but I've got stuff to take care of." He reached through the gate to stroke the side of the big dog's head. Panting while smiling broadly, King groaned as he leaned into Eugene's touch. Soon they were forehead to muzzle. "I think I'd have been a lot better off never leaving you," said Eugene, kissing the dog's wiry-haired face. King offered a comforting lick in return. "I'll be back and we'll make time—"

Headlights appeared to the south. Eugene squinted into the twin beams coming fast under the eastern flank of the bridge.

Jack revved his engine. "That isn't good kid. Let's go," he yelled out his window.

In the heartbeat it took for Eugene to weigh the risks, the low rider screeched to a stop, cutting him off from the SUV. Even in his near panic, Eugene saw the old car was a beauty. Its pearlescent white paint gleamed and its engine idled with a satisfying, throaty note.

Calculating his escape route through the yard, Eugene scrambled up the fence. At the halfway point, King's friendly bark from below froze him in place.

"In the car! I need to see your hands, NOW!" Jack barked.

He held an assault rifle, its mounted flashlight illuminating three Hispanic males, two in the front and one in the back. The driver laid his open hands on the steering wheel. The passenger palmed the dash. The rear seat's occupant simply held his hands up to touch the car's headliner.

"No need to freak out, Dude," said the driver, turning his face to the flashlight. "We just want to check on Eugene. We're friends."

"Hang on, Jack," yelled Eugene, dropping to the ground.

"All right, but do me a favor, kid. Move to the front of the car so I have a clean field of fire."

Eugene placed himself behind the engine block and ahead of the car's inhabitants just in case things should go bad.

"Do I know you?" asked Eugene, trying to see the faces in the backlight.

"We had a run in or two around the block, back when we was kids," said the driver with a heavy Hispanic accent. He cocked his head to better see, but his open palms stayed planted firmly on the top of the steering wheel. "My name's Roberto. You won't remember me, because I could never catch you. You was pretty fast for an Anglo."

"No, can't say as I do remember you. But, half the neighborhood wanted a piece of me back then."

"You met my nephew and his friends up the street a few hours ago," said the driver, jerking his head toward the back seat.

Eugene eyed the young boy with a badly swollen face. "You here to get even?"

"Nah, not hardly. We came to apologize. *Estupido* kid came home cryin' 'cause he got his ass whipped. I told him he got what he deserved, working for them damn *chomos*."

Eugene's brow furrowed. "What's a *chomo*?"

"The *chomos*, man, those kiddie molester freaks. Word on the street is someone was willing to pay for your head. We figure it's the *chomos* because you caught one of their boys. We saw it on TV. You're like a neighborhood hero, man."

"Are you talking about the *Luchadores*?"

"That's our word," spat Roberto. "Those sick *putas* insult our culture by using that name."

"Got it," said Eugene, nodding. "Sorry."

From the far side of the car Jack barked, "Done making nice, kid?"

"You sure you want to go with that noisy *gringo*?"

"He's on my side and he's got pretty good . . . connections."

Roberto eyed the assault weapon with an envious expression. He smiled crookedly.

"Eugene, quit fucking around, Let's go," ordered Jack.

Eugene held up a hand. "Hang on. This is important. These guys are okay." He stepped up to the passenger window for a better eye-to-eye exchange. "I'm sorry for the thing with your nephew."

"Hey, it's cool. Good he learned old guys can still bite."

Still in his twenties, Eugene marveled at being called an old guy. He nodded, though remembering that in this neighborhood, closing in on thirty meant you were lucky to still be alive and out of jail.

"You know the brothers keep all your pictures," said Roberto. "They talk about you all the time."

"Carl and Albert?"

"I worked here part-time after you left."

"That explains King's happy bark."

"Yeah, us junkyard dogs, we tolerate each other." The driver smiled, nodding at the dog. "Once I grew up and got my head outta my *culo*, Carl and Albert got me into some business classes and helped me open my own shop."

"Explains your fine ride," said Eugene, smiling as he eyed the classic old Chevy. He had to blink several times to control a sudden, embarrassing urge to cry. "They're good men."

"None better. Like I said, my name's Roberto and this is my brother, Alejandro." The driver thumped his brother's chest then thumbed toward the back seat. "That sourpuss you met earlier, his name's Richie. He's still got some growing up to do. We're working on that."

Eugene stepped in to shake all three men's hands paying close attention to the young nephew, whose battered face still held a great deal of anger.

"Good to meet you, all of you," Eugene emphasized, catching the nephew's youthful confusion and hopelessness. All at once he understood Carl and Albert and Mr. Condon's heartfelt yearning to take troubled kids under their wing. "Richie, if I survive the next few weeks, I'll talk with Carl and Albert. I might have a project you can help me with in the junkyard . . . but only if you stay out of trouble."

In the front seat, Roberto winked his approval. "He'll be ready whenever you are. And if you need help, call." He held out a business card that Eugene took.

He bobbed his head toward the SUV. "Now I need to go with that noisy *gringo* before his head explodes. *Gracias y adios*. Glad we all survived the bullshit."

"*Vaya con Dios, mi amigo*," said Roberto revving the engine. The Chevy slow-rolled out from under the bridge and smoothly picked up speed heading west on Buchanan Street.

"What did he hand you?" asked Jack, finally lowering his weapon.

"Just his business card. He's an OG from the neighborhood and a friend of the Fodoni brothers."

"You mind if I snap a pic of the card?"

"Why?"

"It's not for the cops if that's what you're worried about."

Eugene held out the card. Jack took a photo with his phone.

"You know them?"

"Yeah, sorta. They came to apologize. That kid in the back seat was one of the kids we tangled with earlier."

Jack raised an eyebrow. "How'd you know they weren't here to finish the job?"

"My dog's happy bark."

Jack and Eugene glanced at the huge dog, ragged but regal as it stood stretched out with its front paws on the fence.

"Dogs always know, don't they?" said Jack.

"I'll take a dog over a human any day." Eugene shifted his feet. "So, why am I off the hook? What changed?"

"Schaefer confessed to the rapes and the cops uncovered a picture of the Ass Clown so I'm guessing they've lost interest in you."

"Wait. What do you mean, *the* Ass Clown?"

"I guess you haven't heard. Ass Clown is a Luchador. The cops have a picture of him. Apparently Condon had some negatives no one knew about."

"Jesus, now it all makes sense. That's what he was trying to tell me. Guess they've got bigger things to worry about than me right now. What the hell else have I missed?"

"I'll explain once we're moving."

"Jack, my friends said the *Luchadores* had a hit out on me."

"Yeah, they probably do. C'mon, let's get out of here."

Eugene climbed in the SUV, relishing the air conditioning as he slid into the cool leather seat. The cab light dimmed then went out when he closed his door. Jack's unshaven face looked tired in the glow of his Smartphone as he dialed a number.

"Hey, buddy, it's me. I've got him . . . Uh-huh, sorry to wreck your beauty sleep, but I figured you'd want to know . . . What? When did that happen? . . . Shit, he'll be a sitting duck over there . . . Well, there's nothing we can do about it now. Hey, we're gonna hole up and grab some shut-eye. Call me if you hear anything."

After Jack stowed his phone, Eugene asked, "What happened?"

"Stupid bastards transferred Schaefer to Maricopa County. He's no longer in Scottsdale."

A shiver coursed Eugene's back. "They'll kill him in there."

"Maybe, but that's out of our control." Jack dropped the SUV into drive and pulled from under the bridge, his eyes constantly scanning their surroundings.

"I'm sorry about Sandy."

"You two date for long?"

Grateful for the darkness hiding his embarrassment, he said, "We dated here and there. Friends for sure, but I don't think either of us imagined ourselves as a couple."

"You told the police you left before sunrise and that you saw nothing suspicious. Have you thought of anything since then?"

"No, I remember the sprinklers came on. I remember I was relieved to see one of us had locked my Jeep. She drove since I was pretty drunk."

"She lock her front door when you left?"

"I locked it. She . . . Well, she—"

"She stayed in bed. I get it," said Jack. "Can't say as I really want to talk about that right now." Jack's hands tightened on the steering wheel. "Wait. It could be important. Was she seeing anybody else?"

"Not that I know of. But I hadn't been to the Prickly for maybe a couple of months."

"Did she say anything before you left?"

Shame flooded in and with it, tears welled. "She said, 'Will you call?'"

Eugene glanced at Jack's flexing jaw. The words every man who'd ever played the one-night-stand game dreaded, "Will you call," hung heavy in the air. "I kissed her and tucked her in, said I'd be by the bar after work . . . She looked really happy . . . Jack, I swear I never hurt her."

"Did I say you did?" snapped Jack.

"No, but—"

"I've seen the pictures. Whoever killed her is a special kind of evil. Trust me, I've met evil and you ain't it."

Eugene reeled at the thought of the crime scene. Forcing the images from his mind, he closed his eyes then shook his head as he slumped into the seat. "God, I'm tired of this bullshit."

"Yeah, me, too," Jack said, turning left onto Grant Street.

Eugene jerked up straighter. He grabbed the dash and peered out the windshield. "Are those townhouses? Where are the projects?"

"Don't know if they're apartments or what. Pretty sure it's still low-income housing, though. How long since you talked to your mom?"

His fingertips tightened on the dash. "Years. Did you ask because she lives here in—"

"No, sorry to get your hopes up. A friend of mine tracked her down. She's squatting in an abandoned house. It's not far."

"Your friend say if she was still a drunk?"

"She is. Can't blame you for wanting to stay away. My brother Chris is on that same track."

"Shit. I keep forgetting you're brothers. All of us at the paper worry about him. Hell of a talented guy, but he never got over losing his wife. And now Sandy . . . uh . . . Has the funeral happened yet?"

Jack's sigh was audible. "Tomorrow morning."

Sorrow and regret knifed at Eugene's chest. "I keep saying it, but, God, I *am* sorry. How's Chris doing?"

"Not well."

"When this is over I'd like to—"

"You can talk to him tonight. We're headed for his place."

Eugene's mouth opened but no words came out. Jack glanced over, the weary look on his face indicating he wouldn't listen to any objections.

"Ah, okay . . . but—"

"Think about it. Where's the last place anyone would look for you?"

"Oh, well. Yeah, uh, that would be it."

They passed through the intersection of 7th Avenue and Grant. Eugene's mind lost focus as he looked out at the industrial wasteland.

"Thinking you should have stayed in hiding?" asked Jack.

Eugene rubbed his forehead and the still sore, but shrinking knot. "A little. I guess I'll have to face Chris sometime. Might as well get it over with."

Jack nodded, keeping his eyes on the road. Eugene looked out at the high rises of Phoenix's downtown. "Did your mystery man say which jail Schaefer was taken to?"

"4th Avenue."

"So, he's in one of those buildings right over there, right now."

"Yep. Psych ward from what I was told. Seems he had a little melt down just before he confessed."

"Oh, Christ. Really?"

"Yeah . . . Hey, sorry. I forgot you two are brothers. If you—"

"No, it's all right. We're only half brothers and I never knew him."

"Still."

"Nah, don't worry about it. Um, I hate to be rude, but I can barely keep my eyes open, mind if I . . . ."

"Go for it. I see a nap in my own future."

Eugene slumped down in the seat and closed his eyes. In seconds he was out.

20

The all-too-familiar stench of stale cigarettes made Pete Cunningham's skin crawl as he stepped into the lobby of the Bali Hi truck stop motel. Midnight brought a whole new level of sleaze to this stretch of Grand Avenue. He knew the biggest sleaze of all, State Patrol Detective Clyde Wrigley, hadn't chosen it by chance. It was here that seven years earlier Wrigley had snared him in a prostitution sting.

After being cuffed and led back to the bed in room 210 of the Bali Hi, Pete had nervously explained that his being in the room with a prostitute was all just a terrible misunderstanding. He was at the motel not for sex, but simply to do research into the dark underworld of sex trafficking exposed by the Luchador case. Wrigley had listened, straight-faced and full of concern. When Pete had finished talking, Wrigley produced a small laptop and fired up a high-def surveillance video.

Pete remembered cringing at the sight of his goofy smile, the bulge in his pants, the money exchange and the awkward small talk that lasted only seconds before the long-legged hooker knelt, unfastened his jeans and planted her lips on his cock. He came within seconds. "Turn it off!" Pete had screamed.

Wrigley had smiled. "Wait, here comes the best part."

In the clarity of high-def, Pete saw the hooker turn to the camera and spit his semen on the floor. "Good gawd, that's sexy as hell," he heard himself say just before the hooker stood and pulled out her own dick. Pete had shrieked like a little girl, pushed the he-she aside and raced from the room, straight into the waiting arms of Detective Wrigley.

Pushing down the awful memory, Pete walked through the motel's dingy lobby and into the near-empty bar. A fat little bartender stood with his back to the door while he watched a Sienfeld rerun.

"Hey, if someone comes in looking for Pete, tell them I'm in the cafe," he called out.

The fat man gave him a thumbs-up without turning around.

Pete strolled down a hall with threadbare carpet into a dingy cafe and took a seat well away from the windows. He ordered coffee and apple pie. Wrigley appeared as the waitress returned with a coffee pot.

Detective Wrigley was a heavyset man who bulged out of his cheap suit. Everything about him was over-sized, from his sausage fingers to his big, bald head ringed by a monk-like fluff of gray hair.

"Can I get you something?" asked the waitress.

Wrigley squeezed into the booth, mumbling, "Coffee with cream." His wide, ruddy face sagged with fatigue. When the waitress was out of earshot, he huffed, "What the fuck happened with Condon and why didn't you tell me about the negatives?"

"How long is this nightmare going to continue?" snapped Pete. "I thought we were done."

The waitress returned with Wrigley's coffee and a small bowl of creamers. "Anything else?" she asked.

"I'm good," crooned Wrigley, maintaining eye contact with Pete.

"Hon, you want your pie warmed up, maybe a little ice cream on top?"

He finally glanced at her. "No thanks, just the pie. No need to nuke it."

As the waitress headed for the pie cooler, Wrigley plucked a creamer from the bowl, peeled back the foil then squeezed it so the thick liquid came out in little squirts. He smiled. "Gawd, that's sexy as hell, isn't it?"

Disgusted, Pete rolled his eyes and gritted his teeth. "What happened to Condon was a horrible accident. And as for the negatives, nobody knew about them."

Wrigley cocked his head. "All I ask for is a little cooperation, Pete. It's not like we're talking about revealing your Deep Throat source here." He sipped his coffee. "Besides you owe me." He added more squirts from his creamer, obviously enjoying his oral sex reference.

Pete held up a hand. “This is all just a big joke to you, isn’t it?”

Coffee to his lips, Wrigley froze. His eyes darkened as he set down the cup. “This ain’t a joke. Knowing about those negatives might’ve saved a few kids a whole hell of a lot of misery. You know damn well those sick bastards never stopped.”

“I told you I didn’t know about the negatives. And, given your department’s corruption problem, I can’t blame Condon for keeping what he had under wraps.”

Wrigley settled back in the booth. “That corruption problem was *one* guy. Ibarra. And we got rid of him. From what I hear, your paper has got its own problems in the corruption department, my *friend*.”

“What are you talking about?”

“Fellig. Who do you think? The more I sniff around that white-trash piece of shit, the worse he smells.”

“We’re on it,” said Pete. “Read the morning paper. Wait, is that why you wanted to meet in this shit hole? Just to bust my balls about Fellig and the missing negatives?”

“Nah, what I really want to know is how that hit piece on Ibarra is coming along.”

“Jesus Christ, you just won’t let go of that, will you. I told you I got a lot of push-back on that because we had already reported his questionable resignation when Scottsdale hired him. Until recently, the newsroom consensus has been that it’d be overkill to rehash the issue.”

“Until recently? Does that mean it’s a go?”

“I’m saying it’s a *maybe* and it’d be facts, not a hit piece. You know a little inside info is one thing. I can’t let you dictate my paper’s editorial content just because you have a hard-on for Ibarra.”

“I see your point.” Wrigley smiled then sneered. “But it’s *your* hard-on that put you in this position. Speaking of hard-ons, I hear the internet is full of ‘em. Hidden camera shit’s popular as hell, if you get my drift.”

“Really? You hate him that much that you’d resort to straight-up blackmail?”

Wrigley choked on his coffee. For a second Pete thought the big oaf might be having a seizure until red-faced, he coughed out, “Ah, hey, no. This is way better than blackmail. This is . . . it's . . . it's black *she-male* . . . Get it?"

Pete sat back with a grimmace.

A fit of laughter erupted from Wrigley. "Ah, hah-hah-heh. And-and with both your dicks out . . . you-you looked anything but straight. Oh gawd, I should write this shit down . . . ."

A look of deathly seriousness curtained down the big man's huge face. He leaned forward and under his breath said, "Fuck your pushback. No more maybes. With Condon gone, you're the boss. Ibarra's ugly mug and a story on page one or your double-dick date ends up on the you-tubes."

Pete crumbled. "I already wrote the damn story, asshole. It's running tomorrow . . . but don't think you had anything to do with it. It's a public service."

Wrigley waved a hand in the air. "Hey, whatever helps you sleep at night."

"I sleep like a baby. In fact, I should be sleeping right now. Are we done?"

"Not quite."

Wrigley shifted in the booth just as the waitress arrived with the pie. "Here you go, sweetie." She slid the little plate to the table with one hand while pouring coffee with the other. "You sure you don't want anything else, Clyde?"

Pete blanched. S*hit! Of course she knows him and what he does. Fuck me.*

"No, darlin'. I'm good. Just need a few more minutes with my old friend Pete."

"Old friend? Hell, he looks young enough to be your grandson."

Pete forced a laugh, "Not hardly."

"You picking up the tab, Clyde, or are you gonna cheap out as usual?"

"I'll take it, darlin'. Why don't you go write me up and I'll meet you at the register in a minute or two."

"Sure thing, and don't be cheapskate on the tip," she said and sauntered her big-boned hips toward the front counter.

"Tip hell, darlin'," Wrigley called out. "I'll give you the whole thing."

Pete cringed at Wrigley's low-brow dance with the waitress.

She snarked back over her shoulder, "I ain't never heard that one before."

Wrigley brightened, turning his attention back to Pete. "So, how're the new owners treating you? Seems like every other day I see a story about layoffs in the news business."

"Just fine. Already got a bump in pay and I expect my interim status will be made permanent this week, so I can't complain."

"Well then, Condon's untimely demise worked out pretty well for you . . . Funny how a few peanut crumbs cleared the way for you to rise to the top."

"Just what are you accusing me of?"

"Me? Nothing, but I'd watch out for Ibarra. He ain't the sharpest knife in the drawer, but I wouldn't put it past him to try to pin something on you."

"Then my *hit piece,* as you call it, will be well timed."

Wrigley smiled as he pulled a five from his wallet and dropped it to the table. "Now you're thinking like a pro. See? This wasn't so bad. I got a little something, you got a little something, and we both go away happy. I call this meeting of the great minds adjourned."

Wrigley hauled himself from the booth. Pete forked into his pie as the detective tapped his sausage fingers on the table with "See ya."

"Not if I see you first," Pete quipped sarcastically.

* * *

The blare of a siren yanked Eugene from his short nap. They were at 7th Street, driving up the slow rise of the bridge over the railroad tracks. Jack pulled to the curb to let an engine company roar past.

"What the hell's going on?"

"Hang on. I'll see if I can pick something up."

Jack reached into an overhead console to turn on a police scanner. The usual chatter crisscrossed the airwaves until they pulled into traffic. Finally, the scanner latched onto a fire channel as the engine and squad that had just passed them by reported their arrival on the scene.

At the crest of the bridge, traffic slowed to a crawl. Red flares blocked both north and southbound traffic on 7th Street. Beyond the flares a firefighter sprayed foam on a jack-knifed semi-tractor-trailer that had broadsided a minivan. A police officer stood in the intersection, circling his flashlight, directing traffic onto Jefferson. Two other officers, one with a canine, stood at the corner, looking into the passing cars, directing some to pull over for closer inspection.

Three sharp warning tones on the scanner preceded a male dispatcher's voice, "ALL UNITS, THIS IS A REBROADCAST—ESCAPEE IS A DEREK SCHAEFER, TWENTY-SIX YEARS, FIVE-NINE, ONE-HUNDRED-SEVENTY POUNDS, BROWN AND GREEN, LAST SEEN EXITING THE WEST ENTRANCE TO THE 4th AVENUE JAIL WEARING BLUE DISPOSABLES."

"Holy fuck! You think this accident is part of that?"

Jack didn't answer.

"Shit, they're checking cars. What do we do?"

"Are you wearing blue disposables?"

"No, but—"

"Then just chill. They aren't looking for you. You got your ID on you just in case?"

"Yeah, but there's a warrant—"

"They've got bigger things to worry about."

As they turned the corner onto Jefferson, the canine officer aimed his flashlight into their vehicle.

Jack slowed and rolled down his window. "Hey, officer, what the heck happened?"

Eugene felt a flashlight beam wash over him. He kept his head craned to the accident, turning to the light only at the last possible second, squinting and irritated, one hand up to block the light beam and hide the damage to his face.

"Keep it moving," barked the cop on Jack's side, waving them on.

"All right, all right," Jack said, shaking his head and rolling off slowly.

Eugene hauled in a deep breath then let it out through pursed lips.

The much calmer Jack pulled his phone and dialed. "Have you heard? Schaefer's escaped . . . Hell, I don't know how. I'm assuming the Luchadores had something to do with it. We just passed a helluva car accident not far from the jail. Don't know if—Okay, call me when you know more. Eugene and I are heading back to Scottsdale."

Eugene shot upright. "SHIT! did you see that?"

"No, what?"

"Out your side. Check your mirror. I think I saw him."

"Saw who?"

"Schaefer."

"You're shittin' me."

"No, I swear I saw something. Back by that church, near some bushes. Turn back and hurry."

"Hold your horses. I gotta do it nice and easy. No need to attract attention."

They hit 10th Street by the time Jack navigated across the five lanes of the one-way street and circled back. The SUV rolled slowly south on 8th.

"Up there. A little further. There, between the brick wall and the bushes."

"Still don't see it," said Jack.

"Just pull over. I'll get out and look—"

"You stay put. I'll check." Jack shut off the engine, pulled the key and exited, crossing in front of the truck to the sidewalk, ambling, then quick-stepping toward the bushes. The SUV's back hatch popped open as Jack thumbed the key fob and motioned for Eugene to come and help.

Five seconds later Eugene stood over a bloody and battered Derek Schaefer. "Is he still alive?"

"Yeah. Got a pulse. Bad gash on his head. Wait. Gunshot wound, small caliber. Hell, here's another. Shit! Grab his feet."

"Shouldn't we call 9-1-1?"

"Think, kid! Better nobody knows we have him. I have a friend, a trained trauma medic. He'll patch him up."

As gently as speed allowed, they slid Schaefer into the back of the SUV. "Get in. If he fights, hold him."

Schaefer's eyes flashed open, his terror obvious. He sent a weak punch in Jack's direction.

"Quit fighting," said Eugene.

Derek focused on him, "Hey, that you, paparazzi brother? Gonna put me on the front page again?" His eyes rolled back and he was out.

"Climb in, kid. We gotta get moving."

Eugene crawled up and pinned Schaefer's arms. Jack held up a pair of plastic zip ties.

"Put his hands together."

When Derek's hands and feet were bound, Jack shot Eugene a hard look. "He wakes up and tries to fight, you subdue him."

"Uh, yeah, sure. I can do that," Eugene replied, staring at his unconscious half-brother. *This is weird as fuck.*

As Jack steered back onto Jefferson, the SUV passed streetlights that offered slow, strobe-like flashes of his half brother's wounded face. His attention flicked between face and chest, checking that he was still breathing. Curiosity and pity alternated in Eugene's thoughts, followed by anger at what Derek had done to his victims.

Oliver Condon's voice came into his mind, loud and clear. "PROVIDENCE FAVORS THE OPEN MIND, EUGENE."

The authenticity of it chilled him. Eugene shook his head, wondering if he might be delirious. When he glanced back to Schaefer, he saw an innocent child.

Oliver's voice returned, "KINDNESS KILLS EVIL."

In that instant he understood why Condon and the brothers had devoted their lives to helping others. Warmth and certainty washed over him. He knew somewhere, in some other world, Condon was watching and smiling.

* * *

Jack pulled into the driveway of an older, ranch-style home not far from South Mountain Park. Through the windshield Eugene saw a compact man in a t-shirt and jeans swing open a chain link gate and point to an open garage behind the house. Jack pulled in and the overhead door lowered on their sanctuary.

As Jack popped open the rear hatch, the man flicked on a bright, hand-held work lamp. "Some retirement, Jack. What the hell are you in to?"

"Hop out, Eugene, and give Terry room to work."

The man set a large, military medic's pack in his place. A folding knife appeared in the man's hand. The flick of the spring-loaded blade brought Derek to life. Panicked, he yelled and thrust his tied hands out as if to fend off what he clearly thought was an attack.

"Whoa-whoa-whoa, son. We're the good guys," the medic said calmly, stepping back as Eugene jumped forward to grab his brother's hands and attention. The medic looked at Jack. "We are the good guys here, right?"

Jack nodded. "You watch the news or read a paper, Terry?"

"No, it's all liberal bullshit anyway. Why bother?"

"Then you haven't heard. Someone murdered my niece. They just tried to do the same to this guy, but I got to him before they could finish the job. If you can patch him up, he might be able to help us take them down."

The two men held eye contact a long moment, as well as Derek and Eugene's attention.

"Well, then I'd better get to work," Terry finally said. He looked at Derek, holding up the knife. "If you're cool with that, I need to cut your jewelry."

Derek nodded and held out his hands as Eugene once again moved out of the way. Terry reached in to slice through the plastic then set about cutting away the papery suit. He ended up on his knees beside his patient, grunting and sweating. The grimacing Derek twisted and lifted to aid him in counting holes.

"Once you get him stabilized, Gracie can do the rest."

Terry huffed and wiped his brow. "Whoa, Amazing Gracie's on the case?"

Jack smiled and nodded.

"Then I better make this pretty or I'll never hear the end of it. Kid, you ever been shot before?"

"No."

"Could have fooled me. First time Jack took a bullet he got all shocky and scared. You're holding up a shitload better than he did."

Jack scoffed then crossed his arms. Derek buoyed at the slanted praise. His last bits of worry slipped from his face. He even exchanged a quick smile with Eugene.

Terry talked as his hands adeptly worked. "Of course, Jack took four bullets and you only took three, so there's that."

Both Eugene and Derek turned a respectful gaze to Jack who rolled his eyes.

"On the surface, looks like you're one lucky son of a bitch." Terry prodded around the entrance wound near his armpit then its exit at his back. "Any trouble catching your breath?"

"No, but it hurts like a motherfucker," croaked Derek.

"Be glad that's all it is," the medic said, pointing to Derek's ribs. "An inch either way or more direct and you'd a been in a world of hurt. As it is, the bullet probably only cracked a rib as it glanced off."

"How about the shoulder and leg?" asked Jack.

"Through and throughs in the muscle. No big whoop. I'll plug 'em and patch 'em, but what gives me the most concern, Derek, is that big, lumpy gash on your head. One eye's a little slow to respond. You've got a helluva headache, right?" Derek barely nodded. "He needs to be sitting up to reduce the pressure in his head. Can one of you drop the back seat forward a little?"

"Got it," said Jack

"Eugene, there's a bag of ice in my beer fridge over there and a box of zip-lock bags in the second workbench drawer. Can you grab them?"

Eugene jumped into action. Soon they had Derek propped at a forty-five degree angle with a plastic bag full of ice bandaged to his head.

"There, that'll do nicely," said Terry. "Now, let's plug those still leaking holes."

"Derek, you feel up to answering some questions?" asked Jack.

"First, answer one for me."

"If I can."

"Who the fuck *are* you?"

"I'm the guy who saved your ass, for starters. Plus, I'm the uncle of the girl Eugene is accused of killing."

Derek's eyes widened in surprise. He looked at his brother.

"He knows it was the Luchadores and not me," Eugene reassured him.

Derek looked back at Jack. "You gonna kill them?"

Jack shrugged. "Only if I have no other choice. Now, how about giving me some answers."

"Shoot, big man."

"Were you in that accident on 7th Street?"

"Yeah, never saw the truck coming. Fucking cab driver picked me up in front of the jail, We drove off then he shot me."

"Don't suppose he mentioned who sent him."

"No, tried to talk all friendly like, but it felt squirrely."

"How'd you get out of the jail?"

"Guard showed up with paperwork. I was processed and walked out the door."

"Guard have a name?"

"If he had a tag on his shirt, I didn't see it."

"What did he look like, White, black, Chinese?"

"White guy, brown hair, average everything else. He wore glasses."

"Could you tell if he was right or left handed?"

Derek thought for a moment, "He kept the paperwork in his left hand, wrote with his right."

"Did you talk?"

"He did most of the talkin'. Said to put on the paper suit and follow him. I thought I was going to a shrink, but the paperwork he had cut me loose."

Derek grunted with pain as Terry lifted a leg to wrap a bandage.

"Leg or ribs?" asked Terry.

"Ribs. Hurts like a bitch."

"I'll wrap 'em with an Ace bandage, but it won't help much. First, I need to plug your shoulder."

Derek nodded, closed his eyes a moment as if collecting himself, then looked at Jack, "What happens to me after you pick my brain?"

"I won't lie to you," said Jack. "You'll have to answer for what you did."

Eugene inserted, “If you help us take down the Luchadores maybe there’ll be a deal.”

“Sure,” said Derek with a fatalistic note.

“You ready to wrap those ribs?” asked the medic.

“Let’s do it.”

* * *

In Scottsdale, Jack circled the block twice then parked on the street to survey the sleepy neighborhood. Satisfied that all was clear, he backed into the driveway of Chris Carter’s bungalow home. A living room lamp glowed warm through a front window. Jack dialed his cell phone.

“I’m coming in. Everything quiet? . . . All right. See you in a few. I’ve got company . . . The photographer plus one. And, Gracie, the plus one is Schaefer.”

Eugene heard Gracie’s loud protests. Jack merely sighed.

“No choice, hon. He’s in bad shape. I’ll tell you more once we’re inside.”

Sitting in the back with his brother, watching Jack in the rearview mirror, Eugene saw exhaustion do a slow dance on Jack’s square, unshaven face.

“Chris isn’t going to kill me or anything is he?” he called from the back.

Jack turned to steer a weary look Eugene’s direction. “Frankly, he talks a good story but doesn’t have the balls. I’m more worried about Gracie. She may just kill us all. And she has the skills to do it.”

When he pressed a button on the dash, the rear hatch opened. Jack exited and stepped to the back to eye his passengers. “How’s the head?” he said to Derek.

“Hurts like a bitch but I’m not as dizzy. This is warmer than piss now.” He slid the ice bag and its wrap off over the neat bandage.

“You got your bell rung pretty good. Been there. It’s no fun. At least you’re awake and making sense. Eugene, you ready?”

“Yeah, let’s get this over with. I need to set things straight with Chris.”

“Well, that’ll have to wait. Apparently he’s incommunicado for the moment.”

"No surprise there. So, your wife's name is Gracie?"

"Yeah, Graciela. A woman who deserves a lot better than me and my miserable family." He drew himself up as if assuming a new level of seriousness. "Listen you two, once we're inside, don't make waves. You'll understand when you meet her." He pointed a meaningful finger at them. "Treat her with respect."

"Understood," said Eugene.

"It's not you I'm worried about. Derek, pardon my blunt edge, but if you run your mouth to her, she'll ring your bell all over again. If she doesn't, I will."

"No problem, dude. I'll play nice."

"Not what I want to hear, *dude.* You won't *play* anything. You will *be* nice."

Derek's eyes blanked as his shoulders slumped, "Yes, sir," he said meekly, his voice instantly sounding years younger.

Jack and Eugene exchanged a quick questioning glance at the sudden personality shift.

Eugene scooted forward to crawl out.

Jack studied Derek. "You able to walk?"

"Yeah, I think so, but . . . I need some pants to cover my underwear."

"How about a blanket? I saw one up front," said Eugene, "I'll grab it."

Derek tightened his lips and rolled forward, "Darn it that hurts," he said, wrapping a hand on his left ribs.

Jack leaned in. "Here, at least let me lift—"

"No, I'll do it."

"Derek, we don't have time for slow. I'll help lift you out then you can try to walk." Jack slid one arm under Derek's naked legs.

Derek went rigid and rolled off, "Don't touch me, you fuckin' perv!"

Jack jerked back, blinking in surprise. "Calm down! You do it, but let's hurry. And keep it down. There are neighbors. Eugene, where's the blanket?"

Silent, in spite of what had to be excruciating pain, Derek scooted forward, hung his legs over the tailgate, set his good leg on the ground and stood. After his first wobbly step, he didn't object to Eugene and Jack each shouldering an armpit as they wrapped the blanket around his waist. Together they hobbled him to the porch, up the steps and to the front door. Jack fumbled for his key but a short, curvy, dark-haired woman swung the door open.

She eyed the threesome as they side-stepped in. "Jesus Christ, Jack! What's going on?"

He didn't answer until they lowered Derek to the living room couch. When Gracie's assessing eyes landed on him, Derek cowered like scared dog and pulled the blanket up to cover his exposed skin.

"Luchadores got him out of jail and tried to kill him." Jack had his woman's attention. "Terry patched him up. Three through and throughs at shoulder, right calf, and left chest that probably busted a rib. Signs of a concussion, but the vitals were good on last check."

Gracie went into action, sitting on the couch next to Derek, "Look at me," she ordered. Derek complied. "I was a critical care nurse for many years. There's nothing I haven't seen. Now I need to check you over. You will *not* argue."

In silence, Derek met her eyes, squinted momentarily then nodded. He awkwardly unwrapped the blanket.

"Thank you, Derek. Jack, go get my medical bag from our bedroom, then find him some clothes."

Jack obediently complied.

"I take it you are Eugene," Gracie said, keeping her eyes on her patient as she placed fingers to his wrist then looked at her wristwatch.

"Yes, ma'am. Nice to meet you."

"Mmm-hmm," Gracie murmured.

Jack returned with a blue nylon bag, a t-shirt and a pair of sweat pants.

"Put it on the couch, Jack. Hand me your flashlight." Jack fired the light and placed it into her outstretched hand. She flicked the beam in and out of Derek's eyes. "One's a little slow. How did you hurt your head?"

"Car wreck." said Jack.

Gracie held up a hand. "Let *him* tell me. Derek, you still have the ability to speak, correct?"

Derek tried to dodge her intense gaze but failed. "Car wreck," he mumbled, tucking the blanket back around his middle.

She held up her hand. "How many fingers?"

"Two."

When she asked, he accurately answered the city and date.

"Sick to your stomach?"

"No."

"Your hair and the bandage are wet. Did you have ice on it?"

"Yes."

"Is there a cut under that bandage, something that may need stitches?"

"That Terry guy didn't say so."

"Well, then I suggest you rest and avoid moving your head." As she talked, she pressed fingers into the bend of the arm below the bandaged shoulder then opened the bottom of the blanket to check over his bandaged leg. "No sleeping. Eugene, you're in charge of watching him. Jack, find a bag of frozen something in Chris' freezer for his head. Loose vegetables would work."

Eugene smiled at Gracie's crisp command of her warrior husband.

Jack hesitated. "Gracie? Where is Chris?"

"On the kitchen floor. You'll probably have to step over him to get to the fridge. I couldn't stop him from drinking, so I let him drink till he passed out. With any luck the asshole choked to death on his own vomit."

"I'm sorry, hon. I'll handle him from now on. Tomorrow, after the funeral, you can head back home. Jeff's coming down to drive you back. Better safe than sorry. When you're ready I'll bring you up to speed on what's happened."

"That would be nice for a *change*." Her sarcasm made Eugene cringe and froze Jack in place. "Eugene, the bathroom is down the hall on the left. You need a shower and I need to talk to my husband."

"I thought I had to watch—"

"I'll stay awake," Derek jumped in.

Gracie flicked them a stern glance. She honed in on Eugene. "Take what clothes you need from Chris' bedroom. He's quite a bit larger than you but do what you can."

"Yes, ma'am, and thank you," said Eugene, heading toward the hall, still marveling at the little woman's commanding presence.

"Eugene," Graciela called, stopping him in his tracks, "according to the news, you may have murdered Jack's niece. Can I trust that this is not the case?"

"Yes, ma'am."

"Go on then. Jack and I will adjourn to the dining room for a little talk. Derek, can you get dressed on your own?"

"Yes, ma'am."

Eugene glanced at Jack, who looked like a middle schooler awaiting a visit to the principal's office. He tried for a sympathetic smile but ended up only shaking his head and continuing on down the hall.

After grabbing a Prickly Pearadise t-shirt from Chris' closet he went in search of pants, but found nothing even close to his size. The quest for underwear proved more successful. Pulling open a dresser drawer, he found two packages of Fruit of the Loom briefs, oversized for sure, but untouched by Chris' nether regions. The removal of the briefs revealed several framed photos placed face down in the drawer. He dared to look and got punched in the gut. Teenage Sandy with Chris and his wife along with others of Sandy as a grown up. *Probably couldn't stand the constant reminder*. He very carefully replaced them. His chest aching slightly, he grabbed socks, closed the drawers then headed for the bathroom.

Never had a shower felt so good. Seeing the street crud pool and slip down the drain lifted a giant weight from his shoulders. He dialed in the hottest water he could stand and let it massage his sore back. Meditating on the night's events, he smiled remembering Roberto and Richie under the bridge. *"You're like a neighborhood hero,"* Roberto had said. Eugene didn't remember the guy from his younger years, but back then he seemed to be on the run from everyone.

Stepping from the shower and still lost in thought, he toweled off. The fogged-over mirror sobered him. He wiped the moisture away and got the first solid look at his battered face. A scab had formed where he'd collided with the newsprint. The swelling around his eye—courtesy of Freddie—had disappeared. The bruise was now heading toward a greenish yellow. A shave would have been nice.

Seeing no disposable razors, he decided he'd intruded enough and emerged from the bathroom feeling like a new man.

Graciela and Jack sat in separate chairs opposite the couch where Derek rested quietly. Two bags of frozen peas hugged his head.

Gracie smiled and nodded. "Well that's an improve—"

A crash in the kitchen interrupted her. Jack leaped from his chair and loped toward the noise with Gracie close behind. Eugene brought up the rear.

Wearing only his underwear, Chris sat on the ceramic tile floor, banging his head against the kitchen cabinets. Obviously knocked from the counter, broken plates littered the floor around him.

"What the hell is wrong with you?" growled Jack, grabbing the distraught man by the shoulders, his boots crunching on the ceramic pieces.

Chris's blood-shot eyes looked up at Jack. "Did you fuck him up good? Is he dead?"

"Hell, no. Now, quit—"

The heavy-set man struggled against the restraining hands. "Then what good are you? Jack Carter, the big poser, the big fucking deal—"

Graciela grabbed a saucepan from the kitchen table. Before Eugene realized what she had planned, water hit Chris square in the face. The saucepan followed, hitting him on the chest before clanging on the kitchen floor, ringing as it spun to a stop. Chris stared at her in stunned silence.

"Get your alcoholic ass off that floor and start acting like a man!" she ordered.

Chris grabbed for the pan. Jack moved to block him. Instead of launching it as a projectile, Chris violently wretched into it.

"Is there a mop?" Jack asked.

Graciela's fierce gaze swung to him. He held up his hands in surrender. "Hold your fire. Hon, I, ah . . . ." He cracked a smile, obviously regretting it the instant it escaped.

"The mop is in the closet. Stick it up your ass for all I care." She turned and stormed from the room, practically running over Eugene.

He flattened himself against the wall just in time. Seeing she wasn't going to turn back, he quietly set about picking up the broken plates.

Jack squatted to eye level with his now panting brother. "Get this straight. Eugene here did *not* kill Sandy. That's a fact. Get used to it. I'm gonna need his help to catch the bastards that did."

Chris lifted his head, stared at Eugene with watery, red eyes. They narrowed as he snarled, "Bullshit."

Jack planted a wide hand on his chest. "Look at *me*. You always said you wanted to be a hero. Well, now's your chance. Sandy's funeral is tomorrow morning. Be a—"

Chris again wretched into the pan then blew spittle from his lips, his whole frame shuddering.

"Did you hear me?" Jack shook his brother's shoulder. "Your daughter's funeral is in the morning. You will be there and you will at least appear to be sober. Now, get your ass off this floor. Clean yourself up. I'll start some coffee. Eugene, I'll deal with my brother's mess. You go watch your own damn brother like Gracie ordered. I'll be out there in a minute."

Eugene followed the no-nonsense orders, padding to the living room. Derek, still resting quietly, watched as he shuffled by to take a seat at the far end of the couch.

The silence thickened. Eugene sighed. "From what I hear, we have the same father."

"Yup," said Derek, taking the frozen vegetable bags from his head, then setting them on the arm of the couch. "I don't need this bullshit, no matter what that woman said."

"Really? How're ya feeling?"

Derek glared at him. "Screaming headache. How about you?"

"I feel better now that I've had a shower."

"What was he like?" demanded Derek.

"Dad?"

"Yeah."

"He was a lying, cheating, jerk, but not near as bad as what you had to deal with."

"How do you know about that?"

"I've heard and read a few things." When Derek's eyes blanked and he stared off into space, Eugene held up his hands. "Hey, sorry—"

"Shut up. Don't want no pity. Ma and the guy I thought was my Pa weren't near as bad as my foster parents." He studied Eugene a long moment. "What did our dad look like?"

"Short, heavyset, brownish hair, but kinda balding. Why?"

"Tryin' to figure out if I ever saw him. We had lots of regulars."

Taken aback, Eugene swallowed to steady himself. "My . . . I mean, our dad cheated on my mom a lot."

"My Pa was a scrapper," said Derek. "Did you have anything worth scrappin'?"

The pieces came together for Eugene in a heartbeat. "Cardboard, lots of cardboard. Did your pa have an old Ford that blew a lot of smoke?"

"Yeah, that was us," said Derek. "We had a regular cardboard stop there for as long as I can remember, like every couple a weeks." Derek frowned. "You had a big dog, didn't you?"

"Yeah, King, a big Shepherd mix. He's getting older, but he's still around. He's been living with the Fodoni brothers since I left."

Derek nodded once then held his forehead a moment, eyes closed. "I remember those guys. They chased us off once or twice."

"I read that your dad passed away. Is your mom still alive?"

"She's in Yuma prison, last I heard. Didn't deserve it. She was kinda slow and Pa would beat on her if she didn't earn her keep. I was glad to start helpin' her out. Know what I mean?"

Silence again reigned. Derek retrieved the now half-thawed peas and placed them back on his head. Eugene thought he looked like he was contemplating a decision.

Out of the blue, Derek blurted, "I raped and beat on 'em 'cause I thought they deserved it."

"You don't have to—"

"Bullshit. You know you want to ask."

"Okay, since you seem to want to tell me. How could you think they deserved it?"

Derek stared at the floor, blinking as if he were assembling his thoughts. "Maybe deserved ain't the right word. Ever been to the dark side?"

"What do you mean?" Eugene asked, already knowing the answer.

"Ever been so mad it felt good to hurt?"

He waited until Derek looked him in the eye. "Yeah, I've hurt people and enjoyed it, but only when I was pushed into a rage."

Derek frowned. "Rage *is* kinda how it starts . . . but, then it feels so good to have the power." He looked away. "Well, once you let it out . . . Well . . . It felt like I was *owed* the pleasure."

Eugene lowered his voice. "You let the dark take control."

"Yeah. Yeah, and it felt good."

Derek sat up, suddenly looking older, stronger and even a bit frightening.

"I know all about the dark." Eugene hurried on, "I have it in me. In fact, I think we all do. Everybody. But letting it have control . . . that's when it costs you . . . I think you know that now."

Derek's shoulders slumped and the childish expression returned. "Yeah, I know. I really didn't have much to lose, anyway." He looked around, uneasy, maybe even fearful. His voice dropped to a whisper, "You don't think that lady heard us, do you?"

21

The simplicity of crystal-vased pink blossoms on white linen tablecloths softened the hotel restaurant's dated brass and glass opulence. Marty Janck, CEO of the Mid-States Investment Group, sipped coffee from a china cup just as the sun peeked over a lush green landscape that stood in stark contrast to the desert locale.

From a line of bungalow suites on the far side of the resort's massive swimming pool, his favorite hatchet man, Steve Spears, appeared. He looked tanned and relaxed in a white cotton shirt, khaki shorts and sandals. *What a waste. Such good looks and not a gay bone in his body.*

"Looks as though the desert is treating you well," said Janck as Spears took a seat at the table. He had a copy of the *East Valley Herald* under his arm. His skin glowed, probably from a recent exfoliation, and he smelled of coconut oil.

"After that little hell hole in North Dakota, this is heaven," said Spears, setting his folded paper on the table. He turned his coffee cup for a waiter who had breezed up, silver urn at the ready.

"Frankly, the heat has me wilting," said Janck.

"Oh, it's not so bad," said Spears. He sipped his coffee. "It keeps the tourists away. I had the whole pool to myself yesterday morning. Frankly, after North Dakota, I could stand a few more days of baking in the sun."

"Consider this week a reward for a job well done," said Janck. "Now, on to the task at hand, the *East Valley Herald*."

Spears tapped the newspaper. "How'd you beat the locals to this little gem?"

Janck smiled, sipped his coffee and sat back in his chair. He straightened the brown and blue checked tie that complimented his pale-blue summer suit.

"That's the beauty of it. It was one of the local chains that clued me in. They wanted to fold it into their other suburban papers, but the previous owner—the unfortunate Oliver Condon—had stipulated a two-year moratorium on his pride and joy being sold to them. So, we buy it, make a nice profit with our more-with-less business model and sell for a tidy sum."

"Nice," Spears said admiringly.

"Yes, I rather thought so. Now you know the drill. A thirty-five-percent profit by the end of the first year guarantees your usual bonus."

Spears gave his boss a doubtful look. "That mark's getting tougher to hit."

"We're first to the table on this one, remember. There's still plenty of public goodwill and dedicated talent to exploit."

"Speaking of exploitable talent, any people problems I should know about? Take this photographer, for instance." He unfolded the paper and placed a finger to the headline above the latest update on Eugene Fellig, fugitive photographer.

"That story made the Drudge Report yesterday and traffic went through the roof. Milk it for all it's worth. Media hero gone bad is the ultimate click bait. The city editor, Pete Cunningham, has already started the ball rolling."

"So, he's on our side?"

"For the time being. He's dealing with some personal issues regarding Condon's death. He could turn when he learns that you, not he, will be in charge of the newsroom. But I have some leverage and he's a realist. As for other possible troublemakers, starting tomorrow the paper's front page will have an advertising bug in the masthead and a banner ad across the bottom of each section front. Needless to say, the advertising department loved it."

Spears laughed. "Goring that sacred cow always brings the whiners to the surface. By the way, if I'm playing managing editor, we'll need a publisher to schmooze the local advertisers and politicians. Have anyone in mind?"

"I hope to seal that up tonight. I'm having dinner with a socialite in the local art scene. He's happy to play along and knows all the right people."

"When do I start?"

"I'll announce your hiring to the newsroom after we lay this out for Cunningham over lunch. Start tomorrow or wait until Monday, if you'd rather let Cunningham take the heat for the new ad policy. In the meantime, please enjoy all the resort has to offer."

* * *

The sound of slamming car doors coaxed Eugene to peek through the curtains of Chris Carter's dining room window. Jack and Graciela had returned from the funeral. Graciela stayed in her Camry while Jack paused to talk with a man in an SUV he'd stationed in front of the house in his absence. Jack returned to Gracie's car, opened her door and together they shuffled for the house.

Gracie's morose tone and Jack's firmly set jaw told Eugene that it had been a miserable affair, probably made worse by the summer heat that had followed them in. Jack stripped off his sweat-soaked coat and tie, tossing them to a living room chair. The silent Graciela, followed close behind, scooping up the clothing before heading for a bedroom.

"Where's Chris?" asked Eugene. "Did he do okay?"

"He held up," said Jack. "Some of his friends from the bar took him off our hands for the time being. Where's Derek?"

"Sleeping off a recurrent headache in the back bedroom. Were there a lot of people?"

"Church was packed. Sorry you couldn't be there."

"Is Graciela okay? She looked a little—"

"She's been better," Jack cut him off. "I'm eager for her to get back home and away from all this. Anything happen while we were gone?"

"Nah, nothing."

"Talk to Derek much?"

"Mostly we compared childhoods, but, man, it's like walking a minefield with him. His emotions are all over the map. Super highs and lows."

Jack slumped into a living room chair, looking tired and defeated, "Did he say anything we can use?"

"He talked a lot about Riley Mitchell. You know he even had somebody follow Mitchell into the gym to check out his leg? Says there's a birthmark right were the big band-aid was in the pictures."

"Don't suppose this guy took a picture for proof. You know he could just be bullshitting."

"I suppose but—"

"I ain't a liar," snarled Derek, standing in the entrance to the hallway. He leaned against the wall to favor his wounded leg. His sleep-matted hair stuck out in all directions.

"Ahh, you're up. How you feeling?" asked Jack.

"Feel like I got hit by a truck."

Both Jack and Eugene cracked small, hesitant smirks at his unintentional joke. Derek's eyes narrowed then softened, obviously realizing the irony of what he'd just said.

"So, if you are telling the truth on Mitchell, convince me. How'd it go down at the gym?"

"He works out at a 24-Hour Fitness near his house in Paradise Valley. Anyway, I paid a towel guy twenty bucks to look at his leg. He got a glimpse in the locker room and he saw a big, purplish blot on his thigh."

"How did you come to know this towel guy?"

"I didn't. Just caught him on a smoke break out back."

"And he didn't think you were a weirdo?"

"Probably, but twenty bucks is twenty bucks. And FYI, he said no to pictures because a camera in the locker room would get him fired."

Jack nodded his acceptance of that explanation.

"Is Mitchell the place to start?" asked Eugene.

"I don't know," said Jack, wearily. He rubbed his eyes and scratched his scalp, obviously finding it hard to think after his miserable morning.

Derek limped to a chair on the opposite side of the room, settled then winced as he tried to find a comfortable position.

"Want the ottoman for that leg?" asked Jack, rising from his chair to push the padded footstool to Derek. "Remember that Gracie said to keep it elevated."

"Yeah, yeah," griped Derek, pinching a hold of the fabric of his oversized sweatpants to lift the leg.

Jack slumped back into his chair, his big frame looking awkward. He crossed his legs and stared up at the ceiling. In the silence, Eugene heard small noises in the bedroom and assumed Graciela was packing.

Jack finally spoke, "First thing we need to do is debrief you Derek, I—"

"That sounds like a job for a perv," said Derek, with an odd little smirk.

Jack shot him a blank look, "What?"

Smiling, Eugene filled in the blank, "Debrief, get it? Briefs? Underwear?"

Levity graced Jack's face for only a millisecond before maturity squelched his near smile. "What, are you guys ten years old or something?"

"Just funnin' with you, big guy," said Derek. "So, why not go after Riley Mitchell?"

Eugene offered Jack a covert wink that said, "See what I mean about the minefield?"

Jack ignored him. "Mitchell is only one small part of what we need."

"He's one of 'em," Derek insisted. "I ain't no scared little kid no more. I get my hands on him, he'll tell us who the others are."

His frustration cranking up his irritability, Jack sat up straight in the chair, "It's not that easy, Derek. He's probably got his guard up. I'm willing to cross a few lines to get what we need, but not—"

"Yeah, well fuck you," Derek threw back at him, "and fuck—"

"You watch your mouth in this house," snapped Graciela, emerging from the hallway. She'd changed from her funeral garb into more comfortable summer clothes.

"Sorry," said Derek, flipping back into his childlike persona.

Gracie brushed past without acknowledging the apology. "Jack, is Jeff ready to go? I want to get back home."

"Anytime you're ready. Need help packing?"

"It's already done."

Jack jumped to his feet. "I'll put your bags by the door."

As he passed her, he wrapped an arm around her middle then firmly planted a kiss on the top of her head. She spooned into him. Together they stood for a long moment lost in their grief and affection.

Eugene watched Derek's intense observation of what he thought might be his brother's first glimpse at real love.

Graciela broke away to turn her attention to Eugene and Derek as Jack headed for the bedroom to collect the bags. "You two will do as he says, no questions asked," ordered Gracie.

"Yes, ma'am," Eugene said. Derek nodded, clearly cowed by her powerful presence.

Jack reappeared, bags in hand.

Gracie settled a hand on his chest. "Jack—much as I want to bring whoever killed Sandy to justice—I don't want it to cost us more than it already has. Promise you won't do anything illegal. I heard what you said about crossing lines and I don't like it."

"Hon, I—"

"No. This is a police matter. Help them, but do not break any laws. The last thing we need is for you to go to jail."

Jack's jaw flexed in frustration. He clearly wanted to tell Graciela that the police were part of the problem, but his respect for her kept his jaw clamped shut.

Jack's phone buzzed with a text. "Jeff's coming to help with the bags. You'll ride in his vehicle and I'll send someone down for your car later."

"He'll have to wait a moment while I give this boy one last look," said Graciela, kneeling to check Derek's dressings and wrap a blood pressure cuff around his uninjured arm.

"Sure thing, Hon. No hurry."

After taking vitals and checking each bandage, she shined a light in Derek's eyes. Finally, she stood, straightened her blouse and announced, "Good eye response and no sign of infection. No showers for another week. That's when you can take off those dressings. My work is done."

"Thank you," said Derek.

Graciela didn't respond. She returned the blood pressure cuff and stethoscope to her medical bag, scooped it up with her purse and headed for the door. "Eugene, you take care of yourself and my hard-headed husband."

"Yes, Ma'am. I will."

"Jack, I want you to promise—in front of witnesses—you won't do anything illegal."

Bags in hand, Jack hesitated, "Hon, we're already harboring two fugitives."

"That's different. You know what I mean. Get what you need and move them someplace safer than here. Jack, I know what you're capable of. Don't let it overshadow your good judgment."

Jack bristled then softened. "Good judgment it is. I'll keep my warrior-self in check."

Gracie met her husband's eyes then moved to him as he set down the bags. She melted in his arms as he pulled her in tight. A light knock at the door had Eugene rising from the couch.

"I'll get it," said Jack. "You two stay out of sight and away from the doors and windows."

After a few whispered words between Jack and Jeff, the three of them stepped out. Graciela never looked back.

In the sudden void left by Graciela's departure, Derek said, "I don't think she likes me much."

"I think she's conflicted between the real you and what you became," said Eugene.

"I-I get that. Do you think we stand a chance? I mean, I know *I'm* screwed for what I did, but maybe putting the Luchadores down would help make things right."

Eugene stared at the floor and nodded.

Jack returned, his body language all business. He gave Derek a long, hard look. "You're a mess. You know that, right?"

"Go fuck yourself."

Knowing he risked another meltdown, Eugene reached out and placed a hand on Derek's shoulder. "Dude, listen to him. He's right. I can barely keep up with all the people in your head."

Derek let out a long, slow breath. His face softened, but his body remained stiff.

Jack continued, "Sandy was my niece and my god daughter. I'm going to end the Luchadores for taking her away. I'll do it, with or without your help, I—"

"I'll help," said Derek.

"Okay, it'll mean some very embarrassing and painful questions. I don't ask them out of disrespect. It's simply intelligence gathering. Think of your answers as bullets in the gun we'll use to destroy our common enemy."

Derek nodded.

"Think you can keep your demons in check and get through this?"

He nodded again.

"Very well then. Let's move to the dining table and get to work."

Settled solemnly at the table, Jack began by asking Derek if he'd prefer Eugene not be present to hear the details.

"No, I want him here. He's smart. He can handle it."

Blood rushed warm and fast to Eugene's face. He mumbled, "Thanks, but I'm . . . I mean, I'm happy to stay. No one's ever accused me of being smart. Lucky maybe but—"

"Nah, you're smart. Just accept it."

For the first hour they talked about the Buckinghams' routine. They talked about the little kids and the big kids and the private internet chat rooms of pedophiles. When Derek told the story of Reggie, the older boy who had taught and protected him only to end up in a landfill, he broke down and buried his face in his hands.

"Jesus, they use the innocent kids' own need to please against them," said Eugene, fighting back his own tears. "That's just pure evil."

"Yeah, evil," choked Derek, wiping snot from his nose and lips. "Little kids don't know any better. When they made me a recruiter . . . deep down I *knew* something was wrong, but I-I . . . still helped 'em. Oh god, they're all in a landfill . . . and I knew what they were doing . . . I'm-I'm just as evil as they are." Derek buried his face on the table and sobbed.

Eugene moved in close, his arm around his half brother's back to hug tight as he whispered, "They're the evil ones, not you. You got away and you stopped the Buckinghams. You're smart *and* brave."

When it was clear Derek needed time to cry it out, Eugene looked to Jack whose face was a mix of resolve and anger. "Chris's got pizza in the freezer," said Eugene. "I'll make a couple. You okay, Derek? Need anything?"

"Just gimme a minute," Derek said, his head still buried in his arms as his hands tugged at his hair.

Wiping his own tears, Eugene headed for the kitchen, thinking of the bullshit he'd endured just to please his own parents.

The kitchen reflected pure depression. Chris' long, boozy nightmare had left it in shambles. A little breakfast nook to one side of the room framed the home's back door and a table piled with Amazon boxes and unopened mail. Holding his breath, Eugene picked up the saucepot Gracie had used to douse Chris who then used it for his stomach contents. He set it in the sink and turned on the water faucet to rinse the vomit into the garbage disposal. Relieved to be rid of that repulsive matter, he opened the fridge's freezer drawer and removed two frosty, plastic-wrapped disks from a stack of frozen pizzas.

The guy's a top-notch chef and this is what he eats at home?

Pizzas cooking in the oven, Eugene returned to the dining table. Derek had regained his composure enough to manage a pitiful smile.

"All right, if you're ready, we need to get back to it," said Jack.

Derek nodded.

"I need to know about the warehouse. Can you handle that?"

"Sure, let's do it. The place was hotter than shit and smelled like a paint factory."

"Paint?"

"Not paint exactly, but kind of chemically. Plus you got your sweat, ass and cum smells," Derek gave Eugene a challenging glance and seemed disappointed at his lack of reaction. "Anyway, we'd be locked in the back of the van, we'd roll in—"

"Did you go straight in," Jack interrupted, "or was there a ramp?"

Derek's brow furrowed in thought, "A ramp, I think. Yeah, we'd kinda go up a little hill and stop. We couldn't see much from the back, but I did see a door roll up before we drove in."

"Electric door or did somebody lift it?"

"Couldn't tell. If we got caught looking around we wouldn't get our candy."

"Candy?" asked Eugene.

"Coke, dude. Buckingham called it candy, like, 'you kids want your candy, you have to be good.' It always pissed me off 'cause we knew we were about to be fucked half to death . . . " He took a deep breath. "Anyway, we'd pull in and I'd hear the door rattle down. Wait, it must have been a manual door 'cause I could hear someone work the chain . . . Anyway, Buckingham would hand back the baggie of coke. We'd suck it up and crawl out. That's when I'd smell the chemicals."

"Okay, you're out of the van. Imagine yourself looking up. What do you see?"

Derek closed his eyes and tilted his head back. "Lots of wood but there was a big light over the mat that made it hard to see."

"Any windows?"

"Not that I could see, but it was nighttime and everything was dark except for the mat."

"What could you hear?"

"Not much. The door going down and the other guys whispering . . . Oh and jets, sometimes really close."

Jack shook his head as he scribbled notes. The fingers on Derek's hands squirmed, but remained clasped together on the table.

"After like a minute I'd hear a creaky door and the Luchadores would—"

"What kind of door, roller or hinge?" asked Jack.

Derek's face scrunched around his closed eyes. "I couldn't see 'cause it was dark. Guess I always pictured a hinge like a creepy door in a monster movie." His scrunched face gave way to a grimace and his squirming fingers clawed the back of his clasped hands.

"Was it a peaked roof like this?" asked Eugene. He formed an upside down V with his hands, "Open your eyes and look."

Derek glanced over. "Yeah, but it wasn't pointy. It was curved," he said, his fingernails leaving tiny, red crescents as he raised his hands to form an arch. Sweat showed in his armpits and Eugene caught a sour whiff of fear.

Jack continued, "How big is the warehouse? A football field? Two football fields?"

Derek's eyelids shuttered and his clasped hands returned to the table. "A football field, maybe . . . So, after the door creaks open, the music starts . . . and-and the Luchafreaks march in." The worm crawl returned to Derek's fingers. Eugene reached out to offer comfort and Jack held up a hand to stop him.

"What kind of music?"

"Lame marching shit, you know trombones and tubas." Faint beads of sweat glistened from his brow. Eugene was sure Derek's nails would soon draw blood.

"Think about the wrestling mat. I couldn't see its details in the pictures. Was there anything painted on it?"

"Just circles."

"No pictures or letters?"

"Nah."

"What were the walls like?"

"Just gray, nothing special."

"Gray blocks or gray smooth?"

"Blocks. The floor was rough concrete."

"Any other doors that you could see?"

"Nope."

"You said it was hot. Was there any air moving like fans or swamp coolers?"

"Nah, just real hot in the summer. Anal Pirate liked it hot and sweaty. I liked the sweat because it made me harder to get ahold of and it slicked up my asshole for—"

"Aw, Jesus," escaped Eugene's mouth.

Derek's eyes flashed open with a familiar rage, "Too much for you, Paparazzi Dude?" His fingers turned to fists. He turned, arm cocked to throw a punch. "I'll rip off yer head, you pansy-ass piece of shit! Come on, you know what I need. Give it to me!"

Eugene just stared evenly, not raising a hand to defend himself. "I'm sorry," he said softly.

Derek blinked, shook his head and blinked several more times. Finally, he swallowed hard, struggling for control. Slowly, he folded his hands and stared into nothingness.

The oven's beep broke the long silence. Sensing they'd reached a stopping point, Eugene asked, "What *is* your day job anyway, Jack?"

Jack set down his pen and relaxed, turning his chair sideways to stretch out his legs. "I run a weapons and tactics training school up north of here."

"Some sort of military cop shit?" asked Derek.

"Some military, some law enforcement, but mostly it's professional body guards and corporate asshole wannabes with money to burn."

Derek cocked his head. "You teach people to kill?"

"First, I teach them situational awareness. But, yes, I also teach them how to deal with a lethal threat. Sometimes you're not given a choice, that is, if you want to live or your responsibilities to live."

"Where do the Luchadores land on your need-to-kill scale?" asked Eugene.

Jack stretched nonchalantly. "Oh, they're right up there . . . but I'm patient . . . in an ideal world they'd get gang-raped in prison for a few years then die slowly of AIDS." Jack cracked a rare smile that coaxed grins all around the table. Beyond Jack's parted lips and shining teeth, Eugene saw something dark and terrifying. *Whoa, this guy's got his own demons.*

The impromptu early dinner-late lunch felt like a family affair. Eugene provided the entertainment, describing his escape from the cops, the bus ride to his old neighborhood, his meeting Fat Freddie and his fight with the gangbangers.

"So, you got that shiner from the retarded guy? Not your fight in the street?" asked Derek.

"Yep."

"He really tore into those little shits," offered Jack. "Looked like a damn junkyard gladiator, swinging a battery cable and throwing lug nuts. I don't think any of them landed a punch."

"Yeah, but I thought I was up shit creek when that one asshole started shooting."

"They shot at you?" blurted Derek.

"Yeah, and they probably would have killed me if Jack hadn't come to my rescue. He knocked the shit out of them with the bumper of his truck."

"Damn, dude, I've got a bad-ass for a brother."

"Nah, Freddie's a nice guy. I couldn't just let 'em kill him."

Jack slapped the table with his palm. "You guys ready to get back to it?"

"Sure," Derek said, still eyeing his brother. "I'll do my best."

While Eugene steadied Derek on a trip to the bathroom, Jack gathered their used dishes, carted them to the kitchen and put them to soak in a sink of soapy water. A few minutes later they were once again settled at the dining table.

"All right then, let's start with an easy one. I have the pictures, but I want to start from scratch. Can you tell me how many Luchadores were at the parties?"

Derek closed his eyes and folded his hands on the table, exhibiting far less stress than when they'd started. "Seven. Oh, they had a helper, too. They called him water boy but we called him the gimp 'cause he was in a leather suit with a mouth zipper."

"Did he walk with a limp?" asked Jack.

"Nah, it's from Pulp Fiction."

"What?"

Derek opened his eyes and smiled, "Probably the best movie ever."

"Never seen it," said Jack.

A wide grin spread on Eugene's face, "The pawn shop scene?"

Derek beamed "That's the one." He offered a low, growling, "I'ma call a coupla hard, pipe-hittin' niggers, who'll go to work with a pair of pliers and a blow torch. I'ma get medieval on your ass."

Jack stared, slack-jawed.

"Trust me, it's a great movie," said Eugene. "The gimp is this guy they kept locked in a box. He wore this studded leather suit with eye holes and a mouth zipper."

"That's the gimp."

"Okay, what did your gimp do?"

"He tended bar. They had a folding table with tubs of beer and shit. Every once in a while they'd knock him around, unzip his mask, make him kneel and you know . . . but Ass Clown never let them really hurt him."

"Ass Clown looked out for him?"

"Yeah, he'd let the other guys mess with him some, but nothing that hurt real bad."

"Was Ass Clown the leader?"

"No, the guy in charge was Anal Pirate. You got the pictures? I'll show you."

Jack spread the pictures on the table.

"This is Anal Pirate," Derek pointed to a heavy-set man in a skull and crossbones mask. "He was the oldest and he always got first pick of the new kids. Ass Clown was like his enforcer. He was the worst. Even the other Luchadores were scared of him. My first time on the mat. Ass Clown and Anal Pirate ganged up on me." Flipping into uneasy, he shifted in his chair. "I thought I was going to die."

Jack didn't let him linger. "You say there were seven, plus the water boy and there was a hierarchy that—"

"What's a higher arky?"

"A power pecking order, like generals and captains and sergeants."

"Ahh, I get it . . . a peckering order." Derek paused for effect.

Jack's eyes narrowed and Eugene let out a smiling hmpff, glad to see silly Derek's return.

Derek continued, "So, Anal Pirate was the general. He made the rules and Ass Clown enforced 'em."

"You said the other Luchadores were scared of Ass Clown. Did they argue?"

"Oh, sure. Sometimes it was over who got what kid but there was this one guy . . . " Derek shuffled through the photos. "Here he is, the guy in the white mask. We called him Mr. Limp Dick 'cause sometimes he couldn't get it up."

"I suppose that was better for the kids," said Eugene.

Derek shook his head. "No, it was bad. This one time when Ass Clown caught Limp Dick fake fucking his kid, he punished him by breaking the kid's arm. Then he jammed his big horse cock down the kid's throat until he passed out. He told Limp Dick it was his punishment for not being a team player."

Eugene stared hard at the table to control his repulsion.

"He actually use the term 'team player?'" asked Jack.

"Yeah, that's what he said. Told him to man up and be a team player . . . The kid wasn't right after that. Mr. Buckingham said he took him to the hospital . . . but now I know better."

Jack and Eugene locked eyes for a moment as if sharing self-control.

Jack tapped a finger on the photos. "Sounds like hazing gone completely bat shit."

"What's hazing?" asked Derek.

"Making someone do something painful or degrading to join a club."

"That's dumb. Why would you want to join a club like that?"

"Good question," said Eugene. "There was a jock at my high school who did that sort of shit. He got expelled for tea bagging a freshmen."

"Tea bagging?" asked Jack.

"It's when one guy puts his ball sack on another guy's face," offered Derek.

Jack nodded. "The ultimate insult."

"Naw," Derek spoke as if lecturing. "That's nothing. A dick up your ass is a lot worse."

Jack coughed. "Ah, yeah, good point . . . Jesus, Derek, I'm no prude, but, damn . . . well . . . My point is, these guys sound more like dominators than pedophiles." He sat forward as if excited with the realization. "The cops have been going at this all wrong. It's not *who* they are but *what* they are."

He plucked his phone from his belt, dialed and put it to his ear, "Hey, it's me . . . Yeah, everything's cool, no problems. Derek's been very helpful. In fact, he may have given us the key."

Eugene glanced to Derek and saw a twinkle of glee in his eyes.

"Can you search the system for cases involving a high school or college sports program that had sexual hazings? . . . Yeah, I know, obvious, right? Can't believe we overlooked . . . Yeah, I know. Chances are they never got caught, but maybe they left tracks. It's worth a shot . . . Oh, and we think the warehouse was near the airport . . . Hang on, I'll ask him." Jack pulled the phone from his ear. "Derek, did you ever tell this to anyone else?"

"Yeah," said Derek, "There was this older guy who talked to me for hours. I told him all of this."

Jack frowned. He put the phone to his shoulder, muffling the mic. "Was he Hispanic?"

"Nah, not Ibarra. I hardly talked to that dumb ass. My guy was old and white and real big."

Relief crossed Jack's face. "Got a name?"

Derek's face scrunched in thought. "It's on the tip of my tongue . . . Nah, lost it. Sorry. Wait, it was a gum name like—"

"Orbit?" asked Eugene.

"Nah."

"Wrigley?" offered Jack.

"Yeah, that's it, Wrigley."

Muffled curses erupted from the phone. Jack's eyes widened. He hesitantly put it back to his ear. "That name means something?" More cursing sparked from the earpiece making Jack wince. He pulled the phone away from his ear. "Okay, I hear ya. Hell, they heard you in China. At least now we know." He set it back against his ear. "Okay. Call when you're getting close. I'll get 'em ready."

A sudden bolt of dread shot through Eugene as Jack ended the call.

"You're working with Eddie, aren't you?"

Jack hesitated then shrugged. "Yes, but—"

Angered and wary, Derek had pushed to his feet.

"You don't trust him. I saw it on your face," said Eugene.

"Stop right there. I do trust him," said Jack, "I'm just being careful."

"Bullshit!" yelled Derek. "He's playing you . . . He's one of them . . . He's gonna pick us up and kill us, just like they killed Reggie."

"Shut up, Derek. Just shut up!" Eugene directed. "Jack, is that true?"

"Shut the fuck up, both of you. Engage your brains. Jesus Christ, think about it. Wrigley played Eddie. He framed his daughter for drugs and threatened to kill her then made him take the fall for destroying evidence."

"I'm gonna hurl," coughed Derek, springing from the table so fast his chair tipped over. He hobbled into the kitchen to vomit in the sink.

Eugene remained at his seat, opening and closing his fists. He waited until Derek appeared in the doorway to ask in a strained voice, "Why did you hesitate, Jack? There's something you don't trust."

"Calm down. I've known Eddie for decades. We were in the Special Forces together. I've trusted him with my life many times." He leaned forward in his intensity. "And by the way, the whole bumbling cop thing was a ruse, Eugene, he orchestrated your escape from the paper."

"Bullshit."

"Think about it. Do you really think he'd have left the back door uncovered?"

Eugene froze, his mind spinning. "Okay, but-but why'd you hesitate?"

"Between you and me, he's getting older and may have lost his edge. The Luchadores got the better of him once already . . . and . . . Well, when that happened he went on a bender. He lost his job, his pension and his wife and kid. He pushed all of his friends away and . . . ."

"And?"

"And I hadn't talked to him until he called to ask for help. So, honestly, I am just being careful."

When Eugene looked at Derek standing in the kitchen doorway, his brother gave a cautious little shrug. "Okay, I'll buy it. Where's he gonna take us?"

"His apartment—"

"Oh, this just gets better," Eugene spit out sarcastically.

"Hang on. It's a secure building and it's the last place anyone would look."

"I thought this was the last place. I don't know . . . Derek, what do you think?"

Not hearing an answer, Eugene stood. A blast of summer air caught him as he looked through the kitchen to see the back door hanging wide open.

Two strides into his run for the back door, Jack shoved past, gun drawn. He cleared the doorway with practiced precision then stepped out, pistol sweeping all directions. He quick-stepped out of sight. Eugene raced to follow finding Jack in the middle of the yard, weapon lowered and cell phone to his ear.

"He's on the run, Eddie. He went out the back door and over the wall. Circle the block and maybe you'll get lucky."

22

Well into their drive back to the little house on the hill, Graciela closed her eyes to the passing landscape and let the white noise of tires on blacktop quiet her mind. Today the mountainous desert vistas she so loved looked mean and unforgiving. She feared Sandy's murder would forever taint her ability to see beauty in this part of the world.

Her quiet lasted only a moment before worry for Jack intruded. She looked to Jeff, his confident hands on the wheel, the desert's reflection sliding over his dark sunglasses. She knew his eyes scanned the horizon for threats. They were the same eyes she'd seen on his arrival at Walter Reed Medical Center. He'd been shot up by God knows who in God knows where. Her time with him had been brief but those eyes had stayed with her and she knew she couldn't be in better hands.

"Not to worry, Gracie," Jeff said. "We'll be home in less than an hour."

"It's not me I'm worried about. These people Jack's after . . . They don't play by the rules."

"Jack's no easy mark. If it makes you feel any better, he'd already made plans to get those two guys out of the house. You didn't need to remind him of the risk."

"Really? Well, paint me dumb then."

"Hey, no need to get snippy. I'm just the messenger. It's a good thing—"

"No, Jeff. He should have said something rather than just managing me."

Jeff let a quick smile escape and shook his head.

They were well out of Phoenix's urban sprawl on Highway 69 just south of Mayer. Heat shimmered from the blacktop ahead and the late afternoon sun still hung high.

Graciela leaned forward to adjust her air vent then settled back into her seat. "Does Jack have other plans in the works that would interest me or is this one of those need-to-know things he's so fond of?"

"Just a few security things, you know, just in case. Nothing set in stone beyond interviewing that Schaefer kid. By the way I talked with Eddie at length on my drive down to Phoenix. Stumbling onto Schaefer was a big break because most of the original interviews were tainted or tossed. Jack should be re-interviewing as we speak and hopefully he'll glean some good intel."

"Jeff, can we trust Eddie? I know Jack feels like he owes him."

"I think so . . . No, I know so. The old Eddie's back. I didn't pull any punches when I talked to him. He's got his footing again and this time he has the upper hand . . . and our help."

Graciela took another deep, calming breath. "I'll just be glad when this is over. I'm getting too old for this bullshit."

Jeff cracked a bigger smile at Graciela's rare use of profanity, "That's my amazing Gracie. Now, just relax and—" Jeff's smile vanished as his focus flashed to the rearview mirror.

Graciela stiffened. She glanced to the side mirror but saw nothing. "What is it?"

"Cop car on our six."

"Are they pulling us over?"

"Not yet. Let's just wait and see. It could be nothing." He tapped a small radio on his belt then spoke to a mic clipped to his collar, "Looks like we have company, gentlemen. Anybody see where he came from?"

"About a mile back. He pulled out right after he saw you," answered the radio.

Surprised to learn that she was part of a convoy, Graciela fought the urge to ask questions.

"Yep, here we go. He's lighting us up. Lead car, find me a good spot to pull out."

Gracie's heart thumped in her throat as they drove and waited.

A low, smooth voice flowed from Jeff's radio, "Dirt road, first right past the Saguaro Trail sign."

"Roger that. First right past Saguaro Trail," echoed Jeff.

"Twenty yards in will put you in good cover."

"Roger that," repeated Jeff, his defensive military persona fully engaged.

He rolled on, pretending not to see the flashing lights until he caught sight of the Saguaro Trail sign. He then slowed, signaled and pulled off the highway, turning on his emergency flashers. The dirt road slanted down and within twenty yards they were hidden in creosote brush and cholla cactus. "Perfect, gentlemen. How long before you're set?"

"Ready in three," said the radio.

"Roger that. I'll go silent now. No need to scare off our prey." Jeff pulled the mic, unclipped the radio, and set everything between the seats.

Gracie craned in her seat to look out the back window. She saw a short, balding State Trooper step from his car while donning his flat-brimmed drill sergeant's hat. Jeff removed his license from his wallet and retrieved the SUVs registration and insurance papers from the center console.

"Let's see what we're dealing with," said Jeff, rolling his window halfway down before placing his hands on the steering wheel with the paperwork held up between his left hand finger and thumb.

The lawman stopped just behind the driver's door, peered in and stretched to scan the back seat. "Shut off the motor and show me your license, registration and proof of insurance."

Jeff cautiously dropped his right hand to turn the car off at the same time he held the paperwork to the open window. "What's up, officer? Don't think I was speeding, was I?"

"Where you headed on such a hot afternoon?"

"Back to the ranch. We've got a little place up near Paulden. Do I have a tail light out or something?"

"Or something," said the trooper. He glared at Jeff's papers for a long moment. "Ma'am, I'll need to see your identification, as well."

"I don't think you can ask—"

"Go ahead, Gracie. He probably just wants to be sure you're legal, right, officer?"

"Legally, sir, I can't ask that question. Let's just say I'd consider it a courtesy."

Jeff looked to Gracie and winked.

"I'll have to reach down and get it from my purse."

"That's fine, ma'am. I appreciate it, thank you."

Gracie handed her license to Jeff who handed it off. The trooper turned away, heading back to his cruiser without a word.

"What's he doing now?" asked Gracie.

"He's in his car talking on his cell phone. Probably confirming his target and requesting orders."

"How do you know?"

"He'd use his radio or in-car computer to run our info, not his cell phone."

"Jeff, are you armed?"

Jeff smiled. "If you're asking if I have a gun, no, but yes, we're armed . . . Okay, he's getting a canine from the car. When the dog alerts, he'll make us exit the vehicle. Just follow my lead and don't worry. Friends are watching. We're just giving him enough rope to hang himself, so play dumb. He can't know we're onto him."

Gracie nodded, her hands stiff and breath coming in short pants.

The trooper and his canine approached the rear of the SUV. The dog whined then yelped.

"There's his bullshit probable cause," murmured Jeff. "Nice and easy, Gracie. No sudden moves."

Gracie nodded, tension clamping her chest.

The man returned his dog to the car. He turned to approach with his weapon drawn. "Driver, keep your hands visible. Open the door through the window then exit the vehicle."

"No worries, Gracie. Jack anticipated this." Jeff lowered his window, extending his hands to open the door with the exterior handle. He smoothly rose to his feet, keeping his hands in front of him.

"Turn to face away. Back to the rear of the vehicle. Drop to your knees and cross your legs. Passenger, do not move!"

Graciela watched Jeff comply, feeling faint as he dropped to his knees. He expelled a grunt when he was pushed to the ground before the cuffs ratcheted.

"Passenger, open your door and exit the vehicle just like he did. Keep your hands where I can see them!"

Fighting to control her trembling, Gracie complied. When she stepped down, she looked to the trooper and saw only the huge muzzle of his pistol. Her eyes darted around the brush as she backed.

"On the ground, now!"

Graciela awkwardly complied, the gravel stabbing as she dropped to her knees. She heard his weapon sliding back into its holster. As he moved close, she caught the odor of strong sweat and cigarettes. He yanked her arms down then to her back to slap the metal handcuffs on her wrists hard enough to make her cry out in pain.

"Hey, take it easy! She's no threat!" yelled Jeff.

"Shut up, ass wipe. My dog alerted on something in that vehicle. That tells me you're likely a drug smuggler." He leaned closer to Gracie's ear. "I suspect that you, *Mamacita,* are in this country illegally."

"You son of a bitch!" spat Gracie, still on her knees, unable to control her fire.

When he reflexively shoved her to the ground, she grunted, trying to keep her face from the rocky desert floor. "Bastard," escaped her mouth before she thought better.

"Gracie, be cool!" called Jeff, writhing and helpless. "Don't give him an excuse."

"That's right, *Mamacita*," growled the trooper. "Resisting. That's my excuse to search you." Pressing a knee to her lower back, his clumsy hands probed and rubbed at her crotch and breasts.

She resisted the urge to kick him. Angry tears welled as she looked to Jeff. He blinked slowly and nodded. The calm on his face cooled her anger as she turned her mind to calculated retaliation.

The trooper stood, jerking her back to her knees. He scratched his crotch, then spat on the ground before her. He moved to the SUV, opened the rear hatch then pulled something from his shirt pocket. "Let's see what got my dog so excited. Ah, what's this? Could this be drugs? Huh, imagine that."

The paunchy trooper's fingers pinched what looked like a small, dark, plastic-wrapped popcorn ball. "Why, I think it's tar heroin and, by golly, this much makes you a distributor. Where do you think my back-up should find it? I'm thinking somewhere down around the spare tire. Spics are generally a little more creative, but this'll have to do."

"All right, we get it. What do you want, money?" asked Jeff, rolling to his side.

"I don't *want* anything. You are drug dealers and I'm an officer of the law. You will go to jail. That's satisfaction enough for me."

"You lying cocksucker," spat Graciela.

"No, ma'am, not me. Although I'll bet you've swallowed a few dicks in your day."

Gracie unsuccessfully struggled to stand.

The trooper laughed. "There you go, *Mamacita*, getting all excited. I knew you wanted it." He stepped close, grabbing her hair.

Jeff, too, struggled to stand. "Leave her alone or I'll fucking—"

"Shut up, asshole."

Gracie lunged forward. Her forehead rammed the man's groin.

"You stupid bitch!" With his dog frantically barking, he stumbled back, looking far less injured than she'd hoped.

After panting a couple of breaths, he smiled diabolically then drew his metal baton from his duty belt. A flick of his wrist opened it to its full length. Grasping her hair to yank her head back, he slid the baton down her face and stared in her eyes.

"Now, *Mamacita,* kiss it and make it all better." He forced her face into his foul-smelling crotch. The grunting man ground into her face.

Gracie could feel his organ swell but the next instant his whole body jerked upward. The fingers in her hair lost their grip. She leaned back and blinked through her tears to see the officer's bulging eyes and red face. His feet were off the ground. Two men in shaggy, netted suits held him. One choked him to unconsciousness as the other relieved him of his baton, pistol and pepper spray.

Jeff rushed past them, a metal cuff dangling from one hand. He unlocked her cuffs and pulled her into his arms. "Gracie, I am so sorry. That went a little too far."

She stepped away, rubbing her wrists. "No, it was my temper, my fault."

After handing the trooper's weapons to Jeff, the camouflaged men hauled the unconscious man to the base of a palo verde tree where they propped his back to its trunk and zip-tied his hands around the tree behind him. They looked to Jeff. He nodded. Then, just as quietly as they had appeared, they melted back into the desert.

Jeff stepped to the cruiser speaking in soothing tones to the agitated canine. He gave a hand signal and the animal melted into whines, sat then stretched out on his blanket, his head on his paws.

On his way to the rousing trooper, he winked at the watching Gracie. "The cruiser's running with the air on and he's got a fan in the corner so he won't over-heat. Beautiful animal, nice that he speaks German." She laughed as he expected.

The trooper coughed to consciousness. Confusion crawled across his face as Jeff pulled the man's pants and underwear down around his ankles. "What the f-fuck . . . Who the . . . aw, Christ, what're you gonna do?"

Without answering, Jeff stood and walked back to Graciela.

"Why'd you pull his pants down?"

"He needs to feel vulnerable," Jeff said, pocketing the dark ball of heroin then donning a pair of heavy leather work gloves.

"Are you going to beat the answers out of him?"

"Nope, just gonna poke him a bit. We don't have a lot of time. Can you turn our vehicle while I get some answers?"

"Yes . . . of course . . . You're *not* going to kill him," she said sternly.

"No, just going to introduce him to the desert," said Jeff, a smile blossoming on his face as he retrieved a small folding shovel from the back of the SUV.

"And what about the dog?"

"I'll call 9-1-1 before we leave."

A beige Toyota club cab pickup rolled up the road coming out of the desert. The driver's tinted window lowered. Gracie recognized the three men inside as members of a military group training at the Breech.

"State boy got a dash or a body cam?" the driver asked, reaching out to offer Jeff what looked like a small video recorder.

"No, I checked. We're golden," said Jeff, jamming the camera into the left breast pocket of his khaki shirt.

"Sorry, I let it get a little out of hand, sir—"

"Had to let it play out to remove all doubt."

"It was my temper and I'm sorry if it complicated things," said Gracie.

One of the passengers leaned over to better see her, a broad smile on his face, "Ma'am you performed admirably, just as expected. He's lucky I didn't drill him when that baton came out. Nobody messes with our Amazing Gracie." The man's contagious smile spread to all the men. Because the nickname always embarrassed her, Gracie rolled her eyes.

"Thank you, gentlemen," said Jeff, "I'm in your debt. Now, slide on down the road. We'll handle it from here."

"Thank you," Gracie called, waving them off.

Jeff pushed her arm down. "Enough. We've gotta move."

"Go do what you have to. I'll turn the truck."

Jeff made a beeline for a tangle of cholla cactus. Working quickly, he stabbed the shovel into a pile of spiny, dry nodules at the plant's base then marched to the watching trooper.

"What's your name?" Jeff asked.

"Why'd you pull down my pants? You some kinda perver—"

Jeff answered by flicking a piece of cholla onto the man's exposed groin. He flinched, automatically closing his legs and driving the barbs in deep.

"Holy Jesus! Oh fuck, you are a bastard . . . Wait, no more! My name's Farley, Devin Farley."

"Who sent you?"

Farley's face blanked and he turned his eyes to the ground as his whole body trembled.

Jeff flicked another chunk of cactus. It snagged the fleshy, white skin on the trooper's thigh. His jaw clamped, the man looked up in defiance. Jeff pressed the wicked needles in with the sole of his boot.

"Aaahhh! . . . Jesus I can't . . . I owed him," the man screamed.

A third nodule of pain flew from Jeff's gloved fingers, it's barbs hooked Farley's eyelid and cheek. Farley tried to shake it off but the wobbling ball of spines hooked into his nose. Childish mewling became sorrowful sobs.

"Oh, shut the hell up and tell me who sent you." Jeff held the shovel out over the trooper's lap and shook off a few more nodules then paused for an answer. When none came his boot drove the needles home.

Standing beside the repositioned SUV, Gracie winced at what sounded like the scream of a dying rabbit.

Snot, tears and drool streamed down Farley's sweaty, red face. Jeff knelt and spoke softly, "Much as I'd like, I can't afford to kill you. But I should warn you, my next logical target is your eyes and mouth."

One poke of the shovel toward his eyes and the trooper melted, "I was just doing a favor for a buddy down in Phoenix. He wanted the lady locked up. Didn't say why. Honest to god."

"What's his name?"

"Clyde, Clyde Wrigley," croaked the hurting man. "I swear, just please, I need a h-hospital."

"Is Wrigley State Patrol?"

"Yes. A detective."

"Is he a Luchador?"

"I-I don't know what that is. He called like an hour ago. I owed-owed him a favor."

"What for?"

"Ah, please. Oh, god, he caught me with an underage hooker. Fucking had me cold."

"Boy or girl?"

"What?"

"The hooker. Boy or girl?"

"Girl. Jesus, I'm no pervert."

Jeff grunted then shook his head and set down the shovel. He pulled the trooper's phone from the duty belt now around his ankles and memorized the last numbers dialed. From his left shirt pocket he pulled the heroin.

"Here's a little something for the pain," he said, flicking open a knife and cutting a small chunk of black onto the knife's tip. Jeff began a sing-song as if coxing a toddler. "Open wide. Here comes the airplane. Buzz buzz, buzz."

When Farley opened, Jeff slid the blade tip deep enough to make him gag. "All right. That's a good little asshole. Now, swallow."

Farley closed his eyes and obeyed.

Jeff produced the video camera and flipped open the screen. He removed a glove and hit the LCD's play button then turned it to Farley.

"This hits YouTube unless you forget you ever met us."

Farley's red, watery eyes narrowed as he nodded.

Jeff stood, sprinkled the remaining cactus then tossed Farley's gun, baton and pepper spray well out of reach. "Now, I'm gonna cut you lose. You move an inch before I'm gone and you'll regret it." He wiggled the recorder.

Farley nodded.

"Gracie, you ready?"

"Yes."

"All right. Wait, our driver's licenses. Where?"

"Shirt pocket. Left side," croaked the trooper.

Stepping close, Jeff slid two ungloved fingers into the khaki shirt. The stab of a cactus barb made him flinch as he yanked the paperwork free. "Jesus that smarts." He looked to the man's crotch, swollen red and oozing blood. "Was it worth it?"

The trooper cast his watering eyes to the ground.

"Nice and easy. No sudden moves. We're almost done." Jeff re-gloved his bare hand and walked to the back of the tree. Plucking two nodules from the ground, he place one in each of Farley's hands and squeezed.

"Iiiiieeeeee! Fuck you! Fuck you, goddamn it. I'll fucking kill you. Aahhh! Aahhh! Huh! Haa! Fuuuuck!"

In one continuous motion Jeff cut and collected the zip tie then bolted for the SUV.

"That was awful," Gracie said as they pulled back onto the highway. "Can't say as I didn't enjoy at least a little of it, though."

Jeff smiled. "The desert is an unforgiving place. Hang on, got one more thing to do."

After punching 9-1-1 on the trooper's phone, he affected an amazingly feeble, elderly voice, "Hello? Uh, say, you might want the police to send someone. I just pulled off the highway to piddle and saw an officer playin' with himself in the bushes . . . Hell no, this ain't a crank call. I think he's on drugs or somethin' . . . I am *not* giving my name . . . He scared the begeezus outta me . . . Okay, yes, he's just north of Mayer, maybe a mile or so. Goodbye, now, I hope he's okay."

Jeff closed the phone, slid its battery free, rolled down his window and threw both into the median.

"Piddle?" asked Graciela, smiling.

"What can I say? I was in character . . . Hey, I made him eat a fingernail-size chunk of that heroin. Was that too much?"

"It'll dilute in his stomach. He should be fine."

"How long before it hits his system?"

"Half hour, give or take."

"Perfect."

23

Alone in the bungalow, Eugene forced down the urge to scream. He was determined not to lose what little control he had left. Jack was supposedly driving the neighborhood in search of Derek, but the sincerity of that effort was in doubt now that he had what he needed.

Vehicle sounds in the driveway caught Eugene's ear. He moved to the dining room window to peer through a slit in the cigarette-yellowed curtains. Jack stepped out and shut the door of his SUV. A second car door slammed and Eddie appeared. Both men's body language said defeat.

Eugene dashed back to the table, not bothering to unlock the door. Hearing a key slide into the deadbolt, he leaned back in his chair crossing his arms. The front door swung open, bathing the living room in summer.

"Did you even try to find him?" Eugene spat as Jack stepped in and faced the dining room.

"What? Of course we tried."

"Hey, Eugene, it's good to see you're safe," Eddie said, with an unusually genuine smile.

"Like you give a shit," snarled Eugene.

Eddie's smile dimmed. He looked tired. His salt-and-pepper hair had seemingly turned more salt than pepper since he'd last seen him.

"Here, I brought you your shit," he said, handing Eugene a plastic bag containing his iPhone and multi tool. "Has Jack filled you in on what's going on?"

"Sort of. He says you're not the dick I think you are, but I'm withholding judgment." He pawed the bag, tucked the multi-tool into a front pocket then thumbed the phone's power button.

"Fair enough. I deserve that." Eddie put his hands to his hips and stood in silence, staring at the floor for a moment then continued, "You know, I needed the Luchadores to believe I was an idiot and that meant shitting all over you. Sorry for that."

"Aw, that's okay. It just cost me my apartment and probably my job. But that's just collateral damage, right? Cops shit on good people all the time to get what they want. No big deal. Anybody got a charger? This phone's dead."

"Hey," said Eddie, his eyes drilling with a steely determination. "Sorry if you think your personal shit's more important than putting an end to a bunch of murdering child rapists."

Suddenly feeling small, Eugene tried for logic. "Letting me in on your plan woulda saved me a butt load of grief."

Eddie looked at the ceiling then at Eugene. "Couldn't risk it."

Eugene shifted in his chair. "At what point did you know I was innocent?"

"That morning when Harry and I met you at the jail. That's when I put my plan into motion."

Eugene met Jack's eyes as one eyebrow arched, challenging him. "Yeah, I can see it now." He looked back at Eddie. "You kinda kicked it up a notch that morning. You went from jerk to complete dick. Did Harry know?"

Eddie didn't even flinch. "Not then, but he does now. Wasn't sure I could trust him."

"Where is he by the way?"

"Driving his family up to my compound in Paulden," Jack jumped in. "Once they're safe, he'll be back."

Jack's phone interrupted. He plucked it from his belt and answered. Within seconds his face turned to stone. "She's unharmed, correct? . . . Okay." Still serious, he marginally relaxed. "Cholla cactus? Heh, wish I coulda seen that . . . You get a name? . . . Okay, thanks for keeping her safe and thank the team. Tell them I owe 'em a big one. And tell Gracie I'm sorry . . . Yeah, yeah, I know. You got her into it, but the buck stops here. I'll be sleeping on the couch for a month. Again."

When Jack ended the call, Eddie asked, "Was I right?"

"Yep, State Patrol pulled 'em over just north of Mayer. Thanks to you we were ready."

"I knew it. Same shit they pulled on my kid. They're safe now, right?"

"Yes, and they got a name after massaging the cop's nut sack with a little cholla cactus."

All three men wriggled in their seats, then smirked at the thought.

"That'd do it," said Eddie. "What's the name, who sent him?"

"Clyde Wrigley strikes again."

"That son-of-a-bitch. I cannot believe I didn't see it. He's one of the few guys I thought I could trust. I even let him sleep on my couch after his wife tossed him out."

"A name's not gonna do much without proof."

"True," said Eddie, "but knowing where to dig will. I'll call the chief and put it in the works."

"Hang on. Let me check my email," said Jack, "Jeff's sending more details. I'll forward it to you." Both Eddie and Jack stared at their little screens, ignoring Eugene.

He counted to ten then demanded, "What are we going to do about Derek?"

Jack and Eddie looked from their phones to each other then to Eugene. They slumped into chairs. Jack held a hand up toward Eddie who explained, "Scottsdale has him back in custody. They picked him up about a block from here."

Eugene's face fell. "Oh, shit. He's done for."

"No, he's the least of the Luchadores worries right now," said Jack. "The move on Gracie means they know I'm in play. They know we have the missing picture and probably that we had Derek. I doubt he's on their radar at this point."

"But it's not fair."

"What, going to jail for rape?" snarked Eddie.

Eugene puffed with anger. Jack stepped in, easing the pressure. "They're brothers, Eddie. Derek needs to pay for what he did, but you know he's a tortured mess for a reason. He worked his ass off to keep it together for us and he's earned our understanding."

Eddie's face went from keen-edged cop to soft-sided human. "Yes, sorry. Sometimes I get caught in the hunt. If it's any consolation, the chief says Derek will stay in Scottsdale for the time being. When his case goes to court, I'll make sure the judge knows how much he's helped. Who knows? Maybe there's a treatment program that could help him with his demons."

"That's about the best we can do for him, kid," added Jack. "You know he needs major help. This is probably the best thing."

Eugene folded his hands on the table, fighting for clarity. He thought about his hopes for Derek, but as the pieces assembled and reality replaced unrealistic dreams, his shoulders slumped. Embarrassed by the sudden rise of tears, he pushed back from the table, stood and lumbered to the kitchen. There he leaned against the counter with his back to Jack and Eddie.

"Eugene," Eddie raised his voice, "I know it hurts but, if it's any consolation, between Derek's admission and the lab results from Sandy's apartment, *you* are off the hook. You're free to do as you please."

Eugene turned back to them using both hands to wipe the sorrow from his face. The brightness faded at the sight of Jack's graying face.

"Sandy's autopsy's back already?" he asked somberly.

"Yes, we had the reports rushed." His fingers drummed on the table to create an audible pause. "Ah, there was a second, unidentified DNA donor."

A terrible shadow danced across Jack's face. His jaw clamped. "What was the cause of death?"

"Jack, you don't want—"

"I'm not some pansy-ass civilian, Eddie. Tell me. *Every* detail. You owe me."

"I owe it to you not to say . . . ."

The glare Jack leveled at Eddie bristled the hair on Eugene's neck.

"All right, if you insist." Eddie cleared his throat and began a monotone, almost machine-like delivery. "Both arms broken at the elbow. Right shoulder dislocation. Ocular and facial petechiae and her hyoid bone was broken. She didn't go down without a fight though. She had offensive bruising and two broken fingers."

"Petechiae," Jack repeated. "That's a sign of strangulation. Was that what killed her?"

Eddie looked long and deep into Jack's eyes as if weighing the risk of what he was about to tell him. "At first blush, yes, but the bruising and tearing in her throat indicate the insertion of a foreign object."

Jack was upright in his chair, his arms crossed and his face holding the fragile, defiant expression of a proud man facing a firing squad. "How about . . . You know?"

"Yes, there is evidence of rape and . . . Shoot me if you want, but that's all I'll say."

Watching from the periphery, Eugene ached with guilt. His pain for Derek weighed heavier on him than his grief for Sandy in spite of her horrible death.

"Attacker's description?" asked Jack.

"Caucasian male. Strong, a little bigger than average judging by the hand impressions left on her neck."

Jack hauled himself from the table, eyes glistening, shoulders slouching, "I'm tired, guys. I gotta go lay down. Eugene, there's an iPhone charger in the kitchen. Eddie, these are my notes from

Schaefer's interview. Near the end Derek told us of an incident at one of the Luchador parties. I think you'll see similarities to Sandy's murder." He nudged a yellow legal pad to Eddie and in the process uncovered the blurry picture of Ass Clown.

In a heartbeat, Jack had his pistol straight-armed at the picture. Eddie and Eugene stared frozen in concerned silence.

"Jack, what are you doing, buddy?" Eddie said in a low, even voice.

"Just picturing what it'll look like. Wake me in an hour if I'm not up." He holstered his weapon and headed for a bedroom.

Eugene studied Eddie. His face looked ashen and his hair even grayer than a few minutes before.

"It's all my fault," said Eddie. "If I'd dealt with the Luchadores seven years ago, Sandy would still be alive."

"And your daughter might not," Eugene offered. "I doubt there's a parent on earth that would fault you for protecting your family and living to fight another day."

"Thanks . . . that helps," said Eddie, although his red-rimmed, basset-like eyes betrayed him.

Eugene pushed the yellow pad toward him. "Have a look at the notes. Like Jack said you'll see some similarities. That foreign object you mentioned was probably Ass Clown, if you know what I mean."

Eddie wilted even more. "Already aware, Eugene. There were details in the report that I left out for Jack's sake. God, if I survive this, I'm done with police work. It's somebody else's turn to wallow in the dirt and frustration."

Eugene tapped a finger on the yellow pad. "Why not go to work for Jack? Sounds like he's got a sweet deal going up north. More play time than nastiness, if you know what I mean."

"He *has* offered, but I'm not in any shape to—"

"Stop it. Don't talk yourself out of it. Do what's right for you for a change."

Eddie stared at the dining room curtains for a long moment. "Maybe I will." As he said it a weary, but genuine smile graced his face. "Maybe I will. Hey, how'd someone so young get so smart?"

Eugene shrugged, feeling embarrassed heat sliding up his neck. "I guess looking at the world through a camera I see some things more clearly."

Eddie nodded stiffly then pulled the notepad to him. When Eugene set a coffee cup at his elbow, he nodded without looking up. Thirty minutes later Jack stepped from the bedroom looking gaunt, red-eyed and wrinkled.

"Feeling better?" Eddie grimaced when he really looked at him. "Wait, don't answer that. You look like someone kicked the shit out of you."

"Funny, I feel pretty good after my nap."

"Looks bad, feels good. You know what that means—"

Jack's face relaxed with a hint of a smile. "Hey, yeah, that's me."

Eugene rolled his eyes. "Real mature, guys."

Jack nodded and smiled, "So, what's the plan? Eddie—I forgot to ask—anything turn up on that sexual hazing search?"

"We found a few things but nothing that fits. Probably a long shot, anyway. Sexual deviance was dealt with differently back when the Luchadores were in school."

Eugene pushed from the table, stood and stepped into the kitchen to retrieve his semi-charged cell phone. After waiting impatiently for the little apple logo to disappear, he opened the email app and messages flooded in as he returned to the dining room.

"Damn, I go off the grid for a few days and my inbox goes crazy." Scrolling through the incoming stream, he clicked on a message from Brinkmann and muttered, "Son of a bitch."

"What's up?" Jack asked.

"The paper's been sold. Cocksuckers are making everyone reapply for their jobs."

"That was fast," said Eddie.

"It's Pete and Condon's money-grubbing family. Christ, they didn't even wait for Oliver's funeral before cashing in."

"Tell me about Pete," said Eddie. "Something about that guy . . . Every time I look at him I want to punch him in the face."

"He's a weasely, brown-nosing prick."

Jack frowned. "Think he has the stones to take Condon out?"

Eugene let his phone clatter to the table, "I thought about that. He has a lot to gain, but he's a chicken shit. He's a lying, manipulating, ass kisser for sure, but outright murder? I don't think so."

"What if the Luchadores had something on him?" Eddie asked.

Eugene straightened. "Hadn't thought of that."

"You know, it struck me as odd when he denied knowledge of the peanut allergy at the hospital," said Eddie. "He's worked for the guy a long time. It had to come up at some point."

"I don't know," Eugene waffled. "Condon was private guy."

"Okay, but somebody in that newsroom is in the Luchador's pocket. I was sure we had him when we arrested Kurt Wragge. It seemed a perfect. . ."

"You arrested Kurt? What for?" Eugene asked in surprise.

Eddie held up the Ass Clown photo, pointing to the blurry hand. "The finger, plus he has the same body type and he had opportunity."

"But Kurt's one of the good guys," Eugene pressed. "He may be rough around the edges but he takes real good care of his little brother. You know Mikey was brain damaged by a drunk driver. Sometimes he gets a little weird, but Kurt manages him."

"Oh, I found that out the hard way," said Eddie, "and made an ass out of myself in the process."

"What happened?"

"When we tried to take Kurt in for questioning, Mikey went nuts. Things got a little rough and it was all for nothing because Kurt lost the finger well after the photo was taken. Look it up on your phone. It was all over the *Herald's* front page."

Eugene shook his head. “Last time I looked at the *Herald’s* front page it was full of Pete’s lies about me. Now that I’m a free man, I ought to have a talk with him, maybe poke around a little.”

“Poke him in the nose and bust his balls,” joked Jack. “That’ll look good on your resume.”

Eugene grinned, fisting his hands at the thought. “Oh, nothing I’d like better, but that would only play into his game.”

The sound of car doors closing outside sent Jack to the dining room window for a look. “Hell, it’s Chris and his friends from the bar. By the looks of him he’s on another bender. You guys don’t need to stick around to see this. Eddie, can you give Eugene a ride back to his car?”

“Sure, but it’s a mess, like your apartment.”

“I don’t care,” said Eugene. “I just want to fall into bed and sleep for about a week. Then I’ll figure out what I’m gonna do with my life.”

“Maybe you ought to hold off on that for one more night,” said Eddie.

“Why?”

“You don’t have a bed and your water’s been turned off because of a busted pipe. Ah, it’s my fault, I pumped the guys up.”

“Well, shit. Maybe I’ll just get a motel then.”

“I’d pay for it, but it might be safer if you stayed at my place tonight.”

Eugene frowned hard at him. “I don’t know. That’d be kinda weird.”

“He’s right, Eugene,” Jack offered. “The Luchadores are desperate now. It wouldn’t hurt to play it safe.”

Eugene’s faced pinched at the thought, then slowly softened.

“Come on, let me start making things right,” wheedled Eddie. “I know some retired cops in the car detailing business and some moonlighting firefighters who’ll fix your apartment. I might even get them to do it as community service.”

Eugene stuffed his hands in his pockets and slumped in surrender, "Okay, but no spooning and no singing Kumbaya."

"Deal," said Eddie.

24

In the palm tree-silhouetted sky at the end of his apartment complex drive, the last rays of sun died in a tangle of telephone poles and wires hanging like spider webs over the squalor of chain link and squat little houses. Kurt couldn't wait for this night to be over.

Smoke from his cigarette swirled up into his eyes and around his smooth, slightly cauliflowered ears. He shifted his weight to lean his back against a wooden post.

Gym bag in hand and goofy smile on his face, Mikey stepped from the complex's thorny and overgrown barberry bushes.

"You got your suit, right?"

"Yuppers," said Mikey, handing his bag to Kurt who tossed it in the bed of his El Camino.

As Mikey crawled in the passenger side, Kurt pulled open the truck's sagging driver's door. He fired the motor with an eye on the driver's side rearview then cranked down the window and flicked his cigarette butt to the driveway. After thunking the transmission into reverse, he backed out into the drive and headed to the rendezvous.

"Are all the guys gonna be there tonight?" Mikey enthusiastically asked.

"Yep, the whole team."

"Are we driving down to Nacho again?"

"It's Naco," he patiently corrected him, "and no, we're meeting the team at a new place."

"Good, that's a long drive. Did Coach get some new assholes?"

"Nope, I'm gonna be the asshole tonight."

Mikey's face pinched, "You're not an asshole. You're the district champ."

"That was a long time ago, Mikey." He glanced at his brother. "Listen, tonight's gonna be a little different. Coach wants me to take on the whole team and teach 'em a lesson."

"You can take 'em. They're all a bunch of pansies."

Kurt smiled. "Yeah, I think I can handle it. Now, I need you to be quiet. I've got a lot of thinking to do on the drive down."

"We going to the warehouse?"

"No. I told you. Coach Bart has a new place, now shhhh." He placed a cracked and ink-stained index finger to his lips to emphasize his need for quiet.

Mikey nodded and turned to stare at the floorboards, mimicking his brother's serious expression.

On the long, slow swerve down the trash-strewn, potholed lane, he let his mind drift back to the day he met the legendary Coach Bart, a man who forged hopeless mining town boys into champion wrestlers.

Fifteen-year-old Kurt Wragge stared up in awe at the championship banners lining the red brick walls of the Copperfield High School wrestling room. Below, a rubbery, green wrestling mat spread out before him.

Not knowing if street shoes were allowed on the mat, he removed his canvas sneakers. He quietly walked past a wooden rack of jump ropes and a line of lockers. The office sat tucked away in a back corner. Through a large picture window and glass-paned door he saw Coach Bart hunched over a metal desk, reading a magazine. He was a deceivingly large man with a barrel-chested girth that made him look shorter than he was. He had brown/blond hair going gray at the temples and wore heavy, black-framed glasses.

Nervous to the point of being unable to catch his breath, Kurt tapped on the glass. Coach's head turned, his fleshy face scowling at the interruption. The man spun his chair, irritably rose and opened the door.

"What is it?"

"I'd like to join the team," Kurt squeaked, embarrassed by the immature crack in his voice.

"What makes you think you've got what it takes?" growled the coach.

Kurt's eyes dropped to the floor, cowed by the man's power. "I don't know."

"Then I suggest you come back when you do."

Kurt turned, wanting to run, wondering what he was thinking coming in here. Something stirred somewhere deep inside and the courage rose up in him. He turned back to look the old coach straight in the eye. "I'm quick and I'm real strong and I know how to listen."

Coach removed his glasses with one hand while two fingers of the other rubbed the bridge of his wide nose. "Uh-huh, heard that before. There's a mop and a bucket in the utility room." The hand dropped and he stared hard at Kurt. "How about you swab the mat? When the team comes in, you watch and stay out of the way. We'll talk after." He turned his back and settled in his desk chair again. "Now, shut the door and leave me to my work."

Kurt closed the door and went in search of the mop. As he swayed to and fro gliding the wet mop over the mat, he glanced back at the office. Trophies and plaques lined the back wall beyond the coach. In the big window next to the door a stuffed and mounted bobcat stood frozen in a silent snarl, its ears back and fangs gleaming.

Wrestlers streamed in, loud and macho, pushing and shoving each other as they strolled over the damp mat to the lockers. Teasing and sharing school gossip, they disrobed. Some were huge and fat, others small and wiry, all looked dangerous as they donned skin-tight uniforms—he later learned they were called singlets—that transformed them to wrestlers.

"You mopping the floor or looking at my nads, faggot?" called a small boy with weird, shiny ears mashed out against the sides of his short-cropped head.

"Mopping," said Kurt, turning his attention to his task.

"Better hurry up then, we start in five."

Mopping finished and the tools put away, Kurt took a seat on the floor under a bulletin board filled with pictures of what looked to be college and Olympic wrestling teams. A brief quiet fell over the room when coach strode from the office and barked, “Begin!”

The wrestlers set off in a sprint around the room, running faster and faster. The coach blew a whistle and the team gathered. Not speaking, merely pointing, he lined them up. They began tumbling and somersaulting from one end of the mat to the other. Another whistle and the wrestlers paired up, grappling and twisting, throwing and spinning. For nearly two hours sweat poured off of them as they moved from partner to partner. The room’s increasing swelter added a claustrophobic air that even had Kurt panting as he imagined being one of them.

“Hold up!” yelled the coach.

The grappling stopped and all eyes turned to Coach.

“We’ve got fresh meat, boys. Darrel, you’re up!”

The small boy who’d called Kurt a faggot, gave a victorious fist pump and smiled, showing two missing front teeth.

The coach turned his attention to Kurt. “What’s your name, son?”

“Kurt, sir.”

“Kurt here, says he’s quick and strong. Let’s see what he’s got. Darrel, assume the defensive position.”

Darrel moved to the center of the mat and got down on all fours.

“Kurt, get up behind him and wrap your arm around his middle,” ordered Coach.

“Sir, I’m not dressed—” The flash of disappointment on the coach’s face stopped his excuse. “Yes, sir,” he said, feeling awkward and out of place in his outlet mall jeans, t-shirt and stocking feet. He stepped onto the mat and knelt. Revulsion swept over him as he wrapped his arms around the small boy’s sweat-soaked singlet, steamy with body odor.

“Don’t be shy, son,” said Coach with iron in his voice. “Mount him like you mean it. Get your manhood right on up in his backside. Show him who’s boss.” He stepped close and placed a hand to Kurt’s ass, pushing forward.

Confused and uncomfortable, Kurt glanced at the encircling wrestlers. They smiled and nodded. Just when Kurt thought this might be a joke at his expense, Coach Bart yelled, “Wrestle!”

A sudden blur shot out from under him. Still on his knees, Kurt was helpless to stop the little wrestler’s backward whirl that brought wrenching pain as an arm snaked under and over to wrench his shoulder up and his head down. Kurt fell forward, his face mashing painfully into the mat as the little wrestler’s legs slipped between and beside his thighs as a hand—*Where did that come from?*—slid under his chest to clamp a forearm and pull. Kurt held his ground, his size and weight the only things stopping his opponent from driving forward and rolling him over.

The stalemate had lasted only a few seconds when coach bellowed, “Whadda ya got there Darrel?”

“Half Nelson sir,” came the answer.

Kurt felt as though his chest were about to burst. He sucked air, but it seemed there was no oxygen in the room. In a flash, Darrel abandoned Kurt’s forearm, spun slightly behind then slid his other arm under and over to match the first, locked his fingers and increasingly applied pressure until Kurt feared his neck would crack.

“Whadda ya got now, Darrel?”

“Full Nelson, sir!”

Kurt absorbed the agonizing pain sure his spine would crack at any second then Coach Bart yelled, “All right, show him the Father Nelson!”

Darrel relaxed his grip enough to slide all the way around behind. Unbelievably, he began humping and howling like a dog on a bitch in heat. All around the team laughed and applauded.

Rage spiked hard and fast. Kurt leaped to his feet, wheeled and grabbed, catching a handful of sweaty singlet. He yanked Darrel off balance, wrapped an arm under his crotch and lifted. Before he could slam him to the mat, Darrel groped and contorted to knock Kurt’s knees out from under him. They went down hard, Kurt’s head bouncing off the mat. He blinked away stars only to see Darrel’s green, singlet-clad ass and balls coming down to grind mercilessly against his face.

"Teabag! Teabag! Teabag," came the muffled chant through the flesh-filled spandex wrapped around Kurt's thrashing head. His strength gone, Kurt opened wide to let the tender, flesh filled fabric fill his mouth. He bit down hard. The 108-pound champion let out an ear-splitting shriek that silenced all but the coach who bellowed with laughter as Kurt's jaw stayed clamped like a terrier on a rat.

"Ah, ha, ha! Well, I think you'd better tap out, say 'uncle' or something, Darrel," chortled the coach.

Darrel punished the mat, slapping frantically. "Uncle! God, make him stop!"

Kurt loosened his jaw, not caring what punishment was about to come. He'd done what he had to.

Darrel rolled off, his hands rushing to his crotch, "Fuck, coach, I think he crushed one of my goddamn balls!"

"Tape an aspirin to it, Darrel. You underestimated your opponent."

"That was an illegal move!"

Coach's face went from childish exuberance to deadly serious in an instant. "Shut yer gob before I knock out the rest of yer teeth."

Darrel shrank back like a beaten dog. "Yes, sir."

"New kid . . . What's your name again?"

"Kurt."

"Kurt, follow me to my office. We're gonna have a little talk."

Certain the principal and his mom—maybe even the police—were about to be called, he followed, plodding through the ring of wrestlers who he was sure stepped aside only because they saw him as dead meat.

Chest heaving, fighting the urge to vomit, Kurt heard the door close as he plopped into a hard metal chair beside the big desk. Coach loomed past.

"Need a bucket? You gonna hurl?"

"No," gasped Kurt, willing his lunch to stay down.

"You're slow and out of shape," said the coach.

"Man. . . I've never . . . seen . . . I mean . . . God, he's quick."

"Explosive is the term I prefer. If you put in the work you could be, too."

Stomach twisting, Kurt barely heard the words. His hands rested on his knees. His chest heaved like a fish, hooked and stranded on shore.

Ever so slowly, clarity returned. The panic drained away as blood rushed to deliver oxygen to his overtaxed muscles.

"Took you a while, but eventually you found your balls . . . Well, his balls anyway."

"Am I in trouble?"

"Son, what happens on the mat stays on the mat. The school gives us a certain amount of leeway when it comes to how we get the job done and this—" He rolled back in his chair to sweep his hand at the gleaming trophy wall "—proves that we do indeed get it done."

Kurt nodded.

"Freshman, correct?"

"Yes, sir."

"You have a brother in junior high and your mom works some long hours at the diner, right?"

Kurt nodded. "How did you know?"

Coach Bart ignored the question. "And you lost your dad a few years back?"

"Yes, sir. He worked in the smelter. There was an accident."

"That's a tough one. Did his passing make you angry?"

"A little, but I got over—"

"You got sent home for fighting the first week of school. And two weeks ago you were sent to the principal for a scuffle by the lockers."

Kurt's eyes narrowed.

"That's right, I've had my eye on you. Winning requires fire in the belly. You need a good bit of anger if you're going to dominate the competition. So, when I spot a kid who's a little angry and willing to stand up for himself, I see potential. Someday I think we'll see your name on one of those banners out there."

Kurt turned his gaze to the banners bearing the names of champions. "I'd like that."

Coach smiled and clapped his hands with a meaty slap that made Kurt jump.

"Welcome to the Copperfield Bobcats, son."

"I'm on the team just like that?"

"It's probationary and, of course, I wouldn't tell anybody about what went on in here today. What happens on the mat stays on the mat, correct?"

"Yes, sir, not a word." Kurt's eyes went to the back wall where metallic statues stood atop gleaming trophies. He imagined himself as a state champion, arms held high in victory. "That's cool. What is it?" Kurt said, pointing to a black fabric skull and crossbones mask stretched over a Styrofoam head.

"That, my son, is reserved for the best of the best. We've had many champions at this school, but only a select few have earned Luchador status."

"How do you earn one?"

"Talent and dedication among other things. It's a special club, joined by invitation only."

"Cool."

"Here's the thing, son. This is important. The Luchadores require absolute secrecy. In fact, if I or any of the other members ever hear of you even mentioning the name, you're automatically disqualified and banned from the team."

"How many Luchadores are there?"

Coach cocked his head and raised an eyebrow.

"Ah, it's a secret. I get it," said Kurt, feeling a special bond forming between them.

Coach Bart slapped him on the thigh, applying a fatherly squeeze. "Get on outta here. Tomorrow I'll have your uniform, shoes and headgear ready. We'll get you on the road to being a champion."

"Yes, sir," said Kurt, beaming.

Under the tutelage of Coach Bart, Kurt became a skillful dominator, terrifying all who faced him. Now, fifteen years later, he stared over the steering wheel of a rattletrap El Camino.

A car horn's blare jerked Kurt from thought. "Fuck! What the hell!" Glancing to the rearview he saw two cars behind, both drivers flailing their arms in frustration. Kurt shot a glance up and down the busy street, saw a hole and gunned it, squealing the tires into traffic. "Cocksuckers," he growled.

"Whatcha think'n about?" asked Mikey.

Kurt's palm smacked the wheel. "Shit. Sorry, Mikey. Just thinking about Coach Bart."

"Is he mad because they arrested us?"

"No, I don't think so."

"I don't like Coach Bart. He's gonna let the other guys hurt you."

"Oh, now I wouldn't worry about it. Coach always knows best." He glanced at his worried brother. "Don't forget you owe him because he paid for your special rehab after the accident."

"I know. I'm sorry."

"That's okay, buddy. Tonight will be a little rough, but things will be a lot easier once it's over."

* * *

Roiling dust glowed red in the El Camino's taillights as they rumbled up the dirt lane to park in front of what looked to be an abandoned ranch house. To the north the harried glow of city lights hovered over the tips of towering saguaros. The image reminded Kurt of his view out the back window of his father's Galaxy 500 as they rolled home after a shopping trip to Tucson.

When Kurt switched off the headlights and killed the motor, Mikey said, "It's dark. I don't like this place."

"Reminds me of home, Mikey," said Kurt, spotting Coach Bart's Cadillac Escalade parked on the side of the house. Opening the door of his El Camino, he caught a sweet, tropical whiff of blooming jimson weed.

Mikey looked west to the San Tan Mountains. "I hear wolves."

"Just coyotes, Mikey. They're more scared of you than you are of them. I'm gonna go in and talk to Coach Bart in private. Sit in the truck for a minute. I'll be right back."

Mikey glanced to the house where yellow light glimmered from somewhere inside. "Okay, but I'm gonna lock the doors."

Kurt grabbed their two gym bags from the bed of the El Camino. He stepped onto the sagging porch and pulled open the splintered and paint-peeled front door. Inside, a jigsaw puzzle of interlocking rubber mats covered most of the living room floor.

Holes in the cheap wood paneling showed wooden studs and insulation. Light from a hissing Coleman lantern cast long shadows. At the far end of the room a white plastic folding table held an orange water jug and a stack of Styrofoam cups.

"That you?" called Coach Bart from the kitchen.

"Yeah. I've got Mikey in the truck, I need to talk to you before he comes in."

Kurt stepped into the kitchen. It's walls were lined with broken cabinets, a shattered sink and a dismantled stove. Bathed in the pale light of a battery-powered camping lantern, Coach stood at a counter wearing pink rubber gloves. He looked like a limp-titted, topless fat woman about to do the dishes. High-waisted polyester coach's shorts covered his middle and white cotton socks and leather sandals covered his feet.

"I thought your brother was staying home tonight," said Coach, looking over the top of his heavy glasses.

"That's what I want to talk to you about. I think we ought to let him drink—"

"Nice try, bucko. We've been over this. You broke him, you take care of him."

"Yeah, but maybe it's time to put him out of his misery. I was thinking, if they find him with the others, maybe they'd think he was the mole in the *Herald* newsroom."

"He's a fuckin' retard. They'd never believe it. Besides if the cops figure out who he is they'll find out how he got hurt. That would lead 'em to me and you. Trust me, they take a second look at you, they'll dig deeper than a few faked medical records."

Kurt stared at the kitchen floor's curling stick-on tiles. A sudden realization gripped him. *Being Mikey's caretaker might be the only thing keeping me alive.*

"Earth to Kurt, you still with me?"

"Yeah, yeah. Just thinking it through."

"Well, quit thinking and leave it to me. You bring his suit?"

"Yeah, of course."

"Well, now you'll have to get him into it and make sure you zip him up tight. Anything short of that and the guys'll think something's off."

"All right, I'll handle it. Is that the stuff?" he asked referring to an ominous brown jar on the counter.

"Yes, I was about to put some in the jug."

"How long will it take?"

"Not long, I mixed some up and squirted it down a stray cat's gullet. The damn thing yowled for less than a minute before it went down. I'm guessing it'll go quick."

"Wait. Mikey's gonna see and hear. How do we deal with that?"

"You're really trying to force my hand here, aren't you?"

"No, just trying to fix the problem I created," Kurt lied.

"Bullshit. The whole thing ends tonight just like we planned. Mikey will return home with you unharmed. Agreed, *compadre*?"

Kurt put his hands on his hips, exhaling a chest full of frustration. "Agreed."

Coach broke a piece of wood from a splintered cabinet frame and motioned for Kurt to follow him into the front room.

He unscrewed the water jug's lid then sifted the deadly granules into the sports drink, mixing it with the chunk of wood. "Here's how we'll do it. I'll talk up the violation of team rules bull crap—"

"The guys are gonna bitch about the lack of fresh meat," Kurt interrupted.

"They will until I tell 'em you'll be their bitch for the night."

"True."

I'll make 'em go three minutes with you then call for a water break. It's hotter than hell and all but Steve are out of shape, so they'll really be sucking air. I'll find some reason to grab Mikey and choke him out before the shit hits the fan. It'll be your job to carry him outside and strip off the suit. Grab some trainer's tape from my bag and use it to make sure he stays put.

Arms crossed and eyes narrow, Kurt nodded approval.

"How big a fight do you think I should put up?"

"Depends," he said, smiling. "How eager are you to lose your cherry?"

"I ain't no fag, coach."

"Well, then I'd make 'em earn it. The harder they work, the more they'll drink. I'll watch over the jug to make sure nobody grabs water early. Do you really think you can take on all five and win?"

"I believe I can hold them off for three minutes. I mean, Wrigley's gonna be a monster but he's got no wind."

"Sure, sure, but Steve Painter's looking pretty good these days. Says he's into some new workout called cross-fit."

"He's definitely a concern, but three minutes? I think I can at least give 'em a run for their money."

"That's my boy," said Coach, slapping a hand to Kurt's shoulder. "Give 'em hell. Now, go get our little retard and get him ready. The guys should be rolling in any minute."

25

Kurt stepped back into the night and motioned for Mikey to come in. Mikey crawled out, eyes peering into the darkness. "Double-time, Mikey. I need to get you suited up. The guys are on their way."

Mikey did as he was told, adding an awkward quickstep to his pace as he climbed to the porch and began to disrobe even before he'd cleared the door. Kurt pulled the black leather suit and a bottle of baby powder from a gym bag.

"Long time no see, Mikey. How's it hanging?" bellowed Coach.

"Good, sir," said Mikey, smiling weakly, "but it's dark and scary outside."

Coach stepped up to tousle his hair. "Well, you're inside with us, now, where it's safe. Get your suit on and get ready. We're gonna have a wild time tonight."

With Kurt's help, Mikey powdered his body and stepped into the legs of the suit.

"You getting fat, Mikey?" joked Coach, "Or is your suit shrinking?"

"You're the fat one," snapped Mikey. He had both legs in and was rising to his feet.

"Hey, not cool," said Kurt. "We don't talk to Coach Bart like that."

"No offense taken, boys. I am fat and I'm getting old. What's got your dick in a knot, Mikey?"

Mikey looked to Kurt for approval. Kurt nodded his okay. "You're gonna let them hurt Kurt. He says he's gonna be the asshole tonight."

"Yes, and I'm sorry for that . . . but Kurt understands that this is a team-building exercise, right?"

"Yeah. Mikey, Coach thinks the team is getting soft and it's my job as district champion to prove it to them. Besides, it'll only be three-minute rounds. I think I can handle 'em."

The boy offered a sullen nod as he slid his arms into his black suit, then let Kurt zip him up the back.

"You ready for the mask?"

He nodded again and Kurt tugged the black leather mask down over his head, adjusting it so he could see and breath. "Mikey, now this is real important," he said, tucking the hem of the mask down into the neck of the suit. "The water jug is off limits. Tonight you and I drink from our own district champion water bottles." He held up a blue plastic bottle and twisted the lid until the safety seal cracked.

Mickey shook his head. "That's just stuff from the store. I'm not a baby."

"Come on, buddy, play along, okay? You still want to be a member of the team, don't you? You know this is all just good fun."

Mikey nodded and took the offered bottle.

"Good, now head on over to that corner and keep quiet. Wait, I gotta zip your mouth—"

"It's hot, don't—"

"Shut yer yap, Water Boy," Kurt ordered through clenched teeth. He shook Mikey's shoulders firmly, adding a close-up, steely-eyed glare that said the game had begun.

Instantly becoming the submissive, Mikey lowered his head. Kurt zipped the mouth shut, turned him and shoved him to a corner of the room.

"I see headlights. You ready, Kurt?" asked Coach Bart.

"Let's do this!" He slapped his hands together and sucked in deep breaths, pumping himself up just as he had before every match. His shirt came off first then he kicked off his heavy, steel-toed work shoes and white cotton socks.

At the edge of his vision he saw Coach watching, arms crossed on his broad, sagging chest. The old man smiled and nodded when Kurt's pants and boxers came down. Kurt turned his back to his icon, showing off powerful muscles sculpted by both the gym and the heavy work of the pressroom.

"You're still the champ," crooned Coach. "God, but you are an amazing specimen."

Kurt kicked his pants to the wall and turned to give his mentor the view in full. The old man's eyes widened, his thin mouth formed an O. He then licked his lips and nodded. Kurt simultaneously leaped in the air, pumped his fist and let out a macho howl.

The front door opened, admitting Clyde Wrigley, Riley Mitchell, Darrel "Doc" Smith, Phil Simon and Steve Painter. They wore street clothes and carried gym bags. All looked angry and haggard in the low-angled lantern light that cast long shadows behind them.

"Nice digs, Coach. How'd you find this shit hole?" asked Doc.

"You can thank Phil for this *shit hole.* Right, Phillip?"

"It's a flip. My company's gonna gut it in a few weeks. Coach asked me to find something a little closer than Mexico."

"Good," said Wrigley. "Those little beaners we've been doing don't have much fight in 'em. When's the fresh meat arriving?"

"You're looking at him."

Five sets of eyebrows raised and their faces grew eager as they turned their gaze to Kurt and his angry, indignant face.

"Kurt?" asked Wrigley. "Because he was an idiot and wore the mask when he did the waitress?"

"That's correct, Clyde. Let this be a lesson, gentlemen. The price for putting us at risk is an all-on-one, dog-pile match," said Coach. "Since Kurt is the only virgin among us, I figured that'd put a little lead in your pencils. What do you think, boys?"

Smiles spread across their faces.

Even Riley Mitchell, stern-faced and doubtful, cracked a grin. "Damn, Kurt. You're the only guy ever to make the team without losing his cherry. I've wanted to split you in two since freshman year."

"You little faggots are gonna have to earn it," taunted Kurt, head down, fists curled and arms flexing. "I ain't no scared little teenager and I haven't let myself go like you pasty-assed losers."

"I still get my fair share of action," bragged Wrigley.

"Busting hookers and johns? What a workout," snarked Kurt.

Wrigley, a former heavy-weight champion, stepped up close, his bulk and raw power menacing. "Coach, are you in the mix on this one?"

"Nope, sittin' it out."

"Good, 'cause I call dibs on busting his virgin ass. Anybody got a problem with that?"

Kurt's balled fist shot up fast, connecting with Wrigley's crotch. The man grunted with pain, his hands reflexively clamping Kurt's shoulders. His forehead slammed down on Kurt's nose. Broken many times in competition, his nose refused to bleed, but that didn't stop the fireworks from bursting in his head. "I'll fucking kill—"

"BREAK IT UP!" bellowed Coach Bart, pushing in between them. "Now, we're gonna do this right. No striking, you got it? Grappling only. And we're going with three-minute rounds."

Both Kurt and Wrigley stepped back, obviously forcing down their hatred, if only for a moment. The rest of the team jumped, clapped, and howled their approval.

Coach smiled as he held up his arms like a game show host revealing the grand prize behind door number two. "Dress out and mask up, gentlemen. Your opponent awaits his punishment."

Shirts, ties, pants, socks and shoes were stripped off and tossed to the corners of the room.

Coach removed Kurt's clown mask from his gym bag and handed it to him. "Looks like you got 'em pumped up. How's the nose?"

Kurt put a finger to the side of one nostril and then the other to shoot snot and clots of blood to the mat. "Fine, Coach." He smiled then stretched his mask wide and tugged it down over his face.

At the far end of the room, naked and pasty in the lantern light, his opponents donned their masks amid pushing and shoving, joking and laughing just like the high schoolers they'd been so many years before. Kurt nodded. *Three minutes? Yeah, it'll all be over in three minutes.*

Kurt glanced to Coach as the old man took care of business. He'd donned his skull and crossbones mask and was adding a few strokes of pressure to the Coleman lantern. He straightened to say something to Mikey as he draped a whistle and stop watch around his neck. He then stalked to the center of the room where he turned his back to the team to offer Kurt a confident wink. Turning to the team, he bellowed, "Wrestlers ready?"

Riley, Phil, Doc, Wrigley, and Steve stepped up in a line, their masks on and their pricks obviously at the ready. Even sad sack Phil, who never seemed into the game, was rock hard and gleeful.

"Three minutes, gentlemen, then we break. Now . . . WRESTLE!"

They were on him en masse. Grabbing and twisting, they became a tangle of grunts, screams, howls of pain and pleasure. The combination of Kurt's strength, speed, and cunning kept him safe for only so long. One arm then the other was pinioned. Kurt mentally drifted, feeling outside of himself as all around the animals angled for position. *How long until Coach calls for the break?*

Sure it was well past the three-minute point, weakening and helpless to hold back the torturous pack, Kurt let out a scream of pain as the ultimate punishment began. Clyde Wrigley howled with gleeful domination.

Teeth gnashing, Kurt turned a pleadingly look to his mentor. Writhing shadows danced over the old man's body. Devilish fire flickered in the lustful, hungry eyes behind his mask. He licked his lips, formed an O with his mouth and slid a hand down into his shorts.

Kurt was twisted and bent, choked and gagged. Still there was no call for a break. He gasped for air, sure he was about to black out. A tunnel of vision opened through the tangle of limbs. Mikey was on his knees with Coach standing over him. *He's gonna let them kill me.*

The whistle blew. The animals released but pain still gripped his body and mind. Kurt fell flat on his stomach then rolled to his back, slimy and spent. He crawled to the edge of the mat, ripped off his mask and vomited.

"Five minute water break and we go again," bellowed Coach.

The words sounded thin through Kurt's thick fog of agony. Kurt curled to a fetal position. He focused on Mikey filling Styrofoam cups with the green "sports drink" poison. The wrestlers' masks pulled up to their foreheads revealed red faces gasping for air. The team swarmed the drink table. Cup after cup was drained. Nothing happened.

"Two minutes! Drink up and get your pansy asses back on the mat!" growled Coach.

Just as Kurt concluded this was all a cruel joke and Coach had indeed planned for them to bugger him to death, Riley let out a primal scream and doubled over. Steve plopped back on his ass, his face a mix of pain and confusion. He yelped over and over like a dog kicked in the stomach. A chorus of death screams filled the room. Doc flopped on his back, arms flailing and legs goose-stepping to an unknown rhythm. Then the vomiting began. Blood and bile splashed as the wrestlers writhed in agony.

"KURT! MOVE!" Coach's voice strained to rise above the cacophony of death and Kurt saw Mikey, limp on the floor with Coach kneeling over him.

Ignoring his own pain, Kurt darted to the black leather crumple on the floor and hoisted Mikey over his shoulder. Coach tossed a roll of tape and Kurt caught it with one hand. The next moment he dashed through the front door, dumped Mikey onto the dirt and tugged off the suit.

Mikey's eyes fluttered open. He frowned as Kurt wrapped tape around his wrists and ankles. "W-what?"

"Hush, Mikey, I'll be right back. I'll lock you in the truck to keep you safe." He lifted him effortlessly, yanked open the El Camino and heaved him in. Adrenaline pumping, he dashed back inside.

* * *

Eddie woke in his dark apartment kicking at imagined rats nibbling at his toes. In his dream he'd been in one of the countless condemned buildings of his childhood, sleeping in a chipped and rusty iron bathtub next to a broken toilet piled high with shit.

Night terrors invaded all the time now that the Luchadores had resurfaced. *Well-deserved guilt*?

Charging on a cable next to a folding metal TV tray, his cell phone lit up with a buzz and a chirp.

"What's up, Harry? Don't you ever sleep? Jesus, what time is it? . . . What? . . . They did? . . . Where? . . . Uh-huh. Yeah . . . No shit? . . . Okay, I'll be downstairs in five."

His ratty recliner groaned as Eddie slammed down the footrest. The chair squeaked as it rocked in the dark. Using his cell phone as a flashlight, he hobbled to the kitchen, stooped over by an aching lower back. His groping hand flicked a wall switch. He dumped a bottle of ibuprofen on the counter-top. Palming a can of flat soda, he washed down three tablets. He dropped into a kitchen chair, holding his head and trying to order his jumbled thoughts. By the count of 30, the caffeine and pain reliever slithered through his blood. His body started to catch up with his spinning mind.

"What's up," said a quiet voice from the bedroom hall. Eddie turned to see Eugene headed for the bathroom.

He pushed to his feet. "Hey, I gotta run. Got a call. Mind if I hit the head first?"

Eugene stopped, eyeing him suspiciously. "What's up? Was that Harry on the phone?"

"Yeah, it's the Luchadores. Apparently they were as desperate as we thought. They did a Jonestown in a house down by the San Tan Mountains."

Eugene stiffened. "Suicide?"

"Looks like."

"I don't believe it. No way would—"

"Shut your mouth and open your ears. Harry just got a call from Pinal County. Unless there's a bunch of naked copycats dressing in Luchador masks, it's them. I'm thinking they knew we were getting close and decided to—"

"I want to come."

"Uh, no, no way. This is police business." Eddie pushed by him to the bathroom and closed the door.

Eugene waited, arms crossed and foot tapping until Eddie emerged to hurry back to his recliner to pull on his shoes. "At least take me to my Jeep."

"No, no time, I gotta go. You can let yourself out or stay and get some more sleep. Harry's probably downstairs already."

Eugene's jaw tightened. "Sure, sure. Go on. I'll figure out how to get home from here."

* * *

Eddie waited at the front door of his complex as Eugene came down surprised that he was still there.

"No Harry yet?"

"Any minute now. Why don't you grab some more shut-eye?"

"Could you?"

Eddie shrugged. "No, guess not."

Eugene thumbed his iPhone to life.

"Who you calling?"

"Brinkmann, not that it's any business of yours. If he doesn't answer this time I'll call a cab."

Harry roared into the lot, cruiser headlights blinding as he rolled up and stopped with a chirp of the tires.

"Sorry, Eugene, no time."

Eugene stepped to Harry's window and motioned for him to roll it down.

"No time for small talk, kid," Harry said.

"No shit. Eddie's back to being an asshole."

"Yeah, so? And no, we can't take you."

"I know. I just wanted to tell you that I don't think the Luchadores would go out like this. Something stinks."

"I'll keep an open mind. We gotta go."

Eugene stepped back, offering a wave to Harry with one hand and middle finger to Eddie with the other. As they roared from the lot, Eugene realized it was 2 a.m. and he was locked out of the apartment.

Fucking cops.

He dialed Andrew Brinkmann's number again. The call went straight to voice mail. Just as he pocketed his cell, it rang with an unrecognized number.

"Hello, this is Eugene."

"Oh my god, you answered. Are you back? Have you heard?" said a woman's voice.

Thinking it might be the paper's summer photo intern, he said, "Amy? I don't—"

"No, this is Olivia. The Luchadores committed suicide. I'm heading down . . . How did you get your phone?"

"Olivia? Oliver's granddaughter?"

"Yes, we met at the hospital, remember? I'm heading down to the scene. Are you?"

"Maybe you haven't heard. I don't have a job and the paper's been sold."

"I know all about it. Are you heading down?" she repeated, her irritation crackling.

"Let's see. No job, no cameras, and I'm stranded miles from my vehicle. So, *no*. Looks like I'm staying put for the time being. And why would I want to shoot for the *Herald*, anyway? The place is gonna go to hell without your grandfather."

"Listen to me. I have cameras. You'd be working for me."

"I don't understand. What are—"

"I'll explain when I get there. Where are you?"

* * *

As they whizzed down the Hunt Highway on the fringe of the San Tan Mountains, Harry spotted the flashing red and blues from two miles out. "Over there, between the foothills. I see lights."

"Where? I don't—"

"Wait, now I lost 'em. How much farther?"

Eddie stared at the scrolling Google map on Harry's phone, "Says ten more minutes."

"Man, I'll bet it's a circus in there."

The two detectives stared into the distance, their cruiser's siren wailing and grill lights flashing. Coming over a rise, they saw a line of television satellite trucks staged off the highway at the verge of a dirt road leading into the desert. Harry shut down his lights and siren then slowed. He pulled up to a Pinal County Sheriff's cruiser partially blocking the road. Yellow crime scene tape draped from the cruiser's side mirror to a bush at the far side of the road. A lanky deputy waved a flashlight, indicating he wanted to talk.

"If you're here for the main event, you're too late, the wrestlers have all left the building," he said with a grin.

Harry showed his badge and flashed a smile, "Yeah, we heard. Couldn't happen to a nicer bunch of guys. How far in are they?"

"About half-a-mile give 'r take. An old ranch house. You'll know it because there's a bunch of cops standing around."

"Anybody here from Scottsdale PD yet?"

"Just the Chief and a PIO. In fact we've got quite a collection of brass and media handlers in there now. I figure they're all having a pow-wow on who gets credit for what and how they're gonna feed the vultures." He tilted his head to the news trucks lining the highway.

"Gawd, but they are a pain in the ass, aren't they? Any of 'em giving you guff?"

"Oh, sure, but we've got 'em pretty well trained. They calmed down once I told 'em the PIO's will talk to them soon. Only one way in and that's past me. So, they don't have much choice. I will say the scenery's not bad though. There's a hard-bodied little blonde with Channel Seven who's been cuddling up to me, hoping to get the inside scoop."

Eddie reached past Harry to offer the deputy a fist bump, "Keep up the good work, soldier. Harry, shall we go see what's left of the Luchadores?"

Harry let his foot off the brake as the deputy lifted the tape. They rolled in, silent with anticipation as the tires crunched on the dirt road. The night sky eerily flashed red and blue above the low, desert foliage. They topped a short rise that looked down on the scene. Generator-mounted floodlights illuminated the small house surrounded by yellow tape and emergency vehicles.

"Circus would be an accurate description," said Eddie. "And media isn't even here yet."

"Looks like this is as close as we're gonna get," said Harry, pulling off the roadway to cozy the grill of the cruiser up to a large bush nearly 50 yards from the house. "You got room to get out?"

"Yeah, I'll make it," said Eddie, opening his door and shoving aside the bush.

The Chief stood with a small circle of officials gathered beside a Pinal County crime lab van parked outside the wide ring of yellow tape. Inside the tape, two lab techs in white coveralls and hairnets documented foot and tire impressions as a third ran a video camera.

Through the narrow view offered by the open front doorway, a naked corpse with agonized limbs lay sprawled on the floor as techs in full hazmat suits worked the scene.

"The Chief looks like someone shit in his cereal," said Eddie, as they approached.

Chief Royal brightened a little on seeing Eddie and Harry and excused himself from the group to take them aside.

"It's nasty in there, detectives. No one's allowed in until the techs give the all clear. At first blush it appears to be a group suicide. They're testing a water jug and cups for poisons. Five victims, all male, all middle aged, naked except for their masks."

"Judging by the lack of fragrance, it happened fairly recently," said Harry.

"Early estimates are a matter of hours. As you can see, at least one of the bodies is still in full rigor."

"How'd they find'em way out here?" asked Eddie.

Chief Royal tilted his head to a paramedic squad where a bright-eyed elderly man perched on the bumper. Beside him a big-boned female deputy in a khaki shirt and dark brown pants nodded as she took notes.

"Scuttlebutt is that he's a neighbor. Paramedics want to keep an eye on him and that first-on-the-scene deputy until it's identified what they stumbled into."

"I take it she's Pinal County?"

"Yes, Deputy Deb Sorensen."

"All right," said Eddie. "We'll mosey on over and listen in."

Deputy Sorensen was finishing up her interview as Eddie and Harry strolled up. "All right, Mr. Sackett. Thanks for your time," she said, pocketing her pen, then shaking the old man's hand. "I think we'll get the all clear soon, so you can head back home and get some shut-eye."

She stood and cast her gaze to Eddie and Harry. They waved, nodded, then made introductions.

"Mr. Sackett here's a neighbor," she offered. "Said his grandkids spotted an Escalade pulling out onto the highway."

Harry took his own notes as the old man retold his story.

"Like I told the young lady, we ain't got no Cadillac types living around here, so I thought I'd come on over for a look. Thought maybe there was some drug dealing going on. I came up the wash. Kept my distance at first. When I didn't see anything moving for the better part a twenty minutes, I came on in for a look. Front door was open and what I saw darn near gave me a heart attack. I called 9-1-1 as I moved back and here I sit. Awful stuff. They're all twisted up and foamy at the mouth."

A man in a yellow hazmat suit exited the house, peeling himself out of his protective gear. Sweaty-faced, he downed a bottle of water then lumbered over to them.

"Looks like you two are good to go. Whatever killed them wasn't airborne, so no worries." He looked over the neighbor. "If you're feeling all right, sir, you can head on home, that is if the deputy here is done with you."

"I'm good," said Deputy Sorensen. "I've got his contact information, if you need it detectives."

Harry piped up, "I've just got one more question. Don't suppose your grandkids got a plate on that Escalade?"

"No, son, no plate. Sorry."

"Thank you, sir. Where you parked?" asked Eddie.

"I'm riding that beautiful blonde tied off over there past the fire engines."

"Excuse me?"

"It's a horse, son. Her name's Ellie Mae and she's a lot quieter than my truck."

"Don't suppose Ellie Mae's last name is Clampett, is it?" Asked Eddie with a sly smile.

The old man arched an eyebrow. "No, but she's just as blonde and twice as pretty."

All three men dared a look to the female deputy who smiled and shook her head. "Thanks for your help, Mr. Sackett. Hope the second half of your night is better than the first."

"I know mine'll be better 'n yours," the old man said, heading for his horse. He called over his shoulder, "You all take care and I'm sorry you have to deal with such devilish business."

Harry looked to the tech who still glistened with sweat from wearing the hazmat suit, "I assume it's safe to enter the house?"

"Yes, but Deb, you're the lead on this until our detectives arrive. Your call on who enters and when."

Deputy Sorensen looked to the Harry and Eddie. "I'll take you in, if you promise not to step on our guys' toes. I'll warn you, it's pretty awful. No decomp yet, but the bodily fluids will set you back on your toes."

"Lead the way," said Harry.

The tech handed out disposable booties, hairnets and gloves as they gathered on the porch. Stepping in through the door, one by one, they edged the room so as not to get in the way of the lone remaining crime lab technician.

All were stunned to silence as they took in the scene. The sharp, warm air in the room still reeked of vomit. Five naked men now in full rigor, lay splayed out around the rubbery mat, their limbs at agonized angles with toes and fingers curled. All were smeared with a foamy, green-brown crust.

"Any word on what they ingested?" Deputy Sorensen asked of the lead technician.

"There's a half-empty jar of sodium cyanide on the kitchen counter and initial tests indicate that's the chemical in the water jug."

"I've read that cyanide smells like bitter almonds," said Harry, making small talk to shake himself from the grip of the horrific scene.

"True," said the tech, "but does anyone really know what almonds smell like?"

All raised their eyebrows and nodded in unison.

"I'll bet they smell like cyanide," said Eddie.

"I smelled almond extract once," said the deputy. "Can't say it smells like much of anything." She edged past Eddie and Harry then crossed the room to the pile of clothing.

"All this has been photographed, correct?" she said to the lead tech.

"Yes, ma'am, both video and stills."

Plucking the first pair of dress pants from the top of the pile, she slid a hand into a back pocket and pulled out a thin wallet. It fell open to reveal a badge.

"Holy shit. Uh, excuse my French," choked out the deputy. "This is a State Patrol badge."

The words hit Eddie and Harry hard. Both of them stepped back.

"No shit? Is there a name?" asked Eddie.

She flipped the badge holder around to look at the ID. "Says he's Clyde—"

"Wrigley," blurted Eddie, his eyes scanning the corpses.

"You know him?"

"Yes . . . and I believe that's him," he said pointing to the largest corpse in the room. "If you lift the mask I'll make the ID."

Deputy Sorensen looked to the tech, "You care to do the honors?"

"Sure," said the tech. "The guy in the pirate mask?"

All three nodded.

The tech moved to the body, knelt and shot one more close-up picture before peeling up the mask to reveal a face deformed by the evil grin of rictus.

"Holy Mother of God," said Eddie. "Wrigley was the Anal Pirate."

"What?" asked Sorensen.

"Sorry, Deputy, it's a nickname given to him by kids he tortured."

"That's disgusting," said the tech, releasing the mask as though it were red hot.

"See that guy over there in the clown mask?" Eddie pointed.

Sorensen and the tech nodded.

"They called him the Ass Clown. Those two were the ring leaders."

"They must have decided to off themselves because we were closing in," offered Harry.

"Excuse me," interrupted the lead tech, "Detective Ibarra, didn't you work with the State Patrol on the original Luchador investigation?"

"Yes, I—"

"Deb, I'm not sure he should be in here." He tilted his head to Eddie, before stepping to the deputy to pull her out of earshot.

Deputy Sorensen's head whipped around. "I'm afraid I'm going to have to ask you two to step out. Our detectives will fill you in on the rest of the details."

Eddie's shoulders drooped. His chin down, he blew out a long breath. "I understand."

"Wait," snapped Harry. "He was set up. The fact that Wrigley is present makes it clear—"

"No," interrupted Eddie. "She's right. Let's clear out so they can do their work. We need to fill the Chief in on what we know. Deputy, you'll note for the record that I touched nothing, correct?"

Deputy Sorensen scanned Eddie from top to bottom then glanced to the floor around him. "Will do," she said, her angry gaze pushing them from the room.

26

As Eugene sat waiting on a stucco wall near the entrance to Eddie's apartment building, he surfed the local news sites on his iPhone. As expected, actual information on the Luchador's demise was thin, but bright graphics and titillating headlines were thick. Disgusted, he stood, pocketed his phone, and stared out at insects swarming in the dim, yellow-orange glow of the parking lot lights.

His phone vibrated and lit up with Olivia's number. A shock wave of anticipation swept through him as he tapped the screen to answer.

"I'm in the complex, but there's about a million different buildings. Where the heck are you?"

"Hang on. Let me look around." He lowered the phone to cast his eyes to the buildings in search of a number or letter. "I'm in front of building C if that helps. I think it's on the south side."

"Okay, I think I've got it. I'm in a white Jeep Grand Cherokee."

"I'm standing by a . . . Wait, I see you. Come on over."

He heard the Grand Cherokee's engine rev as she caught sight of him. The vehicle rolled up in a rush. Pulling open the passenger side door, he saw a blue canvas bag on the seat.

"That's for you," she said. "Hop in."

Eugene picked up the bag, crawled in to settle in the front passenger seat, and set the lumpy bag on his lap.

"You look awful. What happened?"

"Well, let's see, I smacked my head while running from the police, got punched in the eye by a homeless guy and got in a street fight with bunch of gang bangers who tried—but failed—to shoot me. Oh, and I haven't shaved for a few days. All in all, I'll have to say that being a fugitive isn't all it's cracked up to be." He gave her a false smile and lifted an eyebrow.

Eyes wide, Olivia shook her head and blinked as if making room in her brain for all the new information. "You're kidding . . . No, guess you're not. At least the fugitive part's straightened out. Is this where you live?"

"No, this is where Detective Ibarra lives. I was staying here because the police trashed my place. Gosh, these leather seats feel pretty darn sweet. Your Jeep is a lot nicer than my old beater," he said, switching gears and savoring keeping Olivia off balance.

"Square headlights or round?" she asked, her recovery quick enough to toss back her own non sequitur.

"What?"

"You say you have an old Jeep. The headlights aren't square are they?"

A huge grin spread across his face. For the first time he found the courage to really look at her. Her dark hair was pulled back in a pony tail and silver earrings twinkled above the collar of her dark blue blouse.

"Round, of course. A CJ-7 with a straight six and a hard top. Mostly stock."

She smiled. "Respectable"

Shaking off a sudden mix of curiosity and outright attraction, he turned his mind to the bag on his lap. He opened its front flap as she threw the Cherokee into reverse and whipped it around to speed out to the street.

"I'll be darned, I've been looking at these," he said, staring into the bag full of Fuji X series cameras and lenses. "I figured you'd have some little point-and-shoot."

She took her eyes off the road for a second, offering a friendly, but disdainful glance. "Think you can figure them out by the time we get there?"

He reared back, feigning indignation. "It's a camera! Of course I can. Oh, hey! You've got the new, fast telephoto. Nobody has that yet. Sweet!"

This time she kept her eyes on the road and simply smiled. "Grandpa was in Japan last month and got a tour of the factory. He says mirrorless cameras are the future."

"I think he's right and I think I'm in love." The instant the word love left his lips he wanted to haul it back. His ears suddenly grew hot.

"With the cameras, right?"

"Uh, yeah. The cameras, of course . . . Speaking of the future, what did you mean when you said I'd be working for you?"

"*The Arizona Providence*."

"What's that? I haven't heard of it . . . Wait, no. I saw it on the card you handed me at the hospital." He had the second camera body out of the bag and was mating it to the telephoto.

"Actually, nobody's heard of it. We went live shortly after I learned of the Luchador's demise."

"You're telling me you've started an online newspaper? Was Oliver in on this?"

"It's non-profit and online only. It's more of an investigative organization than an actual publication. Grandpa and I have been working on it for a little over a year."

"How many employees?"

"Three for now. You, me and a wicked-smart web developer named Austin."

"No kidding? How—"

"I think we'll be picking up a couple more in the coming days. I'm guessing there will be an exodus from the *Herald* soon."

Mouth agape, Eugene struggled to find words, "O-Oliver saw this coming, didn't he?"

"Yes, not quite in the way it happened, of course . . . And we thought it'd be at least another year but, yes, he did."

"Oliver said the traditional newspaper model will eventually fail. How do we make it work?"

"I like the 'we.' That says you're on board. The 'how' factor is still open for debate, but the business model Grandpa and I decided on is small, lean and focused on investigative journalism. We earn the public's trust with top-notch work and survive on fundraisers, grants and offering our services to other news organizations who've cut their own full-time teams."

Eugene's silence drew Olivia's glance. "What's the problem? You look confused."

"Investigative teams generally don't need a photographer."

"They do, they just don't know it. Grandpa was pretty clear on that. Plus, we're all going to have to wear a lot of hats. This won't be easy. In fact, it may not work at all without Grandpa." She took an audible deep breath. "He was the brains behind the operation."

"I don't know. I wouldn't sell yourself short. I'm impressed with what I see so far."

Olivia rolled her eyes at the compliment.

Both stared silently at the night as they rolled up onto the 202 Freeway.

"Aren't you curious as to why I was staying at Eddie Ibarra's apartment?" asked Eugene.

"Yes, that was odd . . . Just what have you been up to?"

Eugene smiled. "I can't tell you everything just yet, but I will eventually. Eddie's a real jerk, but he's not the guy everyone thinks he is. For that matter, nothing here is what it seems. The Luchadores aren't part of some giant pedophilia ring. From what Derek told us—"

"When did you talk to—"

A horn's honk caused Olivia to swerve as she tried to merge with traffic. "Damnit. My fault." She waved an "I'm sorry" hand at the driver she'd almost hit as he passed with an indignant stare. She then slid in behind him.

"So, when did you talk with Schaefer?"

Eugene smiled again, taking pleasure in the outrage he knew that Pete would feel in getting scooped. "Right after the Luchadores arranged his escape from jail in the hope of killing him. A friend and I stumbled into him by accident. He'd been shot three times and hit by a truck. You sure you don't want to talk about this later? You're about to merge onto the 101 and the 202 is faster."

"Shit!" hissed Olivia as she double-checked her mirrors, signaled and moved over. "Who's your friend?"

"Mind if I keep that a secret for the time being? I didn't know he was a friend. Heck, I didn't even know he was watching over me. I kinda owe it to him to ask his permission before revealing his name."

"Fair enough. This is all off the record. Don't tell me anything that makes you uncomfortable . . . How on earth did you stumble onto Schaefer?"

"Pure providence. My friend had just picked me up from where I was hiding in Phoenix. We were on our way back to Scottsdale and drove up on an accident. Turns out the accident was part of Derek's escape. Like I said, he was hurt pretty bad when we found him, but we got him patched up. We had almost a whole day together before he ran off and got picked up by the Scottsdale cops."

"What did you two talk about?"

"Lot's of things . . . He's really messed up in the head. Huge mood swings. It's like he's three different people, one funny, one mean and one a scared little kid."

"Wow. Well, with what he's been through—"

"Deep down I think he's a good guy, in spite of what he did. Wish you could have seen how hard he worked to hold it together when we interviewed him about the Luchadores."

"A second ago you said the Luchadores aren't part of a pedophilia ring. What did you mean?"

"They aren't pedophiles. They most likely aren't part of some nationwide ring of perverts, either."

"Then what are they?"

"Sadistic dominators, mostly.

"Like whips and chains?"

"Not exactly. They get off on hurting and degrading . . . like locker room hazing taken to the extreme. I don't know what it was like in girls' high school locker rooms but in the guys' it was all about domination. Towel snapping, Nair in the jock strap. We even had a varsity quarterback who got expelled for tea bagging a freshman."

Olivia's face wrinkled with repulsion. "Boys are so weird. Girls' locker rooms weren't much better, but it was more mental than physical. Back stabbing, insults, cliques."

An image of Olivia, sweaty, half undressed and sitting on a locker room bench flashed to mind. Eugene quickly tucked it away. "Cliques were a big thing for boys, too. But imagine if the domination thing got out of hand. Maybe hazing the freshmen turns into tea bagging and then gets exponentially worse."

"High school is such an awkward time for kids."

"I never got into sports much in high school."

"Why's that?"

"I dunno. I think it was the coaches, mostly. I thought sports should be fun. They acted like it was life and death. I just couldn't buy it."

"My stepdad, the *senator,* was a coach." As she said the title she puffed herself up and lowered her voice. Eugene thought it was the cutest thing he'd ever seen.

"The *senator* was a high school coach before he became a politician. He has a shelf full of trophies and awards. You'd think he'd found a cure for cancer, the way he acts."

"Hey, a sports nut and a politician. I'll bet he and Oliver got along real well."

Olivia's eyes widened. "He was sooo disappointed when Mom announced their engagement. It wasn't long after they were married that the feud over control of the *Herald* started. After Grandma died, Mom was all over Grandpa to retire. She wanted his money so bad she even hired a lawyer hoping to have Grandpa declared incompetent."

"No kidding? I never heard anything about that."

"I think it was before you came to the paper."

"So, the power struggle's been going on that long?"

"Yes . . . Eugene, what do you think of Pete Cunningham?"

"Are you asking if I think he poisoned Oliver?"

She winced at the words then nodded.

"You're not alone in that suspicion. The police are looking at him, too. At first I didn't think he had the ball, uh, courage. But then we wondered if the Luchadores might have something on him."

"So you think he—"

"No. To be honest, the guy makes my skin crawl, but I don't see him as a murderer."

"So, this dominator thing, why didn't it come out before?"

"It did but it got covered up. There's this detective named Clyde Wrigley at the State Patrol. He did the dirty work then blackmailed Eddie Ibarra into taking the blame."

"How do you know? Can they prove it?"

"Derek said he told the whole story to Wrigley. Plus, there's another angle, one involving my friend that I can't talk about yet.

Long story short, Scottsdale PD is looking into Wrigley. It'll make a hell of a story once it all comes out."

"Yes, it will," Olivia said, flashing a crooked, confident smile. "And hopefully, we'll get it first."

Eugene returned her smile. "Exactly what I was thinking."

"Okay, so, back to the task at hand . . . Do you think the Luchadores killed themselves because the police were closing in?" asked Olivia.

"Yeah, but something about it doesn't ring true. These guys are self-centered and enjoy the ugliness of what makes them feel good. They wouldn't just end it by offing themselves. They'd want to leave a big, evil scar on someone else."

"Well, we don't know what's at that house. Maybe there's a bunch of dead kids in there with them."

They drove in silence as the 202 loop made its slow arc to the south. Eugene turned his attention to the cameras, scrolling through menu after menu, setting the cameras up to his liking.

"There's a manual in the back of the bag if you need. Oh, and extra batteries, too."

"No, I think I've got it, everything's fairly self explanatory. It reminds me a lot of an old Nikon FM-2 . . . " He pointed the body with the wide angle toward Olivia and fired off a frame just as she glanced his direction. In the low light, the shutter was more of a ka-thunk than a click.

"Got it figured out?"

Eugene lowered the camera, found the play button and looked at the image he'd just taken. "You have your grandfather's eyes."

When he looked back to her he saw tears welling.

"Sorry, I'm really gonna miss him," said Eugene.

Olivia wiped away the moisture. "You and me both. Now, let's get down there and do his last big story justice."

* * *

Eugene searched the eastern horizon for the first hints of sunrise as they slowed and pulled to the side of the road. Of course, news crews crowded the edge of the Hunt Highway ahead of them.

"How do you want to do this?" asked Olivia.

"What do you mean?"

"You want to get out here so you can slip in unseen?"

"No, maybe if we had a second shooter, ah, photographer. But, if I get caught we'll have no pictures. Let's play by their rules and once we're in, I'll figure out something."

"You'll get swarmed if the other media spots you."

"Good point. I'll keep to the shadows . . . Got a cap or anything?"

"In the back under the shopping bags."

He put the cameras on the floorboard, unlatched his seatbelt and turned in the seat. He moved several reusable Costco bags aside to find the cap.

"Oh, man," Eugene groaned. "It's pink." He settled back into his seat, gingerly turning the hat as if it would magically change colors.

"You have a problem with that?" She fought a teasing smile.

"No, no, not at all. I'm comfortable with my manhood." He didn't miss her approving expression. "Just wondering if it'll attract or repel attention." He donned the cap and draped the wide angle camera around his neck. "What do you think?"

She nodded as she pronounced, "I think you look like a weirdo."

"Perfect. A big story like this always brings out the weirdoes. I'll hang back and follow everybody in when they open up the scene. Once we're in, I'll be the last thing anyone's looking at."

"Okay," said Olivia, slowly pulling back onto the road. "I'll park at the far end of the pack."

Eugene tugged the cap low on his face and hunkered down into the seat. They rolled past the long line of satellite trucks lining the highway and parked at the end of the line in front of a Tucson radio station car.

"So far so good," said Olivia. "You have the cameras figured out?"

"I'm good to go. You want to hop out and do a little scouting?"

Olivia nodded, pulled the keys and opened the door, causing Eugene to squint as the dome light flashed on. "I'll be right back."

As soon as the door closed and the light went off, Eugene's phone came to life with a call from Andrew Brinkmann.

"Hey, buddy," said Brinkmann, "Sorry I missed your calls. Good to see you've been cleared. Where you been hiding?"

"Oh, here and there, I'll tell you over a beer when you get time. Hey, where are you?"

"Down south of Queen Creek. Did you hear the Luchadores offed themselves? Damn, I wish you were down here with me."

"I heard. Wish I was there, too. So, the paper's new owners are making everybody reapply for their jobs. Are you okay?"

"Don't know. Hoping I can hang on until I find another job."

"Pete's probably crowing now that he's the managing editor, right?"

"That's the only good thing to come out of this mess. The new owners brought in their own guy. A weasel named Steve Spears. Pete's still city editor and, let me tell you, he's really got his panties in a wad over it."

"Ha! Tripped on his own dick. That makes my whole year. I take it the cops have you corralled out there somewhere in the desert?"

"Yeah, been sitting on the edge of the Hunt Highway for hours. Word is they're gonna let us into the scene in fifteen minutes. Of course, they said that a half-hour ago."

"Some things never change. Call me when you get clear. We have a lot to talk about."

"No shit. You take care, buddy. I hope to see you back in the newsroom."

"Maybe you will, maybe you won't," said Eugene. "I've already had an offer someplace else."

"No shit? Where? Any openings for reporters?"

"Possibly, but I have to keep it on the down-low for now."

"Got it. Okay, I gotta go."

Eugene ended the call, gleeful at the deception. Using his phone as a flashlight he double-checked his camera settings. After he deciphered how to turn on his camera's wi-fi function, he paired both cameras to his phone. A shadow crossed his face and he turned to see Olivia staring at him through the driver's window.

She opened her door. "You ready? The cops say they'll let us in—"

"In fifteen minutes," interrupted Eugene.

"How did you know?"

"I just talked to Brinkmann. He told me they said fifteen minutes half an hour ago."

"Did you tell—"

"Oh, heck no. He's the competition . . . for now."

Olivia bit her plump lower lip. "You really do look like a dork in that cap."

"All the better to screw the competition with, my dear. Hey, looks like the media horde is on the move."

"Let's go, Pinkie," she laughed.

Eugene winced, but decided the sound of her laughter was worth his embarrassment.

27

Eugene pulled the pink cap down low on his face and stepped from the Grand Cherokee. After a good stretch, he checked the settings on his cameras. Again. "Shall we?" he said, growing nervous now that his real work was about to begin.

Carrying a computer backpack, Olivia went first using her phone for a flashlight. They hung back from the pack of eager journalists trudging up the road toward the scene.

"Look at those poor TV bastards," whispered Eugene. "Glad I don't have to carry all that stuff."

"I'm glad I'm not wearing heels like that blonde from Channel Seven. Who wears heels to a desert crime scene?"

The half-mile walk went quickly. Soon they stood at the top of a small hill looking down on the house. Eugene held back and stepped from the roadway.

"What's up?" asked Olivia.

"Just waiting for the pack to get down the hill, so I get a clean scene-setter."

"Ah, good idea. Can you believe all the cars down there?"

"Yeah, and it'll only get worse. Crews will be drifting in all night." He pulled out his phone. "What's your email? I've got the cameras set up to feed my phone. That way I can send you images as we go . . . just in case I push things too far and get tossed."

"I'll send it to you," Olivia replied, working her phone as she walked.

The media gathered before a podium erected about twenty yards in front of the house. Eugene hung back in the shadows as news crews staked out their territory with the thunk of tripod legs. Yellow tape behind the podium fluttered in the night breeze. Bugs swarmed the generator-powered floodlights.

Atop the little podium, microphones were taped and clipped, growing more precarious with each addition.

The Channel Seven blonde sauntered to the microphones and held up a white notepad. "Anybody need a white balance?" she asked, then waited as the camera operators fired their lights long enough to get a reading. She scanned the crowd as cameramen and photographers nodded or offered good-to-go thumbs. The lights went out to save battery power.

"How about a mic check?" called an anonymous voice.

"Check, check, check. One. Two. Three," enunciated the blonde.

Turning from the first hints of pale sky on the horizon, Eugene looked past the media frenzy to the open doorway of the house. Just inside, a blue blanket covered a stiff body. He dropped to a crouch, zoomed in with the telephoto and made four frames just as a serious-looking detective closed the door.

"I saw one body still in full rigor." Eugene stepped closer to Olivia to show her the frame. "They died within the last eight hours, probably less."

"How do you know?"

"Rigor mortis is an eight hour process. The body's still stiff."

"Got it," said Olivia, making a note. "That's kinda gross."

"Where does the *Arizona Providence* stand on dead body pictures?" asked Eugene.

Olivia stared at the house for a long moment. "As long as they're covered, I don't see a problem. This is an important story. People need to see the reality . . . Here comes a talking head."

An older, lanky man wearing the tan and brown of the Pinal County Sheriff's Department stepped to the podium, flanked by a cadre of city and county officials. In the glare of the over-head floodlights, his white Stetson threw a hard shadow on his solemn and weary face. When camera lights before him fired to life, he flinched then squinted as he set a handful of papers on the podium. Miraculously, none of the microphones toppled off.

"Is everybody ready?" he asked, turning on a used-car-salesman smile. Not waiting for an answer, he began. "I'm Ray Mutchler, Pinal County Sheriff and—"

"Hang on," called out a breathless cameraman, slamming his tripod legs and camera into position at the end of the arc of television cameras.

Annoyance crawled over the Sheriff's face. He glared at a tiny Asian woman scrambling to the podium to perch her wireless mic atop all the others. The crowd of professionals heard her apology then watched her scurry toward the late-to-the-party cameraman.

"I'm Pinal County Sheriff Ray Mutchler and—"

"Can you spell that for us?" came a call from the crowd.

Clearly irritated, the Sheriff loudly enunciated, "M-U-T-C-H-L-E-R. At approximately eleven p.m. we received an anonymous tip that led our deputies to the discovery of several deceased males in the house behind me." He swept an awkward hand toward the house.

"Can you confirm that the Luchadores are in there?" asked an anonymous voice.

"I can't comment on that at this time."

"How many—"

The Sheriff held up a hand. "Let me finish *then* I'll answer what questions I can. At approximately eleven p.m. we received an anonymous tip that led us to the discovery of several deceased males in the house behind me. At this time I won't comment on details, other than to confirm that we are investigating the deaths as suspicious."

"Word is that this was a mass suicide and it's the Luchadores in there," said a rumpled reporter Eugene recognized as affiliated with a local radio station.

"I can't comment on that at this time."

A wave of muffled complaints rolled through the crowd. A cameraman next to Eugene growled, "Christ, they make us hike out here in the middle of the night and they're gonna play the no-comment game."

As the Sheriff waved off question after question, Eugene captured a few images of his animated "No comments," He then watched the other still photographers scramble to get their editors off their backs by filing their first images from the scene. Glad not to be rushed, he turned his gaze to the less obvious.

Staring at the north end of the curving line of television cameras, he noticed the glow of a window on the side of the house. He casually moved back into the shadows. Staying well outside the yellow tape, he crept through the dark until he was square with a small curtain-less window. He hunkered down, raised his telephoto and focused. Plain-clothed cops appeared to be running scenarios, repeatedly looking down then pointing to the back of the room.

He made a few frames then cupped the back of the camera to block the light as he played back his frames. Curious as to what the cops were pointing at, he scrolled to the image taken through the front door then magnified it to look at the background. Its lid askew, an orange water jug sat on a white folding table.

At the podium the Sheriff stepped away and a sweaty man in a white dress shirt and tie took his place. "I'm John Walker, Pinal County attorney . . . ."

Eugene zoomed in and made a few frames. He then turned his back to the scene to block the light from his screen as he selected and transferred the best of what he'd taken into an e-mail to Olivia with the note *"Orange water jug on a table. Cops look interested."*

Seconds later she texted back, *"Too bad we can't confirm poison in there. This press conference is a joke."*

Eugene sent, *"Stalling for time. Politics."*

"Think I should ask about the jug?"

"Not yet. They don't know I'm watching."

Settling in for the long haul, Eugene winced as a rock stabbed into his knee. He brushed it away, refocused on the window and waited.

The coming dawn crept softly into the eastern sky, giving the scene an other-worldly feel. Detectives passed back and forth through the window, their faces stern and arms animated. When one paused—perfectly positioned in the window, his chin in his hand—Eugene fired a few quick frames.

Glancing back to the sky and seeing a balance between the pre-dawn blue-gray and interior lights, he captured another scene setter. *Tragedy framed by the morning's glory.*

Eyes sweeping between the pack, the window and the lighter sky, he fired more frames as the sky gradually became light-saturated.

The moment he'd envisioned from the first second he'd seen the house came together in an instant. A weary, overweight detective stepped into view. Eugene let out his breath like a sniper about to fire a fatal round. The detective bent over and came up holding a limp, crumpled object that Eugene recognized instantly as Ass Clown's mask.

The buffer on his new camera filled quickly as his index finger pressed the shutter button firing frame after frame. "Come on, you bitch, catch up with me," he growled, willing the camera to hurry up and write his images to the memory card.

When the camera caught up, Eugene dove back in, firing more discriminately, better picking his moments. A second detective approached, pointing a flashlight. Its beam gave the mask's wild, red hair an air of evil divinity. Unable to hold back, Eugene filled the camera's buffer again just as a hand touched his shoulder.

Without looking back, he set a non-confrontational tone by saying, "Hey, this is awful isn't it?" Then he turned slowly, assembling his plea to what he assumed was a uniformed cop who would insist he move back to the pack.

"Nice to see you're still coloring outside the lines," said Harry.

Surprised to see the man kneeling, Eugene offered, “I’m outside the tape and no one said anything about staying together.”

Harry almost smiled. “You got what you need?”

“Yep . . . Ah, how many are in there?”

“I see you’re with Condon’s granddaughter. Do you trust her to keep me out of it?”

Eugene nodded.

Harry held up five fingers.

Eugene frowned. “That’s three short.”

“Yep, and, FYI, State Patrol Detective Clyde Wrigley’s one of the dead. Now, no way that information comes back to me, you got it? Work his ex-wife. She can probably confirm.”

Eugene’s eyes widened then he blinked his understanding. “Why do me a favor?”

“Just keeping everyone honest. I think you’ve earned a break for putting up with Eddie.”

“I suppose I should mosey on back to the pack.”

“Yep, and I should get to that piss they think I’m taking.”

Eugene rejoined Olivia in front of the podium. “Did I miss anything?”

“Not a darn thing. Half an hour and they confirmed absolutely nothing. No Luchadores no—”

“What gave us the impression it was the Luchadores in the first place? How’d they find these guys?”

“They say it was an anonymous call. I picked up the Luchador rumor from TV. Heck, for all we know, it’s a bunch of illegals up from Mexico.”

Eugene smirked and whispered, “It’s the Luchadores. Here’s the proof.” He brought his camera to life and showed her the picture of the mask framed in the window. When he zoomed in to make the mask clear on the little screen, she gasped.

“Holy shit,” she mouthed in silence.

“Walk with me,” Eugene said, drawing her away from the crowd. “This is strictly off the record—for now—There’s five bodies and one is a cop named Clyde Wrigley. He has an ex-wife who may be able to confirm."

"Jesus Christ. How did you get this?"

"A friend who said I deserved a break."

"Does anyone else have this?"

Eugene shook his head. "Sending you the images now."

* * *

In the soft pre-dawn light, they found a perch a safe distance from the crowd. Olivia furiously tapped at her laptop keys, occasionally consulting her notebook. "Story's mostly done, I need to reach out to the ex-wife. If her Facebook posts are any indication, there's no love lost between her and her husband, as well as the police in general."

"Don't suppose she came right out and confirmed her husband's demise on Facebook did she?"

"Nope, and let's pray to god she answers my call. You want to work your images while I work the phone? I pulled them from the emails and parked them on the desktop. Photoshop is in the dock."

"Sure," said Eugene, rising to his knees to take control of the little MacBook. "Dang, I'm tired. Never should have sat down."

"Yeah, I'm starving and really need a restroom."

"There's always the command center," said Eugene tilting his head toward a large motor home parked just outside the yellow tape. "Maybe if you ask nice, they'll let you use it."

"Fat chance. I get the distinct impression they'd prefer we leave."

Eugene barely heard her words as his fingers went to work on keys and trackpad.

Minutes later Olivia ended what had clearly been a contentious phone call and smiled. "Not enough to publish, but she's been informed of her husband's death. Detectives questioned her for hours, never mentioning the Luchadores."

"So we've just got the picture?"

"That's a lot more than just a picture, Eugene. It's a scoop and a damn good job. If we play the Wrigley card right, we can sucker punch our competition and all involved. These public servants need to remember their job is to protect and serve, not cover their asses and play politics."

Eugene nodded and returned a sullen smile.

"What's the matter?"

"Nothing . . . You just sounded a lot like your grandfather."

Olivia's eyes welled and she wiped at them, "How're the pictures coming?"

"I've got the mask, the body, the overalls and the talking heads. I just need to double check the spelling on the Pinal County Sheriff."

Olivia consulted her notes and fed it to him, squirming and crossing her legs. "I'm really going to enjoy watching them wet their pants when they see our first edition."

Eugene smiled and handed the laptop back. "Do your thing. I'm gonna go find a bush and pray I don't get arrested for indecent exposure."

"Wait. This won't take long, I want you to hit 'send' on our first post."

Thrilled by the offer and glowing with pride at his night's work, Eugene smiled. "I guess I could hold it a little longer."

"Okay," said Olivia turning the keyboard to Eugene. "Once it's up I'll start working social media."

Eugene took a deep breath and discerned the proper on-screen button. "Goodbye, *East Valley Herald*, and screw you, Pete," he said with a grin. "This one's for Oliver." He clicked the trackpad.

* * *

Sunrise brought along the heat. The generators running the floodlights had been shut down. The desert's quiet returned.

Eugene stayed well away from the crowd and watched from the nearby scrub. The media had broken into cliques, yawning, stretching, and rubbing weary eyes as they laughed at stories of past exploits peppered with the dark humor that took the edge off of covering tragedy.

Two plastic outhouses had been delivered and lines were forming. Olivia stayed perched on her rock, eyeing the officials inside the tape, obviously waiting for her story and Eugene's images to incite a reaction.

Within minutes, the phones of the on-air television talent and camera crews began chirping. Wide-eyed, they scanned their peers. The high-heeled blonde traipsed to the crime scene tape and motioned for a police public information officer to come over.

Eugene raised his telephoto for a closer look.

When the PIO's eyes widened, Eugene captured the moment. *That one gets framed and hung on a wall.*

Still clutching the television woman's phone, the PIO did a quick about face and headed for the Sheriff. A law enforcement huddle ensued.

Knowing he would soon be the center of attention, Eugene calmed his tightening nerves with the mantra, *No comment. You'll have to read more details on the Arizona Providence website.*

He pulled the pink cap's brim to shadow his face then strolled up behind Olivia. "I think our first post is having the desired effect," he said quietly.

"You're going to have hat hair if you end up on camera, Pinkie," she quipped.

He gave her a cocky grin. "Maybe I'll just leave it on. I've grown fond of it."

She bit her lip. "You might want to look at the cap a little closer."

Eugene turned from the crowd, removed the cap and for the first time saw the cap's embroidered, *COWGIRL UP!* Below, in smaller letters, it read, *AGRA 2014.*

Turning back to the now grinning Olivia, he said, "This is from a gay rodeo, isn't it?"

Olivia laughed out loud. “I thought you were comfortable in your manhood.”

“Yeah but, this is like . . . well . . . false . . . uh . . . I’ll go with hat hair. Not that I care if anyone is gay, makes no difference to—”

“Just give me my cap back. Your hair will be fine. If all goes as I have planned, you’ll be the last thing on anyone’s mind.”

Eugene handed it over. He scratched his scalp and clumsily combed his hair with his fingers. Olivia’s teasing smile pleased him.

“Looks like we’ve got some action, Pinkie.” She turned to the podium.

28

The Pinal County Sheriff returned to the podium lacking both his Stetson and his car salesman smile. Bright morning light glared through his short, crew-cut hair as he cleared his throat and began. "Is everyone ready?"

Camera crews nodded and offered thumbs up.

"I'm here to give you all an update on the investigation, although I have little new information to offer."

"Other than to confirm that the Luchadores are inside, correct?" asked the blonde from Channel Seven.

The Sheriff held up a hand. "I'm well aware of the photo circulating on the internet. At this time we do believe the Luchadores are involved. But, I want to caution you all to behave like responsible journalists. The taking of that photo violated the trust we placed in you by giving you more than reasonable access—"

"Nobody crossed the tape, Sheriff. The rules were followed. How many bodies are in there? Surely, you've had time to count in the last—what—eight or nine hours?"

"I'm not ready to release that information at this time. It's important to the investigation that we—"

"Aw, come on, Ray. What are you trying to hide here?" said a radio journalist. "Are we looking at a mass suicide, or what?"

Red crept up the sheriff's neck. He paused, jaw flexing. "All I'll say at this time is that foul play was involved. We—"

"This is pretty basic stuff," interrupted the radioman. "I understand the need to keep some things under wraps, but, given the previously tainted investigation, a little transparency—"

"Let me remind you that you are here at our pleasure," snapped the Sheriff. "It is important that some things stay under wraps. This internet scandal sheet . . . What is it again?" He turned to a public relations staffer. "Ah, yes, the *Providence* has hurt this investigation—"

"It's the *Arizona Providence*," said Olivia, stepping forward with her hand raised. "I'm the publisher and owner and I take offense at your prejudicial remark."

The Sheriff lowered his head, snickered and waved his hand. "Well, nice to see you step from the shadows. Why don't you introduce yourself? I'm sure everyone in attendance would like to know who is responsible for the media being pushed back to the highway."

"I'm Olivia Condon and I'd like to remind you that you serve at the pleasure of the taxpayers. I'd also like to remind you that it's our responsibility as journalists to keep you accountable and honest."

The man assumed a condescending smile. "My years-long track record speaks for itself. Wait. Are you Oliver Condon's little girl?"

"His granddaughter."

"Gosh, I remember back to when you were just learning to ride a horse. As I recall you turned into quite the little barrel racer."

Olivia smiled tightly and nodded once.

"Well, Olivia, I'm sorry for your loss. Oliver was a great man. I went hunting with him just last year. Tell me, do you think your grandfather would approve of you hindering a law enforcement investigation?"

"Oh, I'm sure he's smiling down on me right now. Probably beaming with pride. Sheriff Mutchler, you're up for reelection this year, correct?"

"That has no bearing—"

"Do you think the voters would approve of you hiding the fact that a high ranking detective in the State Patrol—a Detective Clyde Wrigley—is in fact one of the deceased men inside that house?"

Previously lounging beside their tripods, the now wide-eyed photographers came to life, lurching for their eyepieces to zoom in on the astonished Sheriff. He gripped the podium and leaned back, blinking from face to face as though the press was about to leap for his throat. “Ah, let me assure you that there is no cover-up. We simply have—”

Questions of who and how and why flew in from all directions as the man stood frozen and unable to cough up even one answer. The County Attorney stepped up to the podium, shoving him aside. “This press conference is over. Ms. Condon, we need to talk,” he said over the chaos of shouted questions.

The questioners fell silent. “An exclusive interview would be lovely,” said Olivia, looking beyond smug to confident. “But, it will have to be at a later date. Right now you owe the public an explanation as to why the cover-up that began seven years ago continues.”

The microphones picked up a barely audible “Fuck” as the Sheriff tried to push back up to the podium. Public relations handlers held him back as the County Attorney raised both hands to calm the crowd.

“In the pursuit of transparency, I will tell you that a State Patrol detective *is* among the deceased and that there are five bodies inside the house. At this time, experienced detectives are pursuing his involvement in both this incident and the previously tainted investigation.”

“Why hide it from us?” shouted the Channel Seven blonde.

“Karen, that is an unwarranted and offensive accusation,” blurted the County Attorney. “We will answer everyone’s questions in good time, just—”

“Hey, isn’t that Eddie Ibarra, the State Patrol detective who was forced to resign?” called an anonymous voice.

Eddie, who had been slouching in the background suddenly stood erect and wide eyed. Those near him inched away.

“Yes, but he’s currently employed by Carlton Royal, Chief of the Scottsdale Police Department. Chief Royal, would you care to handle this question?” The County Attorney stepped to the side of the podium in a move that gave Royal no options.

Royal’s eyes narrowed in thought. As others sidled away, he was left standing near Eddie, arms crossed and one cowboy boot propped on a wooden porch post. His whole body appeared to relax as his boot hit the ground. He strolled up to the podium, his gaze sweeping the hungry journalists.

"Good morning, everyone," Royal started. "For the record, it's c-a-r-l-t-o-n and Royal is common spelling. I'm the Chief of the Scottsdale Police Department. I'll make a brief statement, but will *not* answer any questions. This is not—I repeat—*not* my investigation. I wouldn't dream of stepping on the very qualified toes of Sheriff Mutchler."

Eugene, who had been firing frame after frame of the political bloodletting shifted his aim to Sheriff Mutchler. The pompous prick's eyes looked like they might just pop out of his head.

"I hired Detective Ibarra because I believe he is a fine man who fell prey to the crooked dealings of another, higher ranking member of the State Patrol. That man is likely lying dead in the house behind me. It is my fervent belief that this unfortunate incident confirms my faith in Detective Ibarra and tips the scales of justice in his favor. It is also my belief that the dogged work of both he and his partner, Detective Harry Aronson, moved the Luchadores to this horribly desperate and cowardly act."

The crowd of media stood silent as cameras rolled and clicked. Chief Carlton offered a nod and a simple, "Thank you" then stepped away.

Eugene sidled up behind Olivia to whisper, "You are a rock star."

Without taking her eyes off of Royal, she replied, "No, *he's* the rock star. My god, they tossed him a shit sandwich and he ate their lunch."

"So, what's next, boss?"

"You've got pictures to file and I have another heckuva story to write. But first, I need that porta-potty."

"Is our web developer on duty?"

"I believe so."

"Maybe I should ship him a couple of pictures to tease your pending story."

"Good idea," she said, giving him a smile that made his chest warm from the inside out. She then spun on her heel to head for the porta-potty.

Eugene considered her confident gait, worn boots and western-styled jeans. That total package implied she'd grown up around horses. He looked at the pink cap now poking out of her back pocket and remembered its embroidery's implications. Respect, fear and curiosity tangled. His brain urged caution, yet his heart soared at the thought of just being near her.

* * *

Looking thoroughly defeated by getting scooped, Pete Cunningham, Michael Specht and Andrew Brinkmann sat slumped in the cheap office chairs that now lined the front of what had been Oliver Condon's grand desk. The deceased publisher's mementos and identity had been stripped from the walls, pulled from the drawers, and tossed into storage.

Steve Spears' only personalization of the now dingy little office was a framed Minnesota Twins homer hanky from their 1987 World Series championship. As the trio waited for Spears to come in and dress them down for getting beat on the Luchador story, Pete searched for excuses.

"Did Eugene contact either of you?" he asked, running his fingers through his greasy hair then wiping them over his loose tie and wrinkled shirt.

"He left several messages on my phone last night. All he said was that he'd heard about the Luchadores thing and wished he could be there," said Brinkmann.

Michael humphed. "Apparently he found a ride."

In a growling voice, Pete said, "We can sue the shit out of him for shooting for the competition with our company gear."

"Uh, Pete," Michael tentatively spoke up, "his gear's locked up back in photo. I looked at the meta data on his images. He's shooting Fuji cameras. We're Canon."

Pete sat up a little straighter. "Well, there's still gotta be some sort of—"

"He got the same 're-apply for your job' email we all did," Brinkmann interrupted. "These new idiots did it to themselves."

"The photo intern was there with you, Andrew." Pete jabbed a finger at him. "What was she doing? Standing around with her thumb up her butt?"

"No, she was scrambling to file pictures as fast as she could because that's the new directive."

"A story this big, you should have been there too, Mike," spat Pete.

"I run the desk, asshole. Don't you try to lay blame—"

Steve Spears strode in, tall and chiseled, looking fresh in a white dress shirt and yellow tie. "Good morning, gentlemen," he said, tossing a printout of Eugene's clown mask picture on the desk. It lay there for all to ponder. "Care to explain how we got beat on what was essentially our story?"

"Well, for starters, you fired our best photographer," Brinkmann stated.

Spears settled into his chair and sat back. He folded his hands on his chin, his index finger tapping his lips. "Being asked to reapply for a job is not the same as being fired."

"Semantics," said Brinkmann.

Spears shot Andrew an irritated look then turned his attention to the other two men in the room.

"Mr. Specht, Mr. Cunningham, I'm sure you had people on the scene. Why didn't—"

"We were first online with photos and a brief," said Pete, "as per your orders."

Spears offered Pete a condescending nod. "What do our analytics tell us on morning and overnight traffic?"

"Overall traffic was up thirty percent," said Pete.

"I need the drill-down. How many uniques?"

"We don't have that kind of specificity," said Pete. "I mean, it's not like I haven't tried, but our IT—"

Andrew interrupted, "Mr. Condon didn't want that level of specificity. Chasing hits tends to color news judgment."

"Then how the hell can he sell the online product—"

"Condon didn't believe in the web, said it cost us more than it made," said Brinkmann.

Pete sat up and raised his hand like a school child asking for the bathroom. "We didn't even have a website until two years ago. Even then it was only because I lobbied for it night and day."

Spears gave another condescending nod. "And what was the great Mr. Condon's plan for the future? Everyone knows print is going away."

"Except our print circulation has been steady," Brinkmann offered.

"That's not entirely true," Pete jumped in. "Circulation took a distinct drop in—"

"It dropped," Andrew cut him off, "after you badgered Condon into giving it away on the web. Since then, it's leveled out."

Pete glared at him. "You can't put that on me. People just don't have the time anymore."

Andrew thought he caught the hint of a smile on Spears' face as the man held up a hand. "I realize I've only been on the job for a short time, but I'm wondering if Mid-States Investments was wise to acquire a property so ham-strung by a Luddite like Oliver Condon."

Andrew stiffened and forced a smile. "I'm sure if you'd had a chance to get to know him you would have seen he was a visionary more concerned with readers than popular trends."

"If that's true," said Spears, obviously forcing his own smile, "perhaps it was his absence that caused you to get beat so soundly . . . and by an internet start-up no less. Things will have to change. Pete, the new employee handbooks. Have they been distributed?"

"No, we've been kinda busy."

Daggers shot from Spears' eyes and Pete winced.

"We've never had employee handbooks," added Brinkmann, knowing he was treading dangerous ground. "Mr. Condon was honorable and loyal. We returned his confidence in us accordingly."

Spears gave him his full and unhappy attention. "I'm beginning to question your loyalty to your new employer."

"Am I employed? Your fire-rehire email has left us all in limbo on that matter."

Spears sat forward, placing his slender, tan hands on the desk to irritably drum his fingers. "Andrew, Mike, why don't you step out. Pete and I have some things to discuss. And close the door behind you."

With Specht close behind, Brinkmann took the lead. Shutting the door as ordered, Specht muttered, "I told Condon that little welfare shit Eugene would bite us one day."

Brinkmann wheeled on him, fists balled tight, "God but you are a sorry excuse for a human being."

Specht blinked and stepped back. Brinkmann glared at him for a long moment then turned to face a newsroom looking back with fear and uncertainty. None dared ask what had just occurred. They only stared as Brinkmann stormed from the newsroom.

Slamming open the swinging doors to the pressroom, he came face to face with a weary-looking Kurt Wragge who quipped, "Looks like your day's going about as well as mine."

"You have no idea. Jesus Christ . . . These Mid-States ass wipes . . . The corporate culture . . . " Brinkmann angrily stuttered before getting his focus. "They're gonna make us a clone of every other failing newspaper and squeeze us until we scream. Then we'll be sold from one vulture capitalist to another until we're a weekly give-away littering people's driveways."

Kurt returned a surprised and curious look. "Feel better?"

"A little."

"Things aren't any better out here. I just learned we're switching to a new, cheap-shit paper. The ink's gonna hit that crap and—kablooey—it'll bleed all over the place. I'll never get reproduction dialed back in." Kurt put down the spindle collar he'd been fiddling with and pulled a pack of cigarettes from his shirt pocket. He knocked out a smoke and lit up.

"That cigarette violates about a hundred different laws."

"Fuck it," snapped Kurt. "I got a feeling I ain't long for this job anyway." He knocked out another cigarette and offered it to Brinkmann.

"You and me both." Brinkmann accepted the cigarette and a light. He sucked in a chestful of smoke and blew it out slowly, "God, I forgot how good that is. I quit when my daughter was born."

"Amazing how fast they swooped in to pick Mr. Condon's bones isn't it?"

"You can blame Pete Cunningham for that. Of course, he's been angling for this for a while." Brinkmann took another drag on the cigarette and cast an eye to the press looming not twenty feet away. "Eugene was right. I should have spent more time out here. Much as it scares me, that monster machine fascinates me, too."

"You're welcome anytime. Hell, maybe we can get Pete out here and have a little accident, if you know what I mean."

Brinkmann grinned, unsure as to whether or not Kurt was joking.

The pressman crossed his arms and leaned back against the forklift, wincing with pain as his backside made contact.

"Excuse me for saying this, but you look like shit," said Brinkmann. "You still hurting from that thing with the cops?"

"Nah, rough night at the bar. Too many beers and too many years under my belt. I gotta quit doing that shit. My insides are raw and I think I bruised my tailbone somewhere along the line." He put a hand to his backside and rubbed it lightly. "Speaking of pains in the ass, you heard from Eugene? I figured he'd be back, now that the cops cleared him."

"Ah, you haven't heard. He's working for our new competition. He kicked our ass last night and the new management is none too pleased."

"Whadda ya mean?"

"You haven't seen it?"

"I can barely see past the end of my own nose today."

Brinkmann brought his Smartphone to life, surfing to the homepage of the *Arizona Providence*.

Kurt's face turned deadly serious. "Holy dog shit. What is that? Some sort of decapitation?"

"It's a Luchador mask. This picture is the first real proof that those bastards offed themselves yesterday. Best part is, the news organization Eugene's working for is run by Mr. Condon's granddaughter."

Kurt grunted out an awkward laugh, "Good for Eugene. He was always a street-smart, hustling little dude. Hey, you gonna make the same jump?"

"Maybe, if they'll have me. But that's between you and me. Got it?"

"No worries. Your secret's safe with me. Not like the newsroom types talk to us anyway . . . You know, I'm not surprised those sick bastards killed themselves. Things don't go well for that kind in the joint."

"That's what I hear. Thanks for the smoke. I gotta go outside to call my wife and let her know what's up."

"Come back anytime."

"I think I'll take you up on that. I'd kinda like to see that flying paster thing you guys were talking about . . . before the new guys fire my ass."

"Deal," said Kurt, pulling a rag from his back pocket to wipe his palm before giving Brinkmann's hand a firm shake.

* * *

Mid morning at the pancake house was a busy affair. The coffee flowed freely as did talk of the Luchador's demise.

"Saw you on TV this morning. Breakfast is on me," said Paul Harbin, the night manager as he paused to pour coffee for Eddie, Harry and Chief Royal. Eddie and Harry had wedged in on one side of the booth facing the chief.

"Thanks, but it's against department policy," said the Chief. "Last night was just part of our job."

Harbin nodded. "You wouldn't say no to a little free pie though, right?"

The Chief looked to his detectives, considered the offer and nodded. "I guess we could keep it our little secret."

Harbin started off then paused, resting the hand not holding the coffee pot on his ample belly. "I told you Eugene was one of the good guys. I knew there was no way he was involved with hurting Sandy. I saw his pictures from last night. Did any of you get a chance to talk to him?"

"Honestly, I never saw him," said Harry. "Chief?"

"I did see him briefly, talking with Condon's granddaughter."

Harbin smiled. "Well, if you run into him, tell him we're all eager to see him and we'd like to buy him dinner."

"If we get the opportunity, we'll let him know," said Eddie.

"Speaking of Olivia Condon," Harry offered, "she's quite a looker."

"Smart as a whip, too," added the Chief. "Just like her grandpa."

"And Eugene's hanging out with her. Don't tell the girls," Harbin said tilting his head to the wait staff. "They'll be heartbroken."

All chuckled knowingly and shook their heads in unison.

"I'm gonna head out," said Harbin, "I shoulda gone home three hours ago, but I stayed to help with the rush. My dogs are barking so loud I could use one of Eugene's famous foot rubs."

"Beth would be jealous," said Eddie.

"That she would," said Harbin, "that she would. One of the girls will be over to get your pie orders in a minute." He waved goodbye as he headed for the counter.

"Thank you," called the Chief, "Go home and put those feet up."

When Harbin was out of earshot, Harry got right to the point. "Back to business. Isn't anybody wondering why there were only five guys in the house?"

"It could be that the five were all that's left," Eddie reasoned before slurping in a mouthful of coffee. He looked to the Chief, obviously hoping he'd back him up.

The Chief frowned. "I didn't see any missing fingers, but we'll know soon enough. We have Ass Clown's DNA from the Sandy Carter murder."

Eddie sat down his coffee cup hard on the Formica tabletop. "We don't know for sure about that missing finger."

The Chief squinted at Eddie, "I know you want this to be over as much as I do. Just take pleasure knowing five are gone . . . and don't forget that you've been vindicated."

"Thank you for that by the way, sir. You didn't *have* to come to my defense like that."

"Yes, I did and I was happy to do it." He fingered the rim of his cup. "Have you talked with your mystery friend? He needs to know we're grateful."

"Only briefly. He's got some family matters to deal with."

Worried the Chief wanted to rest on their laurels, Harry blurted, "So, now we just sit back and wait for Pinal County to run the DNA? That could take weeks."

"It is their case," said the Chief. "Let's enjoy this small victory. Lord knows they're few and far between in this line of work. I'm ordering both of you to take a couple of days off. By then Pinal County should have some meat for us."

Harry opened his mouth to object, but the Chief cut him off. "I have no illusions that this is over. Don't think for a second my letting you two catch your breath is my wanting to take a political victory lap. Don't forget those negatives. You missed them because you were overtired."

"Sorry, sir," said Harry, hanging his head as he wiped his plate with a piece of toast. "I *am* overtired, way over tired. My wife and kids got back this morning. I should get home and hug 'em."

"I'm having dinner with my daughter tonight to celebrate," said Eddie, brightening. "You're welcome to come and bring the family."

Harry shrugged. "Maybe another time. The two of us get together and you know we'll just want to talk shop."

"True enough," said Eddie.

"Well, gentlemen, I'm going to take off. Thank you for your hard work and don't forget, no matter which way this goes, suicide or homicide, it was your good work that forced their hand." The Chief stood. "Oh, Eddie, before I forget, you might want to think about petitioning the State Patrol to reinstate your retirement."

"I hadn't even thought about that. It'd involve lawyers—"

The Chief interrupted him, "I'll make some preliminary calls if you like."

"Yeah, I'd like that." Eddie nodded with a sincere smile. "I thought I'd have to work until the day I died. Thank you, sir."

29

In the parking lot of the *East Valley Herald,* Olivia waited beside her Grand Cherokee as Eugene peered at the mess inside his Jeep. He was amazed it hadn't been impounded and still sat where he'd left it. Black fingerprint powder clung to almost every surface. His tool bags lay empty on the passenger seat, their contents jumbled on the floorboards.

"At least they didn't tear up the upholstery." He moved to the rear hatch and pulled it open. "Locks are busted and cameras gone. Hope it wasn't a thief."

"I'll bet they took your gear inside the building," said Olivia. "Listen, I've got a place you can stay. Grandpa had—"

"Nah," Eugene stopped her offer. "I need to get back to my apartment and deal with *that* mess. Probably have a lot of making up to do with the manager."

"I understand. You sure you'll be okay?"

Her concern warmed away the ache in his chest. "Yeah, I'll be fine, though, ah . . . if I find I've been evicted—"

"Just call. There's a lot we need to talk about, anyway. I'm thinking maybe we should head back down to the San Tans later today and check in."

"I'll be good to go in four or five hours. I just need a quality nap." He squinted at her. "I'm going to guess there'll be a lot of running with a staff of three."

"HEY, BUDDY, WHERE YOU BEEN?" called Andrew Brinkmann, striding from the back door of the *Herald* building, arms wide and a broad grin lighting his face. "By god, Eugene, it's good to see you. You really kicked ass last night."

Eugene emerged from a back-slapping hug and laughter to haul Brinkmann around to the Cherokee's driver's side. "I'd like you to meet my new boss, Olivia Condon."

"Nice to meet you," said Brinkmann. "So sorry about Oliver. I really loved that old guy."

She nodded tightly. "Thanks, we're all going to miss him. Wish he could have been there to see what went down last night."

"Oh, I've got a feeling he's watching," said Brinkmann. "Last night as you made Sheriff Mutchler squirm? All I could think about was Oliver's big 'gotcha' grin."

"I remember it well," Olivia said. "Usually he flashed it when he caught me fudging the truth." A small croak ended her comment and tears welled. She briskly wiped them away.

The lump in Eugene's throat shifted to a sudden, surprising sob. Turning toward his vehicle, he planted a hand on the hood and ducked his head. "Well, this is embarrassing," he croaked. Both Olivia and Brinkmann placed hands on his shoulders. He fought for a breath. "I-I can't believe he's really gone."

All three wiped and sniffed awkwardly trying to push down their sudden grief.

Brinkmann straightened first, wiping at his eyes. "We'll get through this."

"Yes, yes we will," Olivia stated with conviction. She deep breathed as she gave a watery nod to Eugene then looked at Brinkmann. "His funeral service is on Tuesday. Are you coming?"

"Wouldn't miss it," he affirmed then swallowed repeatedly to regain control. "I'm sure the newsroom will be there in force . . . whether the new owners want to give us time off or not."

"He'd like that. My mom and stepdad are making a much bigger deal out of it than Grandpa would have wanted, so expect a crowd."

"I'll spread the word."

"Good." She raised her chin, shifting to her business persona. "When you're ready, I'd love to talk to you about coming to work for us."

Brinkmann rapidly blinked then nodded. "I was hoping you'd offer. Let me ride this out for another day or two and run it by my wife. I've got a feeling these yahoos are going to try to make us sign some sort of non-compete document."

"That's silly. It's not like they're a tech company," said Eugene, scrubbing his hands over his face.

Brinkmann shrugged. "I'm sure they'll just want the illusion of leverage. You know, to prevent a mass exodus when they cut pay and benefits. Pete said severance—or probably the lack thereof—was all spelled out in an employee handbook that I've never seen."

"Don't worry about that handbook. It was something Pete was promoting and is *not* enforceable," said Olivia, "I know for a fact that he tried to trick Grandpa into approving it a while back. It never made it off his desk. In fact, that's what put our little project into high gear. Grandpa was no fool. He saw the fine print and knew Pete was in cahoots with somebody."

"Pete's always been a weasel looking out for number one. Karma's a bitch, though." Brinkmann smirked. "Despite his game-playing and judging by the ass kicking he endured a few minutes ago . . . he may be first to get the boot."

Eugene thought of the lies Pete had written about him then remembered his on-again-off-again suspicion that the man had poisoned Condon. "Wouldn't that just be the ultimate revenge," he murmured.

"I'd better get back inside," said Brinkmann. "Ms. Condon, I'll give you a shout after I talk to my wife." He started again toward the door then turned back. "Oh, Eugene, in all the excitement I forgot to tell you. Harry gave us your clothes, your old laptop and such."

"Cool, where's it all at?"

"Your apartment. While we were there, ah, we had a little talk with the manager about your place being trashed. He's pissed, but he understands. And, ah, we kinda took it on ourselves to spruce things up a bit. Sorry we didn't have time to get to the Jeep. Things got a little crazy."

"No kidding? Gosh, thanks, and thank everybody else for me." He again fought a rising lump in his throat. "Tell 'em I miss 'em and that I owe 'em."

"Anything inside in your locker you want me to grab?"

"Nah, I never kept much in there. They got their cameras back, right? I'd hate—"

"Michael retrieved them. They're safe, so the paper's new owners won't have any hold on you."

"Excellent. I-I'm really grateful, Andrew." Eugene opened his arms and they fell into another quick back-slapping hug.

Brinkmann shook Olivia's hand. "I'll be in touch."

As the man headed back inside, Olivia slipped her hand into Eugene's for a reassuring squeeze. He savored the rare moment of feeling all was coming right in his world.

* * *

The alarm on Eugene's iPhone pulled him from his deepest sleep in days, but his head still ached from lack of sleep. He fumbled for the phone, knocking it to the floor. Cursing, he sat up, retrieved the phone and silenced the alarm, He flopped back down to let the world come into focus.

His friends from the *Herald* had done more than a little sprucing up. They'd replaced his old mattress, ripped to shreds by the overzealous cops, with a wonderful new pillow top queen. Even his ruined television had been replaced with a fancy, new LCD. A red bow and a tag attached to one corner held Harry's signature and read, *Sorry for the mess. Hope this helps.* Defying the fatigue headache, he looked around at the evidence of being blessed to have such good friends.

Finally in the shower, grateful the water was back on, he let the heavenly hot water beat on his body then carry his aches and fatigue down the drain. Playing the events of the last few days over in his refreshed mind he came to the sudden realization that he hadn't told Carl and Albert that he was okay.

He hit the speed dial as he toweled dry, "Hey Carl, I'm so sorry I haven't called to tell you I'm safe at home."

"That's okay, son. We've been praying for you. We seen your pictures and figured you got yourself squared away."

"Yes, I'm better than ever. The cops cleared me. Good friends from the *Herald* cleaned up my place and smoothed things over with my apartment manager."

Carl chuckled. "That's good news. 'Course we figured you'd land on your feet."

"Albert's advice about listening to my heart was spot on as always. I took a chance in asking for help and it worked out." He thought of Olivia and sighed with contentment. "I guess beyond the fact that all is well, the biggest news is my new job."

"We was wonderin' about that. You don't work for the *Herald* no more?"

"No. Long story short, politics and greed are taking over in Oliver's absence and it was time to move on."

"You won't have to give up takin' pictures will you?"

"Oh, I'll still be taking pictures, Oliver had a granddaughter named Olivia. She and Oliver saw the changes coming and started an online news operation called the *Arizona Providence*."

"That's a fine name." Another chuckle. "Albert and I always say it was divine providence that brought you to us. Sounds like it's continuin' ta work in your life."

"Yessir, Carl, I believe it so. No matter how bad things get, they always seem to work out. If you've seen the pictures . . . " The memory clenched his stomach. "You know about the Luchadores."

"I have and can't say as I feel too bad for 'em. The world's a better place without their kind."

"I had a chance to talk to Derek Schaefer. What he told me curled my toes."

"My, oh my. Now there's a troubled soul. There's a lot he has to answer for."

"That's the saddest part of this whole mess. Deep down he's a good guy. He just went a little crazy. Anybody would after what he went through. Say, you remember the scrapper with the old, red Ford? He used to offer his wife in trade."

"I do indeed. We chased him off a time or two. Called the cops on him once 'cause he had a kid with him."

"That was Derek. His wife wasn't the only one he was pimping."

Carl let out a long sigh. "Oh, that's too bad. Ah, your daddy . . . is that maybe. . . ?"

"Yessir, best as we can figure. Well, I'd better get moving. Olivia will be picking me up soon. Give Albert my love and thank him again for the advice. Oh, and, of course, for the Zingers and chocolate milk."

The phone beeped in Eugene's ear. He glanced to the screen and saw it was Olivia.

"I'll try to get down there in a couple a days. I'm really missing you all. Give King a good scratch for me. I didn't get enough time with him on my—BEEP—last visit."

"Bye now," Carl said.

Eugene thumbed on the connection to Olivia, glancing self-consciously at his nakedness. "Sorry. I'll be right there."

"Good morn—I mean, good afternoon to you, too," said Olivia. "Get enough sleep?"

"Nope, my head's thumping. I was wrong about a good nap being enough to catch up."

* * *

Wincing at the bright afternoon sunlight with its unrelenting summer heat, Eugene stored his new cameras and old computer bag in the Cherokee's back seat. The front seat's air-conditioned breeze on his wet hair soothed his headache. He deep-breathed the gentle sweet scent of what he surmised was Olivia's talcum powder and awkwardly shifted in the Cherokee's leather seat.

"You look a lot fresher than I feel," he observed, careful not to gaze at her bright face for too long. "So, are we headed for the San Tans?"

"No, TV is still there doing live shots, but law enforcement has sealed the house and all but pulled out."

Eugene's phone interrupted. He recognized Jack Carter's number. "Hey, I'm with somebody. Not free to talk." He glanced at Olivia's eyes now narrowed in interest.

"Are you with Olivia Condon?"

"Yes, we're parked in front of my apartment."

"Well, well. Good for you."

"It's not what you think. She's—"

"Easy on the eyes?" Jack teased.

"Well, yes, I'd agree with that assessment. So, what can I do for you?"

Jack laughed, "It's more what I can do for you. Got a pen and paper?"

"Hang on," Eugene said pulling the ever-ready notebook and pen from his shirt pocket. "Okay, what've you got?"

"Five names."

"Let'r rip."

"Riley Mitchell. That's r-i-l-e-y and Mitchell with two L's. Steve Painter, common spelling. Darrel Smith with two r's and e-l, Phil Simon and you know the last name, Clyde Wrigley."

"Holy shit. How—"

"I've got friends," Jack interrupted. "They want to make sure politics don't get in the way of doing right by Sandy."

"Any thoughts as to why there were only five in the house?"

"Same as what you're thinking. Cutting their losses, hoping we quit looking."

Eugene looked at Olivia as he asked, "Ass Clown and Anal Pirate?" The consummate journalist didn't even flinch.

"Most likely. They're the leaders. My bet is that they traded masks with the deceased."

"Where are you?"

"Went back north this morning after I checked Chris into rehab. Probably won't do much good, but Gracie says we gotta try."

"Yeah, sorry for that. I'm surprised you don't want to hang around down here a little longer."

"Gracie insisted. She's a good woman who knows me better than I know myself. Too much time down there would only cause me trouble. But, I'll be back for Condon's funeral."

"Jack, I have to ask." He met his new boss's eyes. "How much can I tell Olivia?"

"About me? Nothing for now. Keep me out of it. Let's let things shake out. Once it's over we'll re-evaluate. I owe you for using you as bait. Maybe we can grab a beer and talk it through after the funeral."

"Sounds like a plan. Thanks for the info. We'll put it to good use."

"I have no doubt. Take it easy, kid. And watch your back. This isn't over."

"Will do," said Eugene, ending the call.

"Are those names you wrote down what I think they are?" asked Olivia. Her face was flush with intensity, her grandfather's big story look in her eyes.

"Yep, the dead Luchadores. We need to find a computer and start digging."

"I have a better idea. Send them to Austin. He can run rings around us on that front."

Eugene nodded then snapped a picture of his note and emailed it to Austin. The jet like whoosh of the sent email sparked an idea. "Since we're not going to the San Tans, how about taking a run to the airport?"

"Why? What do you have in mind?"

"Some things Derek told us about the Luchador parties. There were enough details that I might be able to spot it on Google maps."

"My laptop's in the back."

"No worries. I brought mine, I'll pull wi-fi from my phone." Eugene unlatched his belt and turned in his seat to grab his old white MacBook.

"That one's seen better days," Olivia observed with a chuckle.

"Hey, be nice. You'll hurt her feelings. She still gets the job done. I loaded her up with RAM and put a new SSD drive in her."

Olivia shook her head. "Tomorrow maybe we can get to the Apple store."

"I'm telling you this one still works." He arched an eyebrow at her. "Being a start-up, shouldn't we be economizing?"

"Yes and no. Grandpa anticipated our needs. He put a pretty good chunk aside for this new venture."

"Good to know we have a sound financial base. How's your family feel about that?" he asked as he opened the screen to type his password.

"Doesn't matter. There's nothing they can do. He set it up so the family can't touch us."

Eugene smiled in admiration. "Covered all the bases. I wouldn't have expected anything less. Okay, Google, let's see what you've got." His fingers set to work, as Olivia pulled into traffic.

"Speaking of family," he said, not looking up, "I'd love for you to meet Albert and Carl. They had a great deal of respect for your grandpa."

"Are they the junkyard owners?"

"Yeah, that's them. They took me in after my real family fell apart. Two of the finest men I've ever known." Typing and clicking, he worked at nonchalance. "Um, the old neighborhood's not far from the airport. I could give you a quick tour. You know, for background on your Pulitzer Prize winning story on my run from police and how the forces of good came together to take down the evil Luchadores."

Olivia threw him a smile as she drove. "Screw prizes. How much can you tell me without putting your friend Jack at risk?"

"A bit . . . as long as I leave out names and a few details. Plus, I'd like you to see where I came from. On the surface it's mean and dirty but you'll meet a lot of good people . . . if you give it a chance."

She nodded, her smile turning to a grin. "I'd like that. I hear a great deal of pride in your voice."

"I *am* proud. It's funny, coming from my world into yours . . . Well . . . When I came to the *Herald*, I was clueless. I had a lot to learn. But most of them were clueless, too."

"What do you mean?"

"Take Carl and Albert, for instance. They started with nothing but an old pickup and they built a huge business. It's not pretty, but they do really well. Yet, the supposedly educated people in the newsroom hear junkyard and think they're losers. What's up with that? Carl and Albert probably have more in the bank and have done more for their community than any of them . . . besides your grandfather, that is."

Rolling slowly to stop at a light, Olivia gave Eugene a long glance that caused him to blush.

"What?"

"Last night you said I reminded you of my grandfather."

"Well, you do. You have his eyes, his brains and his good sense."

"You're a lot like Grandpa yourself."

Eugene's throat tightened. He turned back to the laptop's screen, swallowed hard and blew out a long breath. When she reached for a water bottle in the center console he followed Carl and Albert's advice, listening to his heart. He deliberately touched her hand. Electricity sparked. She opened her palm. He took her hand in his. When their eyes met he pulled her hand to his lips and kissed it gently.

She moaned softly, fluttering her eyelids before leaning back in her seat and pulling his hand to her face.

“We have a lot to sort out, don’t we?” Eugene murmured, his heart racing.

“I think so. No, I know so. This is going to complicate the hell out of—”

The blare of a car horn interrupted. She turned her attention back to the road, lurching from the light as she put both hands on the wheel.

They continued on in silence, heading for the 202 Freeway. The South Mountains loomed in the distance and the low-slung, desert-toned architecture whizzed by as quickly as Eugene’s thoughts and emotions.

When they slowed in the westbound rush-hour-clogged freeway, he broke the silence. “So that gay rodeo cap . . . you, ah . . . . ”

Her face lit up with an impish grin, “It came with a press release packet. I keep it because it really bugs my mother.”

“Ahhh,” said Eugene, smiling and settling back in his seat.

She reached for his hand again, pressing it to her cheek before kissing it and returning it to his laptop keyboard.

“That’s not helping,” he said, adjusting his sitting position to better accommodate his now raging libido.

“Sorry. I’ll try to control myself if you do the same.”

“I’ll be a gentleman . . . for now. But, for the record, let me just say that I fell in love with you the first moment I saw you.”

She looked over at him, a delightful flush creeping up her neck as she said, “The feeling was mutual.”

30

While traveling west on the 202, Eugene scoured Google maps for possibilities. "Derek told us the warehouse had an arched roof. He could hear jets landing and taking off, and sometimes it smelled like paint or chemicals. Grab the next exit. I'm looking at some warehouses just northeast of the airport."

"Papago Industrial Park?"

"No, they're all too new. I'm looking closer to 40th Street. There's some older buildings along there."

After exiting the freeway, they curved north to turn left onto Washington Street then skirted the light rail lines still bustling with activity. At 40th Street they turned south. On their left stood several round-topped metal buildings while on their right stretched the expansive parking lot of a former dog racing track that on Wednesdays and weekends became a giant swap meet.

"Do you think one of those Quonset huts could be it?" Olivia asked.

"I don't know. I got the feeling the place was bigger." He rolled his window down and sucked in a breath. "I smell fiberglass resin. My gut's telling me we're getting close. See Park'n Swap over there?"

"Yeah. I've been there once or twice. Too crowded and hot for me, though."

"When I was like ten, I practically lived there on Saturdays."

Olivia pulled into a driveway cutout and stopped. She cracked open a bottle of water and relaxed in her seat, studying him. "We're taking a break to give your gut time to focus. Tell me more about this." Her free hand swept toward the Park 'n Swap. "What bargain hunting was ten-year-old Eugene doing?"

"None. We were selling. Dad always had a truckload of something that fell off somebody else's truck, if you know what I mean. My brother and I had these cheap sombreros. We'd sit on the tailgate as my dad worked the crowd. This one time Dad bought ten pounds of bananas for our lunch. I ate twenty-three bananas to my brother's fourteen." He chuckled, shook his head then watched her delicate throat work as she swallowed her water. "I got sick as a dog. Believe me, it was a long time before I wanted to eat another banana."

"I'll bet you were a cute little kid. Where's your brother now?"

Eugene's bright demeanor faded. He couldn't keep looking at her. "He's gone. Shot in a drive-by shortly after we moved into the projects."

"I'm sorry. Really. I didn't know—"

"Don't worry about it. It was a long time ago." She handed him the unfinished half of her water. He lifted it as if toasting. "Here's to finding the Luchador warehouse."

Olivia checked her mirror and pulled out. She kept her speed slow so he could assess the area. Maintaining a comfortable quiet, she ignored the rare traffic that seemed to irritably pass her. They passed a mix of industrial, storage and import businesses, all surrounded by chain link.

As 40th Street made a wide turn to the east and skirted the airport property, Eugene twisted to look back the way they'd come. "I don't know. Let's turn around. Maybe this is a waste of time. For all we know it's south of the airport."

"No, your gut instinct is contagious. It just feels like we're close." Her smile made him frown. "Okay, at the very least we can cross reference this area with what Austin digs up on the background checks. Maybe we'll get lucky."

Olivia made a U-turn and headed back north to turn right on Madison where she reduced her speed again to roll slowly through the neighborhood.

Eugene sat straighter, pointing. "That resin smell is stronger here. Look at that boat place over there. That's where the smell's probably coming from."

They drove on, necks craning and eyes scanning for clues.

"Is that a crime lab van?" asked Olivia.

Eugene sat up and leaned to the windshield, "Where?"

She pulled to the curb. "Ahead, maybe fifty yards."

"Yeah, maybe. Hey, I see a cop car, too. Roll by for a look then turn around. I'll take pictures just in case. Could just be a burglary call."

Two police cars and a crime lab van occupied the limited parking space outside a large warehouse with a wide, arched roof.

"Think we should stop and ask what's going on?" asked Olivia.

Backwards in his seat, groping through his camera bag, Eugene paused. "Maybe. Ah, no, let's not. If they know journalists are sniffing around they might release the info and we'll lose our lead." He turned back around, adjusting a camera.

"You set?"

"Yep, let's do it." Eugene propped his elbow in the open window and double-checked his settings as Olivia made a U-turn. He kept the camera out of sight. On their second pass he raised it to fire off five frames, then lowered it inside the door to play back the images.

"Did you get a number on the building?" asked Olivia.

"Let me check the frames."

"I can go back."

"No, I've got it. Does the writer have a pen?"

"Of course."

"4-0-3-6."

Olivia wrote the number on the back of her steering wheel hand then pulled to the curb. She pressed the home button on her phone. Siri's polite, female voice asked for a command.

"Call Austin O'Neal, Mobile."

Austin answered on the first ring, sounding tired. "Good evening, boss."

"Hi, Austin. You're on speaker. I've got Eugene with me."

"Good evening to you, too, Eugene," said Austin. "Nice to meet you, sorta. Great job last night."

"Thank you, sir. The website looks terrific. Your hard work shows. I can't wait to meet you in person."

"Likewise," said Austin. "Hey, are you two headed back soon? I could use some food. My tank's running a little low."

"Can you hang on for another hour? Eugene and I have one more quick detour before we head in. We haven't eaten either and I was thinking pizza."

"Sure, sounds great. I'll order delivery. It'll get here about the same time you do."

"Perfect. I called to give you an address. Could you cross reference it with the Luchador background checks?"

"Sure thing."

She read him the address and added her thanks.

"By the way," said Austin, "I'm really enjoying this new gig. Beats the heck out of coding in a cubicle farm. I just got off the phone with Darrel Smith's brother. He was a bit taken aback, but he confirmed his death. Said there must be some sort of mistake with his brother being there. Said his brother was a respected doctor at Mountain View Memorial."

"A doctor? *Very* interesting," said Olivia. "How about the others? Anything on them yet?"

"As a matter of fact, I've got a little something on each and every one. You want me to send it to your phone?"

"That would be lovely. Seeing any commonalities?"

"Other than age, not really. All were born in the 60's, assuming I've got the right people. Mitchell, Smith and Simon are fairly common names."

"Well, keep digging and calling. I really appreciate it. Once we get confirmation on all of them, we can go live with the story. And if you get time, could you dig into school records? There's a possibility that it all started as some sort of locker room hazing that got out of control."

"I'll do what I can, but school records will be tough, given their ages. Nothing was digitized back then."

"Understood. We'll be there in a bit. We can brainstorm over pizza."

"Adios," said Austin, ending the call.

Westbound on Washington Street, Olivia stared out at the traffic, seeming lost in thought. "Tell me more about your time with Derek. What's his back story?"

"Okay, but some of it's pretty disgusting. No, a lot disgusting. I don't know if you—"

"Eugene!" she irritably stopped him. "I was raised on news, not the glitzy, clean society stuff."

Eugene studied her. "Did you know your eyes sparkle when you're pissed? Consider me put in my place." That got him the smile he wanted.

As they drove on, the sun's glare reflected the bleakness of the city in summer, he laid out all the horrific details of the little kids and big kids and the landfill where the Luchadores buried their prey. The more Eugene told her the darker Olivia's expression. The last few miles of their trek to his beginnings were spent in silence.

Driving up the slow rise of the 7th Avenue bridge, she finally spoke, "I'll never understand how people can be so evil."

"I can . . . and so could your grandfather. I'm sure it's why he helped me."

Olivia shot him a curious glance.

At the top of the bridge where the squalor and misery of his old neighborhood spread out for all to see, he said, "See those warehouses and vacant lots down there?" he tilted his head at the scene.

"It looks less than inviting."

Eugene nodded. "That's putting it mildly, but it was home. Most people see a war zone. They don't realize there are a lot of good people just trying to get by. Before today, how much did you know about me and my childhood?"

"Just what's been in the paper."

"Remember I told you Derek's father pimped out both him and his mother?"

She nodded, keeping her eyes on the road.

"Years ago my father was one of his mother's customers. That's how we're related."

Olivia's mouth dropped open, tears brightening her eyes. She swallowed them into control.

"Turn right on Grant, down here at the bottom of the bridge, then right again at 9th Avenue."

She made the turns. Her body tense, her hands opening and closing on the steering wheel, she looked as if she had questions but couldn't find the careful words.

"Okay, stop right up here in front of the railroad tracks at Buchanan Street." They rolled to a stop. He watched her take in the graffiti-laden desolation. "Remember how I said there's misery, but there's good people, too?"

She nodded.

"Look left and you'll see my family's old warehouse. Long story short, my dad split, the business went under and Mom, my brother and I landed in welfare housing just south of here. After my brother was killed, my mom turned into a drunk."

She turned her attention from the scene to him. "You grew up with a lot of pain."

"Yeah, but I survived. And it all made me stronger." He broke the eye contact. "Now, look right. See that place under the bridge?"

"Yes, the junkyard."

"Those brothers, Carl and Albert, took me in after my life fell apart. Without them, I'd be dead or in jail. They gave me a safe haven, made sure I stayed in school and taught me the meaning of being . . . a good man, like them." He held his hands up as if offering her his world. "So, which part of my life do you want to see first?"

Without comment, Olivia turned the vehicle left. The Cherokee's tires crunched to a stop on the gravel in front of the old warehouse. She straightened as if preparing herself. "Oh, that looks awful. Was it this bad when your parents had it?"

"It was a little nicer, but not by much. You know, it's weird. I've always had my feet in two different worlds. Growing up, I was a middle-class kid, but summers and weekends were spent here battling thieves, junkies and gangsters."

"No choice but to grow up fast," Olivia stated, obviously trying to understand.

"Yeah, while my school buddies strategized football plays, my brother and I strategized shootout and survival scenarios."

"Please say your parents protected—"

"Uh, not really. I was fourteen when I held off a carload of burglars all by myself. Well, I had a shotgun . . . and King, but he was little more than a pup. Mom and Dad and Ray left me to watch the warehouse while they did a job in Las Vegas. Two in the morning some guys tried to break in. I guess they thought the place was empty. They heard King, peeked in a window and saw me aiming the gun at them."

"So, they left, right?"

"Not until they tried to draw me out by trashing an old truck we had out front. I wasn't stupid enough to go out. I just called the cops then took cover in a hallway just like my brother and I had planned. I knew it was me or them. I figured I'd shoot the first one through the door. If they kept coming, I'd fall back behind the heavy metal door leading out to the warehouse."

Olivia bit her full lips into a thin line. "Did they come in?"

"Nah, after they trashed the truck and broke a couple of windows, they moved on. Good thing, too, because I'd have killed them. The cops showed up two hours later."

"Oh, Eugene, no kid should ever have that kind of responsibility placed on their shoulders."

"Kids down here put up with it every day. I was lucky. I only had to deal with it on the weekends and summer break. That is until things got bad."

She looked around. "Well, it seems a bit more peaceful now."

Eugene smiled. "You know how when you sit quietly in a forest you start to see things come to life?"

"Uh-huh."

"Same thing here. You can't see it right now, but this whole neighborhood is crawling with predators and prey. The prey survives by flying under the radar."

She touched his nearest hand and raised it to her lips.

He cupped the side of her face. "We're not done. Roll ahead a few yards. That old church I stayed in kinda hides beside the warehouse."

Olivia did as directed then stared at the little broken down building. "Guess I expected something bigger."

"It seemed bigger when I was a kid. On Wednesday evenings churchgoers would stream in and rock that little building late into the night. I used to watch from that little alley between."

"You really slept in there?"

"Yeah . . . and it was as miserable as it looks. Street life sucks. No car to escape in, no phone to call for help, no one to care when the predators come calling. You live with fear and desperation. Anyone who hasn't lived it can't *really* understand." He grabbed her hand and kissed it. "And I would never *want* you to." Again they locked eyes. "A minute ago you said you couldn't understand people's evil. How much did your grandfather tell you about his service in Korea?"

She frowned. "Not much. He wouldn't talk about it."

"Not surprising. The bottom line is that there's evil in everyone but most people never have to open that door . . . Oliver called it his demon. I call it my darkness."

"Grandpa evil? There's no way—"

"Yes, he talked to me about it . . . but, like me, he had no choice. The thing I've come to understand about evil is that once you open the door, it never totally closes. You want to know a secret?"

"Do I?"

"It'd make me feel better if I told you."

"All right. Go for it."

"Have you seen that video of Derek and I grabbing each other in the street?"

"Yes."

"I told everyone busting his nose was an accident. It wasn't. In the heat of battle my darkness took over and I wanted to hurt him. I *wanted* to hurt him real bad. I'm lucky the cops jumped in."

"I just can't see you or Grandpa that way. You—"

"Trust me. I can hurt people. I have hurt them bad. Once you set that evil loose—when you experience that power—it feels so good it's almost addicting." He turned to look at her and in silence, let the fire of evil glow in his eyes until fear tinged her expression.

"Holy shit, you're scaring me."

"Sorry," he said, vanquishing the anger. He scrubbed his hands over his face as if washing it. "You know why guys like your grandpa and the brothers and I go out of our way to help people?"

"No, tell me." She blinked, looking slightly off balance.

"Because we know evil. We've overcome it in ourselves. We know the only way to hold it in check is to be kind to others. I think of it as planting seeds of good. That's why Oliver went into journalism and I'm sure that's why the brothers took me in."

The fear in Olivia's eyes had been replaced by sorrowful awe. "So if you, the brothers and my grandpa are the sowers of good—so to speak—does that make the Luchadores the sowers of evil?"

Eugene nodded. "I think someone or something forced the Luchadores to open that door and they got addicted to the power. That's why they dominate and degrade and kill. Derek told me as much. He went through the same transformation. After all he'd endured, it felt good to release his demons on those women. Judging by his level of regret, it didn't stick. Dang, I'm sorry for getting all philosophical—"

"Oh my gawd!" screeched Olivia, jerking up in her seat and fumbling for the ignition.

From the void between the buildings a giant emerged, arms in the air and stomping like a bull about to charge, "Ahhh, ahhh, ahhh!"

Eugene unhitched his belt and opened his door.

"No, don't!" cried Olivia.

"Freddie! Hey, buddy, remember me?"

Freddie's feet stilled, his arms lowered and he tilted his head as if to accommodate his lolling eye.

"Olivia, have you got something to eat? Snack bars? Anything?"

"A Payday candy bar. In my computer bag, but, Eugene, get back in!"

"It's okay. Just stay put. That goes for you, too, buddy," he said to Freddie while holding up a hand. "I've got a little something for you."

Slowly he moved to the back of the Cherokee, opened the hatch then retrieved the salty-sweet snack. He held it high and carefully walked toward the big man. A goofy smile spread across Freddie's face. Eugene moved closer, tearing open the candy bar's wrapper. Freddie took the offering gently then shoved the whole nutty log into his mouth at once. His eyes closed as he savored it.

"How you doing, big fella?"

The eyes opened. "Uhh."

"Can I check the cuts on your belly and shoulder?"

"Uhh," he said, slobber running down his chin.

Gently, Eugene checked the bandage on the huge round of flesh hanging below Freddie's tight t-shirt. "That's not near as bad as I thought it was," he said before stretching up to peel back and look under the soiled collar.

The next moment Freddie wrapped Eugene in his arms and held him in a long embrace.

After a series of back pats, Eugene pulled back to mumble, "You take care."

"Uhh."

Waving a goodbye, Eugene returned to the Cherokee.

He found Olivia swiping tears from her eyes. "That may be the loveliest thing I've ever seen," she said. "Is he okay?"

"Ah, yeah, he'll be okay for now." Eugene sniffed at his shirt. "But, he could use a shower." He smiled at the man still standing where he'd left him, drool soaking his grungy shirt. "He's really a sweetheart."

"Can we give him some money? I probably have a blanket—"

"No, he'd only lose the blanket and money would make him a target." He squeezed her hand. "There're hundreds of guys just like him out here and . . . all you can really offer are small comforts. Drive around the block and head for the bridge, there's somebody else I'd like you to meet."

"The brothers?"

"Nah, I didn't see their truck. They've gone home for the day."

"Another homeless guy?"

"Nope, he's got a home."

Olivia smiled and knitted her brow.

As they rolled into the shadow of the bridge and stopped in at the junkyard gate, another giant burst from the shadows. Huge paws hit the chain link, backed by a ferocious, deep-chested bark. Eugene quickstepped for the fence, falling to his knees in greeting.

"This guy's a little more stable," Eugene called, motioning for Olivia. "Come meet my old buddy, King."

Olivia set the transmission into park and crawled out. King barked and wagged a greeting as Eugene scratched the dog's neck and ears through the gate's narrow opening, receiving a tongue bath in return.

"Oh my, he's gorgeous. Awww, the poor old fellow's only got one eye. What happened?"

"Long story. I'll tell you on the way back. Say hello, why don't you?"

"Hello, big guy," said Olivia, kneeling beside Eugene. She offered her downturned hand for him to smell. After his hearty lick, she leaned in to scruff the big dog's neck and ears. Not one to miss an opportunity, King delivered a slobbery facial.

Eugene laughed. "That may be the loveliest thing I've ever seen." He impulsively kissed her cheek. She turned to look deep into his eyes. As if magnetized, they came together in a long embrace and open-mouthed kiss. The sensual moment was shattered by King's whine for attention.

"Ha! Sorry, buddy," said Eugene. "King, I'd like you to meet Olivia. Olivia, meet King."

"Hello, sir," she said, reaching through the gate to again rake her fingers through his wiry hair.

"Oh yeah, that's the spot," said Eugene, seeing King close his eye and lean in. "Hate to short change you, fella, but we've got someplace to be. There's a couple more things I'd like to show your new friend."

When Olivia turned her still heated eyes on him, he stood and cleared his throat. "Plus, we still have sowers of evil to track down."

Olivia came to her feet then bowed to her new friend. "It was very nice to meet you, King. Your subjects are on a holy quest."

Eugene leaned in for one more good scratch. "I'll be back in a day or two, buddy. Keep an eye on the brothers for me." He turned to the SUV and urged Olivia forward, shaking his head. "The hardest part is leaving him behind."

"I understand. King," she called over her shoulder, "I'll make sure he keeps his promise."

Pulling away from under the bridge, Olivia asked, "Is he safe in there? What's to stop someone from just shooting him?"

"Nothing, really. But he's real smart and the brothers have earned the neighborhood's respect. Turn right at the stop sign."

In the late afternoon light, they rolled up and over the tracks in the railroad switchyard. They soon encountered the masses shuffling in twos and threes toward the shelter and food of the community's largest facility serving the homeless.

Olivia appeared to be both sad and in awe. "I never knew there were so many."

"Oh, they'll be rolling in until about 10 p.m. That's when they close the doors. Some are coming to eat, some are looking for a semi-safe place to bed down. I used to eat there when the food stamps ran out. It's really pretty good."

When they turned right onto Washington Street, the landscape quickly changed from misery and despair to opulent glass and neat landscaping.

"I've driven through here a hundred times and I never had any idea all that was just around the corner," said Olivia.

"Most people don't know or they don't want to. The really frustrating thing is that building over there is Phoenix PD headquarters. Over there is the County Sheriff and that's the FBI building right up there."

"All that money and power and right around the corner is murder and mayhem."

Eugene settled back in his seat to simply enjoy looking at her. "Ironic, isn't it? So, now that you know who I am and where I came from, how do you feel about me?"

She gripped the steering wheel, tears welling but held at bay. Regret flooded Eugene's heart. He had hoped the passionate kiss signaled good things, but now braced himself for rejection.

"I think I'm the luckiest woman on the planet," she said, reaching for his hand then pulling it close for a gentle kiss.

31

“So just where is this office of ours?” Eugene asked as they exited the freeway on Lindsay Road in the East Valley suburb of Mesa.

“Just hold your horses,” said Olivia. “It’s a surprise.”

The sun had dropped below the horizon and headlights were coming on as they rolled through peaceful residential subdivisions of terra cotta tiled roofs and eucalyptus trees.

When residential gave way to sparse, towering palms and mobile home parks, Eugene tried again. “Let me guess. You’ve secured a snow bird’s trailer for the summer.”

“Not quite. We’re almost there, though.”

Moments later a beautifully renovated, retro neon sign came into view. Two green neon palm trees lazed skyward as a blue monkey flashed up a trunk in an endless climb for coconuts.

“Ah, the old Tradewinds. Now, that’s a step back in time. I love that old-school sign.” Eugene grinned.

“I love it, too. Say, I have an idea.” Olivia veered into the motel parking lot and rolled to a stop. She looked at him, wriggling her eyebrows above mischief-bright eyes. “What do you think?” She tilted her head to the rooms.

“What? Wait, we don’t have time for . . . “His partial arousal came to full attention. He swallowed hard. “What about Austin?”

“Oh, come on.” Her eyes dropped to his crotch, then slowly slid back to stare into his. She raised an eyebrow. “I’ve been wanting this the whole afternoon. I think you have been, too.”

Without breaking eye contact, she let the Cherokee roll forward into a parking space in front of a room.

Pants constricting his growing excitement, Eugene had to adjust himself. "Ah, are you sure? I mean what about Austin and the pizza? We have work—"

"Oh, we'll get to that pizza. First, I want you to meet the friend who helps satisfy all my curiosities." She placed a hand on his thigh, rubbing gently. "Come on, live a little. I guarantee you'll like him."

"Him? What? I don't think . . . ."

At that moment an older, slightly heavyset man opened the door, waved and stepped from the room. Olivia's grin had Eugene's mind doing flip-flops.

"Come on. I promise this'll be fun." She batted her eyelashes.

Following her lead, he opened his door and stepped out slowly.

"Glad you *finally* made it. Is this Eugene?" asked the man.

"Yes, it is." Olivia sidled up to Eugene and covertly squeezed his butt. "Eugene, say hello to Austin O'Neal our computer guru extraordinaire."

"Hey, Austin, nice to meet you. Sorry we took so long to get here. Olivia's been giving me a *hard* time."

The older man vigorously shook hands. "She's a slave-driver, all right. She'll grind you into the ground if you don't stay of top of that one."

"I'll remember that," Eugene said, leering sideways to see if she'd caught the double entendre.

She again batted her eyelashes. "I like to stir things up, make things happen, and get results." She looked at her computer guru. "Right, Austin?"

His testosterone abating, Eugene shifted his attention to Austin. "You aren't what I expected. Not to be rude, but aren't you a little, ah—"

"Old to be a computer nerd?"

"Well, yeah."

"Oliver coaxed me out of retirement. I'm old enough that Woz and I were in the same computer club back in the day."

"Woz? You mean, Homebrew?" asked Eugene.

"Ah, I see you know your nerd history. Come on in and have a look at our operation while you eat."

When Austin turned back into the room, Eugene stepped into Olivia's personal space. She patted his flat belly above his belt buckle. "Food awaits. I said I had been wanting all afternoon, you know, as in pizza."

"Food works . . . for now," he whispered then followed her into the motel room, his loins aching as he gazed at her backside.

Two battered folding tables stood on dingy carpet still bearing the outline of a pair of queen-sized beds. Contradicting the shabby office furniture were a pair of sleek new iMacs connected to multiple monitors. The contradictions continued to the walls where gorgeously matted and framed black and white photographs hung where cheap, mass-produced oil paintings should have been.

After appreciating the photos, Eugene held his arms out. "Okay, how on earth did you land here? Did the owner give you a good summer rate or something?"

Just by folding her arms, the Olivia-the-Boss persona returned. "Did Grandpa ever talk about a friend named Arthur Smith?"

"Yeah, his street photographer buddy." He turned back to the photos. "Say, this is his work, isn't it? I recognize his style."

"Grandpa set him up here as the live-in manager and artist-in-residence. Really, the whole place is his gallery."

"That's brilliant! Is he around? I'd love to meet him."

Olivia's bright demeanor dimmed. "He's in the hospital. Cripes, I just realized I haven't checked on him all day. I've gotta make a call. Go ahead and start eating."

Austin took a seat at a small table under the room's only window, grabbed a slice of pizza, breaking the strings of cheese before he motioned for Eugene to join him. "I'll fill in the blanks while she's on the phone."

"In case you haven't put it together, Eugene, Art's the guy who printed the Luchador photos for Oliver."

"Why's he in the hospital? Is he sick?"

"Luchador thugs came looking for the negatives. He took a pretty bad beating but never gave them up. If your cop friends hadn't shown up, he might have died."

Focused back on his real world, Eugene felt his anger and darkness rising. He contained it before it had a chance to show. His mind concentrated on eating, swallowing, relaxing. "So, the motel guests, where are they?"

"It's summer. There were only a few. The last of them checked out yesterday. The desk won't take new reservations until the new manager starts in two weeks.

Olivia's bright mood returned as she ended the call. "He's doing better than any of the doctors had hoped. He was even able to identify one of his attackers as Clyde Wrigley." When Eugene snapped his eyes to hers, she nodded. "The *late* Clyde Wrigley."

"That's great news," said Austin, handing her a slice of pizza on a cheap paper plate with a napkin.

"I can't believe Oliver never introduced us." Eugene pointed to the large print showing a fiery-eyed Native American boy wearing a feathered headdress backed by a fluttering American flag. "That's a great moment."

"I remember the summer he shot that," said Olivia, delicately dabbing a napkin to sauce at the corner of her mouth. Eugene had to force his attention back to the photo as she continued, "It's from a parade in Guadalupe. I have a smaller version at home."

Pizza in hand, Austin moved to his desk, "Hey, I looked up the records on that address you asked about."

On his iMac's main monitor, he called up the county's street view photo. "Says that the owner for the last decade or so has been the Jolly Time Amusements Corporation which is a shell set up as a subsidiary of yet another shell. Well, you get the drift. I'll find out who's behind it eventually, but it'll take some time."

"Anything on school records?" asked Olivia.

"Nah, like I said, it'll be tough."

"Hey, I have an idea," said Eugene. "How about the high school Interscholastic Association's website? Wouldn't they have records? Maybe we could spot a name or two."

"Already looked," said Austin. "They only go back to the late '90s."

"Damn."

"How about the *Arizona Republic* archives?" asked Olivia.

"Good thought." Austin's fingers flew to his keyboard. "Okay, looks like they go back to the 1920's." He slid the browser window to separate monitor. "Looks like we've got our choice to search for state champions, players of the year and all-state teams."

"I'll take players of the year for all the money," joked Olivia.

"Whadda ya think? 1970 to, what, about 1980?"

"That'll do."

Just as Austin clicked on the search button a loud knock at the door made all three of them jump.

"You expecting company?"

"No, the motel's closed. They'd go to the office anyway."

"Olivia, I know you're in there. I see your car," said a muffled female voice.

"Christ, this is all I need right now," Olivia said, deflating. She tossed her plate on top of the pizza box, strode to the door and pulled it open. "We're a little busy right now, Mother. Can this wait?"

"That's my girl. Never enough time for family," said Margaret Bartholomew, pushing her way in, her suit-coated, politician husband in tow. The couple leered around the room.

"Mr. and Mrs. Bartholomew, nice to see you again," said Eugene, turning on his best fake smile.

Barely acknowledging his presence, Margaret continued, "So, this is your journalistic endeavor that's putting our future at risk."

Olivia-the-boss folded her arms and hardened her voice, "I'm not sure what you mean."

"Oh, you knew your little game would irritate the *Herald's* new owners. Don't deny it."

"I really haven't given them much thought. I've been a bit busy."

"My, but you are just like your grandfather. Always trying to save the world from an endless line of evildoers."

"Yes, and it's that sort of work that allows people like you to traipse through life without a care."

As the mother-daughter argument got underway, Eugene looked to Austin. His expression said he wished the room had a back door.

"Your mother is concerned," interrupted the senator, stepping forward and using a voice more condescending than forthright, "that your little operation will cause the *Herald's* new owners to sue."

"You of all people should know they have no grounds," said Olivia. "There were no non-competes."

"True, but lawsuits are possible, nonetheless."

Eugene looked the man up and down. Everything about him from the heavy, black-framed glasses perched on his wide face to the expensive suit tailored to fit his imposing girth said phony.

"If they back out of the deal," groaned Margaret, shifting from shrew to victim, "we'll lose a great deal of money. Gordon, get me a chair. I need to sit."

The senator did as he was told, grabbing one of the cheap chairs from the breakfast table and tucking it under her rear. She sat heavily. Eugene hoped the little chair would collapse, but it held.

"The tears won't work, Mother," Olivia recited in a monotone.

"So, what are your plans then? Live off of what Oliver left you and play savior of the world at the expense of your own flesh and blood?"

"You'll be fine, Mother. And this isn't a game; it's very important. In fact, it's so important that I'm willing to offer a compromise that should appease your Mid-States friends."

"And what would that be?" Margaret demanded. The glint in her eyes and set of her mouth proclaimed that, at least in her mind, she'd won the battle.

Eugene wanted to slap the old bitch.

"Grandpa wanted the *Providence* to be a non-profit investigative tool that partnered with other news outlets. We'd be willing to share our work with the *Herald* at a discounted price as a show of good faith. We want them to see us not as a threat, but as a partner working for the public good."

Brilliant. Eugene shifted his gaze from Olivia's simpering mother to her puffed-up politician husband who was staring at Austin's computer screens showing the image of the Luchador warehouse and school sports records. *He's looking for clues to give to the Mid-States vultures.* Eugene stepped into his line of sight, blocking the screens.

"I'll have to present them your offer and get back to you," said the suddenly energetic Margaret as she came to her feet, obviously eager to leave now that she'd been tossed a bone. "Gordon, we'll need to get moving if we're going to make our dinner reservations."

"You're welcome to share our pizza. I think it's still warm," teased Olivia.

"No, thank you, dear. Gordon has issues with gluten."

Ol' Gordo's got a lot more issues than gluten. Eugene decided he'd do a little digging into the senator's past once he was back home and alone.

When Olivia returned from ushering her parents to their car, Austin said, "Thanks for not introducing me."

"Oh, I'm sorry, I should—"

"No, no, I really mean it. Thank you for *not* introducing me. Forgive me, but those are two miserable human beings."

"I need something to wash down the pizza," said Eugene. "Does the motel have a pop machine?"

"Yes, right outside the office," said Austin. "Need change? It's a buck-twenty-five."

"I'm good. Either of you need anything?"

"I'll take a diet Dr. Pepper," said Olivia.

Austin held up a liter-sized big gulp and said, "I'm good."

Under the buzz of the beautiful old neon, the traffic on Main whizzed by, kicking up a hot summer wind from the still baking asphalt. At the pop machine, Eugene's mind raced, consumed with the odd vibe he picked up from the senator.

When he returned to the room, Austin stood behind Olivia as she worked the computer keys with furious intensity.

"Whatcha working on?" Eugene whispered to Austin.

"We have confirmation on all the names and we're going to publish them," said Olivia without missing a keystroke.

"So, the sharing thing with the *Herald*—"

"I'll be happy to share if they're willing to pay. But, I didn't like the way my step dad was soaking in what we had showing on screen. I'll bet he's calling the Mid-States people right now."

* * *

At the wheel of his wife's silver Lincoln Continental, Gordon Bartholomew seethed with anger and more than a little fear. He figured they'd find the warehouse eventually, but what surprised him were the scholastic sports records. *If they figure out the school, I'm cooked.*

"Gordon, you missed the turn," whined Margaret. "And you're speeding. Do you want to get pulled over? My god, we'll miss our reservations and then what will—"

"Marge, shut the hell up."

"Don't you talk to me that way, I—"

"I've had all I can take from your whole goody-two-shoes family."

"Need I remind you that it's my family's good name and more than a little of my money that got you re-elected? You were nothing but a washed up old jock riding the coattails of some stupid trophies when I—"

The back of his meaty right hand caught her hard on the cheek and she let out a guttural croak as her head bounced off the Lincoln's leather headrest. Wide-eyed, she stared out the windshield in stunned silence.

"You will keep that pie hole of yours shut and do as you're told. Understand? Oh, and for the record, those championships were no small accomplishment."

She nodded then reached into her purse for a tissue.

* * *

Andrew Brinkmann yawned, stretched, and leaned back in his desk chair after filing a re-write of the story filed two hours earlier by the *Arizona Providence*. Getting scooped again meant another ass kicking, but that was of little concern to him now.

"Don't get too comfortable," said Pete, strolling up with a handful of printouts. "You still have to tease the story on social media. Titillating it up a little wouldn't hurt either."

"Aw, Christ, Pete, did you feel that?"

"What?" Pete suddenly looked worried.

"From somewhere up in Heaven, Condon just punched you in the nose. Teasing and titillating? *Really*? Is that what we've come to?"

Pete scoffed. "Welcome to modern-day journalism, Andrew. It's all about monetizing eyeballs."

"Buzzwords aren't a business plan, buddy. And tweeting for traffic is like tap dancing on a turd. It's noisy, it stinks, and it's a waste of everybody's time."

"You can't talk to me—"

"The hell I can't. Face it, dick-head, everybody knows you've sold out. You have nothing left here but the enduring hatred of everyone in the room."

"Fuck you and quit arguing. Have you signed your employee handbook yet?"

"Nope."

"Fair warning, *buddy*, Spears is on my ass for this stuff and—"

"Yup," said Andrew, ignoring Pete as he felt the press rumble the floor. "A little early to crank up the press, isn't it?"

"It's the new deadlines. What concern is that of yours, anyway? I don't see any ink under your fingernails."

"I don't have any ink on my ass either, but feel free to look as I walk the hell away from you." Brinkmann stood, forcing Pete to back up a step. He then turned and walked away.

"You'll bring me that signed employee handbook soon, correct?" Pete called.

Brinkmann offered a disgusted shake of his head as he stomped for the pressroom.

* * *

Kurt steered the forklift with its huge roll of newsprint through the clear plastic strips between the pressroom and the paper warehouse. He double-tapped the horn and waved to Brinkmann as the reporter appeared.

"What's up, *compadre*?" hollered Kurt, dismounting the lift and dragging a rag from his back pocket to wipe his hands.

"Don't know how much longer I can take the bullshit," Brinkmann yelled over the slow running press. "You got another smoke I can bum?"

Kurt shook a cigarette from his pack and Andrew plucked it free.

"Light?"

"Nah, I bought a lighter this morning. Guess that's the first step off the non-smoking wagon. So, they pushed up the press runs?"

"Yup, by an hour. How's the newsroom liking that big, ugly ad on the front page?"

Brinkmann grumbled, "Trading integrity for a quick buck. It's all downhill from here."

Kurt offered a wan smile. "I hear ya. Hey, if you don't mind, I've got to get on it or I'll have Spears breathing down my neck tomorrow."

"That's cool," said Brinkmann. "Would you mind if I watched a press run later tonight? I'd like to see that little piece of magic at least once before I'm gone."

"Okay by me. Does that mean your exit plan worked out?"

"Yep, my wife gave the green light."

"Fan-fuckin'-tastic. And your secret's safe with me. Good to see somebody getting off this sinking ship."

"But I'm gonna miss this. Something about ink on paper . . . I didn't appreciate it enough."

"If you're gonna smoke you'll have to go out back to the designated area. They put the kybosh on smoking by the side door. Said it looks bad."

"Perfect," growled Brinkmann, raising a hand as he turned to push through the clear plastic strips leading into the paper warehouse.

The mountains of newsprint made for a sound-deadened stroll as he considered his paperless future. *News is news.* He tried to envision Kurt's future with all the changes coming his way. A hollow balloon grew in his chest. Stepping out the back door and into the night, he saw Mikey sitting alone at the picnic table. The jaundice glow of caged industrial light over the loading dock door illuminated him.

"Hey, Mikey," Brinkmann greeted him as he mounted the picnic table's bench seat to face the odd little pressman. "Kurt's gonna let me watch a press run tonight. I'm kind of excited about it."

"Big whoop. Whadda ya want, a party?"

"Well, no. It's just that I'm interested in what you guys do. I think it's pretty cool."

Mikey nodded, his expression as blank as ever.

"What's your job again? Flyboy? Just what does a flyboy do?"

Mikey shrugged. "Nothin'. I'm nothin'. They said so."

"What's wrong? Is it the bosses? Are the new assholes getting under your skin, too?"

"Kurt's my boss but he's not an asshole." He poked a finger at Andrew. "He's district champion."

"I wasn't talking about Kurt. He's a good guy. I'm talking about the new owners. They're the assholes."

"Good, 'cause Kurt's not supposed to be the asshole. He's the best there ever was."

Andrew fired his cigarette. In the flame's guttering glow, he saw Mikey's empty expression had changed to agony. "I know a lot of changes are coming, Mikey. You and Kurt are a team. You'll be—"

"We don't got a team no more," Mikey shouted. "All the guys got sick. They didn't think I saw, but I did. They all fell down sick."

"I'm sorry, I—"

"Hey, Mikey, there you are." Kurt spoke from the doorway. "What have you two been talking about?"

Brinkmann turned to give Kurt a grateful look. "I think Mikey's worried about layoffs. I told him everything'll be fine and you'll take care of him."

Kurt ambled to his brother's side of the table and patted his back. "Just like I always have, Mikey. Quit worrying."

Mikey nodded, silent and sullen.

"Those rolls of paper aren't gonna spindle themselves, dude. Sorry, Andrew, we gotta get back to work."

"Yeah, I suppose I should, too." Brinkmann swung his legs out of the table and stood, flicking his fresh cigarette off the dock before heading for the door.

"You're still coming out to see a press run tonight, right?" asked Kurt.

"Wouldn't miss it for the world."

32

On the 40-minute drive from Mesa to Paradise Valley, Margaret Bartholomew kept her mouth shut and stared out at the night. *It will pass*, she told herself daring a sideways glance at her husband. His powerful hands were strangling the steering wheel.

As they turned off Tatum Boulevard and began the slow wind back to their desert home, she said, “I’m sorry, darling. I wasn’t thinking. I’ll make dinner.”

He offered no response beyond grinding his teeth and gripping the wheel until his knuckles turned white.

“Gordon, you’re scaring me,” she whined as they pulled into the drive and the garage door rolled slowly upward.

“It’s over, Margaret. You’re nothing but a simpering fool.”

“Don’t talk like that. We’re a team. We need each other.” She rattled out, placing a trembling hand to his face. Seeing no reaction she let it drift down to the crotch of his suit pants. “I’ll do whatever you want. You know I will. Just don’t talk like that.”

Slowly, they rolled into the garage. The door hummed down, softly bumping to a stop. Margaret felt his manhood coming to life under her undulating palm. With pleasured grunts, he lifted his hips. She managed a worried smile as her free hand reached to unbuckle her seatbelt, then his suit pants.

“God, but you are a clueless piece of shit,” he murmured. “You’ve never known needs, you only know *want*. You have no idea what I really need.”

"I-I don't understand. What am I doing wrong?" The vigor of her hand increased. "Just tell me and—"

"Shhh, stop talking," he whispered. Like a striking snake he back-handed her then pulled her head to his lap.

* * *

With the kids put to bed and the master bedroom door locked, Harry and Sarah lay together in the afterglow of a long-anticipated lovemaking session. "We really should do this more often," Sarah crooned as Harry wrapped his arm around her and pulled her close.

"You think they heard us? You got a little loud there at the end," he said in a gravelly voice.

Sarah smoothed her hand along his lean chest and stomach. "If they ask, Mommy and Daddy were just playing tickle monster."

"I think they're a little old for . . . Oh, my . . . Ahhh, don't start something I might not be able to finish."

"Focus . . . You owe me for all the hours you've been putting in at work." She swung off the bed then bent back over him, the fingers of one hand stroking over his flippant smile while the other hand slid south. "Seriously, mister, round two begins when I get back from the bathroom."

He appreciated the bounce of her tousled hair, the line of her back down to her butt, still firm after delivering him two beautiful children. That was all the encouragement he needed.

His phone buzzed from the bedside table. Groaning at the interruption, he still brought the phone to life and scrolled to a new email from the Pinal County Sheriff. Within was a Luchador information dump. Clicking into an attached PDF, he moved through a detailed list of cell phone activity. Hearing a flush, he set his phone aside.

His woman emerged from the bathroom, her measured gait and the distant look in her eyes hinting that their moment had passed.

After a few minutes of kissing and stroking, he raised up to meet her eyes. "Are you thinking about your work or mine?" he asked.

The far away look in her eyes faded until she was again with him. She blinked and smiled softly. "Both really. Pulled here, there. The house, shopping for school clothes."

He traced a fingertip over her face. "Remember when we could go at it all night?"

"Less responsibility back then." She nipped his chin. "Now, we have nothing to prove to one another. Let's call what we have quality over quantity."

He rolled to stretch out beside her, nestling his groin against her hip, his elbow bent, his hand supporting his head so he could study her. "God, I love you." When she sighed with contentment, he delivered a series of gentle kisses that led to longer, more sensual ones. Finally, he whispered against her mouth. "Oh, how I love you." Seeing her eyes closing, he pulled up her covers to protect her from the chill of the ceiling fan's breeze.

Returning from his own trip to the bathroom, he hesitated to marvel at her slumbering beauty. After clicking open the door lock, he glanced down the hall toward the kids' rooms. Lights remained out and silence reigned.

Behind him Sarah's sleepy voice announced, "Your phone buzzed again."

He cringed at the thought of his work once again intruding on their much-needed time together. "I'm not back at work until morning."

"It could be important. Check it." She turned over and snuggled deeper under her covers, mumbling, "It will help me feel safe."

"I did get a list of phone calls earlier." He scooped up the phone but hesitated. "Do you know how much I love you?"

"Yep, and I love you, too. Tonight was wonderful, by the way." A delicate hand waved above the covers. "Now, go do what you have to."

He took the time to put on underwear. Silently walking barefoot down the hall, he paused to peak in on each of his sleeping children, so peaceful and innocent in their dream worlds. An unexpected lump rose in his throat. His fingers gripped his cell phone. *How did I get to be so lucky in this screwed up world?*

* * *

In their motel room office, Olivia and Eugene sat on opposite sides of the little dining table tapping away at their laptops. Austin sat staring at his computer monitors with weary eyes. Yawning, he stretched, pushed up his glasses and rubbed his face vigorously.

"You need sleep," said Olivia. "You've put in a couple of very long days."

"We all have . . . but I've gotta say, it's been worth it. Kind of reminds me of my youth when I thought I could change the world with a few lines of code."

"So . . . you really knew Woz?" asked Eugene. "Do you keep in touch?"

"He invited me out to play Segway polo a few years back. Super nice guy and, man, what a brain. It's no wonder he went on to much greater things than I did."

"Did you ever meet Steve Jobs?"

"Oh, sure. Never really got to know him. He kind of operated on a different plane."

"All right, gentlemen," Olivia-the-boss spoke up, "I say we call it a day. Or would that be night?"

Austin consulted his watch. "A little of both . . . Yep, it's stopping time. I'm gonna head out. Back at it 10 a.m. tomorrow?"

"I say, whenever you get up. The competition is playing 'catch-up' which gives us a little leeway. We've all earned a good night's sleep. Go home, give Donna my best, and tell her I'm sorry for monopolizing your time."

"I think she appreciates having the house to herself again. Having me around all the time . . . Well, let's just say absence makes the heart grow fonder." He leaned to pluck a messenger bag from under his desk then stood and slung it over his shoulder. "You two behave," he said with a knowing wink.

Eugene blushed. "Hey, there's nothing—"

"Stow it, dude. I know a perfect match when I see it. Life is short. Enjoy it while you can. Take it from an old nerd. See you two tomorrow."

Olivia followed Austin to the door, thanking him again for his talent and hard work. Eugene watched her in the doorway as she waved goodbye. There was something about the fit of her jeans and her stance in those cowboy boots . . . Visions of her writhing in sweat-soaked ecstasy flashed to mind. He tucked them away. She'd given some pretty clear signals . . . *But she's way out of my league. Tread lightly, Eugene. Don't screw this up . . . This was a woman who could take on the world and win.*

She locked the door and turned with a naughty fire in her eyes. Eugene met her gaze, suddenly feeling like a deer in the headlights. In two strides she was on him, wedging between his chair and the table, grabbing his shirt with both hands to swing a leg over and settle into his lap. Her eyes blazed into his before closing to moan as she ground herself into his swollen and aching member.

"God how I've wanted this," she whispered, tunneling her fingers through his hair before pulling his face to her chest.

Breathing her in, his hand moved to cup a firm breast and tease an erect and wanting nipple through her shirt. She leaned back to intensely study his eyes then came in for a long, probing kiss. Chests heaving, their hot breath mingling they pushed apart long enough to glance around the room in search of comfort.

"Great, we pick the one motel room in all of Arizona without a bed." His voice was thick as he ground into her heat, prompting her hips to rock with his rhythm.

Lithe as a gymnast, she leaned backwards to the table. Eugene supported the small of her back as her fingers probed a pocket of her laptop bag and came out with a single key on a ring. Wide-eyed, she bit her plump lower lip and dangled the key before him.

"Whatcha got there?" he asked, already knowing the answer.

"Arthur's replacement won't arrive for two weeks. Until then we have all 32 rooms to ourselves."

Hand-in-hand, they dashed from the office. Unable to go any further without another embrace, he spun her around in the middle of the empty parking lot.

She broke away, panting and laughing.

"Which room would you prefer?" Eugene said, sweeping his hands at their many choices.

"Any room but the ones near the office," laughed Olivia. "If Austin comes in early, he'll never let us forget it."

Eugene took control. In one swift motion he had her off her feet and over his shoulder. She shrieked with laughter. In a dead run, he crossed the lot and spun around to let her work the key in the first door he came to.

"I can't find the hole," she chuckled, stabbing at the deadbolt in the dark.

"That's usually my line," he crooned, sliding a hand up between her legs just as she slid the key home.

The door flew open. He fumbled for the light switch, closed the door and tossed her to the bed. She bounced with laughter as he grabbed and pulled off one boot and then the other, tossing them to the floor. She unbuckled and unbuttoned to aid him in slipping her out of her jeans. Standing at the foot of the bed, he paused to take in her beauty. She lay there waiting and wanting, biting her lower lip.

He stripped off his shirt and stepped out of his shoes. Olivia sat up to eagerly assist him with his jeans. One slender hand slid over his lean stomach. She leaned forward to kiss her way down. He groaned and swayed into her touch.

Pushing her back down to the bed, he held her heated gaze as he fumbled for her feet to tug off her socks. After kissing her toes, he let his divine intuition guide his strong fingers in working their magic.

"Oh, my god . . . How—"

"Shhhhh, let's take our time and do this right," he whispered. "We have all night."

* * *

Hours later, they lay sated and sweaty, her leg draped over his thigh and her head nuzzling his shoulder. She danced a finger on his chest then gazed up to his face. "What are you thinking about?" she asked as he looked off into nothingness.

"Lots of things . . . mostly about all the stars that had to align to bring us together . . . I mean, what are the chances?"

"Grandpa would have called it divine providence."

Eugene smiled and met her eyes. "Yes, this is divine . . . sacred, even. I mean, it's like all my other relationships were just practice so I'd know when I'd found perfection."

She stretched up to kiss him as her eyes smiled with the naughty look that made his insides melt.

"The waitresses of Scottsdale will be in mourning over the loss of their masseuse . . . Seriously, where did you learn to do that?"

"My fingers just seem to know where to go and how to make things right."

"This is right . . . and good . . . I wish we could stay here forever and never have to face the ugliness of the outside world ever again." Eugene could feel the tension he'd so patiently massaged from every inch of her body returning.

"Ah, but then we'd miss the beauty of it as well. Seems like we need at least a little bad for contrast so we appreciate the good."

"Speaking of good and bad, what do you think of my stepfather?"

Eugene's stomach tensed. "Promise not to hate me?"

"Of course. What is it?"

"I googled him earlier tonight. Something's off with that man."

"I know. I've run searches on him, too. Only found what I already knew. What did you find?"

"Beyond his campaign site and a bunch of news stories on his work at the capitol, there's not much out there. On his past, I mean."

"Considering his age, that's not surprising. He really bothers you, doesn't he? Funny, I thought you'd dislike my bitchy mom more than him."

"Can't say she does much for me, either." He grinned. "I do enjoy watching you manage her. I about lost it when you asked them to stay and eat a delivery pizza."

Olivia's eyes snapped with that mischievous light. "That was fun. Gluten? Yeah, right."

The heat in his belly blossomed into his chest and he gave into the urge to go for broke. "Guess I'll have to get used to it now . . . Have I told you how much I love you?" He reached his free arm over to brush back her hair. She pressed her face into his hand. "Wait, wait, I feel something calling my fingers." He traced a fingertip down her slender neck and out to the tip of her well-sculpted left shoulder. "Right here," he crooned with a gentle press.

"Oh, oh, that's amazing." She closed her eyes and moaned as he put his thumb to work turning tension to pleasure. His hand slid from her shoulder to gently touch and tickle before he pulled her in tight for a kiss that melted her into him.

"Wait, wait. I feel something calling *my* fingers," Olivia whispered, obviously pulling herself from her ecstasy. She slid a delicate foot up his leg to let her calf press into his growing erection. His response coaxed her fingernails to rake his stomach before moving down to pleasure him. She nuzzled his ear and whispered hotly about what was to come.

* * *

After posting links to Twitter and Facebook on his story featuring the names of the dead Luchadors, Brinkmann cast a bleary-eyed glance to the few people left in the newsroom. He saw nothing but dejection and worry. Pete stared forlornly at his computer while overhead on a muted, newsroom television, a sportscaster delivered scores via subtitle.

For a moment, Brinkmann considered adding to Pete's misery by giving notice, but thought better of it. He needed more detail from Olivia Condon and news of his resignation would be better delivered to Spears.

Something about his odd interaction with Mikey was stuck in his head. *What did he mean about Kurt being district champion? Of what? Were the cops right about him?* He turned to his computer and plugged in a search for Kurt Wragge and sports. Page after page of results came back, all involving a New York newscaster. Typing in Kurt Wragge and Arizona returned many results with the right last name but wrong first name.

Brinkmann felt the press rumble the floor then sensed a presence over his shoulder.

"Hey, we're plating up for the last run of the night, if you're free," said Kurt.

Brinkmann's fingers shot to the keyboard, minimizing the screen. He turned to the pressman and, not wanting to look guilty, said, "Sounds like a plan. Lead the way."

"You'll need these." Kurt handed him a pair of earmuffs.

He pinched the muffs around his neck and followed Kurt to the pressroom, his mind still spinning with bits of information that were all just a jumble of suspicion.

They pushed through the swinging doors out to the pressroom. The warning bell rang and the press rotated ever so slightly as pressmen stepped in and out of the giant mechanical stacks.

"So, you've never actually seen a press run, right?" asked Kurt.

"I've walked by when it was running, but I've never seen the whole process. All the places I've worked before had satellite printing operations."

"Well, you're in for a treat. What you have here is a marvel of mechanical ingenuity. This whole thing is kinda like a big sewing machine. We call this the front end. The paper feeds in here and runs this way and that and somehow comes out the other end a finished paper."

"You call the paper's path the web, right?"

"Yep, there's two kinds of mechanical presses, sheet fed and web. Sheet fed's for pussies. Anyway, rollers steer the paper through this way and that and at some point it passes over a blanket that applies ink to the page."

"Blanket?"

"Yeah, there's offset and letterpress. Letterpress is old school while offset is much cleaner." Kurt stepped to a workbench and pulled an old plate from a stack underneath. The thin metal plate made a warping, songlike sound as he lifted it to the bench top.

"Letterpress goes straight from plate to page. Offset goes from plate to blanket to page and gives you much crisper reproduction."

"Okay, I think I've got it."

"Right now the guys are hanging plates and cleaning blankets, getting ready to print the A section."

"That looks dangerous, the guys stepping into the machine like that."

"It can be if you don't know what you're doing. You'll notice we don't wear jewelry or have any loose clothing. Heck, that tie of yours is an accident waiting to happen. The nipping rings down at the far end would rip off you head if they got a hold of it."

Brinkmann nodded, a trickle of fear running down his spine as he plucked at his shirt buttons to tuck away his tie.

"Don't worry, dude. I won't let you get that close."

"Better safe than sorry."

"True. So, basically what happens here is that ink comes down from the top and water comes up from the bottom. It's mixed and broken down in the roller train and eventually ends up on the plate. The plate transfers the ink to a blanket which applies it to the paper."

"And all that happens inside those tall machine thingies?"

Kurt crossed his arms and shot Brinkmann a hard look, "How'd you know they're called thingies?"

"Oh, I didn't. I-I just—"

"I'm bullshittn' ya, dude." Kurt smiled and pointed to the long line of two-story-tall towers that filled the big pressroom. "Those *thingies* are called units. Each one can print a color, like cyan, yellow, magenta, black. Surely they taught you the basics of printing in journalism school, right?"

"They did, but this is the first practical application I've seen. So, if each unit lays down one color and each picture has four colors, how do you line it all up?"

"Art and skill," Kurt said proudly. "We got this baby tuned to the tiniest fraction of an inch, because that's the difference between great reproduction and crap. Thing is, it changes every day with the temp and humidity and paper stock. You have to make allowances. That's the art of it."

"What's with those funny square paper hats?"

Kurt chuckled. "That's a tradition that goes back many generations. The guy that taught me said it started as a way to keep ink out of their hair. Some of the old letterpress machines were messy as hell. Now we just make 'em for fun and for when school kids come through on a tour."

"Eugene called Mikey a flyboy. What's that mean?"

"Flyboy watches the finished papers come off and pulls the bad ones."

"Where is he, by the way?"

"Maybe out back or in the restroom. He'll show up when he feels the press crank up to half speed. We really don't want him around the mechanicals too much. Thing is he's smart as hell—gifted really—when it comes to machines. But, he's forgetful, too. Out here that's a dangerous combination."

"Hm, tell me if I'm overstepping, but was he born with his dis—"

"Nah, it was a car wreck. Happened when I was a senior in high school. Mom and Dad were killed but Mikey survived. I had college plans, scholarships and such but that got put on hold for Mikey."

"That's a lot of responsibility for a high school kid."

"You just do what you have to for family."

"No other relatives? Where'd you grow up?"

"A little crap hole in the middle of nowhere." Kurt reared back, his eyes narrowed. "Say, you want my whole family history, or do you want to see this baby run?"

"Sorry. Guess I'm just touched by how you take care of him."

"No big deal." He turned away to holler at his crew, "Hey, are we plated up?"

The pressmen leaned out from between the units offering thumbs up as they stepped out to man their stations. Kurt led Brinkmann to a large, beige box labeled *MASTER CONSOLE* that bristled with buttons and dials.

When Kurt put on his earmuffs, Brinkmann followed suit.

"All right, boys, let's run a few!"

A warning bell rang and Kurt pressed a pair buttons that brought the big machine groaning to life. It rolled slowly but in less than a minute, finished, folded pages shuttled out on a conveyor at the far end.

Mikey appeared, looking harried as he lumbered to the far end of the press to man his station.

Over the noise Kurt yelled, "You stay here. I'll be right back."

Brinkmann nodded.

Kurt trotted to the far end to point and holler something to Mikey. He pulled finished pages, quickly examined them then barked orders to his crew who jumped into their work without hesitation. Brinkmann thought maybe they were putting on a show for his benefit, but the focus and pride on their faces along with the precision of their moves reminded him of an America's Cup sailing crew.

After a few more tweaks, Kurt returned to Brinkmann and held out a section front. He pointed to the registration marks and color bar at the bottom of the page. "Perfection," he yelled with a smile, "right out of the gate."

"Looks good to me," Brinkmann yelled back, not really knowing what he was looking at.

Kurt twirled an uplifted finger and the crew stepped clear of the press. Grasping the largest dial on the console, he gradually brought the press up to speed. The low rumble became a hum then a whine.

Kurt made another mad-dash quality check, ordered a couple of tweaks then returned to Brinkmann, "Now that she's running, let me show you a few things," he yelled, motioning for him to follow.

"That's the folder board," Kurt yelled, pointing to a polished, triangular metal surface that creased paper as it slid over. When Kurt tugged Brinkmann's arm, he followed. "Those are the nipping rings." he yelled, pointing to a series of vicious, spinning four-inch thick rollers tugging at the paper. "Down here's the cutting box." A blur of wicked blades cut the pages before spitting them out to the conveyor.

Brinkmann stared in wonder, a twinge of caution tightening his chest. The spinning, whizzing, clanking cacophony of steel, paper, and ink was hypnotic and violent. He glanced at orchestrating Kurt, his mind wondering to the man's designation as some sort of youthful district champion. *Champion of what?*

A firm hand pressed into the small of his back. Brinkmann gasped and stepped back.

"Whoa. Sorry, dude. Didn't mean to scare you," yelled Kurt. "Kinda pulls you in like a moth to a flame, don't it?"

"Yeah." Brinkmann swallowed hard. "Eugene was right. It's amazing."

Kurt grinned, "Let's head back to the other end or we'll miss the roll change."

They arrived at the flying paster reel just in time to see a massive roll of newsprint rotate into the web to be pulled in with a pop as the depleted roll was cut then flapped wildly.

"That's the tour," hollered Kurt, dragging a rag over his hand.

Brinkmann took the cue and shook the clean hand. "Thank you. This was great," he hollered, relinquishing his earmuffs then pushing back through the double-swinging doors leading to the newsroom

When Brinkmann returned to his desk, Pete asked, "Where'd you go?"

"Kurt just gave me a tour of the pressroom. It's pretty cool."

Pete rolled his eyes in disdain and moved on.

Brinkmann pulled copies of the Luchador images from a drawer. As he spread them on his desktop, he noticed a small, yellowed newspaper clipping resting on his computer keyboard. *What the hell?* He carefully lifted it for a closer examination. Brittle and creased inside its lamination, the clipping's age was obvious and it smelled like . . . *leather?* He concluded someone had carried it in a wallet for a very long time. It offered only one paragraph with no date or location other than the name of a school.

> *Copperfield's Coach Bartholmew says rumors of a hazing incident causing serious brain injury to freshman wrestler, Michael Wragge are unfounded. "This was just an unfortunate turn of events," said Bartholomew. "We pray that Michael's recovery is swift and complete and we will do everything in our power to help both he and his family . . ."*

Brinkmann's eyes went from wide to narrow and his heart skipped a beat. He scanned the newsroom but saw no sign of being watched.

"Pete, did you see anyone near my desk?"

The man looked back, bleary-eyed. "No, why?"

"Nothing. Ah, thought someone took my stapler again," said Brinkmann, "but I found it."

Bartholomew and Wragge. What are the chances . . . In an instant the pieces of the puzzle that had started to come together on his walk to the pressroom became a fully formed thought. He studied the Luchador party photos on his desk, zeroing in on the older fat man in the black pirate mask.

"Holy crap, that's him," he whispered. *And Ass Clown has to be Kurt . . . but how?*

A second flash of insight hit him. *The dead men in the San Tans, one of them was a doctor.*

His shaking hands plucked an old *Roget's Thesaurus* from the little bookshelf over his desk. He slid the clipping between the pages for safekeeping, then unlocked his file drawer and dropped the book behind the hanging folders.

33

Bland Muzak played in Mountain View Memorial's emergency room as Brinkmann stepped from the revolving glass door into the small lobby. The front desk was unmanned. In the waiting area, a small Hispanic woman with a vacuum cleaner strapped to her back cleaned the carpet.

A heavy-set woman in scrubs emerged from the doorway behind the desk, a Subway sandwich in one hand, a soft drink cup in the other. Her nametag identified her as ER Secretary. "Can I help you?"

"I have a question regarding hospital procedure," said Brinkmann.

She clutched her sandwich as though he might steal it then sucked on the drink's straw, all while looking him up and down. The suspicious light in her eyes didn't bode well. "Are you a lawyer or something?"

Brinkmann assumed a professional attitude. "No, I'm a newspaper reporter. I work—"

"I can't talk to you," she hissed, then dropped her sandwich on the desk to pick up the phone.

"Wait. Who are you calling?"

"Security, we don't need reporters sniffing for scandal—"

"I'm not sniffing for anything. I don't need specifics on any patient. I just have a general question—"

"HIPAA prevents me from saying anything to you."

"Actually, no, HIPAA laws do no such thing."

Continuing to glare at him, she spoke into the phone, "We've got a damn reporter bothering me up here and he won't leave . . . Good. And please hurry."

As she hung up, Brinkmann looked around. “Is there a doctor on duty? Really, I just need some basic information.”

The woman folded her big arms then looked down the hallway. A security guard authoritatively strode toward them, his eyes focused on Brinkmann.

“What’s the problem, sir?”

“There isn’t a problem, I have a simple question, nothing specific to any patient, just a *simple* question.”

“I’m sorry, sir, but you’ll have to leave. Any questions can be directed to our public relations staff in the morning.”

“All I want to know is how easy it would be to—”

The security guard put a hand to Brinkmann’s elbow. “You’re leaving. Now.”

Brinkmann jerked his arm free. “This is important. What’s wrong with—”

The security guard gripped the back of Brinkmann’s neck, turning him around towards the exit.

“Jesus Christ! I’m going all ready. This is totally unnecessary.”

When they reached the revolving door, Brinkmann deliberately tripped himself, going face first into the wall. He remained standing, but stars edged his vision. He’d hit harder than planned. A warm trickle slid down his forehead. “Look what you did! I’m bleeding! I need a doctor!”

“What’s all the commotion?” said an unseen voice beyond the bulk of the security guard.

“No worries, doc. Just dealing with—”

“Aren’t you supposed to call the police if there’s a problem? Is this man drunk?”

“I’m not drunk. I’m Andrew Brinkmann with the *East Valley Herald*.”

“He’s a reporter,” called out the woman at the front counter. Her disgusted tone implied that this justified the rough treatment.

“Yes, Kate, I gathered that from what he just said. Now, he’s my patient, thanks to Clarence overstepping his *limited* authority.”

“But he was asking questions,” the woman declared defensively.

The doctor eyed his forehead. “That’s what reporters do. Go back to your sandwich, Kate. I’ve got this.”

The doctor, who had salt-and-pepper hair and a bushy mustache to match, glared at the now contrite security guard. The man stepped back.

"I'm all right," Brinkmann said, fingering the spot on his forehead.

"You'll at least need a band-aid for that."

"What I need is a minute of your time to answer a question. Nothing specific to any patients, just a general question."

"Odd time of day for that," said the doctor. He cocked his head.

"I know, I know. It's just that we've been putting in some crazy hours lately with all that's going on."

"Oliver Condon was a friend," said the doctor. "I'm sorry we lost him."

Brinkmann slumped for effect. "Yes, he was a good man. Ah, have you got someplace less threatening and with a little more privacy?" He shot a glance to the still-hovering security guard.

"Clarence, I think they just put some fresh donuts out in the cafeteria," the doctor said with a *get lost* tilt of his head. The security guard puffed and ground his teeth then stomped off.

The man then motioned Brinkmann to follow him into a nearby empty exam room. He pulled on gloves and wet a washcloth as Brinkmann parked his rear on the only chair. Taking a seat on a rolling metal stool, the doctor quickly cleaned his forehead, applied a band-aid then stripped off the gloves, saying, "Okay, ask your question."

"How hard would it be to fake a medical record?"

The interested doctor's expression changed to caution. "Where is this going?"

"As you probably know, the police briefly suspected one of our employees—"

"The Luchador mess, yes, I read that in the paper. We aren't talking about specific people here, correct?"

"Correct," said Brinkmann.

"And we are not on the record, correct?"

"Correct. Hypothetically, say I'm a doctor working at an unnamed medical center and I want to insert an inaccuracy into some random person's medical record. How hard would that be?"

"Hypothetically, not hard at all. Just pull the record, then handwrite or type it in."

"Really? There's no checks or balances?"

"Well, no, not really. Of course, the paperwork would have a trail, such as nurses notes and such. It would be hard to fake all that unless the staff were in cahoots."

"Nurses notes?"

"The intake nurse always makes notes. You know, vital signs, the patient's description of their problem, allergies, relevant history. The doctor then collects their own data and observations."

"Would the police dig that deep?"

"I don't know. You'll have to ask them. The medical record is private information belonging to the institution. It has to be legally accessed."

"Thank you. That's really all I needed." Brinkmann shrugged, more than a little embarrassed. "Sorry for the disruption."

"That's it? Really? Oliver would have tried to pin me down on something more specific, like whether there were ever problems with the paperwork of a certain doctor recently tied to the Luchadores."

Brinkmann brightened. *Doc's tossing me a bone.* "What would you have told him?"

"I'd have told him to go pound sand."

Brinkmann laughed out loud. "I'm really missing him right now."

"We're all missing him. The city is much the poorer for his absence." The doctor offered his hand and Brinkmann gave it a firm shake as they stood in unison and exited the room.

"One thing I can tell you about this Smith fellow. Something totally separate from his association with this hospital. He cheated at golf."

Tilting his head to meet the doctor's eyes Brinkmann offered a questioning glance that was answered by a wink.

* * *

Harry winced at the chill of faux leather on his naked back as he settled into his living room recliner with a laptop, cell phone and case notes in hand. The pulse of his charging laptop's LED and the glow of the DVR clock were the only lights in the room until he opened the computer and cringed at the bright screen.

When his eyes adjusted, he went straight to the email from Pinal County and zeroed in on a PDF list of Clyde Wrigley's phone calls. *Well, shit. This won't do me much good.*

The PDF offered page after page of numbers, dates and times going back six months, but associated no names with the numbers. *Not exactly the quick-look-and-back-to-bed I was hoping for.*

About to give up and turn the lists over to the techs in the morning, an idea sparked. After turning on a table lamp, he flipped through his case notes. He ran searches for each number he'd collected during his interviews. The first match was a call to the Tradewinds Motel. *Well, that's more proof that Wrigley was involved . . . not that it will make any difference now.*

After several more searches, all of them fruitless, Pete Cunningham's cell number came up a winner. He noted dozens of calls, from Wrigley to Pete with none from Pete to Wrigley. He speed-dialed Eddie, who answered on the first ring.

"You're looking through the Pinal County crap, aren't you?" said Eddie.

"Yeah, sorry about the hour. I didn't think—"

"Hey, not to worry. I got up to pee and couldn't go back to sleep, then Pinal County's email comes in. Trouble is, it's raw data—"

"I cross referenced with numbers from the case notes and found maybe three dozen calls from Wrigley to Pete Cunningham in the last six months."

"Interesting, but he was the lead investigator on the original Luchador case."

After a moment of silent consideration, Harry said, "Shit. You're right. I'm an idiot. They could be legit."

"Except that I knew Wrigley. He'd do anything to avoid talking with the press."

"But Cunningham still has an out."

"I think it'd be worth asking. I'd like to see his reaction. That guy's hinky all the way around. I'm willing to push his buttons."

"Let's make it our first stop in the morning. You're picking me up, correct?"

"That's what I remember. Your kids and wife all well?"

"Yeah, been a terrific couple of days. How was dinner with the daughter?"

"Outstanding. She's got a new job and a new boyfriend. Things are smooth right now."

"I'm happy for you."

"Get some sleep. We'll get back to tracking down the bad guys in the morning."

* * *

Kurt's fear had blossomed to near panic at glimpsing search results for "*Wragge and sports*" on Brinkmann's computer. Finishing up the night's work, he found himself flinching every time something sounded the least bit off. With the final press run and preparation for the next day complete, he slipped from the pressroom into the dark, unoccupied advertising department where he settled into a cubicle and dialed a phone number.

"Who is this and why call at this hour?"

In a whisper and working hard to keep the panic from his voice, Kurt said, "It's me, Coach. We have a problem . . . Mikey slipped up and it's all falling apart. I told you we should have—"

"Come to me with solutions, not problems. What's your plan?"

"It's time for the fallback. I think Brinkmann is onto us."

"How?"

"I saw on his computer. He was googling my name and sports. It's only a matter of time before he finds something that puts us together."

"I wouldn't count on that. It was a long time ago, way before the internet. I paid a lot of money to some very talented people to make any mention of the incident go away."

"Coach, there are still people alive who remember. What's to stop them from posting something new? And, well, it's not just the search. He was in the pressroom tonight asking a lot of questions about the past. I fed him the usual drunk driver BS. What if he digs into medical records? He's smart. He'll figure it out."

Coach Bart let out a long, frustrated breath. "I stopped by my stepdaughter's office tonight. She had that Eugene Fellig and some old fart searching sports records, too. They had a picture of the warehouse . . . Maybe it is time for the fallback . . . I worry though. It's our last play. If it goes bad, there's nothing left."

"Can't we just disappear? What about South America?"

"Pipe dream at this point, son. I'd like nothing better than to divorce this Condon bitch and disappear. That scenario is at least a year off. Shit! Well, we had no way of knowing that little cum receptacle Derek would screw us all by going off the deep end."

"We should have taken care of that problem years ago."

"Hindsight's twenty-twenty, son. There were risks in that, too."

"I guess it's up to me to throw a 'Hail Mary' then."

He heard the Coach's heavy sigh. "Afraid so. Do you have a game plan?"

"Yes, sir. I've scouted both houses, planned my route and pulled together my supplies . . . You know, this is a big job. I could use some help if—"

"No, absolutely not. We can't risk anyone making a connection between us. That could ruin our last hope of confusing the trail."

"Mmm-hm."

"Don't you start questioning my motives. I have all I can handle in managing my idiot wife and stepdaughter . . . Seriously, it's time to man up . . . Just remember, I love you, son." For the first time in his life Kurt thought he heard a hint of desperation in Coach Bart's voice.

"Love you too, Coach. Sorry I questioned you. I'll make you proud."

"See you on the other side of this. I'm trashing this phone, so don't try to call. I'll contact you when the heat subsides."

After wiping tears and collecting himself, Kurt slipped back to the pressroom, grabbed a freshly-printed front page and spread it out on the workbench near the control console.

"Whatcha doin?" asked Mikey, looking far less dour than he had at the picnic table.

"Just make'n a hat, bud. Gonna give it to that reporter fella we had out here tonight."

"That's nice. Sorry I was a grump."

"That's okay, Mikey. We all have bad days. You want to come with me to give it to him?"

"You said I can't go in the newsroom."

"It's okay just this once. It's late and the big bosses are gone."

Mikey brightened. "Okay. Is Eugene up there, too?"

"Not tonight. It's just that Brinkmann guy."

Mikey nodded and watched as Kurt began folding.

"Can I make one, too?"

"Sure. Make one for both of us so we match."

Their project started out looking like paper airplanes, but after a minute or so of folding and tucking and folding some more, the little square hats were ready.

"C'mon," Kurt said, donning the hat Mikey had made for him.

Together they marched into the nearly deserted newsroom. Pete shot them a worried look and approached.

"Is there a problem in the pressroom? Spears will be on my ass—"

"Nah, it's all good. We just wanted to give Brinkmann an honorary pressman's hat. He was our guest tonight out on the floor."

Pete's worry became a curious sneer. "Oh, he's gone. He ran out for something. Don't know if he's coming back tonight."

Kurt felt both worry and relief. Then his stomach tightened when Brinkmann pushed through the newsroom's front door, fingering something from his forehead and tousling his hair. Dread of the inevitable punched Kurt in the gut. Tonight would not be as easy or pleasurable as killing the waitress.

"What's up, guys?" Brinkmann asked when he reached his desk. "What can I do for you?"

Kurt thought he saw a hint of fear on the reporter's face. "Mikey and I made you a little something. It's from today's front page. Andrew Brinkmann, you are officially an honorary pressman. Mikey, do the honors."

Childlike glee spread over Mikey's face as he stepped up to present the paper hat. Brinkmann played along, smiling and bowing before placing the hat on his head. "Kurt, what is it you say before you crank up the press?"

"Let's run a—"

"Let's run a few, Mikey!" said Brinkmann, and Mikey squirmed with excitement.

"We're thinking of grabbing a beer at the Prickly. You're welcome to stop by," said Kurt, probing for information while considering whether he'd choke Brinkmann out then kill him or just drop him with the tire iron he had tucked away at home.

"A beer does sound good," said Brinkmann, "but I've probably got another hour here and I've had a heckuva long couple of days. Sorry, guys. Maybe another night."

* * *

Kurt hustled Mikey through the pressroom and out to his Harley. He broke the speed limit several times en route home. Together they pushed the bike up the sidewalk in front of their duplex apartment and around to their tiny backyard. Focusing his mind on his options, he let Mikey chain it to the gas meter near their Budweiser charcoal grill.

Once inside the apartment, Kurt exaggerated a yawn. "Hey, I'm beat I'm gonna hit the sack early. I'll get your meds. You know I need to see you take them so you don't forget."

After rolling his eyes, Mikey grabbed the TV remote and flopped on the couch like a teenager home from school.

Kurt went to the kitchen and came back with a handful of pills. The mix included blood thinners, anti-seizure meds and a muscle relaxant needed to counter complications of a brain injury that was the result of a freshman hazing gone too far.

Mikey downed the mix without looking, not seeing the Rhohypnol that would put him out for hours. As Kurt settled in next to his brother, he swept empty beer cans from the coffee table to make room for his feet. They watched Mikey's favorite show, "Big Bang Theory" for only minutes before the drugs put the kid out.

In the bedroom Kurt donned dark, oversized clothing atop his uniform shirt and pants, then slipped into a cheap pair of canvas and plastic discount store shoes. Weeks before he had secured a Central Market paper bag from Pete's neighborhood grocery store. He filled it with a black ski mask, a wad of rubber nitrile gloves taken from work, cheap cotton gardening gloves, a rag and a plastic trash bag. The heavy tire iron would have to be a last minute add so as not to tear the sack.

After making sure Mikey was out, he grabbed his boots, tucked the bag under his arm and clutched the tire iron as he walked for the El Camino.

The city sky glowed like the phosphor of a dying television tube as he drove to Brinkmann's home. Turning into the reporter's neighborhood, he prayed he hadn't taken too long. A pair of late-night joggers disappeared around the corner. Across the street an old man walked a Golden Retriever.

Flipping off his radio and rolling down his window as he neared the house, he breathed in the scent of oleander blossoms and something else. *Was that night-time cereus in bloom?* He fought a shiver rising up his back recognizing fear and anticipation were tangling his thoughts.

His chest tightened upon seeing Brinkmann's side of the carport empty. He concentrated on drawing in three long, calming breaths. *Yes, I think that is cereus.*

One more round of the block showed nothing but dim light in sleepy houses. He slowed, pulled to the curb two houses down then extinguished the headlights and motor. His fingers deftly tore off the plastic cover of the truck's dome light and removed the bulb. It hadn't worked in years but he couldn't make one mistake.

Blood coursed in his ears and the El Camino's cooling exhaust ticked as he watched the mirrors and scanned the empty street. He amped himself up for the fight for his life, the take down of a full-grown man. A man who could send him to prison where the torture he'd experienced at the hands of his teammates would be a daily occurrence. His bruised and torn insides still ached.

The rubber gloves went on first, followed by the garden gloves and ski mask that he wished was the clown mask that had so deliciously terrified the waitress. The tire iron felt solid but a little off balance. There would be blood, maybe lots of it if what he'd seen on TV was anywhere close to reality.

Move, move, move! Coach Bart's voice echoed in his head.

The heavy driver's door groaned as he shoved it open and crawled out. It groaned again as a nudge of hip closed it. The paper bag, boots and rag went into the truck's bed. Tire iron in hand, he skirted the overgrown oleander bushes hemming Brinkmann's driveway. He backed into the dagger-shaped leaves until he was all but invisible.

The neighborhood came to life as he waited. Every barking dog and distant siren quickened his heart. A bug crawled up his pant leg. He pinched at it. He wished he'd smoked a cigarette on the drive over. In two layers of clothing, sweat trickled into his eyes as he gripped and re-gripped the tire iron.

What did Brinkmann drive? A Chevy Cobalt? Yes, a red Cobalt. Fuck me, let's get this over with.

Headlights appeared at the end of the block. He leaned further back into cover. The car turned into a driveway two houses short. The motion sensor light over the neighbor's driveway flashed on. Kurt took shallow breaths. He shifted his weight causing dead leaves to crackle like firecrackers underfoot.

Just get your neighborly ass inside, mother fucker. Come on, move, move, move. He'll be home any second and I . . .

The neighbor stepped out and slammed his car door. Keys jingled, the man coughed and the front door opened and closed. The motion sensor light went out.

Another pair of headlights appeared, moving slow. *This is it. This has to be it. Choke him out first then hit him? If I just hit him he could scream.* The headlights kept coming. *I'm sweating like a pig. Will it soak into my over shirt? Will they find my DNA? Fuck me, just fuck me. Too late now. I'm not going to prison.*

The dark green leaves glowed bright in the sweep of Brinkmann's headlights as he steered into the drive. Exhaust fumes filled Kurt's nostrils as the red Cobalt idled under its little carport roof. Kurt leaned forward as Brinkmann swung open his door. A dark messenger bag came out first. Then a foot appeared just before Brinkmann rose to his full height and stepped to the back of the car. He parked his butt on the trunk and lit a cigarette.

He stopped to buy smokes. No wonder it took so long.

After two long drags Brinkmann flicked the butt to the street and turned to walk inside.

Kurt exploded from cover, in range in two long strides. Brinkmann turned just as the crook of the tire iron slammed in just above his left ear, cratering his skull.

Kurt's adrenaline-fueled brain barely heard the guttural "Uh" as Brinkmann crumpled to the concrete, rolling to his back, mouth yawning and legs jerking. The second stroke crushed nose and cheekbones and eye sockets. Stroke three felt solid and deep. Stroke four registered as mushy and wet. Strokes five, six and seven were pure blood lust.

Chest heaving, he pulled himself from his murderous fog. His vision widened. He stared at the twitching limbs and a growing pool of blood. *What a useless pile of shit. What kind of man goes down without a fight?* The thought filled him with an evil exultance. He stood over his prey wanting to roar in victory, but froze when, at the edge of his vision, he caught the movement of a dog walker passing under a streetlight two blocks away. His mind turned to the next task at hand.

34

Heading for the El Camino parked in the shadows between two streetlights, Kurt's eyes scanned the surrounding homes looking for any lights coming on or nosy neighbors peaking from windows. By the time he reached his vehicle, his blood-spattered outer layers were loose and the ski mask off. He heeled off the cheap shoes then lifted the boots from the truck bed. Still wearing the gloves, he wrapped the shirt and pants around the bloody tire iron then shoved all into the Central Market bag. The thin shoes, nitrile gloves, ski mask and the rag he used to wipe his exposed eyes went into the trash bag. He threw both receptacles onto the seat.

Behind the steering wheel again, he rechecked the bags, counting off the items to make sure all was correct. He ran through his mental checklist as he pulled the El Camino from the curb. Relief swept over him that the least controllable portion of his game plan was complete. But the night was far from over.

The 2 a.m., traffic made for a 30-minute drive into Phoenix. Turning left off of McDowell at 11th Avenue then left again on Willetta Street, he rolled past Pete Cunningham's bungalow home. Pete's Nissan sat in the drive in front of the dark house, not in his backyard garage. The site conjured a ripple of excitement and fear. This was a risky opportunity he couldn't pass up.

Pulling to the curb across the street, he donned a fresh pair of rubber gloves, reached into the paper bag and retrieved a bloody gardening glove. *Ten seconds, fifteen at the most and it'll seal the deal.* Nothing moved on the street. He heard the echo of Coach Bart's voice, *"Go, go, go. You can do this."* Heart in his throat, he threw the truck into park, exited and quick-stepped to Pete's car to grasp the black plastic door handle with the bloody glove. Back in the El Camino he deposited the gloves in their proper containers.

Turning left again at 9th he steered into the alley behind Pete's house. Slowly, silently his vehicle rolled past trashcans, weeds and the occasional spray of graffiti. Just as he reached the ancient, paint-peeling garage in Cunningham's back yard, an orange cat leaped across the alley. Nothing else moved. Once again he parked and cautiously stepped out. Five seconds later, the Central Market bag was on the ground between a sagging wooden fence and the old garage.

Relief melted into the rush of exhilaration he could only compare to lust's satisfying ejaculation. Savoring the sensations, he pulled back out onto McDowell. Windows up and the air running at full blast, he ran his fingers through his hair, a broad smile crawling across his face. He palmed a Bob Seger tape from the treasured case on the seat. The tape slid easily into the old El Camino's cassette player, serenading him as he triumphantly rolled away in the night.

* * *

Kurt stared down at the drool puddling on Mikey's shirt. The kid hadn't moved an inch. The "Big Bang Theory" marathon continued amid the room's litter of fast food bags and empty beer cans. Kurt kicked off his work boots then stripped off his uniform pants, socks and shirt. Scooping up a half cup of detergent in the kitchen, he carried it and the clothes to the bathroom to mix all in the bathroom sink to soak as he took a hot shower.

The hot water beating down enhanced the recall of every sight, sound, feel and smell of his victory. The vibration of metal crushing bone vibrated once again up his arms. His blood pulsated in his ears recreating the dying noises of the defenseless Brinkmann. The exhalation of lust surging through his blood sent his hand down his soapy torso to pleasure himself to ultimate satisfaction.

Content and feeling the first hints of weariness, he pushed back the shower curtain and stepped out. He toweled off as he sidled up to the sink. It took only moments to hand wash and rinse his clothes. After wringing them out, he flipped them over the shower curtain rod to air dry. Steam had fogged the medicine cabinet mirror. His palm wiped it away revealing his smile and muscled reflection. *Coach will be so proud.*

After rinsing the sink and tub with hydrogen peroxide, he put on clean underwear, a two-day-old pair of uniform pants and a shirt. He scrutinized his boots. They appeared free of incriminating evidence, but just to be sure, he took them to the bathroom for a hydrogen peroxide rinse.

Finally, he grabbed the trash bag with the mask, rubber gloves, thin shoes and rag. He stopped by the fridge for a beer then exited the house to his backyard where the handy red Budweiser grill waited. He nestled the last bits of incriminating evidence in with the ash and spent charcoal. As he doused the compact pile with lighter fluid, he glanced at the surrounding oleander bushes and mulberry trees on two sides. The only exposure was to the neighboring duplex's yard. His neighbor, a bull dyke nurse worked overnights so she wouldn't be home for hours.

A flick of flame from his lighter and the grill's contents went up with a whoosh. The foul black smoke emitted would not be noticed by anyone in the small hours before sunrise. As if mesmerized by the flames, he watched and sipped his beer. When satisfied that the gray-black lump was reduced to untraceable pieces, he stirred it in with the ashes with a thick mulberry twig. One long swallow finished his beer. He then extinguished the grill's smoldering mass with a long, satisfying piss.

The still drooling Mikey remained unconscious on the couch. Kurt dropped down beside him and fell into the deepest, most worry-free sleep he'd had in weeks.

* * *

"Harry, you're phone's buzzing like crazy," hollered Sarah, through the bathroom door. "Caller I.D. says it's Eddie, you want me to—"

"Yeah, go ahead," Harry hollered back, still drying off from his morning shower.

"Hi, Eddie. Harry's just getting out of the shower. I'll hand him the phone."

"Thanks, Sarah. Sorry to call so early, but it's important."

"I figured. Here you go," she said, cracking the door and shoving the phone into the steam.

"Hey, sorry," said Eddie.

"No worries. What's up?"

"That reporter Brinkmann's been murdered."

"What?"

"Chief just called. Beat to death in his driveway. They think sometime early this morning."

"Luchadores?"

"That's the obvious assumption, but they're still working the scene. I told the Chief about Wrigley's calls to Pete Cunningham. He's dispatched units to pick him up."

"I'll meet you at Brinkmann's house. Did he have a wife and kids or anything?"

"Wife and a little girl. Not sure of the age."

Harry's stomach clenched. "Shit. Witnesses?"

"Nothing yet."

"Shit. Okay, what's the address?"

Harry answered Sarah's questions as he dressed, trying hard not to let her sense his seething anger. *Time off? We shouldn't have taken time off until we knew they were all accounted for.*

"Just in case, keep the doors locked and don't let the kids go out," Harry instructed. "Maybe it was a bad idea to bring you back so soon."

"No, Jack's wife, Graciela is a wonderful woman but we were intruding. Besides, this is our home."

"I really don't think you'll have a problem, but—"

Sarah confidently patted his chest. "I have my cell phone and pistol handy. The kids know what to do."

Harry smiled and wriggled an eyebrow, "You have no idea how hot that makes me. Seriously though, I'll ask that they keep a patrol car in the area, just in case."

A deep though hasty kiss and a quick hug of the kids settled Harry on his way out the door.

* * *

As expected, crime scene tape blocked both ends of Brinkmann's street. TV news crews assembled on the west end, their cameras and tripods forming a line at the tape. Above, a news helicopter circled. Harry waved to a uniformed officer who lifted the tape so he could drive under.

Eddie was already on the scene, their unmarked cruiser parked at the curb three houses west of Brinkmann's small home. In the driveway a small army of crime lab techs combed the scene, placing small numbered plastic tents by anything that could be remotely related.

A blue tarp covered Brinkmann's remains and knee-high, orange plastic fences were set up to keep anyone other than law enforcement from taking pictures. Eddie stood next to the Chief beside a large arborvitae bush near the Brinkmann family's front door.

"Anything new?" asked Harry, strolling up the drive and taking it all in.

"Not a goddamn thing," said the Chief, one hand holding a suit coat slung over his shoulder, the other pinching his chin. "I know what you're thinking, Harry, and you're right. I was a fool to let up until we knew we had them all."

"There's no way we could have known," Eddie offered.

"But I should have known Brinkmann would keep pushing. The man was relentless."

"We think our perp hid in the bushes," said Eddie, pointing to the oleanders lining the drive. "Broken branches and trampled leaves."

"Footprints?"

"Nothing worth casting."

Harry stepped to the body and bent at the waist to lift the tarp. He grimaced at the clotted lump of bone and brain matter that used to be a head. "Jesus, somebody's got anger issues. Are we even sure it's Brinkmann?"

"Wallet, driver's license and press I.D. were intact. Wife recognized the clothes and the messenger bag."

"Is she inside? Where's the daughter?"

"Wife's inside with a female officer. Maternal grandmother picked up the daughter about twenty minutes ago."

For the first time Harry noticed the pink-chalked hopscotch squares partially covered in thick, dark blood. "She didn't see this, did she?"

"Mom says no. Says she got her back inside and dialed 9-1-1 before the daughter saw anything. We made sure everything was covered by the time the grandma got here."

"Did the wife think it strange that her husband didn't come home?"

"Let's go ask her," said the Chief, turning to head inside.

Pulling open a screen door with heavy metal bars that matched the bars on the home's windows, the Chief knocked lightly on the partially-open front door. Eddie and Harry followed him in. The three men nearly filled the small, messy living room.

Janice Brinkmann, red-eyed and puffy-faced, perched on the edge of the living room couch next to a female cop who covertly tried to wipe her tears and keep a tissue in the new widow's shaking hands. Mrs. Brinkmann wore a white uniform shirt with a plastic nametag and dark blue, polyester pants.

"Our deepest condolences," said Harry, conscious of the over-used, "sorry for your loss," phrase from the network TV crime dramas.

"I'm sorry the house is such a mess," blubbered Mrs. Brinkmann. "It's just that I work early and Andrew works late." Her breath hitched and her eyes lost focus as she rambled on. "The paper's new owners have really been pushing. We're worried about layoffs, you see . . . ."

As her voice trailed off, her pupils dilated as though she realized for the first time that her husband was gone for good and his job worries were a moot point.

"So, it's not unusual for you to go to bed before Andrew arrived home?" Harry asked, trying gently to pull her back from a ledge of inconsolable despair.

"Uh, no, not unusual." She blinked away tears and tilted her head like a dog trying to comprehend. "Of course, his not being next to me when I woke up, that . . . well . . . ."

She crumbled, burying her face in her hands. When the female cop put a hand to her knee, Janice dropped her hand, screaming, "NO! IT'S NOT POSSIBLE. THAT'S NOT HIM. THERE'S BEEN A TERRIBLE MISTAKE." Twisting away, she shoved her face into the couch. Her shoulders heaved as she sobbed.

The female cop, a sergeant named Kelli Maxwell, looked to the Chief and shook her head as her own tears trickled down her face.

The Chief swallowed and hardened his expression. "No enemies beyond those he investigated for the paper, ma'am?"

Janice shook her head, not turning to face them.

Harry followed his boss's example. "The metal bars on the front door and windows, what were those for?"

Wild-eyed, Janice came to her feet. "FOR THOSE GOD DAMNED MURDERING CHILD MOLESTERS. WHAT DO YOU THINK?"

"I'm sorry I—"

Her voice dropped to a growl. "The hell you are. My husband and a lot of other good people risked everything to root out those bastards seven years ago. What did you do? Absolutely zip. Nada. Nothing."

"Ma'am, that wasn't—"

"Get out of my house. Take your worthless guns and badges and fancy retirements and get out!"

"I'm sorry, ma'am. We'll be on our way," said the Chief. "I-I just don't think you should be alone. Would it be all right if Sgt. Maxwell stays, at least until your friends or family arrive?"

Janice mechanically nodded. The three men turned to the front door, looking and feeling like scolded, trash-eating dogs.

Large, solemn men in white jumpsuits bent over Brinkmann's body zipping a black bag. Harry, Eddie and the Chief stepped back into the too bright morning. A middle-aged, diminutive woman stood nearby, making notes on a clipboard. A white, Maricopa County Coroner's van had been backed into the driveway, its back doors open.

"Hello, Jolene," the Chief greeted her, "Good to see you're on this. I know it's early, but can you see anything out of the ordinary?"

"Nothing you probably don't already know. Blunt-force trauma, probably a metal bar of some sort. Tire iron's my first thought. Killer's likely right handed. Hold up, guys," she said to the two men bagging the body.

They stepped back as she donned latex gloves. She knelt to unzip the bag, pushing the black plastic aside. The sun glistened off the shattered and bloodied skull. When the three lawmen stepped close, she pointed at the side of Brinkmann's head.

"See the indentation above the left ear?"

All three cops nodded.

"This strike likely took him down. You can see the cratering shows the width of the weapon. It's deeper right in here, see?" She ran a finger along the wound. "Like the bend of a tire iron. Our perp's likely male, right handed like I said, average height, strong."

She moved to the oleander bushes and reenacted the attack. "Simple, really. He hides in the bushes until our victim arrives. Waits until the victim's back is turned. He steps out, the victim turns and he drops him. Victim never had a chance to fight back. I see no defensive or offensive wounds on the body."

"Caught him by surprise and clocked him," said Eddie, shaking his head.

Jolene continued, "His first strike to the temple likely would have killed him, but something urged our killer on. I see a lot of rage in the way he destroyed the face."

"Where do you put the time of death?" asked Harry.

"Liver temp says sometime after midnight, maybe 2-3 a.m."

A crime lab tech combing the drive with a black light and a spray bottle of Luminol gave a whoop that drew everyone's attention. The three investigators hurried to her side.

"What have you got?" asked the chief.

"Part of a shoe print, see? Probably stepped in the castoff. It's quite faint."

All stared down at a faint, zig-zag pattern glowing up from the drive.

The Chief humpfed. "Not even enough for a shoe size. If this is all he left behind we're up the creek. Let's hope the neighborhood canvas turns up a witness or a security camera."

"Eddie, come here," said Harry walking back to the oleander bushes. "Let's walk this through. Say you're the perp. How do you get here . . . from wherever you came from?"

Eddie scanned the landscape and turned to peer through the carport into the Brinkmann's back yard. "Block wall behind the house, no alleys. I'm parking on the street."

Together they walked to the end of the drive. A hoard of media now lined the tape at both ends of the block. Feeling the attention of the cameras, Harry bristled.

He looked down at the cigarette butt with its plastic evidence tent. "Partially smoked cigarette. Didn't smell smoke in the house."

"He had a pack in his bag." Eddie knelt and used a pen to roll the butt over. "Yeah, it's the same brand."

Harry crossed his arms and looked up and down the street. "Which way did you come in, the east or the west?"

"West side, came in off of Hayden."

"Me, too. So, you-the-perp do a drive by, maybe go around the block once or twice. Where do you park?"

"I'd go past my target, maybe park one or two houses down."

"Why?"

"I'd have the cover of these bushes on my approach and I wouldn't have to cross in front of the house."

"Makes sense." Harry put his hands in his pockets to reduce photo ops for the cameras. "So, he parks, slips into the bushes and waits. Brinkmann comes home, takes a couple of drags on a cigarette, tosses it to the street, turns to go in and our perp whacks him."

"Yeah, that's about it. Am *I* missing something?"

"How'd our guy know when to arrive? Waiting in the bushes would get old pretty quick."

"I've known guys who could wait in hiding for days. Not that this is the work of a pro, but I'm just saying."

The Chief joined them. "Initial look at his phone shows no calls or texts after 9 p.m. and no personal email after 11 p.m."

"We've secured his desk and computer, correct?" asked Eddie.

"Yes, uniforms are at the paper and techs are either there or on the way. We've got uniforms canvassing the neighborhood."

* * *

Pete Cunningham stood in his kitchen, scratching his balls through his boxers as coffee dribbled from his Keurig. On the living room TV he could hear SportsCenter deliver the previous day's scores. He yawned as the coffeemaker wheezed the end of its cycle, then pulled his coffee cup free of the device. A loud knock on the front door jolted him from his sleepy morning haze. *What the hell? It's too damn early.*

Coffee in hand, he poked his head into the dining room. Through the living room's picture window a huge black man stared at him through the glass. A flash of fear jerked his hand, sloshing hot coffee on his fingers. Only after the man pointed a stern finger and tilted his head to the door, did Pete realize it was a cop. *Shit, shit, shit. They spotted Wrigley's phone calls.*

Pete stepped from the dining room just as another loud knock sounded at the backdoor. This time the coffee spilled down the front of his Scottsdale Independence Day 10-K t-shirt. Cursing the pain, he set the cup to the dining table then lurched for the front door. When the deadbolt came free and he turned the knob, the cop shoved in.

"What?" Pete whined, "You can't just—"

"Pete Cunningham?"

"W-what? Did someone break into my car?"

"Are *you* Pete Cunningham?"

"Y-yes, that's me."

"Are you alone?"

"Yeah. What's going on?"

"Do we have permission to search your home?"

Pete blinked then scanned the room. "Uh, yeah, I guess. I've got nothing to hide. What the hell is going on?"

"I'm going to cuff you for your protection and ours until we have a better understanding of the situation. A detective from Scottsdale will be here shortly to explain. Do you understand?"

Hands going to his hips, Pete puffed his chest. "You can't just waltz in here and cu—"

The world blurred as the big cop grabbed Pete's wrist and, with a quick bend-and-twist had him over the back of the couch. The metal of a cuff closed around one wrist.

Pete grunted with indignation. "I'm a journalist, you—"

"Sir, I'm detaining you," the big cop spoke quietly, as if patronizing him, "until we have a better idea of what's going on." He ratcheted the second cuff before pulling him upright and steering him around the couch to sit down.

Pete's skinny, white legs shook. *God, what do they know?*

The cop keyed the mic clipped to his left epaulet, "Bravo fifteen."

"Go ahead, fifteen," answered the dispatcher.

"We're code four. He's in custody. He's given permission to search the property."

"Ten-four, fifteen."

"*What* is going on?" Pete demanded.

"The detective will be here soon, sir. He'll have answers for you."

Two more uniformed officers entered. They looked to the much larger cop. Although the man didn't have stripes or bars to indicate a higher rank, he carried himself with an air of authority.

"We've got consent," he said, pointing to the body camera clipped to the front of his uniform shirt.

Seeing the camera, Pete's mind flashed to Wrigley's video with the he-she hooker at the motel and wondered if the crooked cop had left an in-the-case-of-my-demise time bomb. *What if he wrote everything down? They'll never believe I didn't know he was a Luchador.*

"Hey, fella, Sorry for the gruff greeting. Lemme fix your glasses. You mind?" The cop's demeanor and voice came off as much friendlier now that Pete was at his mercy.

Pete pushed his chin forward and the cop nudged the glasses into place.

"Thanks." Pete studied him a moment. "You're just bullshitting about not knowing what's going on, aren't you?"

The towering cop shrugged. "To a point. Scottsdale asked us to pick you up because there's been a homicide."

"What? When? Who? My god . . . Am I a suspect?"

"You'll have to wait, sir. That's all I know at this time." His head came up. "Hey, how'd the Diamondbacks do against Chicago?" he asked with a head tilt to the television where SportsCenter droned.

"Won, five to four in thirteen innings," said Pete.

"Cool. You see the game?"

"Nah, I was at work."

"Mr. Cunningham!" said Detective Luke Jeffers, entering through the front door. "Are you up to speed on what's going on?"

"They just told me there's been a homicide."

A uniform cop entered and pulled the big cop aside to show him something on his phone. Pete shivered when the big cop's eyes widened and he pulled Jeffers in for a look.

Jeffers' bright, young face darkened. He turned to Pete, "Sorry to have to break it to you, Pete, but Andrew Brinkmann was murdered sometime early this morning."

Pete jerked and shook his head. He rapidly blinked as his brain tried to catch up. Sucking in a calming breath, he pulled himself upright. "Suspects?"

"You for one. Word is you and he argued in the newsroom last night."

"That was nothing. We argue in the newsroom all the time." Pete felt Jeffers' eyes examining his every move. His own eyes darted sideways to the black cop's body cam. He licked at lips that were suddenly parched.

"Thanks for the assist," Jeffers said to the black cop. "You taking him to county?"

"Yeah, 4th Avenue jail. That is, if you're done with him."

"That's all I have for now. He consented to the search? I brought paper with me if not."

"Yessir. Got it on camera, but a warrant's always better. I'll make sure to send you the video clip after we get him booked."

"You're booking me? For what?" shouted Pete, lurching forward to stand.

The big cop shoved him back down. "Easy there, little fella."

Pete flinched at his condescending shoulder pat. "I did not have anything to do with Brinkmann's death."

"Well, then you don't have anything to worry about," said Jeffers. "Just take it easy. We'll get this sorted out. Ah, Officer, Miller is it?" Jeffers looked at the big cop's brass nameplate.

"Yessir," The man shook Jeffers' offered hand.

"Officer Miller, transport whenever you're ready and thanks again for the assist. I'll head to the jail after I see what else forensics turns up here."

"No problem and you're welcome. I'll tell 'em to get an interview room ready for you. Booking'll probably eat up an hour, so take your time."

As the wide black hands reached for him, panic swept over Pete. "NO! You're not taking me anywhere."

"Ah, now," crooned Miller. "Don't make me work up a sweat this early in the morning. You wanna give me a hand?" he spoke more crisply to the nearby uniformed officer.

"No! You're not," Pete tried to squirm away from the hands shoved into his armpits. As they lifted, Pete raised his feet to make himself heavy. "Wait! At least let me get some pants—"

"Too late for that, sir."

"No!" Pete's voice shrilled a high-pitched condemnation. He spread his legs wide, hooking the lamp table, sending it tumbling. In the ensuing grapple for control, his boxers came down.

"Sir, you're about two seconds from adding resisting arrest," ground out the big cop, his massive hand pressing Pete's face to the floor. "Now, it's obvious you're not gonna win here, so save yourself some trouble and *cooperate*."

Pete gave up and went limp. "Not helping isn't resisting," he whined as he was yanked back to his feet. His head banged on the screen door then a shoulder smacked a post. “All right, I’ll help!” They never slowed.

At the sidewalk he saw the television cameras trained on him and he wished like hell he’d been given the dignity of pulling up his underwear.

35

Olivia was already in the shower when Eugene woke. He fumbled for his pants to retrieve his ringing phone. Caller I.D. said it was Harry.

"Hey, what's up?" mumbled Eugene.

"Where the hell are you?"

"I'm at our new temporary office in Mesa."

"Is Olivia Condon with you?"

"Yeah, we . . . both came in early. Have you got news? Why the questions?"

After a short pause, Harry said, "Hate to tell you this, buddy, but Andrew Brinkmann's been murdered."

Eugene's mind shut down for a moment. He whispered, "What did you say?"

"Andrew Brinkmann. He was beaten to death in his driveway early this morning, I'm calling to make sure you're okay."

"Shit . . . Are you sure?" He pushed his free fingers into his eyes. "Goddamn it, I told him to watch his back . . . He's dead, for sure?"

"Yes, Eugene. I'm sorry. I know you two were close. No problems on your end, correct? Nothing out of the ordinary?"

"Yeah, yeah, we're fine . . . You think it was—"

"Luchadores? Too early to tell. I'm probably talking out of school here, but it's coming out anyway. Pete Cunningham has been arrested. He—"

"Arrested?" Eugene almost shouted. "For what? He—"

"Shut up and calm down. I'll tell you."

Eugene jammed his fingers into his already tasseled hair. "Sorry."

"This is off the record, right? I'm sure the Chief will hold a press conference this afternoon, but you can't print—"

"Off the record. Go ahead."

"There's a connection between Pete and Clyde Wrigley. Phone calls, lot's of them. And we have very strong evidence that Pete killed Andrew."

"What kind of evidence?"

"I can't say."

"That son-of-a-bitch. How did he do it?"

"Can't say anything beyond blunt-force trauma."

"Why are you sure it was him? He's not a killer. Hasn't got the spine. A liar and a backstabber, sure."

"You said yourself he'd do anything to save his own skin. We think the Luchadores were blackmailing him."

"Wait. So, he was the mole in the newsroom? You think he killed Oliver?"

"No way to tell. He's at the 4th Avenue jail in Phoenix. We have people over there interviewing him now. Listen, I gotta go. Remember, you didn't hear any of this from me. I only called to check on your welfare."

"Got it. When's the press conference?"

"Call the PIO. They'll know more. Gotta go. Take care."

Eugene dropped the phone to the bed as the reality of Andrew's death hit home, He moaned, "Fuck me. Fuck me!"

Olivia pulled open the bathroom door, steam billowing from around her toweled head. "What's wrong?"

"Andrew's dead."

Her eyes widened. "Andy Brinkmann?"

Eugene nodded then pulled on his shirt. He hurried to the motel room window and cracked the curtain to cautiously look outside.

"What? What are you doing? Are we at risk?"

"Harry called to see if we were okay. He said Pete killed Andrew. Hit him with something. They have evidence."

"Jesus Christ, this is outrageous!" She yanked the towel from her hair and went in search of clothing. Pieces had been tossed every which way last night as they had rushed into the room, laughing, groping and probing.

Eugene continued to study the motel, its parked vehicles and its surroundings. "Yeah, and for all we know, somebody came for us, too. And they couldn't find us in the office because we were in here screwing around for real. God, I'm an idiot. What was I thinking?"

Olivia froze, holding one boot. "What do you mean?" she asked in clipped words.

"Just what I said. Jesus, I drop my guard for just one night and all hell—"

"So, we refocus." She took a quick breath and resumed dressing. "This is beyond awful and couldn't come at a worse time." Hands on hips, Olivia asked, "Where do we start?"

Eugene let the curtain close. He hung his head a moment, struggling to push down his growing darkness and its urge to strike out, take revenge, make life hell for someone else for a change. The memory of Andrew Brinkmann's face appeared then faded. Eugene growled, "I really do not want to go to his house and take pictures of—"

"Eugene, look at me." He did, seeing Olivia-the-boss back in control. "I'm not sure we need to do that, anyway. We need to stay focused on the missing Luchadores. Let's get to the office, turn on the TV and get online." She tossed him his clothes. "If they were blackmailing him, he's a pawn, so we're still looking for three."

As hard as he fought to keep his anger tamped down, he still fisted his clothes and snarled, "We should just shoot the bastards in the head when we find them."

She blinked then stared harder at him. "Where the hell did that come from?" She cocked her head and cautiously asked, "You do know you'd only end up in jail, right?"

He looked at his clothes instead of her. His words came out low and cold. "Done correctly, no one would ever know."

"But," She snapped her fingers to make him look up, "*you* would know *and* remember. I think that's your darkness talking and not the *real* Eugene Fellig."

"I really don't give a shit what you think." He continued dressing, aware of the darkness swirling in his mind, more a cesspool than a tornado. "This little game you people play, this false sense of security everyone is so fond of, is deadly."

Olivia gaped, her hands again on her hips. "Just what do you mean, *you* people?"

Frustration and grief pushed the words out before he could stop them. "Rich people. People of privilege. You and Andrew . . . and everyone at the goddamned newspaper. You've never had to face real evil, let alone live with it *every* day. You think laws actually protect you." His anger hitting its crescendo, he surprised himself again by shrilling, "Oh, here, let's make this a gun-free zone. That'll keep us safe. Jesus Christ, people are idiots. Evil doesn't give a shit about gun-free zones."

Olivia's disappointed expression and withdrawn body language told him he'd gone too far. He ignored her distress and turned his attention to his shoelaces, yanking at them and muttering obscenities.

"What're you going to do, Eugene?" she demanded in her prim self-righteousness. "Go bust some heads? Get some answers and go on a killing spree?"

"If that's what it takes to stop these assholes, someone has to do it. Kill them before they kill us." He jabbed a finger at her. "That's what this is you know, a fight for survival."

Olivia took a shaky breath. "You have no car."

Eugene ground his teeth and stared over her head with murder in his eyes. "Minor problem."

"I wish I'd seen that chip on your shoulder before I crawled in bed with you."

He grunted. "That isn't a chip. It's a shitload of hard-learned, life-and-death lessons."

"The hell it is. This is always going to be a problem, isn't it? You're so convinced that *normal* people look down on you. But, it's really the other way around isn't it?"

He shook his head. "Trust me, people like you are *not* the norm. Your sense of reality is skewed because you can afford to distance yourself from the world's nastiness."

"God, but you are a pompous ass."

"You are the smartest, most incredible person I've ever known and loved." When she jerked in surprise he pushed on. "Yeah, loved, but you've never looked death in the face. Evil comes in a heartbeat when you least expect it. It's asinine to believe cops do anything but react."

"Five Luchadores are dead because the cops—"

"You really believe that? The reality is that your grandfather handed 'em to the cops on a silver platter . . . and they let 'em go. It's only because Oliver and Andrew refused to give up that they were forced to cut their losses by killing their own. That's reality, little girl."

He ignored her slumping onto the edge of the bed, but he couldn't ignore her silent tears. His own throat burned. "Sorry if I'm being an asshole, but if Andrew . . . his voice broke, "had just *listened* to me, he might still be alive."

"What do you mean?"

Eugene moaned and slumped onto the bed beside her, burying his face in his hands.

Olivia leaned in and put an arm around his back. When he tried to pull away, she persisted, whispering softly, "I'm sorry about Andrew . . . I'm sorry about everything in your life that sucks."

Eugene croaked, "I told him to watch his back, maybe get a gun or at least pepper spray. To at least become more aware of his surroundings. He called me a gun nut and said that's what the police were for. Well, guess what that got him. He-he . . . ." A great wail of grief came out from somewhere deep inside. He leaned into her. She rubbed his back and nuzzled his head.

Finally, after a long, hitching breath Eugene said, "I am so sorry. I didn't mean . . . about you. It's just—"

"No, you're right. We've been far too careless. Did you see anything when you looked outside?"

Her question refocused him on the present. "No, coast was clear as far as I could tell, but we're too isolated here." He returned to the window. "We should probably be someplace more public, at least for today. Harry said to call the PIO about a press conference."

"Okay, you go take a quick shower. I'll call the PIO and I'll call Austin to let him know what's going—"

"I hear a car. Get down!" Eugene barked.

She dropped to a crouch, eyes wide.

"Get to the bathroom. Stay low. Put some walls in front of you."

Olivia crab crawled for the bath. Eugene dropped to his haunches below the window. He carefully tipped the table, putting the thick, round top between himself and the front wall. Slowly he moved the curtain just enough to see out.

His laughter brought an angry shout from the bathroom. "What's so goddamned funny?"

"It's Austin. He's armed with a weird croquet mallet or something."

Olivia walked to his side as he righted the table then joined him in peering at the parking lot. "I think that's a polo mallet. Oh my, he looks scared. We'd better let him know we're okay."

"From here? He'll know what we've been—"

Olivia pushed open the door and called to Austin.

He spun on his heel with the mallet held high. Lowering it, he hurried toward her continuing to nervously glance around. "Have you heard? They killed Andrew Brinkmann this morning." He nodded a greeting when Eugene appeared at her shoulder. "You two have any trouble? Is that why you're hiding away from the office?"

Going for honesty, Eugene awkwardly stuttered, "Uh, no. We, uh . . . Last night got a bit—"

"Got it," Austin stopped him, a hint of a smile relaxing his face.

Olivia scowled at the two men. "Everybody inside, please."

Eugene eyed the long-handled mallet that looked far from threatening. "Why didn't you just call?"

"I was going to." The older man turned his back on the rumpled bed. "Then I thought 'What if they're hiding and the hit men hear the phone ring?' "

"Considerate of you," said Olivia. "As you can see, we're fine. In fact, we were just headed to the office to get a better idea of what's going on."

Austin lifted the side of the window curtain to check the surroundings. "You think Andrew uncovered something good and they offed him for it?"

"That'd be my guess," said Eugene. "But, the cops seem pretty sure it was Pete Cunningham. They think the Luchadores were blackmailing him. I sure wish I knew what Andrew had on them. Maybe we should call Millie and get a little insight—"

"Cripes, I forgot to tell you," said Olivia. "The new honchos let her go. Now, there's a recording when you call the newsroom."

"Idiots," Eugene declared. "The newsroom will fall apart without her. Those people are complete fools."

"Come on, you two." Olivia opened the door and peered around. "Looks clear to me. Let's make hay while the sun shines, as in while our competition's being fools."

The two men flanked her as they quickly crossed to their office. Austin frowned at Eugene when Olivia opened the unlocked door. He merely shrugged in return.

"You have your laptop don't you, Austin?" asked Olivia, firing up the office television.

"Got it in the car. Never leave home without it."

"It might be wise to work someplace a little more public for the next day or so,"

"Good idea. Library maybe?"

"Or maybe a Starbucks," she suggested.

"I've got something better in mind," said Eugene, smiling. "Who likes pancakes?"

Austin and Olivia nodded.

"There's a great place near my apartment. Let's go get my Jeep then head over. Once we're set up, I'll take a run by Andrew's house. With any luck somebody from the Herald will be there and I can sniff around a little."

"Good thought," said Olivia. "But they'll be at Grandpa's funeral this afternoon, don't forget."

The group's bright demeanor suddenly dimmed.

"Oh, man, with everything that's going on I almost forgot. Where are they holding it again?" asked Eugene.

Distaste washed over Olivia's face. "My mother's mega church up in north Scottsdale. Like I said, they're making it a huge blowout. It'll be everything Grandpa would have hated."

Eugene sucked in a heavy breath and let it out. "Ugh, that's too bad. Maybe once they finish with the spectacle, we can pull a group together after and go have a drink in his honor."

Olivia cocked her head at him, a sad smile softening her face. "Yes, he would've loved that. All right then, I'll run you to your Jeep. Austin, you want to follow—"

"Hey, that's Pete, isn't it?" Austin pointed at the TV.

All eyes turned to the television where two cops carried a screaming man to a car, his mid-section censored with an out-of-focus blob.

"Looks like Pete's arrest." Eugene's satisfaction colored his words. "Couldn't happen to nicer guy. Wow, he's screaming like a little girl."

"Is that his—" Olivia flipped a hand at the screen.

Eugene laughed. "Yeah. Oh, that just makes my whole year."

* * *

Pete Cunningham squirmed on his interrogation room chair. Nervous fingers plucked at his coffee-stained t-shirt and jail-issued blue paper pants as he blubbered, "I-I keep telling you. I had nothing to do with Andrew's thing."

"That *thing* is murder," Detective Jeffers enunciated carefully, sizing up his prey, strategizing how he'd reel him in, shove him off balance and push the shit out of his buttons. "What, Pete? Are you so ashamed of what you did that you can't even call it by the correct name? Murder?"

"It wasn't me. Good God, I could never do something like that. Andrew and I argued about social media bullshit. That's it. After he stormed off, I went back to work."

"Where'd he go? Back to his desk?"

"No, I think he went to the pressroom to cool off. Then he came back for a while before leaving the building for some reason. Later, maybe an hour, he came back again."

"Did he say where he went?"

"No, we were all doing our own work. I heard Kurt invite him out to the pressroom to watch them print the paper."

Jeffers listened and made notes, nodding to keep him talking. When it appeared that Pete had his feet back on the ground, Jeffers went on the attack. "What is it that gets your rocks off? Looking at little boys, Pete? I mean, I'm a man. When I see a beautiful woman—heck any woman—I can't help but flash a thought of what she'd be like in bed. Is it like that for you and little boys?"

Pete's jaw tightened. He glared at his interrogator. "You sick bastard, I am not one of them."

"You've told me nothing to convince me otherwise." Jeffers tapped his pen on his pad. "In fact, with the TV stations and YouTube replaying your little meltdown in front of your neighbors, the whole world knows you're a sick freak."

His face reddening, Pete fidgeted. "I don't know why I'm even talking to you. I'll sue your ass. Your department will pay for the way you publicly humiliated me and tarnished my professional image."

"We can call for a public defender if you like," Jeffers said, dancing just shy of the Miranda line, "or you can drop a dime on a real lawyer. I figured your paper would send Rosenthal over . . . but I guess they don't have as much faith in you as they did in Eugene."

The muscles in Pete's jaw flexed.

"Then again, he was little more than a person of interest. Street smart kid, that Eugene."

Pete scoffed. "Goddamn white trash, that's what he is. You want a suspect, look at him. I'm pretty sure he and his serial rapist brother were working together."

"Really? Yet here *you* sit. Let's see," Jeffers counted on his fingers, "five dead Luchadores, Brinkmann, and . . . say, you had motive to kill Oliver Condon, too. That makes seven counts of murder. And God knows how many counts of child molestation." The detective frowned and flipped back through his notebook then looked up with cold eyes. "And some of them were murdered, too. I'll bet the cons are already lining up for a turn at your bony butt."

Getting his second wind, Pete pushed out his big chin. "That'll never happen, because I'm innocent. All you have is my little argument with Andrew and phone calls between me and the lead detective on the original Luchador case. You've got nothing because there is nothing. I'm not an idiot. You're desperate and trying to trick me."

Jeffers shrugged. "You strike me as a fairly smart, college type who can recognize a good deal when he sees it. We know the Luchadores have a history of blackmail. Could be they forced you to kill Brinkmann. If that's the case, I'm sure the court will take that into account."

Pete sat back in his chair and stared at the ceiling. He huffed and slowly shook his head. Obviously reaching a decision, he sat up, placing his forearms on the table and met Jeffers' eyes. "In the interest of clearing this up, I'll tell you what was really going on between me and Clyde Wrigley. And, no, it's not what you think, though I can see how it might look suspicious."

Hiding his glee, Jeffers said, "The truth? That'd be refreshing."

Pete leaned forward in his sincerity. "I accidentally stumbled into one of Wrigley's prostitution stings while researching a story. Once he realized that we were both on the job, he cut me loose and apologized. As one professional to another, I agreed to keep him apprised of any new developments in the Luchador case. Of course, at the time I had no idea what he was."

"There now, that wasn't so hard was it? You were being noble—really—showing a courtesy to a fellow professional who took advantage of your trusting nature."

"Yes, and I truly feel terrible about that." Pete tapped his pointer finger on the table for emphasis. "Condon would have frowned on my working with police, of course. *But,* everybody knew his brand of journalism died well before he did."

Fighting the urge to grab the insipid prick by the collar and pound his face, Jeffers said, "So, it started with noble intentions, but went south. Were they blackmailing you? Did that force you to kill Brinkmann?"

Pete's face twisted with frustration. "No-o-o, that's not—"

Out of patience, Jeffers interrupted, "I'll bet it was quite a shock to learn you were helping a murdering child molester. Getting pinched for poking a prostitute was bad enough because that puts Pete-the-prick in a preeminent pickle." His palm slapped down on the table. "Hey, maybe I have a future in the word business. I hear there's going to be a city editor opening at your paper."

Pete deflated. "That isn't funny."

"Neither is murder." He let his voice turn cold again then leaned over the narrow table getting in Pete's personal space. "Do you really think I'd waste my time charging an arrogant prick like you if I had anything less than incontrovertible proof that you're a killer?"

Pete blinked and licked his parched lips. "What the hell are you talking about?"

Jeffers pulled his Smartphone from his belt, turned it to Pete and swiped through pictures of the bloody evidence collected from his backyard.

Eyes still defiant, Pete leaned back in his chair. He exhaled a heavy breath before leaning forward again. One finger pushed up his glasses as Jeffers swiped to the image showing the blood on his car door. He clasped his now shaking hands and pressed them into the table. "I am smart enough not to leave such blatant evidence so accessible. Think about that. I'm being framed, just like they tried to frame Eugene."

"So now Eugene's innocent? A minute ago you had him tried and convicted."

"I was making a point and, obviously, a wrong one. That's clear as day now that I'm in the same predicament." He relaxed, his eyes pinched as if his brain had finally settled into logical analysis mode. "I'll lay out exactly what happened, plain and simple for you. Andy and I had one of our everyday spats, I finished my work at the paper, went home and went to bed. While I was sleeping, someone killed

Andy and planted evidence to frame me. Next thing I know some big, black cop is beating on my front door."

"Tell me, Pete, did you panic and try to hide the evidence . . . or did you think you were so smart that we'd never catch you?"

"I. Didn't. Kill. Andrew. You've got to believe me."

The determined Jeffers wagged his head like a dog with a bone. "So, did you mean to kill Condon or did you just think the anaphylactic shock would give you cover to steal the picture of Ass Clown?"

Red drifted up Pete's neck and into his face. Tears welled in his eyes. Shaking fingers slid under his glasses to wipe them away.

"People are getting murdered all around you, Pete," Jeffers pressed on. "You're on the hook for six. Condon would make seven. Do I need to remind you that Arizona still has the death penalty? They'll strap you to a table and stick a needle—"

"If I tell you what really happened to Mr. Condon, will you believe me when I tell you that I had nothing to do with the Luchadores or Andrew?"

Barely able to swallow his surprise as his nimble brain zipped through the catalog of evidence gleaned from Condon's office, Jeffers nodded. "A little truth would go a long way right now."

"I've been under a lot of pressure from Condon's family. They had a very good, limited-time offer on the table from Mid-States. Newspapers all over the country are dying. I worried that if we didn't take the offer, no one would buy us and in a year or two, we'd be done."

"Better to cash-out now than lose everything later, right?"

Pete nodded. He pulled his glasses off his face and rubbed the tears from his eyes, then leaned back and stared at the ceiling. The detective recognized the signs that the man was clearly struggling to hold off a total breakdown.

"God, this is hard," Pete murmured.

Jeffers decided to twist the knife. "Harder than a needle in the arm? Just say the words, Pete. I can see you're barely treading water.

If you just meant to make Condon sick, get him out of the way for a little while so you could save his pride and joy—"

Pete's nostrils flared. "Yeah . . . I just needed him out of the way. I had a chocolate donut. It had peanut sprinkles. I let a couple of little chunks fall into his cup. At the last minute, I thought better of it and tried to get to him to take it away." He rubbed his temples. "He took a drink before I could stop him."

"Did you know he had that Epi pen?"

"Yeah, I knew it was right there in his jacket. I figured he'd get sick, but I could stop it before it got too bad. I thought a health crisis would buy me that time, maybe even bring him to his senses. Offers like the one Mid-States was making just don't come around much anymore."

"So, he drank the coffee and you grabbed the pen, right?"

"I honestly never thought the damn peanuts would come anywhere close to killing him." Pete sat forward, intense with his sincerity. "I mean, I have a sister who's allergic to bees. She'd get sick and have trouble breathing, but it never got bad enough to kill her."

Jeffers played the logic game with him. "So, you're familiar with the Epi pens. You knew it was in a case in his coat. You grabbed it and handed it to Eugene, correct?"

After nodding, Pete pressed his face into his hands, the glasses dangling from his fingers.

"Did you read the instructions ahead of time?"

Energy drained, he raised his head but didn't open his eyes. His voice came out in a flat monotone, "I read them, but I know how they work from my sister. I tried to hand it to Eugene, but the idiot dropped it."

"He said it fell out of the case."

"Yeah, because he fumbled it. It fell out and rolled under the desk. He grabbed it and jabbed it into Condon's leg."

"Just how it's supposed to be done, right?"

Another nod. "The only thing I can think is that Condon's heart gave out before the medication had an effect. Christ!" Pete finally broke down. His tears flowed as he placed his head on his arms on the table. He mumbled, "I really loved that old guy. I am so-so sorry."

Almost as wrung out, Jeffers put a gentle hand to his shoulder and rubbed. He let him cry until the man calmed and sat upright, swiping his shirtsleeve across his eyes.

Jeffers counted to ten to give him focus time then got back to the business of documentation. "If you're ready, I just need to make sure I've got the details right."

Pete nodded.

"I've got you handing the pen in its case to Eugene, it fell out and he retrieved it. You watched to make sure he made the injection correctly."

"That's how it went."

"So, how do you explain *your* fingerprints on the pen? You said you only touched the case."

Recognizing the trap, terror then anger flashed in Pete's eyes. "Lawyer, right now. I'm not saying another word."

Jeffers closed his mouth and tapped the pen on his notepad. He wanted to ask so much more, but it would have to wait. He shoved to his feet, "Been real nice talking with you, Pete."

* * *

"Nice job, kid," said Eddie when Jeffers stepped from the interview room. "You worked the piss out of Pete-the-Prick."

"Thanks. I was nervous going in, but he's such an asshole that he made it easy."

"Here's the big question, kid: Is he one of them?"

Jeffers didn't hesitate, "Nah, he's too stupid. They must have had some heavy shit on him to get him to go straight for Brinkmann. Can you envision him taking a tire iron to somebody's head?"

Eddie shrugged. "Desperate men do desperate things."

Jeffers looked through the mirrored window at his fidgeting perp. "Well, what do you think? Let him cook a little before we give him a phone call?"

"Yeah, give him time to think about it. He knows a lot more than he's saying. That whole prostitution bust thing is a pile of crap. Wrigley never did anyone a favor, especially a prick from a newspaper."

* * *

Still reeling from a night filled with nightmarish pleasures mixed with worry, Gordon Bartholomew hauled himself from bed and plodded for the bathroom. Mentally running all the possible outcome scenarios, he figured Kurt's chances of success were slim to none. He'd already made plans to throw the ex-champ under the bus, if need be.

The bigger worry was his wife. If his aching balls and the scratches on his back and shoulders were any indication, he'd brought out her inner demons. She started out uncertain but domination had lit her up. Her transformation had been a textbook example of his coaching style. Anger to fear, fear to surrender, surrender to desperation. Out of desperation a champion or, in her case, an insatiable wildcat was born. He'd left her sweat-soaked and tangled in the sheets, balled into a fetal position.

In the shower with the hot water stinging his wounds, he reveled in the night's feral sights and sounds. *Inside that civilized kitten lurked a wildcat! Who knew? Maybe she liked acting out that part of herself. . . just like my guys liked freeing their lurking animals.*

His dress slacks bulged with excited anticipation as he walked from his bedroom down the hall to hers. Her door hung slightly ajar. He pushed it open and was surprised to see her bed neatly made and the light on in her bathroom.

Margaret Bartholomew sat perched in front of her vanity makeup mirror wrapped in a silk robe and applying a cream to her face.

"Good morning, darling," he crooned.

His greeting went unanswered as she worked the cream in around her eyes, giving special attention to a developing bruise.

"Sorry if I went a bit far last night. I don't know what got into me." He moved close then stroked her shoulder. She flinched away from him. "I'll make breakfast and coffee. Any special requests?"

"No."

"I really am very sorry for pushing you so far. If it's any consolation, I thought you were amazing."

She finally met his eyes in the mirror. "You're sick, Gordon. You need professional help. Now, go do whatever it is you're going to do. We won't speak of it again until after the funeral. Then we're going to have a serious talk about our future."

He blinked at the burst of angry fire under his sternum. His hands fisted as he fought the urge to grab her by the hair. His mind flashed an image of holding her over that vanity while he gave it to her twice as hard as he had the night before. Two cleansing breaths pushed down his lustful rage. "Yes, dear, we'll address your problems with me later. I'll be ready to go to the church whenever you are. Until then I'll be in my den."

36

Carrying computer bags and still laughing about Pete's arrest, Eugene, Olivia and Austin stepped into the bright and bustling Pancake Palace.

"Welcome to my home away from home," said Eugene as the waitresses swarmed in his direction.

"My gawd, it's so good to see you," said Beth Carpenter, leading the pack. "Are you okay? Have you heard about that reporter? I told the police you could never have hurt Sandy."

"I'm fine, everybody. Thanks. Beth, Mary Ann, Jennifer, I'd like you all to meet Olivia and Austin. Given what happened to Andrew, we thought we should work in a more public place today. Who's managing dayside?"

"That'd be John. I'll grab him," Beth offered.

As she sped off, Eugene looked to the remaining wait-staff. "Man, it's good to see all of you. Was it the two detectives from Scottsdale that were here?"

"Yes," said Jennifer. "I heard they asked Beth all sorts of weird questions."

"Gosh, I'm sorry for that—"

"Morning, Eugene," called the manager as he waded through the crowd. "Beth tells me you need to set up in back. Go right ahead. Nobody's back there today."

"Thanks, John." He flicked a hand at his cohorts. "Meet Olivia Condon and Austin O'Neal. We—"

"The *Providence* people," John crowed, moving in for handshakes all around. "You folks are really kicking butt and taking names.

Welcome. Honored to have you. I'll personally get you set up." He held onto Olivia's hand. "You're Oliver's granddaughter, correct?"

"I am. Pleased to meet you."

"The pleasure is all mine. Your grandfather was a heck of a guy. I'm really sorry we lost him. Terrible thing, just terrible."

"Thank you for that," said Olivia, "I really appreciate it."

* * *

"You seem to be quite the popular fellow." Unpacking her computer bag, Olivia glanced from Eugene to the waitresses the manager herded away after getting them set up.

Eugene grinned. "Yeah, great bunch of people."

"And Beth is very pretty."

Eugene rolled his eyes. "Okay, we dated, but she's married now."

"Time out, you two. This isn't junior high. We're here to work," said Austin as he fired up his laptop. "Is there a wi-fi password, Eugene?"

"Nah, it's open." He fingered the camera hanging from his left shoulder. "I'm gonna head over to Andrew's house, if you two are set."

"Don't you want to eat first?" Olivia asked.

"Nah, I'll grab a sandwich to go. I'm eager to start poking around. I'll keep you posted if I find anything."

Olivia locked eyes with him and spoke in her most authoritative boss voice, "You be careful. You're still in the cross-hairs. I'll keep you updated with what we find on this end. Watch the time. We have a funeral."

"Yes, ma'am."

Austin snickered. It was her turn to roll her eyes.

* * *

Scanning the lot for threats, Eugene stepped from the Pancake Palace and headed toward his vehicle. He munched an egg and sausage sandwich while trying not to think about Andrew or the afternoon's funeral. Memories of his night with Olivia were a better alternative.

Fingerprint powder still smudged most of the hard surfaces of his Jeep. He cursed the overzealous cops as he fired the engine, once again noticing the lifter tick. It felt like a lifetime had passed since his breakup with Trish. Her image gave way to Olivia's sated expression. A warm glow swept over him.

"Live in the moment, Eugene," he warned himself as he pulled onto the street.

* * *

The tape blocking Andrew Brinkmann's street had come down. A long strip of yellow still draped across Andrew's yard and driveway. Local TV crews occupied the far side of the street, waiting to do their live shots for the mid-day newsbreaks. Eugene pulled up behind a van from Channel Seven. He crawled from the Jeep's cool interior into the day's mounting heat. No one looked his way. He studied the visuals of the area as he opened the back hatch to retrieve a second camera from the broken lockbox.

"Hey, Eugene, sorry about Andrew," said a feminine voice behind him.

He hadn't escaped notice, after all. He turned to find the intern Amy Becker, loaded down with a confused jumble of still and video equipment.

"Hi, Amy. How's the staff holding up at the paper?"

"It's not good. Everybody's looking to get out. This mess with Pete and Andrew was kind of the last straw for a lot of us. This new Spears guy they brought in is nothing but a head chopper. He doesn't have a clue about who we are and what we can do."

"You know," he rechecked his cameras so he didn't have to keep looking at her anxious expression, "it's quite possible that Pete's being set up just like I was."

Amy shook her head, "One of the TV guys told me they found bloody clothes and a bloody tire iron hidden in the backyard at Pete's house. Did you see the video of his arrest?"

"Who didn't? Guess there was one good thing to come out of this mess. He got taken down a peg or two." He sighted through one camera then the other as if trying to decide his visual approach. "So what are you still doing here? There's not much going on."

"A few hours ago I snagged some stills of Andrew's wife leaving with a female officer. She looked awful and I hated myself for shooting it. Spears wants me to stay on the scene in case she comes back. He's really hoping for a grieving wife and kid video."

"Classy," he scoffed.

"I'll hang out, but if she comes back with her daughter, my cameras are gonna have a malfunction."

Eugene smiled his approval, "Good for you . . . So the new guy's into video?"

"They want video and stills of everything. It's all about advertising and it's like tripled the workload. Spears says we have to be revenue generators to justify our existence or reporters with iPhones will replace us. You're lucky you got out when you did."

Disgust showing, Eugene put a camera to his eye, zoomed in and fired just as the torn police tape fluttered over the dark blood stain on the driveway. "Who's taking lead on the Luchadores now that Andrew's gone?"

Amy huffed out a little laugh, "Charlie Hastings has it. They took him off the copy desk and put him on the street."

Eugene cringed but said, "Well, he's smart and experienced."

"Yeah, but he hates it. He's retirement age. I don't see him sticking around for long. I think Spears is pressuring anybody with longevity, know what I mean?"

He played back the bloodstain image on the camera's LCD. Zooming in to check focus, his stomach twisted at seeing the childish chalk drawings. "You gonna stick it out? Could be a chance to turn your internship into a full-time job."

"I don't know. I loved this place until . . . well . . . Don't suppose the *Providence* will be looking for another shooter in the future, will they?"

He finally looked at her, noting the uncertainty and hope warring in her eyes. "I kinda doubt it, but you never know. It'd be worth asking Olivia." He took another quick survey of the news crews and the empty house. "I'm going to grab a scene setter and move on. Are you going to be at the funeral this afternoon?"

"Yes, but unfortunately Spears has his fingers all over that too. He's got Specht shooting stills—"

Eugene stiffened. "They put a camera in Mike's hands again? Who's running the desk?"

"He gets to do both. Overloading another old guy. You get the drift."

Eugene shook his head.

Amy continued, "So I'm both video and stills with an emphasis on video. Spears wants us to live stream Senator Bartholomew's eulogy. Won't that be exciting?" She rolled her eyes for emphasis.

"Oh, geeze," he groaned. "I heard it was gonna be over-the-top bad. What a jerk. Playing politics with a great man's funeral."

"People are saying it's payback for Bartholomew arranging the takeover. Disgusting, huh?"

* * *

In the computer tech department on the fourth floor of Scottsdale Police headquarters, Harry stared in wonder at a wall full of monitors. Eddie nudged him to listen as Ken Stoops droned on with his technical explanation of his team's details gleaned from long hours of internet sleuthing. Harry only wanted simple and relevant, which finally came.

"I've been chasing your sports team theory. So far, nothing. Only Wrigley and Mitchell were born in Arizona. The others are from Texas, New Mexico, and Colorado."

"Where'd they go to college?" Eddie asked.

Stoops pointed to a screen showing the breakdown, "A variety of Arizona colleges. U of A, ASU, NAU."

Eddie rubbed the hint of beard stubble on his chin, "So they met in high school or before. They go off to college, but not so far away that they can't meet for their monthly, ah, entertainment."

"Here's the interesting thing," said Stoops. "You'd think they'd start showing up in the DMV records around high school, but there's nothing."

"Wrigley's law enforcement background check has to show something," Eddie pressed.

"Nope. Somebody went to a lot of trouble to scrub these guys clean. Between birth and college, these guys don't exist." A sly grin lit the computer geek's face. "But here's the thing, leaving holes is almost as good as leaving tracks. It raises suspicions and pisses us off."

"Pete Cunningham have any holes in his record?" asked Eddie.

"Nope, he's good. I looked at him first thing this morning. Kurt Wragge on the other hand is another teenage ghost."

"Oh, man, that's good work," said Eddie, clapping his hands while wiggling out an odd little happy dance. "What made you look back at him?"

"Chief Royal got a call from a doctor at Mountain View Memorial. Brinkmann was there asking questions about Wragge's medical records last night. That and Brinkmann's browser history shows searches for Wragge, sports and Copperfield High School."

"Then that's the key!" Harry said, with a clap of his hands.

"Not so fast," said Stoops. "There is no Copperfield High in Arizona. The only Copperfield I can find is in Texas."

"One of the Luchadores was born in Texas," Harry quickly pointed out.

"They have no record of any of our guys attending."

"Well, shit," Eddie sputtered. "Whadda ya think, Harry? Go pick up Wragge and sweat it out of him?"

"Wragge's disappeared," Chief Royal said as he entered, Millie Mansfield at his side. Both were dressed for the funeral.

All stood to greet them.

"Hi, Millie," Eddie spoke softly. "How are you holding up?"

"I'm quite well, taking it a minute at a time. Thank you for asking. The important question is do you have any leads on Andrew's killer?"

Impressed with her fortitude, the men exchanged quick glances. Nothing like a tough survivor to apply pressure.

"We were just taking a hard look at Kurt Wragge. Chief, sir, you said he disappeared?" asked Eddie.

"I sent uniforms to his apartment and neither he nor Mikey are anywhere to be found. Here, Mildred, let me get you a chair."

All four men in the room scrambled for chairs. Obviously touched by the gesture, Millie made a point of taking the chair offered by Eddie. "Now, what did I hear about Copperfield High School?" She looked directly at Eddie.

"It's from Andrew's search history. Unfortunately, there are no Copperfield High Schools in Arizona."

Millie placed her purse in her lap and stared at the computer screens, taking it all in. "I wonder where Andrew picked up the Copperfield tidbit?"

"That's what we'd like to know. Can you think of anything, ma'am?" Harry asked.

She scanned the computer screens a second time. Harry could almost hear the wheels in her brain turning. "Have you gone through Andrew's notes? He was very meticulous."

"We did, but found nothing specific," said the Chief. "We can go down to the evidence room for a look, if you like."

"You looked at them yourself, Carlton?"

"Yes, every notebook from the last two months. His handwriting's a bit sketchy, so maybe if you—"

Millie looked back at the screens. "Have you called the school districts in the southern half of the state?"

"No, we just searched online," said Stoops, sounding like a student fearful of a scolding.

"Oh, that damn internet," scoffed Millie. "It's atrophying our collective brains."

All four men nodded, none daring to offer a rebuttal.

"Why the southern half of the state?" Harry dared to ask.

Millie shot him an incredulous glance, "Copperfield implies a mining community. Most of them are down south, like Bisbee, Clifton, Morenci, and so on. Copper's always been a boom and bust industry. The state's littered with mining ghost towns."

"So, you're thinking the school no longer exists," said Stoops.

"Consolidated most likely. Families arrived in the boom years and disappeared in the bust."

"Any big ones come to mind?" asked Eddie.

"No. If Oliver were still alive, he could have listed them off the top of his head. That man read five Arizona newspapers a day, cover to cover."

"How about the *Herald's* archive?" asked Eddie.

"No, we were too local. The *Arizona Republic* would be better. Wait! You have a treasure trove of institutional knowledge coming in for the funeral. Newspapermen and women from all over the state. I'll pose the question to them."

"Excellent," said the Chief then looked to his men. "In the meantime, start calling southern school districts and working families and friends." He smiled gently at Mildred. "Shall we grab a quick lunch before heading to the church?"

* * *

After sending his photos from Andy's house and passing along the information regarding Pete's arrest to Olivia, Eugene returned to the Pancake Palace.

"How was breakfast?" he asked.

Not taking her eyes off of her laptop screen, Olivia answered, "Outstanding."

She and Austin sat side by side with their open laptops at a large table in the back room of the busy restaurant. The remnants of their breakfast had yet to be collected by the wait staff.

"We are about to go live with another update," said Austin.

"Andy's murder?"

"No, that went up 30 minutes ago. This one's regarding that warehouse by the airport," said Olivia. "Austin tracked it back to Phil Simon, one of the Luchadores."

Eugene's breath caught. "Nobody else has that yet, right?"

"Not that I've seen. Thanks for passing along that evidence tidbit from Pete's house, I was able to confirm with the PIO at Scottsdale. Sounds like they have him cold."

"Has he confessed?"

"Unfortunately, they wouldn't reveal that little detail. They probably won't until tomorrow morning's press conference."

"Tomorrow? Why—"

"Grandpa's funeral. Everything's on hold."

"Makes sense. Speaking of that, don't you need to get to the church soon?"

"I need to run home to change. We just wanted to get this up first."

"How do you want me to handle . . . I mean, am I working it or—"

She cut him off, "What would you prefer? It's totally up to you."

Eugene leaned on a chair back. He'd pushed the funeral from his mind. Only now he realized that he might need to work it rather than just attend to mourn. He raised his burning eyes to meet hers. "I think I'd be more comfortable working. The cameras kind of act as a buffer, if you know what I mean. You're there but on the other side of the lens."

Obviously touched by the welling tears, Olivia nodded. "I'm sure Grandpa would approve. I'll touch base with you when it's over. Maybe we can arrange that drink you were talking about."

"Okay then." Eugene took a deep breath and exhaled. "Guess I'd better get home to change, too. Where is it again?"

"Green Valley, up on Cactus Road. Do you know it?"

"Yes. Well, I guess I'll see you up there." As he said the words he felt a necessary distance growing between them. She was family and he was an employee. It would be a difficult afternoon. The easiest way to get through it would be to play their respective parts. He would be the best-damned photojournalist on the planet.

"Austin, are you going?" asked Eugene.

"Wouldn't miss it."

"All right then. I'll see you both on the other side."

* * *

Eugene stared at his closet. For a moment he considered wearing the thrift shop polo shirt he'd worn the day he'd walked into the *East Valley Herald*. He held up the shirt. *Oliver would like it.* He smiled at the memory of how scared he'd been following the old man to his office and how the man's intense but understanding gaze had filled him with hope. With an aching heart he put the shirt back in the closet and selected something less sacred.

* * *

Green Valley Evangelical Church had been built to look like a Southwestern mission with a modern flair. Its parking lot was a sea of cars when Eugene arrived. Instantly feeling out of place in his old Jeep, he searched for a parking space among the shiny new SUVs and luxury cars. Even the television live trucks lining the drive to the east side of the building looked better than his transportation.

Finding a few working class vehicles in a far corner of the lot, he pulled into an open space. A feeling of dread and weariness fell over him as he crawled out into the heat. His feet trudged to the back of the Jeep to retrieve his camera gear. With his new canvas camera bag slung across his body and his new cameras dangling from each shoulder, he made a beeline for the TV trucks where he could blend in with the media crowd.

A mix of condolences and curiosity greeted him.

"Are you working today?" asked a veteran cameraman from KPHO.

"Yeah, I figured it would be easier, if you know what I mean."

"Good call. Sorry for your loss, man."

"Thanks," he said, looking around. "Any restrictions on us in there?"

"The pastor says we have free rein. He just expects us to be respectful and do our best to stay low-key."

"Got it," he said. *There's nothing low-key about any of this.*

He followed the thick river of television cables to a side door. When he stepped in, he was stunned to see the three huge video screens mounted above the stage that was awash in blue light. The screens played a memorial slideshow to the crowd already filling the sanctuary's movie-theater style seats. A young Oliver Condon in military dress flashed on screen, followed by images of him in civilian clothes holding a shovel at the groundbreaking of the *East Valley Herald* building.

On the far side of the stage, a group of string musicians played light classical music. Nearby, the empty front row awaited Olivia and her family. He wondered if he would have the wherewithal to capture images of her grief.

You're working, Eugene. This is just like every other funeral you've covered. Do your job.

Considering his usual low-key presence a kind of cloak of invisibility, he slipped past the seats lining his side of the stage and dropped to his knees behind the line of tripod-mounted television cameras. Immediately, he calculated his angles of view. From here he would be able to work the pulpit and swing to the family in the front row.

Heart thudding in his chest, he quickly looked away from the stage to the balcony. It too was filling. Soon the church would be standing room only. He scanned for friends in the crowd and saw Only Jack, looking uncomfortable and out of place in his suit. *I wonder where the Herald crew is?*

When he turned his eyes back to the stage, he saw it, not more than twenty feet in front of him. Oliver's casket, draped with an American flag and surrounded by a cascade of flowers.

His breath caught. Goosebumps rose on his arms. He shook off his shock and turned his attention to his cameras. That put him in newsman mode. He concentrated on anticipating moments and composition. Standing, he stepped clear of the TV cameras and made an image of the stage and the casket.

Unsatisfied with the angle, he quick-stepped to the church lobby and climbed the staircase to the balcony. Oliver's smiling face loomed large on the screens while below them, piercing the somber blue stage light, a shaft of warm light bathed the casket with an ethereal beauty. *Oh, Oliver, you would've lovded this image.*

Rushing back down to floor level, he was glad to see his spot on the floor still open. He settled back to his knees to patiently wait. A flute had joined the strings. It played a haunting melody that abruptly ended.

A hush fell over the sanctuary. Warm lights fired to illuminate the center aisle. A military honor guard advanced the colors, saluted and stood at parade rest at the far side of the stage. Six somber family members filed in led by Margaret Bartholomew, Olivia, then the senator who looked ruddy-faced and as pompous as ever.

Watching through his camera's viewfinder, Eugene pressed the shutter button, picking his moments as the family formed a line in front of the casket. One by one, each placed a hand to the gleaming cherry wood.

When Margaret and Gordon Bartholomew stepped back, Olivia lingered, her eyes filled with tears, glinting in the light reflecting off the casket. Eugene fired three frames then lowered the camera and switched to the wide angle to capture the scene in its entirety.

A solemn minister walked down the aisle to the first row. After greeting Margaret, Gordon and Olivia in turn as they took their seats, he then stepped up to the stage and took a seat with three other officiants behind the pulpit to the left of the casket.

Majestic pipe organ music fired. The minister stood and the crowd rose with him. On the overhead screens lyrics to "King of Love My Shepherd Is" appeared superimposed over a picture of prairie grass at sunset. On the far right of the stage, a resplendent choir began to sing and the crowd joined in.

As the hymn came to a close, the minister stepped to the pulpit and signaled for the crowd to sit. "Good afternoon, everyone. Today I'll be reading from Deuteronomy 29:29. 'The secret things belong unto the Lord our God, but those things which are revealed belong unto us . . . .'"

Eugene made a few obligatory frames then blanked the minister's words from his mind to concentrate on visuals. Moving around to the back of the stage, he captured the sweep of the church and the officiants haloed in light. Next he zeroed in on the family, making an image of them framed between the pulpit and the flowers surrounding the casket.

Margaret looked like an old blind woman behind her sunglasses. She held a tissue in her right hand that she occasionally raised to dab under her glasses. *Crocodile tears.* Olivia stared teary-eyed at the casket, seemingly unaware of the trickles down her cheeks. He made a few frames then lowered the camera.

The minister had finished his reading and had moved on to a more personal sermon, referencing Oliver Condon's great achievements and his generosity to the community. Eugene returned to his spot on the floor. After two more hymns, a family member Eugene did not know stepped up to the pulpit. His ten-minute commentary made the room laugh and cry. He turned a moment to look at the casket, bowed his head then returned to his seat.

Olivia's grief took on a brittle, nervous edge. Stunning in her black dress, she wiped her face with both hands and stood. Since she never wore much make-up, not even mascara smeared. She carefully mounted the steps, crossed the stage to the pulpit and drew herself up with a deep breath. Her glittering eyes scanned the audience then she began. Eugene made a few quick frames before lowering his camera to listen.

"My grandfather was the kindest, most gentle man I've ever known. But when it came to his love of community, he was a warrior for truth. For nearly half a century he devoted himself to holding the powers that be accountable." In the spotlighted stage, all saw her graceful neck as she painfully swallowed. "But, what he loved most of all was telling the good stories of his community. He had an incredible talent for seeing the fleeting, everyday moments that needed to be appreciated. He instilled that vision of kindness in all who worked with—not for—him."

Perfect and profoundly true.

"Grandpa was old school. Newspapering was not a business to him. It wasn't about web traffic or circulation or ad revenue. He knew all that would take care of itself as long as he stayed true to his readers. You proved him right for 47 years."

"He will be sorely missed. We are all the poorer for his passing. I thank you for coming today and I hope that after this service you will all take a moment to pray for him and . . . " Her voice cracked. She swayed and gripped the pulpit for support. "Raise a glass in his honor to wish him well."

Stepping back and crossing the stage to return to her seat, she left silence in her wake. Eugene realized he'd stopped breathing and his own face was wet. He took a shaky breath then glanced to the front row where the senator looked on in awe and anger. *Let's see you follow that, you slimy son-of-a-bitch.*

The man collected himself as he consulted his notecards. He hefted his girth, straightened his suit coat, and headed to the pulpit looking a little off balance.

"Thank you for that, Olivia," he began. He arranged his cards on the pulpit before clearing his throat. "And I too thank you all for coming . . . My relationship with Olivier was an interesting one, for you see I too have devoted myself to community, but occasionally our visions were at odds. That's as it should be. It is the fourth estate's job to keep those in power honest and accountable. He certainly did that. Over the years we had countless respectful debates. Every now and then he was able to sway my opinion on matters of great importance. He was indeed a great man, both in intelligence and in his love of community. I'll miss his counsel greatly."

Eugene glanced to Olivia. She appeared tense and furious but then relaxed as if relieved the senator had finished. Her eyes narrowed and her chin came up when he continued.

"But fear not, people. Oliver's legacy is in good hands."

Eugene stiffened. *What the hell? Where's he going with—*

"I've met with the *East Valley Herald's* new owners and spent a great deal of time talking with Steve Spears, the paper's new managing editor. Although he is younger, I believe he too is a man of great vision."

Eugene caught movement in the crowd at the far end of the stage.

"He may be new to the community, but I believe he has the same commitment to—as newsmen and women always say—afflicting the comfortable and comforting the afflicted."

A small group from the Herald's newsroom gathered at the foot of the stage.

"Ah, welcome. Yes, please, all of you come down," said the obviously nervous senator, waving his hand at the people moving down the aisle. "This is the staff of the *Herald's* newsroom. Please come on down let the community see you."

The group had grown to fifteen or more and were led by Millie Mansfield and Charlie Hastings.

"Oliver would be—"

"Don't you dare assume to speak for any of us, especially Oliver!" shouted Millie with a shake of her fist. Grief overtook her anger. Her shoulders fell with her fist and quiet crying could be heard as Charlie Hastings put an arm around her for comfort. Then in unison, the group turned their back to the senator and stood in silent protest.

"Well, ah, yes, I can see this is an emotional time for all of us," said the senator, through a clenched jaw, as he unsuccessfully attempted to again arrange his notecards, his hands shaking with rage. "The family and I thank you all for coming." He stepped backward from the pulpit then lengthened his strides all the way to his seat.

Glowing with pride at having captured the senator's desperation for all eternity, Eugene moved from his position to join his colleagues' protest. Tears streaming down her smiling face, Olivia shook off her mother's attempt to stop her and moved to Eugene's side. The group stood their ground until the church began to clear. When no one else joined them, they climbed the steps and crossed the stage to form an arced line, all staring at the casket containing the remains of a much beloved man. Tears flowed freely as one by one, each placed a hand on the casket. When all stood connected, together they said, "Rest in Peace. Goodbye, Oliver Condon."

37

"I don't have much time. Mother's waiting for me. Are you coming to the graveside service?" asked Olivia, as Eugene stepped from the church.

"I hadn't even thought that far ahead. I don't think so." He looked down to where she clasped his hand. "I've said my goodbye. Is that . . . ?"

"Yes, that's just fine, Eugene. I'll catch up with you after. Are you going out with the group from the *Herald*?"

"Charlie Hastings said we're welcome to join everyone at the Rusty Spur in Old Town, after they get the paper out tonight. Said it could be sooner if Spears starts chopping heads."

"I don't think that'll happen right away." She looked around, trying to spot lingering *Herald* staff. "They were amazing, weren't they?"

"Yep, pretty courageous bunch risking their jobs like that. Your stepfather looked furious."

"Priceless. I can't wait to see your pictures. Any chance you could—"

"Already talked to Austin. Told him I'd file pictures from my car. He wanted me to ask you about a story."

"Tell him he'll get an emailed brief from our new reporter in an hour or so, but it won't have a byline."

"Who's our new reporter and why—?"

"Charlie Hastings called me right after I left the restaurant this morning. Said he'd whip up a quick story on the down-low, so I wouldn't have to. I offered him a job and he's giving his two-week notice tonight."

A grin spread across Eugene's face, "That's fantastic."

"Olivia Condon, get in this car now or we'll leave you here!" shouted Margaret Bartholomew.

Olivia shrugged regretfully at Eugene, started to turn then looked back at him.

"You never said where you were going."

"I thought I'd drive into Phoenix and spend time with the brothers before they go home for the day."

"And King, too?" she asked, talking and walking backward for the funeral home limousine.

"He'll get some much needed scratching . . . because he's been such a good boy."

She grinned at his intentional replay of one of her comments during their night at the Tradewinds. "Can I meet you there?"

"I was hoping you would," he said, waving her goodbye.

* * *

"How dare you have anything to do with those rude low-lifes," harped Margaret Bartholomew as Olivia closed the door. They sat facing each other on the limo's opposing rear seats.

"That was the most embarrassing moment of my entire career," snarled the senator, staring out the dark-tinted window.

"For the record," snapped Olivia, "you did it to yourself, hijacking Grandpa's funeral like that. What were you thinking?"

"Don't you talk to your father—"

"He's *not* my father!"

Her mother dabbed her tissue under her sunglasses. "You won't be happy until you've totally ruined our deal with Mid-States, will you?"

"Your problems stem from those you choose to crawl in bed with, Mother. And would you *please* take off those ridiculous sunglasses?"

Margaret pushed the big glasses up the bridge of her nose with a defiant jab of her finger. "Just what are you trying to say?"

"Nothing, Mother. All I want to do is get through the afternoon and be done with this."

"You're coming back to the church for dinner, aren't you?"

"No, I won't. After the cemetery I'll be joining Eugene and his family."

Gordon's upper lip curled in distaste. "That's fitting. His mother's a drunken whore."

Olivia stared at him a long moment. "Not his mother. I'm going to meet the men that raised him, the Fodoni brothers."

"Ha! Even better. Darkies in a junkyard. Talk about crawling into bed with low-life scum—"

"You are a racist pig," Olivia snapped. "For the record, I'll take hardworking, self-made men over a politician any day. They earned what they have . . . unlike you."

"That is uncalled for, young lady," Margaret whined. "To maintain family accord, I suggest you shut your—"

"Or what?" she cut her mother off. "You'll stop the car and make me get out? Wouldn't that look good on the evening news?"

"Both of you, just shut up," Gordon ordered then crossed his arms as if holding in his temper. "Let's get through this. We can argue later."

Clasping her hands in her lap until her fingers turned white, Olivia stared out the window. She refused to acknowledge her mother's whimpers.

Finally, the limo rolled to a stop in the cemetery. Bagpipes played "Amazing Grace" as the family emerged. Not a word was spoken as other mourners moved forward to escort them in their trek across the cemetery's well-maintained grass. A large green awning shaded the short row of family seating and Oliver's flag-draped casket. A fawning funeral director guided Margaret to her place then placed Olivia next to her. The tight-lipped Gordon nodded to the respectful gathering as he settled in the indicated chair beside his step-daughter, rather than at his wife's side.

The minister spoke a few words before offering a short prayer. Marines in dress blues slow-marched forward along both sides of the casket, crisply turned toward it and lifted the flag in their white-gloved hands. At the head of the casket, the officer of the funeral detail executed a slow-motion salute.

Despite bracing herself, Olivia still flinched at the nearby, three-volley 21-gun salute. She held it together until the finality of a lone, distant bugle played the aching notes of "Taps" that conjured heartfelt sobs. Through tear-blurred sight she watched the Marines fold the flag with military precision. The officer clasped the folded triangle to his chest and stepped back. His detail slow-marched from under the awning before he walked to position in front of Margaret, knelt and reverently placed the flag in her hands. Olivia stared at her grandfather's casket as the man softly offered the Marine Corps' and President's thanks for Oliver's service. He stood, performed a slow-motion salute and crisply followed his detail.

Her skin crawled as Margaret and Gordon wrapped their arms around her. She initially wiggled to shake them off but they persisted. She then realized the seating arrangement and the group hug had been orchestrated for the line of cameras she had subconsciously ignored.

When the casket was lowered and the crowd began to disperse, Olivia scanned the crowd. On the periphery she spotted her grandfather's good friend, wheel-chair bound Arthur Smith, holding up a camera. When she raised her hand, he lowered the camera and gave her a nodding smile.

In the privacy of the limo, all remained silent. Margaret lifted her glasses for the first time to wipe away tears. Olivia thought she noticed a bruise under her left eye.

* * *

Eugene pulled into the Fodoni brother's yard and killed the engine. The moment the door opened, King was on him. He was glad he'd changed into an old t-shirt and blue jeans because the old guy's big paws left streaks of junkyard dirt down his front. It felt good to be home.

"How was the funeral?" asked Carl Fodoni, as he rounded the battery pile with the fender of an old Chevy in hand.

"Awful and beautiful at the same time," said Eugene. "Is Albert in the office? I want to tell you both all about it."

Carl set the fender on the oily ground. "Get down, King. Give me my turn." When the dog dropped to his butt, he wrapped his ancient arms around Eugene then followed the hug with a hearty handshake. "Come on in. I do believe we have some Zingers and chocolate milk. Figured we'd be seeing more of you."

"Perfect," Eugene said on a sigh.

"There's my boy," Albert called as they entered the office. "How was the funeral?"

"It was interesting, I'll say that."

"Say, you didn't have any trouble last night, did you? We read about that reporter friend of yours."

"No, no trouble on my end. Turns out the weasel in our hen house was Pete Cunningham. They arrested him this morning for killing Andrew. Damn shame. Andrew was one of the good guys. We were pretty close."

Albert cocked his head as he studied Eugene. "But you don't think it was Pete what killed Andrew, do you? I can hear it in your voice."

"Nah, doesn't ring true. Takes a lot to sneak up and kill a man face to face. Pete doesn't have it in him. I think the truth will come out eventually." He frowned at the two men. "Hey, I figured to see you two at the funeral. What happened?"

Carl looked to Albert. "Well, we read about all the goings on and figured we'd be outta place. Can't say as I thought the goings-on was what Oliver would have picked for himself. We figured we'd visit the cemetery on Sunday. Pay our respects and say our own words then."

"You figured right, but you missed a pretty good show. Oliver's daughter and her politician husband tried to make it all about them." He loosed a sly grin. "But the good folks at the Herald didn't let 'em get away with it. Let's sit down and I'll tell you all about it."

Seated at the old chrome and Formica table and washing down Zingers with chocolate milk, Eugene detailed what Olivia had said at the church and how the senator had stumbled. His face glowed with pride in describing how the *Herald* staff had stood up to the senator en mass. "For a bunch of sheltered, white-collar folks they really showed some courage."

"You thinking about goin' back to work for the paper? We miss seein' your pictures in print."

Eugene considered it for only a heartbeat. "Nah, I'm afraid I'm done there. The new owners are gonna bleed it and sell it. I'm better off sticking with Olivia. She's got a good plan. Speaking of Olivia, she said she'd meet us here after while. I'm really looking forward to you all getting to know each other."

Carl looked to Albert, both growing smiles. "So, is this you bringin' home your best girl to meet the family?"

Heat suffused his face. “Yeah, I guess it is. This one’s special. We even survived our first fight this morning. It was dumb but we came to an understanding.”

Albert shook his head. “I don’t know. You workin’ for her and all? Family business can be a hard row to hoe, ‘specially when you ain’t exactly equal.”

“She’s got a good head on her shoulders. And, hey, it worked out good for the two of you.”

“True enough,” Carl said. “When’s she comin’? Maybe we oughta clean up a little.”

“Nah, no need to put on airs. She’s down to earth just like her grandpa.”

“Well then, since you got your workin’ clothes on what say you come help me pull another fender off a ’69 Chevy C10? Got a fella in Chicago champin’ at the bit for the sheet metal.”

“Let’s get to it. Been too long since I had a wrench in my hand. If we get time, I want to check the valves on the Jeep. It’s got a little lifter tick driving me nuts.”

* * *

You’re sick, Gordon. You need professional help.

The memory of Margaret’s words had added heat to Gordon Bartholomew’s simmering rage all afternoon. His embarrassment at the funeral had brought his rage to full boil. The awkward dinner and way too long ritual of repetitive condolences at the church just added fuel. By the time they arrived home, he had turned into a ticking bomb in search of a reason to go off.

Margaret hadn’t said a word to him since leaving the dinner. Last night she’d been a firecracker, but now she looked absolutely ancient. *What a useless, wrinkled pile of shit.*

Following her inside, seething with anger and disgust, he watched her place her purse on the kitchen island then take a seat at a little kitchen desk to hit play on their blinking answering machine. A long string of condolence calls were deleted unheard. Then the voice of Carlton Royal yanked at Gordon’s already frayed nerves.

“Hello, this message is for Mrs. Bartholomew. You have my deepest condolences for your loss. Knowing you’ve had your hands full, I wanted to wait until after the funeral. I was hoping I could send someone over to talk about last night's incident. Could you give me a call at your earliest convenience? Thank you." He went on to recite his private cell phone number.

"Margaret," he said her name with icy control, "surely you didn't call the police over our little adventure last night."

She hit the pause button on the machine. "No, I did not. I assume he wants to learn more about Peter Cunningham." She hit play. More condolence calls were erased.

Gordon paced. "Well, I certainly hope you didn't. That's the sort of salacious gossip the press would use to crucify me."

"I didn't call them." She glared at him over her shoulder. "But, if you ever lay a hand on me again, I will. And as far as your public image is concerned . . . " Her expression turned smug, "You looked like such a doddering old fool at the church, I don't hold much hope for your political career."

His body exploded before his brain realized he was moving. It was as if he was standing outside of himself as his huge fist crashed into her face. She sailed to the kitchen's hardwood floor, eyes lolling.

"Here, let me help you call the police!" he screamed, ripping the phone from the desk. He then landed on her with his full weight. The crack of ribs was delightful. She managed to put up a hand in defense but it was no match for his fury. The phone came down on her face again and again. "Call the cops now, you cunt! Go ahead, call them!"

Chest heaving and his blood lust receding, he numbly realized there was no going back. A sense of finality came over him.

Margaret groaned and coughed, blood bubbling in her mouth. Gordon watched in fascination. *She's not dead . . . Oh, how delicious.* He wrapped his thick hands around her neck and squeezed, relishing the site of life draining from her wide eyes.

Chest heaving, he rose from her corpse to grope for the cell phone in the pocket of his suit coat draped over a kitchen chair. Peering through his blood-spattered glasses, he dialed.

"Hello?" answered Kurt.

"It's me."

"Hey, Coach, surprised to hear from you so soon. Hope I made you proud. Everything looks good to—"

"They're onto us."

"What? How—"

"No time. Pack a bag. We're heading for Mexico. It's all arranged," he lied. "We'll lay low with our friends then catch a boat down to Ecuador."

"But I thought—"

"Stop asking questions!" he shouted.

"Okay-okay, Coach. Where do we meet?"

"A junkyard, 9th Avenue and Buchanan in Phoenix."

"Eugene's place?"

"Yes, we have one more loose end to tie up."

"What about Mikey?"

"Bring him, of course. We'll need his help."

* * *

As Eugene and Carl walked in from the salvage area, Olivia's classic, open-topped Willys flat-fender Jeep pulled into the junkyard. Carl pulled a two-wheeled dolly laden with a tool box. Eugene carried the recently removed fender. Dirt streaked his shirt and sweat stung his eyes.

"That's a pretty little flat fender," said Carl, as King let loose his happy bark and bounded for the Jeep.

"The woman driving it ain't too bad, either," quipped Eugene.

King parked his paws on the Jeep's doorsill, whining with joy over a vigorous neck scratch.

"Well, now I'll have to agree with you there. King likes her, too."

The sun had dropped low enough to shine in under the bridge. Its backlight sparkled off her ponytailed hair and outlined her slender body clad in blue jeans and a white cotton blouse.

"Howdy!" yelled Eugene with a wave.

Leaving Carl behind, he hustled to place the fender outside the office. Albert poked his head out the door, eyeing the young woman waiting beside her Jeep.

"She's here," Eugene happily stated the obvious. "Come on and let me introduce you."

Grinning from ear to ear, Albert stepped out.

Eugene led the way to their visitor. He came to a stop in front of her, intentionally looking over the vehicle and not at her. "I didn't know you had an old Willys. She's a beauty."

"It was Grandpa's favorite. I learned to drive a clutch in this when I was 14. Seemed like the perfect day to take her for a spin and blow out the cobwebs."

"Good call." He finally met her eyes.

When they both grinned, he wondered if she could hear his thundering heart. Albert and Carl arriving broke the spell.

Eugene beamed with pride and swept his hand toward the two men. "Olivia, I'd like you to meet Carl and Albert."

"Very nice to meet you," Albert said, shaking her extended hand.

Carl examined his own hand then rubbed it on his pants, "I'd shake, but I brought a little of the yard with me."

"A little oil and dirt never hurt anyone," said Olivia, again thrusting out an insistent hand.

Carl beamed, gave her hand a delicate shake.

Olivia pulled him into a hug. "Wonderful to finally meet both of you."

Carl eased away, eyeing her. "You know, you're the first young woman Eugene's ever brought home."

Eugene rolled his eyes as Olivia shot him a glance, saying, "That's good to know."

"Well, what say we get out of the heat," Albert suggested. "We got comfortable chairs and cold drinks in the office. Restroom's just down the hall to the right if you need it. Carl, maybe we oughta pull the gate shut for the day. No point in tempting the neighborhood with that pretty little Jeep. Say, what's the year, 1952 maybe?"

She rubbed an affectionate hand on the Jeep's fender. "She's a '53 with the hurricane engine. Grandpa and I installed an overdrive in her a few years ago."

The brothers offered Eugene a smiling nod of approval.

"I'll get the gate, Carl," said Eugene, "You go on inside and cool off, but don't start telling stories before I get there to defend myself."

As he strolled for the gate, he heard Albert start in. "He ever tell you 'bout the time he ate 23 bananas?"

"At the Park n' Swap, right?" She laughed and his insides melted. "I have heard that one, but I'm hoping to hear more."

"Well, there was the day," Carl offered, "he and his brother found big buncha red, white and blue rubbers at the landfill—"

"Now, Carl," Albert interrupted, "don't be forgettin' we got a lady here."

"Oh, don't worry about me," said Olivia. "I tricked Eugene into wearing a gay rodeo cap at a press conference the other night."

The brothers' cackling laughter drifted to him. Eugene shook his head as he pulled the gate closed and wrapped it with the chain.

As he stepped into the office, Carl was finishing the rubber story, "Every car on the block had a patriotic prophylactic a hangin' off its antenna. Made for quite the sight."

* * *

Eddie and Harry had returned to headquarters after the funeral. Millie called with news that a retired reporter from the *Tombstone Epitaph* remembered the school had been consolidated into the Sierra Vista district around 1983. Being so late in the day, calls to Sierra Vista went unanswered.

"We'll try again in the morning," said Harry. "We might even have to take a drive down there to talk to the locals."

"We still don't know what led Brinkmann to Copperfield in the first place," said Eddie. "It's still early. Maybe we should go back to the paper and ask around. I hate to go home with this hanging."

A short while later, Eddie and Harry pushed through the glass doors into the *East Valley Herald* newsroom. With no one at the front desk, they pushed through the little swinging door.

"Hello," Harry called. "Anyone home?"

Heads popped out of cubicles. Charlie Hastings waved and approached, "Can I help you?"

"We're trying to get a better handle on what happened last night. Pete Cunningham told us that Andrew watched a press run. Shortly after that, he went to Mountain View Memorial to ask about your head pressman, Kurt Wragge."

"Wragge hasn't surfaced here has he?" asked Eddie.

"No, no sign of him." Hastings looked around. "There's a skeleton crew in the pressroom, if you'd like to talk to them. I suppose you should check with Spears, first though."

"Check with me for what?" said Spears, approaching from across the newsroom. He had a briefcase in hand and looked like he was about to leave for the day.

"We'd like to talk to your press crew about last night, mind if we—"

"Do whatever you like," Spears impatiently interrupted him. "I've got to catch a flight to Chicago."

Harry could see the frowning Hastings wanted to ask why but held back.

"Charlie, give them whatever they need," said Spears as he pushed through the swinging gate to leave.

Hastings folded his arms and rocked on his heels. "Well, that was interesting."

"We heard what happened at the funeral," said Eddie.

"I gotta say I rather enjoyed that aspect of this otherwise awful day." Hastings said. "Follow me."

In the pressroom they learned that Andrew's visit had been uneventful. The lead pressman for the day, Jerry readily cooperated. "Yeah, Kurt gave him the tour, showed him the different parts of the press then he went back to the newsroom."

"You haven't heard from Kurt or Mikey have you?" Harry asked.

"Nothing beyond their calling in sick this morning. Kinda weird though. Neither of them ever called in sick before. Not really Kurt's style. He'd show up even when he was draggin'. Just the other day, he was lookin'n beat to shit. Said he'd had a hell of a night at a bar, but he still showed up to work."

"What day was that?" Eddie asked, his pen poised over his notebook.

Jerry thought for a second, "Night before last."

Harry and Eddie exchanged a glance.

"What?" said Jerry.

"It's probably nothing," said Eddie. "Thanks for the help. If you think of anything, give us a call." He handed Jerry a card.

"Anything else guys?" asked Hastings as they pushed through the doors heading back to the newsroom.

"Mind if we hang out at Brinkmann's desk to think things through?" asked Harry.

"Go right ahead. Wish I could be more help—" Hasting stopped mid-stride.

"What, did you think of something?" Harry asked.

The blood drained from Hastings' face. "I just realized . . . The morning Kurt showed up dragging was the morning after the supposed Luchador suicide."

All exchanged knowing glances then Hastings continued on his way, shaking his head.

Harry took a seat at Brinkmann's desk and leaned back in his chair. He closed his eyes, putting himself into Brinkmann's head. He imagined working the phone and the computer then opened his eyes to gaze around the newsroom while his mind wandered. "Pete would have had a perfect line of sight on this desk."

"Would have been able to hear his phone calls, too," said Eddie.

He took a seat in a stackable chair, focusing on Brinkmann's cubicle wall lined with old press passes, political campaign pins and his daughter's artwork. The desktop was empty but for the phone and loose cables that had been connected to his computer. On the shelf over the desk was a picture of his wife and daughter, an Arizona Diamondbacks bobble head of Randy Johnson, an AP Stylebook and a dictionary. Eddie picked up each item and examined it.

Harry pulled the pencil drawer all the way open. All the papers and cards and post-its had been taken into evidence, but pens, pencils, paperclips and coins remained.

"We've been through all that," Eddie pointed out.

"I know, I know." Harry continued his search, anyway.

He took out his flashlight and shined it to the back of the drawer then pulled open the letter drawer and did the same. Lastly, he opened the file drawer. Empty file folders hung on a metal frame. Harry thumbed through them then pulled them out for a better look. A Roget's Thesaurus sat at the back of the drawer.

"There's something the techs missed," said Harry. "If he was as meticulous as Millie said, this would have been on the shelf with the dictionary."

Eddie offered a doubtful look as Harry plucked the thick little paperback from the drawer and cracked it open. A small, laminated newspaper clipping tumbled out.

38

Olivia's laughter warmed Eugene's heart as they traded stories around the old chrome and Formica table in the junkyard office. The funeral now in her past, a heavy weight had obviously lifted from her shoulders.

"Remember that story I told you about how Mom and Dad had me stay overnight to guard the warehouse?" asked Eugene.

Olivia nodded.

"I didn't tell you the cool thing that happened the morning after."

Olivia waved a hand for him to get on with it.

"After the cops left, I couldn't sleep. Around sunup, King and I went out to the loading dock. We liked to watch the trains in the switchyard at sunrise. After the miserable night I'd had, the morning seemed extra beautiful. Well, we're sitting there watching the switchyard come to life and I noticed this shiny silver train parked on a siding."

"I ain't never heard this one," said Carl. "Was it the Amtrak?"

"Nope, this one was different. Boxcars and sleeping cars mixed together. Out of one of the boxcar doors I see this funny, snakelike thing poking out and moving around like an octopus arm. It wasn't until I put binoculars on it that I realized what it was."

Eugene looked around the table and saw all three were eager for the answer.

"What was it?" asked Albert.

"An elephant."

Olivia shot him a "you're bull-shitting me" look as Carl cackled, "Ah, the circus train."

"Yep, the Ringling Brothers were in town for the weekend. I locked up and walked over. Got to hang out with the circus people all morning. We ate breakfast in the dining car then I helped them feed the animals. It was amazing. They were so cool that I wished I had a camera so I could share it with everyone. I realized right then and there that I wanted to be a photographer."

"And a fine one you turned into," declared Carl. "Say, I think somebody feels left out." He pointed to the picture window behind Olivia.

She turned to see King smiling and panting, his big paws perched on the window sill. Behind him, the sun had fallen below the horizon. The fire-red sky framed the sparkling high rises in the distance.

"My, what a handsome old fellow, and that view of downtown is absolutely stunning."

"Yessiree, that's why I put in that big window," said Albert. "Nothin' better than sittin' here and watchin' the sun set on a hard day's work."

King's happy expression suddenly turned to concern. His focus whipped to the front gate. He disappeared from the window. A heartbeat later the air filled with a series of ferocious barks.

Eugene stiffened.

"Neighborhood kids?" Olivia asked.

He glanced at her and shrugged to calm her nerves.

"Sounds more like his stranger bark," Carl said as he rose from the table. He went to a curtained window with a view of the gate. One hand dropped to his right pants pocket. Eugene saw the bulge of his .38 snub nose.

"Huh, some fellow with a fancy white Escalade," Carl told them.

"Really?" Olivia mumbled. "That's what Gordon drives."

"Your stepfather came here?" asked Eugene.

She scoffed. "I sure hope not. Leave it to him to ruin a perfect evening." She joined Carl to peer out the window. "Good lord, that *is* him. What could he want here?"

Uneasiness blossomed in Eugene's chest. "I suppose we should go see."

"I'll put King on his tether," said Albert.

Olivia glanced at Eugene then back out the window. "Maybe if we just ignore him he'll go away."

"He's seen the Jeep. He knows you're here. Besides, for him to come all the way down here, it must be important."

Eugene and Albert went outside with Olivia on their heels. "I'm sorry, guys," she said. "I apologize in advance for his intrusion. He's not a pleasant man."

"No worries," said Eugene. "We need to head back to Scottsdale, anyway."

"Okay, we're good," hollered Albert when he had King fastened to a long rope attached to the back of the building. The dog's barks had diminished to a still audible vicious growl.

Eugene and Olivia approached the gate.

After turning off his vehicle and its headlights, Gordon Bartholomew stepped out of his SUV. He looked completely out of character in a blue t-shirt and old school, high-wasted coach's shorts.

"What do you need?" snapped Olivia as Eugene unlocked the gate.

"Your mother is beside herself with concern," said Bartholomew.

"Mother is always—"

The instant the gate chain clanked free, Bartholomew pushed through, pointing a Beretta pistol square at Eugene's face.

Not in the least intimidated, Eugene looked into his eyes glittering behind his glasses in the dim yard light. The pieces to his mental puzzle came together in an instant.

"Anal Pirate," Eugene announced.

"Pleased to meet you," Bartholomew snarled. "For the record, I've never liked that name. I prefer Coach Bart. Now, both of you get your asses back or I'll drop you right here."

"Stop it right now!" Olivia shouted, as she lunged toward her stepfather. His free hand reflexively punched her in the face. She crumpled to the ground. The gun barely wavered before Eugene's eyes.

Eugene pushed the vulnerable Olivia from his mind to concentrate on the threat. *Weak, off-balance stance. Not a trained shooter. Beretta nine millimeter, double action. Christ! How many rounds?*

Kurt and Mikey appeared from behind the SUV. Kurt aimed a Colt revolver at the downed Olivia. "I'd do what he says, Eugene. Coach Bart don't mess around."

To be heard over King's renewed barking, Bartholomew shouted, "Hey, you two darkies, show yourselves or I'll gut shoot both of 'em. And don't even think about turning that dog lose."

Carl and Albert lumbered from the shadows, hands out to their sides, the ineffectual overhead yard light shadowing their faces.

"Now, I think we should all head inside where it's cooler," said Bartholomew.

"Why? You're just going to kill us anyway," Eugene goaded.

In the dim light, death sparkled in Bartholomew's piggish eyes. Heart pounding in his ears while the world slowed to a crawl, Eugene focused on the gun's mechanics. As Bartholomew's index finger began the long, first pull on the double-action trigger, he imagined the springs tensioning as the hammer rocked back.

At the last possible fraction of a second, Eugene screamed, "Hey!" then jerked to the side and closed his eyes to the muzzle flash as the gun roared. "All right! All right!" he screamed. "Olivia, get up and do what he says."

The still-stunned Olivia had pushed up to a sitting position, her mouth dripping blood. Deaf in one ear, Eugene prayed that the cops' shot tracker system had registered the gun blast.

"That's a good boy," said Bartholomew. "Now, face me and walk backwards to the office. No, don't help her up. Let the bitch do it on her own."

Olivia struggled to her feet, swayed a moment then mimicked Eugene backing slowly. Kurt, Mikey and Bartholomew followed.

"Hurry up! Move it!" ordered Kurt.

Complete dread played on Mikey's face.

He's the weak link.

Eugene's cell phone rang in his pocket. "Leave it be," said Kurt, urging them to keep moving.

"So what's the plan, Kurt? Go out in a blaze of glory?" asked Eugene. *Office. Shotgun under the counter.* "You can't possibly think you'll get away with this."

"Nah, Coach Bart's got it handled. He—"

"Shut up!" bellowed Bartholomew.

Olivia's cell phone rang, almost immediately followed by the office phone ringer echoing out over the yard. A siren sounded in the distance. All were punctuated by the frantic King's frustrated barking.

Eugene smiled. "They know, Kurt. Cops are coming. Leave now and you might have a chance to get away."

Bartholomew slammed the barrel of his gun across Eugene's cheek. He doubled over. Stars burst before his eyes but he still launched himself forward. His right fist slammed into Bartholomew's crotch just before his left fist jacked a crushing blow to the big man's nose.

The assault rocked him back but Bartholomew repositioned his gun on target, insanely screeching, "Party time! Kid's fast as you, Kurt. Shoot the bitch. Take the fight out of him."

Kurt's aim wandered as Carl and Albert stepped close to shield the shocked young woman.

"No!" screamed Mikey. "You said it has to look like a robbery!"

"So I did," sputtered Bartholomew, swiping at his bloodied nose. "Good thinking, Mikey. You go in first with the old niggers. If one of 'em makes a move, yell, and I'll finish this one right here."

On the far side of the building, King yapped and howled.

Eugene considered the damage to Bartholomew's face. His swelling nose leaked blood onto his lips. His glasses were bent. He kept moving his head as if trying to focus better through the off-kilter lenses.

Mikey cautiously side-stepped into the office. Carl and Albert followed.

"All right, Olivia, my dear, your turn."

Ashen-faced, Olivia obeyed. Kurt followed her, never lowering his gun.

Eugene's mind spun with calculations. *The door's the pinch point. We're separated. Now's the—*

Two loud blasts sounded as the office flashed with fire.

Eugene ducked then lunged upward for Bartholomew's pistol. More shots sounded in the office. His hands wrapped around the man's thick wrist. Eugene twisted to slam his back against the out-of-shape body. Stumbling backward they collided with the office's exterior. Eugene whipped his head back with all his might. Glasses and cartilage crunched. The gun roared.

Despite being old and flabby, the man was monstrously strong. A big arm swung around for a chokehold. Eugene tucked his chin so the massive trunk of flesh wrapped his face instead of his neck. For a blind instant, they danced, Eugene's sweaty face sliding from under the arm as the former wrestling coach wrapped a leg around his and pushed forward. The world became a slow-motion tumble. Eugene released the gun hand and wrenched sideways. The old man's bulk hit the dirt face first.

Eugene squirted out and scrambled to the open door. He prayed Carl and his .38 had gotten the better of Kurt. He fell through the opening and rolled clear as three blasts from Bartholomew's gun splintered the wood below the front counter. On all fours, Eugene scrambled for the shotgun only to find it gone.

Two slow, heavy footfalls resonated through the floor. In his narrow view from behind the counter, Eugene saw either Carl or Albert's legs sprawled and motionless beside the table. Beyond, Kurt lay propped against a cabinet, holding a bloody hand to his chest, blinking slowly. Acrid smoke hung heavy. Outside, King yapped.

"Kurt! Get your ass up and let's finish this!" Bartholomew ordered.

Kurt tried to move then grimaced and fell back.

In the window that looked out at the gate, Eugene watched the reflection of Bartholomew's wide form edging toward the counter. Eugene's searching hand found a heavy car part. He popped up from behind the counter and threw. The old man fired. Both missed their target. Bartholomew rounded the counter. He spread his stance and viciously smiled down at Eugene.

"You lose," he growled, again taking aim.

Hands out, Eugene stood slowly. Judging by the old man's swollen-faced squint, he was half blind without his glasses. He stepped closer, his sneer radiating his enjoyment of the misery on Eugene's face.

Playing for time, Eugene said, "It's power and control that get's you off, isn't it?"

Bartholomew ignored the question. He licked his bloody lips and hollered over his shoulder in a coach's demanding voice, "Kurt, I can't see to drive. I need you, son. Dig down and find the strength."

In his peripheral vision, Eugene was surprised to see Kurt roll to all fours. The injured pressman collected his revolver and staggered to his feet. Blood stained his chest and his left thigh. Dragging his wounded leg, he hobbled across the room. Coach tossed the car keys to the counter. Kurt retrieved them and struggled for the doorway.

"God, but you are magnificent, Kurt. Son, can you make it?"

"I got this, Coach. I won't let you down."

When his minion was out of earshot, Bartholomew actually grinned. "It isn't about sex. It's the look on their face when they know I own them."

Eugene actually shivered. "Like you own Kurt and every other vulnerable kid that looked up to you?"

"Every leader needs his useful fools. Mine would do anything for me—"

"No!" shouted Mikey, stepping from the bathroom hall with Albert's short-barreled, pump shotgun aimed at Bartholomew.

Wary of the gun's wide shot pattern, Eugene edged back. *Albert keeps birdshot in the chamber and buck in the magazine.*

"Point that somewhere else, you retard!"

The gun roared. Tiny, 8-shot bee-bees peppered the old man and shattered the big picture window beside him. Stumbling back but keeping his feet, Bartholomew shuddered. Blood bloomed on his shirt and trickled from his face as he issued a high-pitched, pig-at-slaughter scream. As he raised his pistol to return fire, Eugene jumped forward.

A growling streak of fur and teeth sailed through the shattered window. The handgun fired just as King's huge jaws clamped around the thick arm. The two combatants went down in a growling, squealing pile. The gun clattering free.

Still standing, white-faced and wide-eyed, Mikey dropped the shotgun and ran for the door.

King was in full blood lust, ripping and tearing at Bartholomew's face. The man's strong arms wrapped around the dog, attempting a crushing squeeze. Pushing down the darkness that urged him to kill, Eugene kicked the pistol away, spun, grabbed King's collar and kicked at Bartholomew's ribs until he released his death grip on the dog.

For the briefest of moments there was nothing but King's tugging and choking against his collar and a moaning gurgle from the pathetic old man as he wiped at his eyes.

"Easy there, Eugene," said a voice from the doorway. "It's me, Roberto, from the other night."

Seeing the friendly face lifted a crushing weight from Eugene's shoulders. He dropped to his knees beside his dog and began to wretch. Between gasps for air, he managed, "A guy . . . went . . . out . . . ."

"We got the little dude. He—"

"No . . . Another . . . Don't hurt the little guy . . . He helped."

Roberto jumped into action, pulling a pair of Vice Grip pliers from a pocket. Straddling Bartholomew, he wrenched and pulled until he crushed a finger from each hand in the plier's locking jaws. The battered old man squealed with pain.

"Callate pendejo," Roberto muttered, then kicked him in the ribs before turning his attention to Carl, still sprawled face down on the floor.

"*Gracias Madre Santa,* he's still breathing." Rolling him gently, Roberto pulled off his t-shirt to apply pressure to the wound. Carl's eyes fluttered open and he groaned with pain.

"Eugene?" cried Albert from the bathroom.

"I'm here. Carl's hit! Where—"

"I'm here, too," called Olivia, "We're okay."

"Come help. Call 9-1-1!"

"Already did," Olivia said as she and Albert hurried into the office. "I hear sirens closing in." The adrenaline in her voice ran down as she took in the bloody scene.

"Roberto," said Eugene, "your guys armed? The cops will—"

"Nah, my boys are cool."

Olivia edged toward Eugene and threw her arms around him and the whining King. Albert scooped up his shotgun before kneeling to grasp his brother's hand.

Two gunshots sounded in the yard. Shouts followed then an engine roared and tires screamed.

"Stay put!" Eugene ordered. He ran for the door to peer out over the battery pile.

Kurt was at the wheel of the Escalade. Driving in reverse, he rammed an arriving police car, knocking it out of action. He threw the SUV into drive, cranked the wheel and lit the tires, glancing off a gatepost as he spun around, jumped a curb and raced down the street.

An SUV with blindingly-bright off-road lights, slid to a stop to block Buchanan Street. Kurt stood the Escalade on its nose. More cop cars had shoved and scraped around the damaged cruiser to close in from behind. Kurt revved the 420-horsepower engine and rocketed the Escalade forward. Three sharp gunshots sounded. The Escalade veered to the right, slamming into a telephone poll. A tall silhouette appeared in the headlight glare to rip open the door and pull Kurt's limp body from the SUV.

"Kurt's down! It's over" yelled Eugene over his shoulder at the office doorway. "Whoa, whoa, the cops are coming in hot. Put King in the bathroom or they'll shoot him. Lose the shotgun! Just lay down and do what they say!"

Exiting the office, Roberto yelled something in Spanish. His three companions holding Mikey in the yard dropped to their knees in the dirt and put their open hands over their heads. Mikey followed their lead.

"We've got a gunshot victim in here. We need a squad!" yelled Eugene as he and Roberto dropped to their knees and put their hands on their heads.

Cops swarmed in, guns out and barking orders as they slammed everyone to the ground, grinding their faces in the dirt and cuffing their hands. Seconds ticked.

"We're clear!" yelled a cop. A moment later, paramedics ran past the cuffed and prone Eugene and Roberto.

"Sorry I didn't get here sooner," Roberto mumbled.

"Hey, you beat the cops. How did you know?"

"That noisy gringo, Jack called and said you was in some shit."

Eugene smiled and shook his head. Two pairs of dress shoes appeared near his face. They were the same shoes he had seen when the cops had him on the floor of his apartment days before.

Harry knelt and chuckled. "Good to see you're still with us."

"Good to see you, too, Detective. Carl's in the office. He's been shot but he's awake and breathing. Eddie's mystery friend, Jack is down the street. He might need some help explaining."

* * *

A Phoenix PD command vehicle had set up under the bridge just outside the junkyard gate. Heavily armed SWAT team members milled near the Police RV, doing little more than looking good for the media horde that had descended.

Still reeling from the shootout, Olivia had pulled away from Eugene when he'd tried to comfort her after she'd heard of her mother's murder. Just as quickly, she'd broken down and sought comfort in his arms.

Carl had strong vital signs. He was awake and talking when paramedics loaded him into a squad for transport. Albert had held his hand the whole time, only letting go when the police insisted he stay behind for questioning.

Gordon Bartholomew had departed in cuffs and strapped to a gurney, howling that he was deserving of better treatment. Between the shotgun blast and King, the damage to his face had stunned paramedics who commented that he'd likely lose the sight in at least one eye.

Animal control had come for King, but went away empty-handed after a spirited, chest-poking conversation between Chief Royal and a man Eugene recognized as the Phoenix Police Chief.

Mikey sat cuffed in the back of an open squad car as Eddie and a Phoenix PD sergeant interviewed him.

King sprawled at Eugene's feet, a bowl of water nearby. A leather leash had replaced the rope he'd gnawed through. Agitated and panting, every quick movement or loud sound brought up his hackles. Eugene knew that bringing him back from his feral darkness would take some time.

Phoenix PD had interviewed each of them separately. Now Eugene, Olivia and Albert sat together in folding chairs outside the office while forensic technicians cataloged the interior.

Harry and Chief Royal approached. "I understand you've all given statements to Phoenix PD. We'll glean the details from them, but could I bother you for a brief rundown of what happened?"

Each spoke in turn, laying out the details of their fifteen minutes in hell. Albert was brought to tears in describing his brother's firing on Kurt before leaping the counter and retrieving the shotgun only to get hit by Kurt's return fire.

"So, he got you the shotgun. How did Mikey end up with it?" asked Chief Royal.

"I got hold of it just as Eugene scrambled through the door. Couldn't risk a shot with him in front of me so Olivia and me fell back to the bathroom."

"Falling back is putting it lightly," quipped Olivia, coming out of her silence.

Albert smiled. "Heh, I was a little worked up. Sorry for pushing you down by the toilet but them thin walls weren't gonna stop a bullet."

"Albert, you were a guardian angel who swept me off my feet and kept me safe. I'm forever in your debt." She reached out and squeezed his hand as he wiped at his embarrassed face.

"But how did Mikey get the shotgun?" asked the Chief.

"I took a chance and followed my heart," said Albert. "Mikey was in the hall. He actually helped push us into the bathroom. Once we was hunkered down, I looked at him. I could see in his eyes he wasn't like the others. He put his hand out for the gun and said, 'He won't shoot me.' I just knew what he was gonna do."

All sat in stunned silence until Eddie approached with a stoic and un-cuffed Mikey at his side.

"Thank you, Mikey," said Eugene. "You saved lives. You're a good man."

Mikey burst into tears. "No, I'm not," he cried. "I tried to make it stop, but Coach was a bad man. He killed the team and he made Kurt do bad things and now Kurt's dead." He turned to bury his face in Eddie's chest. Eddie pulled him in for a hug.

"How did you put it together, Harry?" asked Eugene. "I assume that was you calling our phones."

"Yes, it was. But, hm, I just realized something. Mikey, it was you that gave Andy the newspaper clipping wasn't it? Is that how you tried to stop them?"

Face still buried in Eddie's chest, Mikey nodded.

Harry went on to explain their finding the clipping and how it tied all the pieces together. "We sent units to Bartholomew's house." He glanced at Olivia. "What we found put us in the hunt for you."

Eddie added, "It was Charlie Hastings who told us where you were going. When you didn't answer your phones, we called in the cavalry."

Eugene stood and walked to Mikey. Glued to Eugene's side, King followed.

"Listen to me, buddy. I love you, Mikey. You did good, hero-good. I'm really sorry about Kurt. He wasn't bad, just lost."

Mikey turned to face Eugene and he pulled him into his arms. After a long moment, King nuzzled and licked Mikey's hand. Mikey leaned back "Can I pet your dog?" he asked in a whisper.

"You betcha," said Eugene. "But be real gentle. He's had a rough night."

Mikey sat down in the dirt and King showered him with kisses.

* * *

Derek Schaefer discovered that prison life was not as miserable as expected. His first six months in the joint had been a hellish series of fights won and lost, but over time his refusal to be anyone's bitch earned him the luxury of being left alone to do his time.

Three years into his sentence he'd been ordered to work in the laundry, loading carts and transporting bedding and uniforms to the cellblocks, rags to the auto shop, and linens to the kitchen.

His freedom of movement allowed him to start a small-time hustle by trading his sexual talents for commissary credits and the makings of grilled cheese sandwiches.

Each night after lights out, he rolled toilet paper into tight little bowls to use as fuel for his aluminum foil prison hotplate. Each morning before the cells opened and the prisoners went to their jobs, he parked himself in front of his stainless steel toilet and cooked. Assuming a guard didn't happen by, which would force him to flush the whole works, the sandwiches were then handed off to a block worker who sold them for a cut of the action.

The work was mainly a distraction. He was biding his time and working on a much bigger dream. On the tiny plastic television he'd bought with his grilled cheese and blowjob funds, he followed Gordon Bartholomew's progress through the system. The trial had taken months. The man's sentence meant he'd die old and broken in prison. Derek dreamed of hurrying that process along.

After years of watching and waiting, word finally came down from a friend in the know that Bartholomew would be transferred to Derek's facility. He set to work, quietly calling in favors and trading sex to civilian workers to make sure his target would come into his laundry-duty orbit.

Derek had spotted Bartholomew two weeks before as he delivered rags to the auto shop. The old monster had been assigned oil and lube duty, spending much of his time in one of the shop's three service pits where he worked on prison and civilian vehicles.

On what he hoped would be his final day on earth, Derek woke with a smile. Before grilling the sandwiches so that all appeared normal, he penned a short note to Eugene, thanking him for his monthly visits and expressing his wish that life had been different. He folded the paper and wrote *To My Brother Eugene* on the outside, then placed it with his meager belongings.

When the cellblock doors opened, he stepped out and strolled off to work. He happily endured the pat down from guards before exiting his block. As he stepped into the outdoor chain link passage that led to the laundry, a beautifully bright and sweet-smelling spring morning greeted him.

In the laundry, after another pat down and a count, he went to work loading carts, keeping a close eye on the rags destined for the auto shop. When the rag cart was loaded and weighed, he grabbed it and set off. A squeaky caster made the cart difficult to steer, but it was music to Derek's ears, playing right into his plans.

Another pat down and a cart inspection greeted him as he entered the auto shop. The air was sharp with chemicals. A pneumatic impact wrench whined and hammered in removing a tire.

After passing a line of tall, rolling toolboxes, he waved hello to one of the civilian mechanics. "Hey, I've got a squeaky wheel pulling the cart to one side. Mind if I hit it with some WD-40 from the cabinet?"

Not bothering to look at the cart, the mechanic said, "Go ahead."

Derek pushed down the line of workbenches. Pausing to refill the rag boxes at each, he scanned the area for his target.

Bartholomew stood at a workbench at the far end of the shop. A grease gun in one hand and a clipboard in the other, he looked over the day's work orders. A chunk of his nose and most of one ear were missing. His graying, short-cropped hair had gone pure white. Derek pulled his eyes away to look over the room. Seeing no one watching, he tipped a trigger-start propane torch into his cart and concealed it under the rags.

Bartholomew left the workbench. To Derek's horror, the man walked straight for him. Derek turned and bent down to a rag box. Bartholomew walked past, oblivious. Heaving a sigh of relief, Derek stood and moved on to collect the last item.

The hazardous materials cabinet stood tucked between workbenches on the back wall of the auto shop. After checking to be sure the civilian mechanic was still present to defend him, he opened the cabinet doors, retrieved a gallon of naphtha parts cleaner, and tucked it into the cart. He then grabbed the WD-40 and sprayed the wheel.

The guards drank coffee while making small talk, paying little attention to their charges.

At the far end of the shop, where Bartholomew had been standing minutes before, Derek filled the last rag box. He paused to remove the naphtha can's cap. Weapons assembled, he turned to see Bartholomew step down into the center oil change pit under an ancient, three-quarter ton prison pickup truck.

Derek moved on, pushing down his excitement as he made a beeline for the center pit. No one noticed when he nonchalantly plucked the can and torch from the cart then descended the pit's narrow concrete steps.

Shooting Derek a cursory look, Bartholomew growled, "Whadda ya want?"

One good eye glared, the other glistened milky white. The pit's tight confines made the old perv look even more ominous than Derek remembered.

He swallowed hard, his resolve weakening in the shadow of his childhood horror show.

Shocked recognition washed over Bartholomew's face. He growled out, "You don't have the stones, you little cum stain."

Certainty took hold. From somewhere deep inside a smile rose up to blossom on Derek's face. He lurched forward, squeezing the can, dousing the old monster with chemical. For one acrid, eye-burning instant they stood frozen. Then Derek doused himself. Coach's face twisted in fear. He went on the attack just as the torch sparked to life.

Consumed by a suck and a whoosh of air and flame, they fell to the oil and grease-stained concrete with Coach Bart's powerful hands squeezing Derek's throat. The fireball consumed hair and clothing then flesh.

Derek savored his peace, feeling no pain as his darkness turned to light. He simply smiled into the face of evil as the flames took it back to Hell.

—THE END—

Born in Storm Lake, Iowa, Kent's family moved to Arizona when he was five years old.

A 1977 graduate of Phoenix Central High School, Kent worked at several Arizona newspapers both as a staff photographer and photo director.

In 1984, he married Deborah Shanahan, a reporter for the Arizona Republic. Their daughter Alison was born in 1988. In 1990, they moved their family to Omaha, Nebraska. Their son, Nathan was born in 1991. For ten years Kent worked as a commercial and editorial freelancer, building a thriving business before taking a staff photographer position at the Omaha World-Herald, where he still works today.

Kent Sievers' first novel, LITTLE MAN, a thriller set in the homeless community in Omaha, Nebraska's north downtown, was published in 2013. You can purchase it by following the links on his website at www.kentsievers.com.